DANA EVYN

THE SHATTERED MIRROR

THE MIRRORED TRILOGY

This book is a work of fiction. Names, characters, places, and incidents either are products of the author's imagination or are used fictitiously. Any resemblance to actual events or locales or persons, living or dead, is entirely coincidental and not intended by the author.

THE SHATTERED MIRROR
The Mirrored Trilogy, Book 3

CITY OWL PRESS
www.cityowlpress.com

Cover Design by MiblArt. All stock photos licensed appropriately.

Page Edges by Painted Wings Publishing.

Edited by Danielle DeVor.

For information on subsidiary rights, please contact the publisher at info@cityowlpress.com.

Paperback Edition ISBN: 978-1-64898-676-5

Hardback Edition ISBN: 978-1-64898-576-8

Digital Edition ISBN: 978-1-64898-876-9

PRAISE FOR DANA EVYN

"*The Other Side of the Mirror* is an imaginative story about a woman discovering her place among fae royalty and a war with a false king, the world-building and magic moved the narrative quickly and heightened the love story at its core." — *Florence A. Bliss, Author of Taken by His Sword*

"A story of loss, love, and trauma. Evyn's creativity is shown through invoking emotions within us— and leaving us wanting to know what happens in her second book, in which Eva's final fate, and that of both the human and fae realms, may be revealed." — *Racheal Chie, Strange Horizons Magazine*

"A mirror is just a mirror, right? What if it wasn't? Dana Evyn has created a world on the other side full of adventure, magic and danger." — *H.E. Scott, Author of The Reckless Apprentice*

"*The Mirror in the Mountain* is a fantastic romantasy adventure. You cheer for soulmates Bash and Eva as they face off against one of the most truly terrifying villains I've encountered in a long time. This story is full of steam, spice, and a big-hearted cast of multi-layered characters. It's a heart-thumping and nail-biting ride—a journey not to be missed. Bravo to Evyn on this unputdownable story." — *Leslie O'Sullivan, Author of A Kingdom of Souls and Shadows*

Never believe in happily ever after.

To everyone who went through the mirror with me.
Thank you for the adventure.

AUTHOR'S NOTE

Your mental health matters. Please be mindful that *The Shattered Mirror* includes the following themes: Explicit sexual situations. Torture, blood and gore, imprisonment, and on page death. Memory loss. Viruses, needles, and unwilling injections. Agoraphobia and claustrophobia. Suicidal thoughts. Almost drowning.

The dog is fine throughout the entire series, I swear...

Everyone else is fair game.

For full content warnings please visit danaevyn.com/content-warnings

MAYIM
AGADOT
THE FAEWIL

RONIX
RA
VEN
ESTERRA
IMYR

CHAPTER 1
TOBIAS

The sky feels far too large when you've spent so long in a cage.

My breath snagged, my feet skidding to a stop as if there were an invisible barrier across the stone archway that led from the Solearan castle I had grown up in. The courtyard before me was too open, the pale, blue sky seeming to expand exponentially as I struggled to draw in a breath. My heart pounded in my ears as I tried and failed to force one foot forward.

The sky felt endless, even as something small and trapped inside me berated me that it meant freedom.

Big breath in. Count each second. Breath out and count the same.

I sucked in a quick, boxed breath, my father's voice saying that familiar four count in my head just as his voice had done so many times in that dank dungeon cell. But I was free—free of that awful place, free of that godsforsaken mask whose weight I could still feel on my temples, even months after it last held me hostage.

Safe. Free…

Why did it feel like I never truly would be?

Four years in that dank dungeon. Four years that I had been buried beneath the white stone of Morehaven, trapped and unable to find a way out. No sun, no fresh air, no light.

I dreamt of that cell every night. The slow drip of the dank walls, the endless darkness. Hopelessness tinged with utter despair.

The torture of Aviel draining me of my power, over and over, and over again. The cold stone beneath me as I lay there, too weak to move.

The taste of iron. The blood dribbling from my mouth when he was finally finished with me.

Screaming myself hoarse and yet not being able to speak a single word. The mask that still weighed against my face in every nightmare.

It had become routine to wake up shaking and terrified each night, unsure if my escape was some sort of cruel fallacy that my mind created in a last-ditch effort to stay sane.

I startled as a crisp breeze caressed my cheeks, then closed my eyes with a shudder. Months had passed since I had been freed by my sister, Eva Maris, also known as the High Queen of Soleara. It had been months since she had led an army to the mountain prison of Adronix to end Aviel for good. Months since we had returned to Soleara—the northern kingdom of Agadot—and my mother's crown had been passed down to me.

I had been a child when I left this kingdom along with my family to flee to the human realm. And I had been a child when I returned on my Seventeenth—the birthday when a fae's magic manifested—and was pushed through a mirror by my mother seconds before she was murdered. I had spent more time in Aviel's dungeons than within these walls as an adult. It was almost ironic that now, I could barely stand to leave them.

My heart pounded in my ears as I managed a cautious step forward. The world tilted strangely. With a sharp gasp, I retreated back inside the doorway. My vision narrowed to the stone around me and my shaking hands.

Thankfully, I didn't have any observers at this early hour. I pressed my forehead against the side of the archway, my hands grasping at the unforgiving stone, feeling its grounding presence beneath my fingertips. Cold, harsh stone had been the only thing I had felt for so long. I had hated the way it leeched what little warmth I had in those dank dungeons.

Here I was reaching for it instead of embracing the crisp air that whipped around my face as if in reprimand.

Wincing, I made myself let go. I had to get a hold of myself already and control this awful, irrational fear, this pathetic, gnawing weakness. I had to if I was going to function as the King of Soleara…or just function, in general.

They deserved better than what I could give them—deserved better than me pretending I was anything other than broken.

They deserved someone better than me, period.

While I had spent days on horseback to reach Adronix during those final days of battle, those nights on the road had been spent shaking in my solitary tent, trying to calm my racing heart before the next day began. The open-air ride to Adronix had been torturous after being stuck inside those dark stone walls for so long. It was all I could do to stay in my saddle as the sky expanded around me, my vision blurring as my gelding galloped after the mare in front of him.

I spent my time concentrating on the surrounding trees to ground my spiraling thoughts, sucking in each breath in a careful four count to keep myself from panicking. Forcing myself to focus on my purpose, on my duty, and on my revenge as my horse carried us forward—hiding the fact that I sat frozen and silently hyperventilating beneath my hood.

Quinn always seemed to find me whenever my fear became too much. She would chatter about nothing in particular in a way I suspected was designed to distract me. I wondered if she knew how many times her presence alone had stopped me from unraveling.

That relentless urge to keep moving had been the only thing stopping me from falling apart. Without that momentum propelling me forward, I had hidden myself away as I tried and failed to piece myself back together. My solitude did nothing to keep my terror at bay as my dark thoughts tried to drown me.

Did my people think I was a recluse or simply inattentive? Granted, I was little more than a figurehead with Soleara's new system of governance, but I was an especially useless one. A royal hermit holed up in my family home high on the mountain peak. Akeno and Thorin had long since stopped extending offers of companionship, knowing it would only earn them another polite refusal.

I had, however, repeatedly rebuffed Pari's efforts to rekindle our friendship upon my return to Soleara. She had nearly been as persistent as Quinn in checking up on me.

Pari knew me better than I wanted to admit. After all, she had been the first Solearan I met in this realm—my first real friend here. I had been freshly seventeen and scared out of my wits after my parents were killed in front of me and I had fallen away from the flames through the mirror in our living room. I thought I had lost my mind when I ended up in a forest without any real understanding of how I had gotten there.

If it hadn't been for Pari, Akeno, and Thorin's search party finding me before Aviel's supporters did first, I would likely be dead right now, or worse. Probably eaten by something somewhere in the Faewilds or brought to Aviel before I knew what he was and turned into his puppet.

The trio had taught me who I was, and what I had to fight for. They had trained me in my magic and armed me with my history. And I had rewarded that debt by getting captured by the very evil they had tried to save me from, then returned more broken than any leader had a right to be.

It didn't help that they could barely look me in the eye after my return. I knew they tried to save me from Aviel—and had put Soleara's secrecy at risk to do so. One Solearan soldier ended up in a cell next to mine after one such attempt had gone awry. I hadn't been able to stop what happened next.

The moment he realized he could be used against me, he had slit his own throat. I hadn't even been able to beg him not to do what was already too late to stop, not with the mask that stole my voice. I could barely even scream as his body hit the floor.

Aviel had left him there for days. His sightless eyes watched me in silent condemnation as his blood seeped into the stone. They only dragged his corpse away after the guards couldn't stand the stench any longer.

There were no more rescue attempts after that. At least none that made it that far.

Every day, I prayed the next face I saw in those cells wouldn't be one I knew—and every time it wasn't, the relief I felt at seeing strangers was quickly followed by the familiar sting of self-loathing. Aviel never allowed his prisoners to live for long.

But the three Solearans who originally saved me from the forest had survived without me—thrived even, as had Soleara. Then they had saved Eva from Aviel and helped save us all during the battle of Adronix.

They deserved far better than my shortcomings.

And Quinn? She was better off without me too.

The sky seemed to bear down on me, brightening in intensity as I forced myself to look up. Sweat dripped down my back as I made my legs walk back into the courtyard. All my focus fixed on one step, then the next, despite the growing buzzing in my ears.

I had to get over this. I should've already.

I closed my eyes as soon as I reached the practice yard, the darkness behind my eyelids like a cool balm to my racing thoughts. Trembling, I fell into the familiar motions of a form my body knew by heart, trusting that balance and breath and movement would chase my demons away. Yet I could feel the taunting caress of the morning sun on my cheeks, reminding me of the endless openness surrounding me.

Clenching my jaw, I tried to focus only on the light itself. There was something about the sun's light, something that had always helped me recharge and find some semblance of fortitude even before I knew the connection to my magic. I had always felt my best as the sun rose, usually baiting my grumpy night owl twin as she woke up bleary-eyed and grumbling. After my capture and imprisonment, in that dark, dank cell with that damn mask blocking even the hint of light available from reaching my face, its warmth was now a foreign, painful reminder of the comfort it had once held.

The warmth of my magic rose within me as if aching to reach out the world I refused to reenter. I shoved it back down.

My light still felt wrong. Tainted. It felt forever stained by the ways it had been stolen and used against so many innocents—and against those I loved.

Aviel had robbed me of that comfort. And I had lost the ability to set apart the light that had once given me peace, the light that was solely *mine*, after so many years of it being used to hurt me.

One last, lasting cruelty to add to a long list of mistreatments.

My magic didn't understand my self-flagellation. Magic needed to be used. And I had spent far too long with it blocked not to know that it needed to be released. Add that to the fear that open space brought, and it was no wonder I was on edge.

Shaking my head, I forced everything away and focused on the present.

I *had* missed this. I used to dream about this freedom even as I wondered if I would ever experience it again. The fresh air in my lungs. The smell of the earth, the breeze. The soft give of the ground beneath my feet instead of moist stone. I missed it all so damn much, even with the ever-present twist to my stomach that accompanied each step.

My body moved by rote from one position to another, but my mind refused to still. I was panting far too hard for the casual warmup as I reached the final stance.

Light footsteps broke the silence. Reluctantly, I opened my eyes—though I already knew who would be there.

Quinn Sagray smiled up at me. For one precious moment, the sky seemed to melt away.

The tight curls of her light-brown hair waved wildly in the wind, backlit and glowing in the sunlight. Her white linen pants and tight, sleeveless top only made her look that much more angelic, a stark contrast to the black I wore head to toe. Her arms were darker than usual from time spent in the sun, as was the teasing peek of tawny skin beneath her keyhole neckline. The sunflower amulet I had never seen her without sparkled in the light, the yellow diamonds glimmering like sunlight captured in stone.

Quinn was undeniably beautiful. She had been for as long as I had known her—since my first breath, as she liked to say since she was born seven days before Eva and me. And now? This realm suited her. She carried herself with a quiet confidence—grounded not in ego, but in a clear, unwavering understanding of who she was.

But what made her truly beautiful was her mind. It was the way she made me question the world around me, the way she turned the ordinary into something meaningful. There was something uniquely breathtaking about the way I could always see the gears turning behind those startling amber eyes.

My sister's best friend mirrored between Morehaven and Soleara so often I rarely knew which kingdom she spent the night…not that I was keeping track of where she slept. When she was here, she stayed in the room down the hall from me. Despite the number of visitors at my parents' mountain home, I could pick out the sound of her footsteps from any other. That unremarkable cadence imprinted further upon my brain every time she walked past my closed door.

I could usually hear her tinkering with her experiments late into the night, long after we both should've gone to sleep. Her room was more a mad scientist's lair than sleeping space, experiments bubbling in beakers I had been surprised she had been able to find in this realm. When I asked her about them, she had simply arched an eyebrow and said, "We live in a world full of actual magic, and you're impressed I was able to procure a few beakers?"

Her ensuing smile had left me too tongue-tied to press her further.

I spent most nights locked in my room to avoid running into her and passed my time at the castle during the day. Yet Quinn always seemed to find me when it came time to train, just as she had during our journey to Adronix.

"I thought I'd get a workout in before it's time to go." Her sunny smile grew wider, pulling me from my wandering thoughts. "I should've known you would beat me out here. Can I join you?"

"Sure," I grunted, inwardly wincing at my lack of eloquence. Even months later, I wasn't used to speaking at length. The pain that once accompanied every word had ensured that. I had been conditioned into silence, into compliance, that iron mask choking off my voice until even my screams were silent...

I refused to go where that thought led. Clearing my throat, I added, "What have you been working on?"

She tilted her head like she was surprised I made the effort of that simple pleasantry. "Just trying to understand more about the intersection of magic and medicine."

From anyone else that sentence might have sounded grandiose. From her, it was simply a statement of fact. I raised an eyebrow, my tone droll as I asked, "Is that all?"

Quinn shrugged. "There are so many diseases in the human realm that could benefit from this sort of research, if it turns out to be successful. Not that disease has been eradicated here either, but the treatments..." Her eyes lit up, and I couldn't help but be utterly charmed by her excitement. "The way the healers here can fix things with magic is one thing, but the way they use magic to imbue treatments with those cures...if there's a way to mass produce those, it could be huge. And I didn't spend all those years working on my doctorate to stop researching now."

Many would have if they found themselves in another realm and were best friends with its High Queen. But that wasn't who Quinn was. It was easy to remember the girl I knew before all of this: effortlessly kind and always the first person to offer to help. My sister's best friend, and mine, too.

After all, our trio had been inseparable until my death.

It was no surprise that she had found a career that was aimed at helping people, or that she had healing magic. Nor was it a surprise she had kept at it, even here.

She tapped her foot impatiently. I repressed a smile. Even when we were kids, Quinn had never been able to stay still.

When she walked past me, her arm brushed mine. The fleeting touch seemed to emanate down my entire body, leaving me frozen in place. Her amber eyes sparkled as they met mine. I almost missed the training sword she tossed at me as I found myself momentarily lost in them.

She raised her sword. "Ready?"

I nodded mutely.

If freedom meant having nothing left to lose, then I had been so, so foolish to believe I had ever been freed.

CHAPTER 2
QUINN

Tobias Maris was a paradox. A strange mix of a boy I once knew better than I knew myself and this cold, distant king who had become a virtual stranger. Ever since he had come back into my life, we had danced around each other, both careful not to get too close. We lived in the same quiet house yet never shared a meal.

The only real time we spent together was to train, a usually silent affair unless I coaxed monosyllabic answers out of him. At least he allowed that much, despite his attempts to avoid me and everyone else.

I knew we could never be what we once were. Not because of what he had been through—though I was sure he thought that—but because if he realized what I was hiding from him, he would never look at me the same again.

And yet, despite myself, I couldn't seem to stay away. Not when he needed me. He was hurting, that much was obvious, and not in a way I could easily heal. I wasn't the only one who noticed, just the only one who couldn't seem to handle the thought of him facing his trauma in his own time.

Tobias wordlessly passed me a cool glass of water before filling his own. His eyes were downcast, his face too pale as the flush from our sparring faded, like something had sucked the life from him. He stared down at his glass, his gaze unfocused as if he was reliving some unknown horror.

The water trembled slightly.

Suddenly I was desperate to fix whatever had caused that look—to banish whatever ghosts haunted him.

"If you keep practicing, you might manage to beat me one of these days."

It was a refrain I hadn't said since we were kids. He had been so easy to rile when our parents started training us, so competitive despite his easygoing nature. I had said it to him after every sparring session—win *or* lose—to his perplexed amusement.

Tobias's lips quirked, his eyes meeting mine for a split second before he looked away. Then his expression turned carefully blank, like he had forgotten himself for a moment. Maybe we had both slipped through time for a heartbeat to when he was a boy with a carefree smile and I was a girl he wasn't afraid to share it with.

The Tobias I knew in high school was quick to laugh, and even quicker to get others to do so. He lived with an open heart, was witty in a way that never poked fun, and was rarely seen without a cajoling grin. Along with his sister...he had been my best friend.

Sometimes it felt like that boy died in Aviel's dungeon.

"We should probably get ready," I said, trying to catch his eye once more.

Tobias gave a short nod, his eyes still downcast like he was actively avoiding my gaze. Then he turned on his heel. His long strides ate up the space between us and the stone archway leading indoors as I struggled to keep up. Though, based on the speed he hurried forward, maybe he was trying to get away from me.

Even during our journey to Adronix, his haste felt more like he was running *from* something rather than toward our destination. It wasn't so much that he was going somewhere—it was like he was fleeing something he couldn't bear to face.

Tobias seemed to relax infinitesimally as he crossed the threshold, his posture less guarded as he waited for me just out of reach of the sun. In the shadowy hallway, he was more imposing than usual. He had grown since those gangly teenage years; his broad shoulders muscled in a way that strained against the fabric of his clothes and so tall I had to look up to meet his eyes. The angles of his face were more dramatic than the boy I once knew, his strong jaw covered with dark stubble. No hint remained of the laughter that once lived in the crinkles around his eyes, his mouth.

This Tobias was the epitome of icy composure. For a second, I wondered what it would take to break it. Whether that calm was genuine, or merely a carefully constructed façade stretched over something brittle, just waiting for the right pressure to fracture.

My eyes lingered on his unsmiling mouth before meeting his impenetrable gaze. Before he could run away again, I asked, "Are you excited?"

Tobias blinked, like he didn't understand the question. "For?"

I rolled my eyes. "The wedding."

Getting the most innocuous information from him nowadays was an exercise in patience. My annoyance, however, abruptly faded when I remembered that his silence was likely a vestigial instinct from his imprisonment—an ingrained habit formed when even the slightest slip could have cost his sister her freedom.

Tobias gave a noncommittal shrug, though a muscle flexed in his jaw. "I don't think that's what they call it here. Besides, Eva and Bash have been bonded for months now."

His voice was deep and raspy, like it was still out of use. The low timbre of it sent a shiver down my spine.

"Okay fine," I teased, refusing to let his obvious lack of excitement dim my own. "Are you excited for their very belated bonding ceremony then?"

He almost smiled. The ghost of it played at the corner of his lips before it vanished. His voice was soft as he said, "She deserves some happiness after everything."

A shadow crossed his face. I reached for him unthinkingly, but he had already walked away, leaving my hand raised midair as he continued down the hallway. I took a second to follow, almost glad he walked away before something stupid came out of my mouth like how much he deserved happiness too.

Swallowing the lump in my throat, I hurried after him to the enormous, rose-gilded mirror that would bring us back to the mountain summit high above us and the house that had started to feel like home. I could use a shower before we left for Morehaven, not to mention my bag. Most of what I had packed were gifts since my dresses for the weekend were waiting in my room in Morehaven. Eva had insisted I call one of the many empty rooms in the castle mine though I preferred spending the night here to be close to my experiments.

Tobias stopped in front of the mirror, staring impassively at the ripple that started at its center as I came up beside him. I was stuck on my frustrating inability to read him anymore when he spoke again.

"I don't know how she stands it."

The candor in his tone caught me off guard. "Stands what?"

"Living there. In that *place*."

Tobias's voice had gone gravelly, full of loathing on that last word, though his face still betrayed nothing. His gaze was far away as he no doubt relived the memories of the castle we would soon return to.

My cheeks heated. Of course, Tobias wasn't *excited* to return to Morehaven after being imprisoned there by the monster who slaughtered his parents. Just because Eva had found a way to divorce the trauma that had happened to her there with the home she and Bash created didn't mean that Tobias had done the same. Not when he had spent years being tortured within its walls by the False King.

"They did redecorate," I mumbled lamely. "Found a way to make that castle theirs and not his. Don't you think so?"

Tobias's lips pressed together as if he struggled to find the right words. "It doesn't change what's beneath."

Had the dungeons that had held him prisoner been destroyed? I found myself wishing I knew the answer as his hand drifted to his opposite arm, absentmindedly rubbing the spot where he had once been chained.

Hesitantly, I reached out to him again, giving him time to pull away even as I hoped he wouldn't. His sleeve had ridden up, revealing the thick, layered scars banded around his wrist. My healing magic rose to my fingertips automatically to fix the injury. An intrinsic response though logically I knew it was too late to do anything about it.

"If you want to talk about it, I'm here," I murmured, my hand slipping into his. It wasn't the first time I had said those words to him.

I didn't expect a different answer. Maybe some part of him knew the offer didn't go both ways.

The silence stretched unbearably. I braced myself for him to push me away, just like he had when we first returned from Adronix—any semblance of our friendship vanishing along with Tobias himself.

His hazel eyes flickered as they finally met mine, the gold encircling their pupils more pronounced in the dim light. I could sense the way his heartbeat quickened, even as I made my magic draw back. A flash of something pained crossed his face as his throat struggled to swallow.

Tobias's mouth parted slightly. For a split second I allowed myself to hope that he would finally let me in enough to help him…

Laughter abruptly pierced the silence. Voices echoed behind us, loudly chattering about the preparations that needed to be made before the bonding ceremony.

The haunted look Tobias wore when he thought no one was looking disappeared in a blink. I winced as that blank mask slid firmly back into place. He ran his free hand through his chestnut hair, hopelessly mussing it, the long strands falling over his eyes.

"We should go," he murmured. He looked down at where my hand still held his. The faintest hint of color reddened his cheeks.

I started to pull away, but his fingers threaded through mine before I could. There was a slight change in his expression—a crack in the stone. The gold in his eyes gleamed as he released a measured breath, then gave me a slight nod.

Together, we stepped through the mirror.

I stumbled as we reached the other side. The strange vertigo of this form of travel wasn't something I would ever get used to. Tobias's grip tightened, keeping me upright. He let me go the second I was steady. I could still feel the warmth of his hand atop mine, the way my skin seemed to tingle at his touch. His own hand closed into a fist as he scanned me from head to toe, as if making sure I was safely intact from the half-second journey.

His fingers flexed as he backed away.

I clasped my hands together, rubbing my thumb across the back of my hand. "I don't know if I'll ever get used to the casual teleporting," I said with a nervous laugh. "Though it does beat the stairs."

The dark tunnels from the Solearan castle up to the once-secret city atop the mountain weren't for the faint of heart.

"I know what you mean," Tobias murmured, gesturing for me to keep walking.

Despite his longer legs, he slowed to stay beside me as we walked up the staircase that led to our shared hallway. He paused as we reached my door, leaning against the wall beside it so his body formed a long line. I had a sudden flashback to him waiting outside of my math class for me, though he had been far lankier then. He had filled out in our years apart —during the years I had grieved and wondered who he might have become.

He tilted his head like he was trying to figure me out, his biceps stretching the sleeves of his shirt as he crossed his arms.

"Thanks for walking me to my door," I said before he could walk away again.

Tobias glanced down the hallway then back at me, deadpanning, "It *was* out of my way."

I grinned far too widely in response. "Was that a joke, Maris?"

He looked almost as surprised as I felt, though it was short-lived. "Of course not, Sagray."

But I didn't miss the quirk of his lips before he turned away, striding down the hallway. For a heartbeat, I felt breathless as I realized just how much I had missed him.

Sometimes I would get a glimpse of the boy I knew rather than the stranger with the same eyes. Sometimes it seemed like he might be reaching back rather than shunning all attempts to bring him out of his self-imposed isolation.

Sometimes it was like no time had passed at all.

Still smiling, I called out, "I'll meet you downstairs, okay? We can leave to Morehaven together."

I might not deserve his friendship. But he deserved the chance to heal—and if I could help him, I would.

A slight dip of his head was all the acknowledgement I got before he disappeared into his room.

CHAPTER 3
TOBIAS

Returning to Morehaven filled me with an aching sense of dread. It hadn't taken long to shower and gather the few things I would need for the weekend, leaving me to stew in my unease. Eva kept a room ready for me in Morehaven that I never used if I could avoid it. My suit for the ceremony was already pressed and waiting as well as a closet full of clothing I had never worn—though I had no doubt would fit me perfectly.

Snagging the book I had been reading from my bedside, I tucked it under one arm before heading downstairs to wait for Quinn.

I wondered fleetingly if there was any way out of attending. But even if my sister didn't want me there, which was obviously not the case by the number of missives I had gotten from her leading up to the event, it was important that I attend as the king of one of the kingdoms under her rule.

After spending most of her life in the human realm, Eva had struggled since the war to show that she belonged in her new role. Despite coming out of the Choosing with a crown on her head and the magic of the land coursing through her, the misinformation Aviel had spread during the war had perpetuated even after his death. Many were still wary of the young High Queen whose formative years had been spent thinking she was human. It didn't help that she was changing the order of the faerie realm with her push toward democracy.

Despite the positive reception from the other rulers of Agadot, Aviel's former supporters had switched from outright attacks to a whisper campaign questioning the foreign ideologies Eva brought with her from the human realm. Nevermind the fact that a representative form of government was working perfectly well in Soleara and was entirely based on our mother's blueprint.

And I knew my sister, despite our years apart. A public bonding ceremony in Morehaven wouldn't have been her choice. It was calculated; a political strategy my mother would've been proud of after all those strategy sessions at our kitchen table growing up. Eva hadn't done a public ceremony after becoming High Queen, not when she had been focused on the rebuilding effort. With the vocal minority of those who sought to dethrone her growing louder, this ceremony was a show of unity and a reminder of who had been chosen to lead by the magic of the land.

She was smart to host it at the seat of her power. The entire event was obviously meant to help legitimize her rule, and helpfully featured the former King of Imyr, who had been born and raised in this realm. Eva and Bash may have already been bonded, but this was a chance to show their shared strength and extend a hand to those who remained wary of her competence and integrity.

I could do this. I *would* do this, for her.

After so many years of failing her, it was the least I could do.

My stomach roiled, but I forced my feelings down. Locking my fear away in a carefully constructed cage deep within me was second nature by now. Focusing inward, I blocked out everything that plagued me behind protective ley lines, compartmentalized within the thick mental shields I had spent every day of my imprisonment perfecting.

For four long, dark years I held that line, even as my own blood and magic was used to betray me—betray *her*. All I could do was hope those shields would be enough to keep even the slightest detail about my sister, and the then-hidden kingdom of Soleara, from the monster that forced me into that mask. Aviel had done everything he could to force his way through short of killing me. Each attempt to breach my defenses left me certain he would finally go too far and finish the job.

As I listened to the steady drip of moisture in that musty cell day after endless day, I had prayed that those mental walls plus the fortitude of sheer stubbornness would be able to keep me from breaking entirely.

Somehow, those carefully built compartments—my mental prison in which I was the warden of my own memories—held strong, even through the years of torture that now blurred into a cacophony of pain and helplessness.

Surely, I could handle two days of simply holding myself together for a wedding.

And yet, I couldn't stop the dark thoughts that stole through my mind every time I closed my eyes or the cold sweat that clung to me as I jerked awake, still shuddering from the nightmare of memories that were all too real. I suspected those feelings wouldn't stay hidden for long. No matter how deeply I buried them in the back of my mind, they would keep clawing their way out now that I was free, battering against the barriers I had erected against letting myself feel anything at all.

After so many years of repression and dissociation, I no longer knew how to live without it. I had no intention of losing control because doing so would mean falling apart. And I had no desire to let myself relive my worst moments or to let myself feel anything at all after the pain I had been through. But something told me this teetering equilibrium would shatter the second those emotions found a weakness to take advantage of—a fracture to slip through, like a crack in a mirror.

I raked a hand through my hair, catching a glimpse of myself in the enormous mirror that stood against the far wall in my childhood home. While I had filled out since my imprisonment, the sleepless nights had left me sallow, the shadows under my eyes a witness to the weight I still carried. My naturally tan skin remained a sickly shade of pale from my reluctance to go outside.

During the long, solitary days, I had taken to reading both as an escape and to learn about everything I missed. The latest volume tucked under my arm was a book about the magic behind the creation of these mirror gateways.

It was intention and magic, just like everything else. But I had been surprised to learn that gates could only be made by those with Celestial magics, and their creation mostly tied to royalty. Though anyone powerful enough could close a gate, at least temporarily, creating one took a blood tie to the land itself. The mirrors at each of the five cities had been a joint effort by some of the original monarchs of Agadot, each traveling to each other's realms to create the pathway home. The few others created generally had a single destination, such as the mirrors leading from the mortal realm to the forest entry of the Faewilds.

This mirror was once only linked to the castle below. Eva had created the pathway to Morehaven. Creating a new gate was incredibly draining, and she had taken several days to recover despite drawing on the magic of the land. According to the book under my arm, those who were untrained often didn't survive the effort of pouring their power into making the link. And here I was, uncertain whether I even had the strength to walk through this one again—back to the epicenter of everything that plagued me.

Morehaven. Even in my head, the name sounded like a curse.

Aviel was dead. And my sister was waiting for me, with her soul-bonded *anima* and their coterie of friends—all of whom would obviously do anything for her. Despite all that had happened to her, Eva hadn't let it turn her into a worse version of herself. She had not only survived Aviel's torment, she had *won*. After avoiding her carefully worded missives checking in on me, it was the least I could do to show up when it mattered.

At least Quinn would be right alongside me. Though with how easily she saw through me, I wasn't sure that was a good thing.

I had always been drawn to her. It was a fact that hadn't changed despite my efforts to push her away. When we were kids, she had been the person whose approval meant the most. Even now, the pain on her face when I shut her out cut deep, despite knowing she was better off without me in her life.

There was something endearingly unique about her unwavering optimism every time we crossed paths—a reoccurrence I couldn't entirely blame on her. Maybe it was her need to help others mixed with a backbone that refused to bow that kept her from leaving me alone like the rest of them. Or maybe she knew that some silent part of me still needed her. After all, she had a talent for seeing through things—a gift of discernment I had always trusted, even if it was now working against me.

If there was anyone who could break me, it was her.

As if the thought had summoned her, Quinn appeared, nearly running into me as I started forward at the same moment. On instinct, my hand clasped behind her back, my book tumbling from my grip with a heavy thud as my other arm firmly wrapped around her waist. Her breath caught, and I realized I was holding her in a dip more suited to a ballroom than a rescue.

There was something about her amber eyes that made it feel like they were pulling me in. Like if I didn't keep up my guard, I might fall into them and plummet headfirst.

I quickly righted her, my cheeks hot as I consciously released my hold on her. And yet I couldn't tear my gaze away.

Her natural curls framed her heart-shaped face like a halo, the simple, burgundy dress she had changed into accentuating every curve. An embossed leather belt with laces up the front cinched around the small of her waist, pushing up her breasts. The off-shoulder neckline revealed enough skin to make my mouth water.

"Sorry," Quinn said breathlessly, a matching flush rising on her cheeks.

Unable to form a response, I grunted like that band was still around my neck, though for once, its hold on me wasn't the reason my words felt stifled. Then I walked toward the mirror without looking back.

I hated every step away from her, even as I fought to forget the warmth of her in my arms, the enticing curve of her waist beneath my palm, and the ties of her belt looping around my fingers like one tug would be enough to unravel it. Her floral scent was like the sunflower she wore around her neck brought to life—vivid, alive, and impossible to ignore.

Skidding to a halt a few steps from the undulating mirror, I realized that Quinn had once again saved me, if only momentarily, from the memories that were now flooding me once more.

Quinn's voice cut through the silence. "You're reading about mirrors?"

I turned to see her holding my book in her hands, flipping through the chapters. She paused at a dogeared page. I held out my hand expectantly.

Quinn tilted her head. She seemed to look right through me, seeing everything I didn't want her to see. "Why?"

"I–I like to understand how things work," I admitted, caught off guard by the intensity of her curiosity.

She came closer. "Have you tried it? Opening a gate?"

I nearly fumbled the book in surprise as she passed it back to me. While it was comforting to read about a way my magic could be used without causing harm, it was best my power stay contained. I knew exactly how destructive my light could be.

"No," I said gruffly, looking away.

"I'd love to borrow it when you're done," Quinn murmured.

I could feel her eyes on me as I turned back to the mirror. My hand clenched the book so tightly its spine cracked.

Quinn walked right up next to me, so close I could feel the heat of her arm as it dangled a hair's breadth from mine. Despite my efforts, I found myself hoping that she might reach for me again like she had before our trip through the mirror earlier—that those nimble fingers would weave between mine and unravel the sudden paralysis that gripped my own.

Right now, my feet may as well have melded with the stone at the thought of willingly walking back into Morehaven.

As if sensing my trepidation, Quinn gave me one of those bright, perfect smiles. I had learned long ago to keep every thought and feeling from my face. And yet, her smile never seemed to fail to make my mouth tug at the corners in response.

Maybe I'll be able to get through this. At least if she stays by my side.

Before I could think better of it, I reached for her. A shock danced between our fingertips. Our eyes met, something inscrutable passing between us.

I tried not to think about how much it felt like her hand belonged in mine as Quinn pulled us both through.

✧

I hated this fucking castle. Eva and Bash had obviously worked hard to update it, like that could wipe away the memories ingrained within its gleaming façade. They had done a good job, too. It was beautiful in a way I almost wished it wasn't. Color and life had taken the place of the endless white marble that used to be the main feature of this entrance hall. But after what my sister and I had both been through here, I couldn't help but think of the skeleton of what remained under the new furnishings.

The familiar weight of Morehaven dragged me into memory before I could stop it, yanking me down into its depths. Terror clawed up my throat as I thought of the dungeon that had been my home for four endless years. The inescapable agony of being collared and helpless nearly brought me to my knees…

Quinn's hand squeezed mine, pulling me back to the present. I was trembling, clutching her hand so hard I was likely hurting her.

I immediately let go.

It was an effort to keep my expression empty as her eyes traced over my face—though I knew it was already too late to feign indifference. She gave me a sad sort of smile.

Slowly, I sucked in a breath to a careful four count, then held it in my chest. It was an effort to force everything I felt down somewhere deep inside me before letting my breath out to the same slow count. Only when my shoulders relaxed on my exhale did Quinn look away.

My sister rushed into the great hall a moment later, an enormous smile on her face. Her eyes were bright and glowing with happiness. They were the same hazel with flecks of gold as mine, a trait we had both inherited from our mother. Though Eva's ability as High Queen to draw from the magic of the land now made those flecks swirl excitedly in an echo of the gold crown she could summon at will.

The world owed her a happy ending. After everything she had been through, everything she and her *anima* had been forced to overcome to reach this day…they both did.

Quinn quirked a brow at the leathers my sister wore. "I realize you're not about to walk down the aisle yet, but I was under the impression the festivities leading up to a bonding ceremony didn't include a fight."

Eva laughed, the gold around her pupils swirling with languid contentedness. "Just finished training…I'm still getting the hang of drawing on the magic of the land, and I figured these couldn't hurt." Her mouth quirked. "Hopefully there won't be any fighting tonight, considering it's just a dinner with the people who mean the most to me."

I hid my wince. With the way I had avoided her these last few months, I had no right to be included in that group.

Eva winked. "Maybe tomorrow at the big event. As much as I wish we could keep the actual ceremony small, apparently, high queens are expected to throw a party every now and then." She exaggeratedly wrinkled her nose. "With how long our bond has been in place, you'd think it wouldn't matter, and we could stay focused on the rebuilding efforts…"

"Joy is worth celebrating," Quinn said solemnly. "I'm not surprised the realm wants to take part in it, especially after what you did for them."

Leave it to Quinn to always know the right thing to say.

My throat was tight as I nodded. Eva's smile widened as she met my gaze. Sometimes it felt as though no time had passed, that innate understanding formed in the womb leaving little to explain aloud. Other times, my twin still seemed like a stranger, those stolen years hanging heavy between us.

I was well aware that distance was entirely my fault.

Eva grimaced. "Please don't remind me about half the realm coming to celebrate...I'm just going to keep my eyes on Bash and rely on Toby to get me down that aisle."

Toby. It was still strange to hear that childhood nickname, the one no one but my sister ever called me. Especially now that the queen who said it was so far removed from the little girl who had coined it.

At least she hadn't brought Bash along so he could awkwardly act like my friend. I may have forgiven him for the part he played in bringing me to the False King, considering he thought he was doing the right thing. But I hadn't forgotten whose shadows had bound and gagged me before he unquestioningly laid me at Aviel's feet. I had ignored Bash's efforts to reach out—though by doing so, I hadn't treated him any differently than anybody else.

"How are things going besides that?" My question felt forced, like I was trying to play a part and couldn't remember my lines.

A line creased between Eva's brows. "No outright attacks since Aviel's death, though I almost wish I had a physical enemy to face instead of the whispers about my legitimacy. It's been a war of disinformation after the False King's outright lies when he was trying to discredit Bash and me." She let out a heavy sigh that made me feel bad I asked. "It's worse in Mayim and Esterra, where his supporters were able to blend back into their lives. It doesn't help that there are plenty against the democratic ideologies they say I brought with me from the human realm, even though Mom was the one to create that blueprint."

It was part of why opening Soleara to outsiders was so important. My kingdom was a model for the representative form of government Eva hoped to put in place for all Agadot. The legacy of our parents' rule was a thriving kingdom that showcased the importance of giving power to the people—and a voice in how their realm was run.

Change was never easy, especially with the fae, but those not swayed by Soleara's example at least understood the need for checks and balances to keep a tyrant like Aviel from ever stealing the throne again.

"I'm working on laying the groundwork for allowing those who aren't

Celestial to be able to enter the Choosing," Eva added far too nonchalantly. I had no illusions the process was simple. "From what we've discovered, the barring of Elementals traces back not to the Seeing Mirror, but to a Celestial High King intent on keeping his lineage in power. I assume Quinn told you since she's been helping me research?"

Quinn's smile faltered, but Eva didn't seem to notice. She gestured for us to follow her before Quinn could reveal how cowardly I had been in avoiding her.

Eva cleared her throat. "How's Soleara?"

My footsteps stumbled as I looked down at the floor. I supposed retiling was low on the list of priorities with so much else to be rebuilt…but I hated that white marble. It was a perfect match to the hallway my limp, drugged body had been dragged down every time I was brought to Aviel so he could feed upon my power. He was always careful not to take too much, unlike the others imprisoned with me.

I had quickly learned not to grow attached to anyone in the cells near mine. Their fates always ended with him sucking away their lifeforce to feed his own, their screams echoing down the sterile hallway.

With a shudder, I took a step forward. Only then did I remember my sister had asked me a question. I opened my mouth wordlessly, but Quinn came to my rescue.

"Our people are happy, especially now that our borders are open to the rest of the realm." Quinn gave a casual shrug. "There's been a flurry of curious outsiders. Tobias has been busy."

Her eyes darted to mine, the only tell of her partial truth. Most of my job was signing approvals and sitting in on the occasional meeting, intentionally keeping myself at a distance from the hum of real life and the crowds that set my nerves on edge. "Busy" was technically true, but it hardly captured my self-imposed isolation.

The Solearan senate on which Pari, Akeno, and Thorin sat had done a perfectly good job of running the city without me, and I had no desire to throw my weight around. I may have been a figurehead, but magical or not, paperwork was still the way of the world to my eternal chagrin.

"And you deserve all the credit for the warmth of their welcome," I said quietly.

My praise was met with a slow smile and a hint of a blush on Quinn's cheeks. Eva's eyes narrowed as she slowly looked between us.

Maybe I shouldn't have been surprised when Quinn returned to Soleara after the war. It had been her home once too, after all. Even so, I had expected her to stay with Eva in Morehaven in the aftermath of everything. Instead, she had shown up one day, dropped off her things at the room down the hall from me, and gotten straight to work.

I may have been king, but she was the leader Soleara needed, the main ambassador to the foreign dignitaries that arrived to discuss trade, and an advocate for those who needed it. *She* had been the one to push to allow tourism now that Soleara was no longer a secret, though Pari had been quick to echo the motion at the ensuing senate meeting. And she had been the one to ensure that transition had run smoothly, despite her own projects and endeavors.

Sometimes I wondered if there was anything she couldn't do—and who exactly was taking care of her while she was taking care of everyone else.

"Tobias?"

Eva had a strange look on her face, like that hadn't been the first time she said my name. I realized I had been staring too long—at Quinn, who was staring back at me with wide eyes.

I cleared my throat, turning to my twin. "So, do I need to give you away?"

Eva scrunched her nose. "Nothing quite so mortal. But I was hoping to have both of you up there with me. Rivan, Yael, and Marin will be standing up there with us too."

"Of course we will," Quinn said immediately.

I wasn't going to read into that 'we'.

Quickly, I nodded my agreement even as I fought to keep my face neutral. Quinn wasn't interested in me like that. She had never shown the slightest sign of wanting anything beyond friendship in all the years we had known each other. And even if she finally noticed the unrequited feelings I had tried and failed to suppress since I was a teenager…I was a mess. My first thought wasn't whether my answer to my sister was *yes*, but if the ceremony was going to be held outdoors. Because if it was and thousands of onlookers were there to witness my terror at simply standing beneath the sky…

If I could pull myself together long enough to fight a war, I could do it for one event. Though there was something different about focusing on my revenge and my sister's imminent survival. It had been easier to let my rage propel me forward while disassociating from the rest.

This was an entirely different type of battle. One I couldn't avoid without making everyone more worried about me than they already were.

Eva and Quinn continued discussing the ceremony as I shuffled along beside them, nodding when necessary. At least Quinn would be at my side tomorrow. Though having her next to me during what was likely to be a very romantic bonding ceremony would be excruciating in a different way.

I hadn't been able to avoid the ache in my chest now that she was back in my life or the way my tongue tied when I was around her even worse than it usually did. The excruciating mix of guilt and longing I felt from the moment I first saw her again had completely overwhelmed me. It had been an effort to hide it away, even after so long doing so. Like Eva, I had kept Quinn locked away deep in my mind, my heart, so Aviel hadn't known to use her against me...

She was safe. I hadn't broken. And I hadn't endangered the lives and well-being of the two most important people in my life despite abandoning them.

But having her back in my life...it was unbearable. I heard her laughter echoing up to my room from the planning sessions she ran in my kitchen, could see her curls bouncing around the corner as I watched her return to her bedroom, wafting the sweet scent of her with them. Her room was so close to mine I half wondered if my dreams about her would lead my feet down our shared hallway and raise my arm to knock...

I would never deserve her, not even if I did the work to put myself back together, but there was no denying the fact that Quinn had broken out of the cell that held her, and I didn't know how to put her back in.

CHAPTER 4
QUINN

Visiting Morehaven for my best friend's wedding was a welcome escape, though I was careful not to phrase it that way to Eva. It wasn't that I disliked my time in Soleara. Far from it, especially with the influx of problems to solve as the city welcomed outsiders for the first time in a century. There were few things I loved as much as a good challenge.

Pari, Akeno, and Thorin had accepted me into their inner circle without hesitation. I had met them not long before they had helped Eva escape from Aviel's clutches after he brought me to Soleara, and they had welcomed me as one of their own ever since…or at least, Pari had until recently. Without them, I knew we wouldn't be here today, let alone attending Eva and Bash's bonding ceremony.

Our group was often found together in Tobias's kitchen late into the night. Once, I had gone to sit at the empty chair at the head of the table only for the entire group to tense and look at the stairs. I had quickly rerouted to sit somewhere else, though the chair remained vacant.

They had been surprisingly helpful in gathering what I needed for a few experiments, as evidenced by the mini laboratory that had overtaken my room. I had even taken a trip to the mortal realm with them, returning with a few "borrowed" supplies from the lab I had once worked for, though I left a generous anonymous donation from my abandoned bank account in the mortal realm to ease my guilt.

It was fascinating seeing the minutia of blood and magic, the microscopic way my blood cells seemed to shine with a magical layer of protection. Fae were unlikely to fall sick with so much as a cold with the magic of the land inherent in their blood. While I knew I had to be careful with my research—Pari's overreaction to the barest details left me certain of the taboo I was ignoring in my endeavors—I wasn't about to stop if it could help people.

Before long, I had to move my clothes as well as my bed into the room next door as my makeshift lab expanded. Tobias hadn't cared when I asked, only mumbling, "No one else is using it." I had a bad habit of not making it to bed when working late, often passing out beside my notepad, a pencil still resting against my lips. Though when I woke up, I usually found myself in my bed, still wearing yesterday's clothes, with a fresh glass of water on my bedside table.

I didn't have to guess who tucked me in. After all, he was the only one it could be. Not that he had ever acknowledged it.

But I refused to obsess over the enigma that was Tobias Maris today. Getting ready with my best friend felt like old times despite the vastly different circumstances. The fun of it remained the same, and I was sure I wasn't the only one who needed to escape from our new responsibilities. We both needed this chance to celebrate together and reconnect.

"Penny for your thoughts?"

Eva's teasing voice broke into my reverie, and I nearly smudged the kohl I was using to line my eyes. "Good luck finding a penny in this realm."

She rolled her eyes. "Quinn Sagray, I should've known you were fae long ago from your inability to answer an easy question with a straight answer."

I grinned at her. "Pot, meet kettle."

Eva shrugged as if to say, *fair enough,* her eyes twinkling with mirth. She reached down to scratch Phantom behind the ear. The giant black dog usually followed Bash around, his fur blending into his master's shadows. Today he was curled up at her feet. His snout nuzzled into Eva's hands, likely searching for a treat, as she let out a laugh. "For whatever reason, he won't leave my side today."

Phantom let out a loud grumble, like he knew we were talking about him. Eva scratched along the length of his back.

It was good to see my best friend so happy. She was owed a lifetime of it.

"I'll let you off the hook for the penny," I said impishly. "No need for bribery between sisters." My voice softened. "I was thinking how nice it is to be back together, without anything looming over our heads. And that we really ought to do more girls nights once you're officially Mrs. Ataren."

Eva laughed. "Who says Bash isn't becoming a Maris? Never mind the fact that I've never heard a fae use an honorific."

A fair point. With the exception of titles, as evidenced by the High Queen across from me.

"Count me in for a night off," Eva continued, looking wistful. "Just you and me. Maybe a few friends too…Yael and Marin could use a break with everything they've been doing for the rebuilding effort, and I've been meaning to catch up with Pari if you wanted to bring her along." She reached for my hand, squeezing gently. "Or we could keep it just us."

I wondered if Pari would come if she knew I would be there. She was still outwardly friendly to me, but it wasn't the same. The secret I had foolishly admitted to her had changed something between us.

It had been a mistake. I should've told Eva first—and now found myself even more scared to fess up. Instead, I had run away to Soleara, both to research and to avoid my best friend without looking like I was doing so. Eva had been through enough, and I refused to be the cause of any more strife. Besides, after Pari's reaction, I wasn't eager to test our friendship—or worse, cause any problems for her reign if it came out that Eva knew and kept my secret.

I should tell her. Pari had been pushing me to do so, though I had a feeling it was to make sure she wasn't the only one who was keeping an eye on me. And I would…*after* the wedding.

"Might as well mix it up," I said, squeezing back. "Make it a monthly thing for whoever can make it."

Eva grinned. "Or we could double date. Anyone catch your eye that you haven't told me about?"

Her tone was too casual in a way that made me feel like I was hiding something from her, though I wasn't. At least not about my love life.

"Like I've had time to date lately," I said with a laugh. "Thorin introduced me to one of his friends, who took me out for a drink a while ago, but we didn't hit it off." It had been months ago, and though he had been perfectly nice and more than a little handsome, I hadn't felt an inkling of interest.

"Akeno tried to set me up with someone too, but she just wasn't my type." Actually, she looked almost exactly like one of my ex-girlfriends. At the end of the night, she kissed me on the cheek, laughed at my obvious disinterest, and told me she would be happy to stay friends.

Eva went back to curling her hair, the fire magic imbued wand automatically flaring to life as she held it, adding, "So there's no one you're planning to dance with tonight?"

I slowly swiped on a rose-colored lip stain, pressing my lips together to even it out. For a heartbeat, a pair of familiar gold-flecked eyes flashed through my mind. A familiar figure deftly spun us around the dance floor, a gravelly voice whispering in my ear as those broad hands pulled me closer…

Clearing my throat, I muttered, "I'm sure Rivan's a good dancer."

Eva hummed noncommittally, brushing out her curls with her fingers.

"Though we should get him and Pari to take a spin together," I added thoughtfully. "For two people that seem to get along with everyone, they sure seem to rile each other up."

"*Right*?" Eva turned to me. "Do you know the story there? Bash had no idea what I was talking about when I mentioned it."

I shook my head. "Pari brushed me off when I finally asked. But I got the feeling there's more to it."

"I couldn't agree more," Eva muttered conspiratorially. "In fact—"

She let out a hiss of pain, dropping the curling wand to the floor. Phantom let out a loud whine, nudging at the back of her legs.

I immediately ran to her side, picked up the curler, and set it safely on the dresser. My magic roiled under my skin even before I scanned her for injury, sensing the need. Eva winced, lifting her opposite hand. A burn reddened the back of it.

"I'm usually not this clumsy. I just—" She grimaced down at the angry mark. "My mind must be elsewhere. You'd think an event like this wouldn't make me nervous after everything that's happened, but I keep thinking how much I preferred leading an army to planning a wedding." She laughed, but it sounded strained. "You should have seen me earlier when the seamstress came for one last fitting. I thought she stuck me with a pin on purpose because I couldn't keep still."

"Let me," I murmured, the bluish glow of my magic passing from my fingertips to cover the mark.

Eva let out a sigh as the burn disappeared. "Thanks. I know I should be able to do that for myself now…but for some reason, calling the magic of the land seems to be easier in life threatening situations."

I knew she was already stretched too thin, but with my friend's penchant for danger, it was past time she learned how to heal.

"We should take some time to practice your healing gifts now that the rebuilding efforts are finishing up," I offered. "After your bonding ceremony, when things calm down a bit. With Marin and me teaching you, I bet you'll have a handle on it soon enough."

Eva nodded, then paused, glancing down at her left hand where a message appeared above her rose-shaped scar. I read the iridescent note over her shoulder.

Is everything okay, hellion?

The quill tattooed on Eva's opposite palm seemed to come to life as her pointer finger touched the space where the message faded away. She smiled to herself as she wrote back, the bliss in it making my own heart want to burst.

I'm fine, worrywart. I'll see you soon.

The Eva I knew back in the human realm hadn't ever let herself open up to anyone. She hadn't allowed herself to *like* anyone, let alone stop guarding her heart long enough for it to turn into love. It was gratifying to see her so free, as that *anima* bond healed something within her that had long been broken.

A blush colored Eva's cheeks. I glanced down to see a new line of iridescent writing shimmering on her palm.

I can't wait to see you in your dress. And to tear it off you later with my teeth.

Eva looked up at me like she had just remembered I was there before promptly choking on air. I dissolved into giggles as Eva tried to hide her hand behind her back, as if I hadn't already read the words there. She broke a second later, laughing until tears shone in her eyes.

When I finally caught my breath, I walked toward the closet with a half-snorted, "Well, we better not keep your *anima* waiting. Though tell him that ripping your dress tonight would be nothing short of sacrilege. I can't wait to finally wear mine."

I had sent my measurements to my chosen sister months ago and had loved going through each revision of the seamstress's sketches. For tonight's dinner, I was wearing a perfect pale-yellow dress I helped design myself, and for tomorrow, a ball gown so breathtaking it had brought tears to my eyes. Its voluminous skirts fell in cascading layers of silk and tulle, and the bodice glittered with hand-stitched silver embroidery. Both featured tiny crystals that caught the light like dew at sunrise. Ever since my fitting a few weeks ago, I had been itching to slip into the final versions.

Before I could reach the handle, Eva caught my hand. I turned to see her suddenly serious face.

"I wanted to tell you how thankful I am that you're here," Eva said, sincerity ringing in each word. "I wouldn't want anyone else by my side this weekend."

"Besides your betrothed," I added jokingly, even as tears welled in my eyes.

She smiled devilishly. "You came first, and he's well aware of that fact."

"We're family, you and me." I took her other hand in my own so that they were both clasped together. "I wouldn't miss this for the world."

To my surprise, her skin felt clammy. Nerves perhaps—after all, she was about to host half the faerie realm in the coming days. A prickle crept up the back of my neck, my magic roiling inside me even as I tried to brush aside my unease.

There *was* a hint of shadow under her eyes and a certain heaviness in the way she was talking. Knowing Eva, she had likely put in too many sleepless nights lately with everything going on.

Before I could ask her if she was okay, she squeezed my hands. "Always forward?"

I smiled reassuringly. "Never back."

CHAPTER 5
TOBIAS

This trip to Morehaven couldn't end soon enough. I couldn't handle the ghosts and memories that haunted this palace, the way they found a way past my carefully crafted mental shields at every corner. I had been grateful for the excuse to return to my room to change for tonight's dinner, if only for the chance to be alone.

The second I closed the door behind me, I sank to my knees, utterly drained. It took all my effort to center myself enough to get back up. Even so, I spent so long fortifying the walls of my mental shields and checking for any cracks in the stone that I had to rush to get dressed.

Thankfully, I still managed to be the first to arrive. I didn't want anyone to see the effort it took to force myself from the doorway.

Dinner was set up on the balcony, to my dismay. The long oak table was covered in early spring blooms, their fresh floral scent filling my lungs with each breath. Tiny lights hung overhead like strings of fireflies, and candlelight cast a warm glow over the golden table settings. Long-stemmed glassware sparkled in the setting sun; each crystalline goblet shaped like a blossom and filled with bubbling wine. Musicians warmed up somewhere nearby, soft, melodic notes drifting through the air.

I couldn't help the tremor that coursed down my spine.

The world was too bright. Too brittle.

The waning sunlight tauntingly played across my face as I struggled to count out my breathing. The dichotomy of its light and the knowledge that there was no roof in between me and it warred with my control. My next breath in turned into a gasp as I tugged at the suddenly too tight collar of my shirt, fighting for air.

I needed to get a hold of myself before someone found me like this.

Somehow, the endless sky above only made me feel more boxed in. Below me, the cool white stone of Morehaven gleamed ominously, like it might swallow me whole.

I gritted my teeth. I was safe, I silently reminded myself. I was *free.*

I would never be trapped here again.

My inhale caught in my throat, my panic mounting despite myself. The ghost of the band still scarred around my neck seemed to tighten. I dug my fingers into the white stone of the railing, resisting the urge to scream.

A sinister part of me wanted to leave a mark. To break that seamless stone as I had been broken.

My magic surged at my fingertips, trying to fight the nonexistent threat. The effort of holding it back heated my blood, the searing pain grotesquely familiar…

A movement in my periphery brought me back to myself. My gaze locked with Quinn's. In an instant the heat, the pain, the crushing weight of it was gone. Her presence was a force all its own—one that had always proved impossible to resist.

Today, it would have been easier not to notice the sun than not to notice her, and I couldn't tear my gaze away. Her pale-yellow dress was like sunlight personified, just like the person who wore it. Her fingers nervously bunched her skirt as she came to a stop, the muscle of her thigh visible through the long slit that ran up one leg. A swirling pattern embellished the flowing, liquid-like fabric, small beads casting delicate reflections like sunbeams through stained glass. Her one shouldered neckline featured two thin, yellow straps that lay flat against her darker skin.

There was a gentle buzz in my ears as the world seemed to narrow around her and her alone. My head was full of forbidden thoughts as I drank in every detail. The curls of her hair that seemed to form a halo around her head in the dying light, the way that dress effortlessly hugged the curves of her body, the regality of her posture, the glow of her amber eyes…

"Tobias?"

It took a long second to realize my sister had joined us, let alone that she had spoken. "Yes?"

Eva looked at me askance. "I was just saying hello."

"R-right," I stammered. "Hello to you too."

For once, I hoped she attributed my ineloquence to the years spent without a voice, rather than the real reason.

Quinn smiled at me, and that buzzing sensation returned. "Ready for tonight?"

I forced myself to respond coherently this time. "Something like that. Is tonight the fae version of a rehearsal dinner?"

Eva grimaced. "Just a dinner among friends. I thought we would do things how I would've done them before the entire realm joins us tomorrow."

She wore a champagne dress that brought out the gold in her eyes. The silver-star necklace our parents had given her glinted at her collarbone, but my gaze caught on a pair of matching earrings resting against the curls of her chestnut hair—likely a gift from Bash.

The large black dog that usually followed Bash around sat behind her like her own personal shadow. Phantom's ears were perked at attention, his tail raised and still as he sniffed the air. Strange for a dog that I had only seen asleep at Bash's feet or begging for a treat.

Phantom whined low in his throat, and Eva reached over to scratch behind his ear. I took the opening to really look at my sister, my brow furrowing as I did so.

There were circles under Eva's eyes that I didn't remember from our last visit, a slight pallor to her tan skin despite the warm weather. She looked nearly as sleepless as I knew I did.

"You okay, sis?" The words were out of my mouth before I could stop them. "You look tired."

Eva's mouth twitched. "Gee, thanks. I've been busy. The rebuilding is a continual process, magic or no, and I *have* been planning a wedding..."

She sighed heavily, and I immediately felt awful.

"I just meant...I hope you aren't running yourself too ragged. If there's something I can do to help..."

Eva smiled, though something about it seemed off. "Thanks, Toby. I'm glad you're here."

Get it together, you absolute idiot.

"But you look lovely," I quickly added. "I mean it." I cleared my throat, letting my gaze flick over Quinn's yellow dress once more. "You too, Sagray."

"Thanks," Quinn said dryly, though there was a blush decorating her cheekbones that hadn't been there before.

A few waitstaff walked in with covered trays. Quinn moved closer to me to get out of their way, her arm brushing against mine. The casual touch would have meant nothing with anyone else, but from her it felt excruciatingly intimate.

I closed my eyes, allowing myself a single moment to center myself. To breathe her in.

When I opened them, Yael and Marin had walked outside. Both wore bright, celebratory colors—Yael in a flowing, one-shouldered turquoise jumpsuit, Marin in a blue lace dress adorned with silver flowers. Rivan and Bash followed, the latter of whom stared at my sister as if she was the only one in the room. Rivan's dark green doublet shimmered slightly in the light, and Bash's black jacket had golden embroidery to match his *anima*. Shadows blended into his sleeves, though one brave strand swooped forward to curl around Eva's exposed ankle.

Bash took Eva's hand, yanked her against him, and kissed her soundly. Yael brought two fingers into her mouth and let out a loud whistle. I looked away to give them some privacy—then immediately regretted it when it brought my focus back to our surroundings. The skyline seemed to widen, the space above me simultaneously pressing down while beckoning me into bright oblivion.

The greetings and chatter faded into the background as the group walked to the entirely too exposed table in the center of the balcony. Clenching my teeth, I focused on putting one foot in front of the other as I followed Quinn to our seats.

The menu in front of me blurred together as I reached for my goblet of wine, thankful it was already poured. I rarely resorted to drinking, not when the lack of control was more disconcerting than the open sky. But I had a feeling that a glass or two might be the only way I would make it through the evening, let alone tomorrow's main event.

Yael exclaimed loudly about the décor as she settled in across from me. I had barely noticed the faerie lights hovering slightly above the table, the fresh eucalyptus that stretched along its length and the bright begonias dotting the greenery.

"It's nice seeing you out and about," Yael said brightly as she caught my eye. "It's been too long since you've visited."

She winced just as Marin gave her a pointed look. I had a feeling that Marin had kicked her under the table.

My jaw worked as I weighed my response. "It's nice to see my sister."

"I imagine it's still novel to be together after those years apart," Rivan added, looking at me knowingly. "Especially here."

Marin grimaced slightly. "I imagine Tobias's experience puts our venue in a different perspective."

Making sure to school my face in the aloof veneer I had long since perfected, I finished my glass, then focused on pouring another. I couldn't stand their sympathy. The gentle hesitancy of their words, the way their kindness and compassion rankled, despite knowing it was well meaning.

Quinn's leg brushed against mine. "I'm glad we could all get together to make some better memories here, especially with Bash and Eva the reason why."

Except Quinn, of course. As always, she excelled at being the exception. She expertly steered the conversation away from me and my obvious discomfort, turning the discussion back to the impending nuptials while I tried not to focus on the darkening sky.

Quinn smiled cheerily, lifting her goblet. "To finding the person who makes your heart feel whole."

"Cheers to that," Yael said jovially, clinking her goblet against hers.

"To the happy couple," Marin added. "And your future happiness as well."

The clink of goblets echoed around the table. I shifted slightly, lifting my goblet gently against Quinn's.

"To happiness," she murmured, those amber eyes softening. I nodded, unable to bring myself to respond, yet entirely unable to look away.

Did she feel that same pull that I felt whenever I looked at her? I had spent years learning an unimaginable level of control. In fact, each day of it was still carved in an endless tally on the stone wall of my cell somewhere deep beneath us. And yet the beckoning of her amber gaze was a lure I couldn't escape. It was a siren's call, a longing that never seemed to ebb.

I was standing on a precipice, fighting the urge to leap and falling anyway in a strange sort of vertigo.

Bash got to his feet, smiling as he took Eva's hand. He brushed a kiss against the scar on her palm, then the back of her hand before raising his goblet. "To my *anima*. My perfect match, and a High Queen unlike any other. I will never stop loving you, no matter what the future brings. As long as you're by my side, I have no doubt that these years will be the best of my life."

Glasses clinked again, and I took a deep swig of the lush red wine, forcing a tight-lipped smile to my face when my sister glanced my way. I should've made more of an effort to reach out these past few months. Gods knew we had both been busy, Eva especially as she worked to coordinate the needs of everyone and everything that needed help after the war with the False King. But the relief on her face at seeing even that poor effort made the wine turn bitter in my mouth, settling in my stomach like a stone.

I should do better. She warranted that much from me after the way I abandoned her following our parents' deaths. I could invite her to visit Soleara again and make a real effort to reconnect this time, even if that meant I had to play host. I was well aware she was giving me space "until I was ready". The group that congregated in my kitchen wasn't nearly as quiet as they thought they were, especially after a few drinks.

Plus, Quinn could use the company. Though she had made friends with Pari, Akeno, and Thorin, she spent far too much time alone. Lately, she barely even had time for them. She worked on her experiments late into the night and stayed shut in her room almost as much as I did. I often walked past her door to see light streaming through the crack at the bottom, my fae hearing straining to understand her mutterings to herself.

Despite all Quinn was doing to help everyone else, I knew she could use someone to assist her. Someone to help her take notes, based on the pen marks often covering her hands, or at least make sure she remembered to take a break and eat. Every time I considered offering my own services, my fist had frozen in front of her door before I could knock, my throat tightening until I risked choking on my tongue.

Then I fled like the coward I was, locking my door behind me—moving my blanket to the floor to avoid the too-soft bed before I could close my eyes.

At least my nightmares hadn't woken her. In a cruel imitation of their contents, the fact that I was unable to cry out with that mask muting my voice meant that while I woke up from them drenched in sweat and trembling, my silent screams stayed trapped in my throat.

"Tobias?"

With a start, I realized Quinn was offering me a basket of bread, her eyes flickering with concern. The others had started eating, paying us no mind. Rivan loudly shared a story about his mother accompanying him to assist the Esterrans rebuild after the coup that had nearly taken down King Elias and his *anima* Noam.

Hastily, I took the basket.

A current traveled between us as our fingers brushed, the static nearly making me drop it. I placed the basket on the table before murmuring a quiet, "Thank you."

"It's nice sharing a meal together. I wouldn't be against doing it more often, you know...like old times." Quinn sounded hopeful but resigned, like she already knew what my answer would be.

I was careful not to let any reaction show on my face. We never dined together despite living in the same house half the time. She seemed to think it was an accident, a result of our schedules. Or maybe she realized I was avoiding both the intimacy of dining with her and the inevitable attempt at getting me to open up to her again.

Likely the latter. After all, she *was* the smartest person I knew.

Either way, I had no plans to stop. It was hard enough to maintain my composure.

"Just like old times," Eva chimed in. "Except less training beforehand."

"We can fix that," Rivan interjected to a chorus of groans.

Eva laughed, shaking her head. "When we were teenagers, the three of us would spend every Saturday training. Whoever was the overall winner got to pick what was for dinner."

That felt like a different life. Those happy, carefree kids, full of casual banter and high school drama. Not that most high schoolers spent their weekends fencing in their parents' secluded backyard, running drills and playing strategy games.

"Luckily, Tobias and I had the same taste in pizza toppings," Quinn said with a conspiratorial grin at me that made my stomach flip. "Whenever Eva won, we had to suffer through pineapple."

"A travesty," I muttered.

"Truly," Quinn agreed with faux seriousness.

She winked at me, and my cheeks burned.

"We'll have to host a pizza night in Soleara soon," Quinn said as I looked down at my plate. "It's been too long since you've visited, Eva."

"You and Tobias can take us hiking," Eva said brightly. "I bet the wildflowers this time of year are beautiful. I've been looking for an excuse to get lost in the mountains."

It was an effort to hide my horror at the prospect.

Quinn lifted her goblet. "Glad to hear you're not into hiking alone anymore." She glanced my way. "That would be fun. There's too much of Soleara I haven't explored yet, and so much more to see now that the winter's finally thawed."

I carefully laid my fork against my plate, unable to stomach another bite. The thought of going outdoors for fun, let alone spending the day beneath the open sky, made me want to melt into the stone beneath my feet. And turning them both down? It would be yet another excuse I would need to make in a long list of excuses. Another disappointment to add to the rest.

My vision blurred. It took longer than usual to wrangle that familiar helplessness, the dread that never seemed to ebb.

Picking up my wine, I downed the rest in a single gulp. Then I coldly pushed everything I was feeling deep down, picturing the cell to hold them. With an effort, I shoved everything behind those bars until I heard a key turn in a lock.

"I wonder if there's a path to the top from the outside of the mountain," Eva mused.

This time, the words floated past me. I would make an excuse when the time came, and they would go without me. It was better for everyone that way.

"I thought we'd fixed your danger-finding streak," Quinn said with mock dismay.

Bash let out a heavy sigh. Eva elbowed him in his side.

"I wouldn't have you any other way," Bash murmured. He lifted Eva's chin with the crook of his pointer finger before pressing a kiss to her lips.

Quinn glanced toward me, something in her expression faltering as our eyes met. I knew what she would see—the mask I slipped on like a second skin, like the one I spent so long hating had never been cleaved from my face.

Something deep inside me reached for her like a lifeline, the feelings I buried straining to escape the prison I created for them.

I looked away.

CHAPTER 6
QUINN

Tobias leaned against a pillar, nearly blending into the shadows. He was dressed almost entirely in black—from his leather boots to his billowy black shirt, the top buttons carelessly undone. His silver-embroidered jacket now hung from the back of his chair, though the night air had cooled as the last bit of sunlight faded from the sky.

A pale white band scarred his throat, the match to his sister's, in an eternal reminder of what they both had suffered. He rarely wore a shirt that covered it, perhaps to avoid the feeling of constriction. But as he brushed the mess of hair falling into his face away with one large hand, it was the taut muscles of his neck and the way his biceps bulged against his shirt that made me unable to look away.

As the sun set, a trio of musicians armed with string instruments had set up on the other side of the balcony. The lively sound of violins and the deeper bass of a cello echoed into the cool night air.

Bash and Eva swayed to the music, entirely lost to the world around them. Eva looked lovely tonight, her gold dress glowing in the dim light. The craftmanship was exceptional. The flowing fabric curved around her sweetheart neckline and cinched delicately at her waist. An underlying pattern of golden roses shone beneath the surface. Off-the-shoulder sleeves clung gently to her arms, and an asymmetric slit revealed the length of her thigh as Bash dipped her.

Eva laughed, and I couldn't help my smile at her joy. Bash stared at her so adoringly my heart ached.

I knew how much he loved her from the moment we met. He had nearly broken her door down in his impatience to get to her after her escape from Aviel in Soleara. And I didn't think he had taken his eyes off her since, like his entire universe revolved around her.

It wasn't just the way he looked at her that confirmed my trust in him—it was the way she softened in his presence. Even after everything she had endured, she could let herself breathe around him. It was more than simply an effect of their *anima* bond, which allowed them to sense each other's emotions. He gave her a sense of calm I hadn't seen in years, a quiet happiness that spoke to something like devotion. It was the kind of steady, all-consuming love that asked for nothing but gave everything in return.

Drawing in a breath to rally my nerve, I strode toward the shadows.

Tobias raised an eyebrow as I approached. "Didn't feel like dancing?"

"Maybe I was waiting for the right dance partner," I said with a smirk, wondering if he would take the hint.

Tobias nodded slowly, a divot forming between his brows. "I'm sure you'll have your pick tomorrow."

He sounded resigned. Did he truly not realize my implication or was it something else—the thought of the event itself? In all my time in Soleara, Tobias had largely remained out of the public eye, content to delegate where he could as he worked behind the scenes. Except for our bouts in the training yard, I could barely remember the last time I had seen him outside the castle walls.

Was it the socializing, the crowds...or was there more to it?

"I wasn't talking about tomorrow," I said softly.

I stepped closer, my eyes catching on a button that had come undone on his sleeve. Tobias stiffened as I reached for his wrist, barely seeming to breathe as I refastened it. He was disconcertingly close, the faint, almost smokey scent of him—like charred cedar—making me feel dizzy. My cheeks heated from the weight of his gaze on me, though I didn't raise my eyes from my task.

"There," I said, backing away a step. "Wouldn't want to ruin your outfit. You look...nice."

The corner of his lips twitched, as if fighting a smile. "I look better than that, Sagray, and you know it."

I raised my eyebrows. "Full of yourself, are we?"

"Why shouldn't I be?" He gave me a far too charming half smile I hadn't seen since we were teens. "After all, *you* can't seem to keep your eyes off me."

There was something heady and intoxicating about the way he looked at me that I couldn't even blame on the alcohol.

Two could play at that game. "Funny, I was just about to say the same thing about you."

I could have sworn he blushed. Tobias stumbled slightly as he took a step toward me, then grabbed the side of the pillar to steady himself.

My mouth dropped open before splitting into a grin. "Tobias Maris, are you drunk?"

Well, that explained the brief hint of levity.

Tobias looked affronted even as he swayed on his feet. "I had three drinks. Maybe four. I am absolutely…"

He staggered back against the pillar. A laugh sprang from my throat.

"Maybe," Tobias confessed with a hint of surprise. "I haven't exactly had time to build up my tolerance."

"I promise I won't take advantage of you," I said teasingly, even as the reason behind his inebriation struck home.

Tobias's eyes widened slightly, then he shook his head like he was attempting to clear it.

"I'll admit to…tipsy." His words slurred slightly. "Though I'm not sure if it's helping."

His eyes flicked upward, his expression going distant like some buried memory had surfaced. A rough swallow tightened his throat, his shoulders folding in as his gaze grew haunted. White-knuckled fingers curled onto the stone pillar like he was searching for a handhold, a lifeline.

I said his name in a desperate attempt to pull him back to me. "Tobias?"

He flinched, his eyes meeting mine like he had forgotten I was there.

"I was just giving you a hard time," I said gingerly. "It's okay to let loose every once and a while. Honestly, it's nice to see you lighten up for once."

Tobias blinked once, then again. Shaking his head slightly, he focused his attention back on me, his voice shaky as he whispered, "Then distract me."

"Okay," I immediately agreed. "What do you want me to—"

"Dance with me."

Tobias said it urgently, like it was a need rather than merely a want—like my denial might break him. He held out a hand, eyes wild with a mix of panic and raw vulnerability.

"Of course I will," I said simply, slipping my hand into his before I even finished my answer. "I asked you first, didn't I?"

His body tightened like he was bracing himself. Slowly, I placed my hand on his shoulder, meeting his eyes as his other hand wrapped around my waist. He cradled me gently, his fingers curling around my hand like I was something precious.

Tobias took a deliberate breath in before he led us onto the makeshift dance floor, slowly letting it out as he met my gaze. I could feel the other's eyes on us as we swayed in time to the music, my best friend's sharp gaze among them. But I didn't dare look away from Tobias—not when he needed me.

Eva had been so worried about her brother after the way he had spent the past few months shutting everyone out. I knew she had hoped that my choice to stay in Soleara might lead him to open up to me. And yet, despite our bedrooms sharing the same floor and our silent training sessions, the distance between us felt staggering.

Maybe I was taking advantage of him, in a way. But for once, his guard was down, and I wasn't about to push him away.

His hand moved to the exposed skin of my back. A shiver ran down my spine as a strange sort of shock passed between us.

Tobias's gaze fixed on mine. "Do I make you nervous, Sagray?"

"No," I said bluntly. "You're just an interesting mix of who you were before and who you are now. I'm never sure which one I'm going to get."

He stared at me unblinkingly, his head tilting as if weighing my words. "Who am I now?"

"Hard to tell. You've been avoiding me."

The accusation slipped out before I could stop it. At least my voice was low enough not to be heard over the music and laughter on the other side of the balcony.

I suppose this counted as part of the distraction.

Tobias's jaw flexed. "How very astute of you."

I blinked. "You're not even going to deny it?"

"I wouldn't dare insult your considerable intelligence," Tobias drawled. Then he smirked, a hint of that one-sided dimple creasing his cheek. "Now are you going to let me lead?"

Stiffening, I realized he wasn't wrong. I was practically pulling him around the dance floor with how much I was resisting. Swordplay and fighting, I knew. Dancing was another story.

After all, even when we sparred together I was still in control. I wasn't used to letting someone else lead.

"Don't change the subject," I snapped, though I made myself relax into his hold, allowing him to take charge.

We always had that sort of relationship. The snark, the casual, easy banter that usually had Eva rolling her eyes at us. Or at least we had. Now, he could barely look me in the eye most days.

Tobias raised his brows in mock innocence. "Here I thought we were just trading facts."

He spun me around, the move catching me off guard, before pulling me back into him. I stumbled against him, our bodies pressing together in an awkward hug. Tobias stiffened like he didn't know how to reciprocate that kind of affection anymore. Then his head dipped, his voice a low rumble as he whispered, "But I'm not avoiding you right now, am I?"

My breath caught. I leaned back just enough to look him in the eye. "Drunkenly dancing wasn't exactly what I had in mind."

"I don't know," Tobias murmured, his eyes darkening as they zeroed in on my face. "I don't exactly mind it."

Tobias twisted us, his hand tightening on my waist before he gently lowered me into a dip. Time seemed to stand still as I stared up at him. I wanted to trace the slight curve of his lips with my fingertip—to feel that hint of happiness on a face that was usually so expressionless before it disappeared again.

My breathing quickened. A deep flush stained his cheeks as he brought us back upright.

This…this was *him* for once. Or at least a glimpse of him. I knew he wasn't the same kid I had grown up with, nor did I want him to be. But I was so sick of Tobias acting like the boy who used to laugh with me was as dead as he once pretended to be.

And I missed him.

"Well, I wouldn't mind if you stopped avoiding everyone who cares about you." The words came out sharper than I intended, and I immediately wished I hadn't said anything at all. I could practically see his walls slamming down. Something sank in my stomach as he pulled away.

"Spare me, Sagray."

The night felt so much colder without his warmth surrounding me.

"You should talk to someone. Please." I wasn't above begging if it meant getting through to him. "It's been months of this, and I can only watch you wither away for so long."

He took another step backward. "No one's asking you to. I'm fine. And I don't need you to save me."

"I'm not trying to—"

A bark cut me off, then the crash of broken glass. My head whipped around, my feet already moving in a blind urge to help.

My heart lurched at the sight of Eva half-fallen against the table, her goblet in shards on the ground. Wine spread around her, soaking into the hem of her dress. Bash was there before I could blink, helping her back to her feet.

Tobias and I ran to the table along with the others, any hint of merriment forgotten. Phantom barked again with more urgency, his ears pinned back as he nudged Eva's hand with his nose.

"I'm okay," Eva said, a little shakily. "I must have had a little too much wine—"

"Eva...you're bleeding."

My chest constricted at the concern in Bash's voice. A cold wave of dread surged through me as Eva reached up to touch the trickle of blood underneath her nose, smearing it across her upper lip.

Eva let out a hollow sounding laugh as she looked at the red on her fingertips. "Not sure what sort of omen this is before a wedding." She smiled, though it seemed shaky as she amended, "Bonding ceremony, that is."

Bash passed her a glass of water. Eva waved him away as she took a long sip. Red mixed with its contents in swirling circles.

I reached for my healing magic, but a buried part of me stirred—eager and almost insistent that I use it. I took a step back, clenching my hands into fists.

"Let me see," Marin said, moving closer. Magic glowed at her fingertips, its color an innocuous green.

Eva spat out the next sip. Blood dribbled down her chin, growing worse with each passing second. She swiped at it with the back of her hand, only succeeding in smearing it across her face. Tobias silently passed her a cloth napkin. She gave him a grateful nod before pressing it against her nose.

"It's just a nosebleed," Eva whispered as if reassuring herself. The napkin steadily reddened as it soaked through.

Marin gently rested her hand over Eva's face, healing magic flowing from her fingertips. Her face turned grim, her expression tightening as she worked.

A few drops of dark red dripped onto the pale silk of Eva's dress, the marks slashing over her heart. My stomach dropped, a sudden sense of fear making my heart pound.

I stepped forward, my eyes trained on the flow of blood that showed no sign of abating. It was an effort to keep my voice calm as I told her, "You'll be okay. Between Marin and I, I'm sure we can fix this."

Eva swayed on her feet. She was pale...too pale. Sweat beaded at her brow, her breathing far too labored. Her arm dropped to her side, the bloodied napkin falling to the marble floor. "I...I think something's wrong."

Bash pressed his hand to his forehead with a small groan of pain. Then his gaze shot to Eva. The agony in his eyes stole my breath—a reflection, I knew, of what Eva must be sharing through their bond.

"Eva."

Time slowed to sluggish heartbeats as she started to fall. Bash lunged for her, but Tobias was closer.

He caught her just before her lifeless body hit the floor.

CHAPTER 7
TOBIAS

She still wasn't awake.

Bash held Eva's hand as Marin and Quinn worked in tandem, occasionally murmuring hushed vitals to each other, I could barely hear them over the alarm bells ringing in my ears. Phantom lay at Eva's feet, refusing to move despite the chaos around him.

Quinn wasn't panicking. No, she jumped right into action the second Eva fell, checking my twin's pulse as I held her in my arms. I hadn't been able to breathe until Quinn confirmed Eva was alive, the blue of her magic washing over Eva like a phosphorescent flood.

All I had been able to do was stare at the blood staining her chin, a fresh trickle spilling across both her cheeks into her hair. At least I had the wherewithal to follow Quinn's curt order to bring Eva upstairs to her room once they were able to stop the bleeding. Now I was simply standing here, useless. Powerless, again. Worthless and waiting for any sign that my twin would be okay.

She was my sister, my responsibility. I failed her once…I wouldn't do so again.

"How c-can I help?"

I didn't let myself outwardly react to the stutter that returned when my guard was down, though I inwardly cringed at the sound of it. It was an aftereffect of those long years deciding whether it was worth the pain of using my voice. Though it was better most of the time...worse when I hadn't been speaking in a while, as I was prone to do. Stress seemed to be the main culprit, and right now I was beyond terrified.

At least Quinn was too distracted to notice the stutter or didn't care.

"Wet washcloths," Quinn said briskly, wiping her forehead with the back of her hand. "Cold for her forehead, and a warm one to wipe the blood off her face."

I hurried to obey, nearly tripping over my own feet as I returned with a bowl of warm water along with a few hand towels. Bash silently took the cold towel from me, carefully folding it before placing it on Eva's sweat-damp forehead. Then he got to work wiping the dried blood from her face, his hand shaking.

At least the bleeding had stopped. That had to be a good sign. But from the pallor of her skin, the quickness of her breathing, and the fear on the two healer's faces, I knew this was far from over.

Unease curled tight around my ribs, making my heart pound. Eva looked like the slightest thing might break her.

"She's burning up," Marin whispered. I realized belatedly there was an unspoken ask behind the words as shadows unlatched the windows, opening the two closest in unison. Yael lifted her hand, and a steady stream of cool night air blew past me, rustling Eva's hair.

"I don't have a lot of experience with disease in this realm," Quinn said with a calm I envied. "But something about this feels off."

Marin nodded tiredly. "You're not wrong. Fae can normally fight off the illnesses that plague the human realm. This sort of reaction is rare, especially with the speed of its onset. Which isn't to say that there isn't still disease here, but the magic of this realm usually keeps it from becoming life-threatening." Her features pinched as concern crept into her expression. "Whatever this is, it isn't something I've treated before."

Eva let out a small moan and the room fell silent.

Bash lurched forward, his thumb stroking her cheek. "Please hellion. Open your eyes for me."

I held my breath, silently praying she would obey his plea. But there was only the strained sound of Eva's breathing as her *anima*'s shadows pushed the damp hair back from her forehead.

Bash's voice shook as he looked at Marin. "Is there something we should give her? Someone else who can figure out what's wrong?"

I don't think I had ever seen Marin look so helpless. "We could request help from Mayim. Queen Sariyah may be able to send a few of her healers with more experience fighting whatever this is. They'll want to be notified of any potential new virus anyways."

Quinn glanced my way. "The water magic in the Western Kingdom naturally lends itself to more healers—something to do with water's natural resonance with healing. There's a Healer's Enclave there full of fae that specialize in this sort of thing."

It was a detail I vaguely remembered being told once. Somehow, she had seen my confusion through all the chaos.

"I'll see what I can do," Rivan said with a firmness that told me he wouldn't fail. He turned on his heel before running out the bedroom door. Part of me wondered if he would send a missive or run straight through the closest mirror and drag an unsuspecting healer or two back with him.

Yael cleared her throat. "We should let people know there's no way the bonding ceremony's happening tomorrow."

Inwardly, I winced. Eva had spent so much of the little time she had planning this—not for herself, I knew, but for those around her.

This timing couldn't be coincidental.

I didn't want to put my suspicions into words just yet. Though the worse she got, the harder it was not to.

Bash blinked at Yael like he had entirely forgotten why we were all here. "Could you…"

"Of course," Yael replied before he could even finish his thought. "And I'll let Dianthe know not to expect Marin and I back anytime soon. Imyr will be in safe hands. I can take care of anything needed here, so you can focus on Eva." She looked over her shoulder as she hurried after Rivan. "I'll be right back to help cool her down. That breeze should last for now."

I offered Bash another damp towel, exchanging it for the now soaked one he had been using. He dropped it into the bowl, blood immediately turning the clear liquid dark red.

Quinn stared at it, her teeth sinking into her lower lip—an anxious habit I remembered from our teens. I had known her too long not to recognize the look of an idea forming.

Her expression cleared, replaced by a steely resolve. "Do you have any syringes handy to draw some blood samples? I want to run a few basic tests." Her brow furrowed. "I borrowed a centrifuge the last time I visited the human realm that I managed to power, though I don't exactly have the resources of a full lab here. My magic might help make up for what I'm missing though. I'll also need a throat swab to see if I can detect any pathogens, though I can fashion something myself—" She cut herself off as she realized Bash and Marin were staring at her in horror. "What is it?"

"It's just…you've seen how blood and magic can be used," Marin said slowly. "Bloodletting isn't…it's not a request many in this realm are comfortable with."

I knew better than most what blood magic could do. Aviel had stolen my blood to track my sister down in her dreams. My teeth ground together at the insinuation Quinn would use it for anything of the sort, let alone that she was capable of dark magic.

Quinn let out an exasperated noise. "I'm not trying to hurt her. I'm trying to *save* her."

"I know," Bash said hoarsely. "And if it helps her, I'll find what you need myself. But you need to be very, very careful her blood doesn't fall into the wrong hands."

Quinn's gaze softened. "Of course."

Eva's breathing hitched, and Bash's gaze immediately went to her. I didn't miss the way his hand trembled as he brushed a stray curl away from her cheek, tucking it gently behind the point of her ear.

I turned from the intimacy of the gesture, looking back at Quinn. "Let me know how I c-can help." Not that I knew what I was doing. "If you need a pair of steady hands while you work, or help gathering supplies, or… anything…"

My voice trailed off awkwardly, the last word pleading. I had been stuck on the wrong side of the mirror underneath Adronix, trapped in that dungeon while Aviel hunted her, and unable to help my sister far too many times already.

I wouldn't be sidelined again.

Quinn drew her lip back between her teeth, thinking. "Getting the supplies I'll need from the mortal realm will take time. But if that's our only option, then we'll just have to travel as quickly as we can."

Riding through the Faewilds sounded like the worst sort of torture even with the canopy of trees overhead. I would do it without question for Eva. For Quinn, who I wasn't about to let take that journey alone. Her imploring look would entice me to follow her anywhere, really.

Marin swallowed hard, looking a little nauseous. "I didn't destroy the syringes Silvius left behind…or anything else for that matter, just in case it helped lead us to him. He still hasn't been seen since before Aviel's death." A fact that lingered like a thorn I couldn't pull free. "I blocked off his laboratory with a ward. Maybe there's something in there to save you the trip?"

Aviel may have been my torturer, but Silvius's inventions—the band that stole my magic, the mask that silenced my voice—paired with his utter indifference to the pain his experiments caused was, in a way, far worse. It was an effort not to flinch at the casual way Marin said his name, like invoking it would somehow elicit his attention.

Unless it was already too late for that.

"He has a working lab here?" Quinn sounded as shocked as I felt. "And no one thought to tell me this sooner?"

"I was planning to have it destroyed," Bash said, his gaze never leaving Eva's face. "But I didn't want to until that bastard is found, in case we missed any clues about his disappearance in his belongings."

"At the very least, it'll be more sterile than the setup I have in Soleara," Quinn said hesitantly. "Tobias and I can go gather what I need, assuming it's not too hard to get there?"

If Silvius had a hand in this, that would be the best place to confirm it. If I didn't find anything down there, I could at least tell Quinn my concerns without panicking the entire group for no good reason.

My magic burned at the thought of returning below this castle, even though we wouldn't go near the dungeon. I clenched my fists. The heat of my fingertips seared into my palms, the burn welcome as the pain drove away the fear threatening to consume me.

"I'll come with you to take down the wards, then come back," Marin said. She turned to Bash. "Try to keep her cool. A lukewarm bath might help…I'll go get it running. If she wakes while I'm gone, make sure she drinks some water. With the way that fever's already spiking, she's at risk of dehydration."

Bash nodded. Marin walked into the adjoining bathroom, the sound of flowing water the only sound until it shut off.

When she returned, Bash barely seemed to notice. Shadows swirled in his irises, the only sign of life as he stared blankly at Eva, like her absence was tearing out the very heart of him.

"I can barely feel her." He sounded breathless, like he was breathing for both of them. "I don't understand why she isn't healing herself. The magic of the land…it saved her before."

Quinn sighed, her shoulders slumping. "It was a conscious decision when she called it to heal herself and Rivan. Maybe when she wakes, we can get her to try."

If she wakes. I knew better than to say the dark thought aloud. Not when we are all already thinking it.

Bash set his blood-covered towel aside, then reached back for Eva like he couldn't bear not touching her even for a second. His thumb stroked against her cheek before resting on her temple. "We spent so long not knowing. Fighting what we were because we thought we knew better. Losing that time together." He drew in a shaky breath. "And then I almost lost her to Aviel…only for this to happen."

"You're not losing her," Quinn said, her voice soft but firm. "We won't let that happen."

"I can try to dreamwalk to her…as long as whatever's affecting our bond doesn't block that too." Bash's shadows stroked down Eva's limp arms as if gently trying to wake her up, a storm swirling in his eyes. "It feels like a fog I can't fully penetrate. Something impermeable, and I think it's worsening."

Marin leaned over the bed, pressing two fingers against Eva's brow. She frowned as her magic flowed from her hands in a greenish glow. "I think I can sense what you're talking about." She swallowed hard. "Let's go so I can get back quickly."

Quinn nodded, then looked at Bash. "Do you need help getting her in the bath?"

A curved shadow supported Eva's head as Bash gently lifted her into his arms, two more slipping off her shoes. "I've got her."

He brushed a kiss against my sister's forehead in a gesture so intimate that it felt like I was intruding.

Marin tilted her head in a silent invitation to follow. Quinn reached the doorway first, then glanced behind her, making sure I was following. Our eyes locked, her fear so sharp it carved into me as we hurried down the hall.

✧

I could feel every step downward in my bones. My body screamed at me to turn back around, my magic heating beneath my skin like it was trying to escape. The faint screaming in my ears got louder the further down we got, until it was all I could hear.

Marin stopped short, and I snapped to attention. We stood in front of an iron doorway. There was no need to tell us where we were. A greenish glow spread around the edge of the iron as Marin removed the wards blocking Silvius's laboratory from entry. With a grunt, she yanked one of the doors open. The sound of iron against stone froze me in place.

"You know where to find me," Marin said tersely before turning on her heel.

Quinn started forward, and I forced myself to follow. There was no telling what traps Silvius might have left behind, even if Eva's friends had already given it a once-over. I wouldn't let her go in there alone.

The counters were silver, the walls white. A solitary window allowed the moonlight to stream into the room, dim lighting flaring to life once we passed the threshold. For some reason, I had been picturing a mad scientist's lair, not this sterile scene. Quinn rummaged through the identical silver cabinets, laying out an assortment of medical implements. I turned away from a tray of syringes that made me feel queasy to look at.

It had been bad enough walking into the depths of Morehaven as I pictured the dungeon and the mask and the cell that had caged me. At least the mask had been eradicated. Silvius had only ever made one, a fact he had told me almost proudly, like I should be impressed by the uniqueness of the iron pressing against my face with tortuous claustrophobia.

An ornate desk lay against the far wall, covered in orderly stacks of leatherbound notebooks, evenly spaced handwriting labelling the spine of each one. A glass of water still sat half-drank by a few loose pages of notes, like Silvius had left in a hurry. I shuddered as I realized the open page included a labeled drawing of the collar that had left a permanent brand around my neck. The scar stood in stark contrast to my skin—eternally pale like the thin band had succeeded in sucking even the pigment from my flesh.

The thought that this was the place where Silvius created the torture instruments that had trapped me here made my stomach turn. He and Aviel had done a lot to me in that dungeon: stole my freedom, my dignity, and my blood. But Silvius stripping me of my voice—robbing me of even the words to defend myself—might have been the cruelest of all.

Now wasn't the time to dwell on that, nor let that fear keep me from helping Eva now. If Silvius was behind this, those notes were the best place to start.

I closed my eyes, pushing away the fears I couldn't bear to face, resealing my darkest memories into the mental dungeon I had recreated stone by stone. With effort, I trapped them behind the same bars where some scared part of me still screamed.

When I reopened my eyes, I was calm, if detached.

Quinn flitted around the room, anxiety in every hurried step. The panic in her expression immediately threatened that indifference despite my best efforts…especially when her lower lip trembled.

I made myself walk away from her, turning my back as soon as I reached the desk. The leather notebooks were in no apparent order, so I picked up the closest one, rifling through it. It detailed Silvius's experiments with the serum he used to keep Aviel's prisoners unconscious for transport…or worse.

The last page crumpled in my hand as I thought of how it had been used on my sister. My magic sparked from my fingertips along with my rage, nearly igniting the paper in my hands. Blowing out a careful breath, I pictured four walls closing around that feeling, the clang of a metal door reverberating through me as I put the memory of her terror back where it belonged.

My hand trembled as I picked up the next notebook. My mental cell doors shook as I reached the page detailing Silvius's trial and errors when working against different magics. It didn't note their names—he likely never knew them—but his test subjects were obviously some of the prisoners I once shared a dungeon with, never to return. They had been reduced to numbers and brief descriptions to compare their sex, physical strength, magical ability, and susceptibility to what Silvius put them through. He had experimented on them, *tortured* them, only to release them to Aviel when he was finished, who stole their life force along with their magic.

Breathing in, I forced the thought of their suffering away on the next exhale, that calm colder than before. Another page, another deranged experiment. This one focused on a collar meant for total control, though it seemed like his attempts at forcing his subjects into subservience had limited results.

The scar circling my neck seemed to tighten as I read, as if taunting me. If Silvius had managed to give Aviel my free will, we would be living in a very different world right now. And if he had used it on my sister…

I reached for another notebook, thumbing through it more rapidly as if skimming the horrors he created might make it easier to read. This one had to do with fae biology. My fingers spasmed, my pace slowing as I reached the detailed notes on blood magic and its uses. It came as no surprise this was part of his research. When Aviel had failed to break me through torture alone, it was Silvius who suggested the best way to find Eva was through the blood tie that linked us.

The memory tore through me faster than I could contain it.

Iron bit into my skin as I strained against my shackles, trying desperately to move away from the empty syringe.

"Stay still," Silvius said irritably. "Or I'll ask my king to drain your magic until you pass out again."

I struggled harder, bucking against my bonds as that needle neared my vein. He would win eventually. But I would make him work for it.

"Have it your way," Silvius sneered.

I braced myself, knowing what would happen next...

"Tobias?"

I startled, dropping the notebook so it landed open on the desk. Closing my eyes, I emptied my mind yet again, locking that memory back behind iron bars. Cursing myself for setting it free, I chained the emotions that came with it somewhere so deep underground that no one could hear their screams.

"Tobias," Quinn said more urgently.

I opened my eyes, then froze. The proof was right in front of me. I coughed, choking on air in my haste to speak. Quinn rushed over to me, her voice cutting through the silence as I fought to form words.

"What is it?"

I pushed the notebook toward her, turning it so she could read the neatly scrawled writing that made it hard to breathe. She picked it up, scanning the page with a growing frown. I watched her eyes widen, her mouth forming into a wide O as those amber eyes found mine.

"I think...I think this is all connected," I rasped. "We need to tell the others."

CHAPTER 8
QUINN

I clutched the notebook to my chest, balancing the tray of supplies I had gathered in the other. Tobias took the tray from me before I could protest, his fingertips brushing against my own.

It shouldn't have made my pulse skip, but it did.

"I can carry that," I said belatedly.

Tobias shrugged nonchalantly, still the gentleman I knew he had been raised to be despite everything. "Just because you can doesn't mean you should." He nodded at the notebook in my hands. "You can bring that though."

He seemed to be avoiding looking at the phlebotomy kit I found…not at the vials, the disinfectant, and the gauze, I realized, but the syringes we would need to draw Eva's blood. I didn't remember him having a fear of needles when we were younger…

My stomach dropped as I realized the reason why. Rage quickly took its place.

Of course they had drugged him during his time here. At the very least, they had stolen his blood to create the bloodlink Aviel used to reach Eva in her dreams.

If he was now afraid of needles, he had good reason—one that made me want to tear Silvius apart for his role in it.

One of the syringes slid slightly as Tobias started walking to the door, and he blanched, his throat bobbing just slightly. The tips of his fingers went white where they tightened against the tray. I caught a fleeting glimpse of his tortured expression before he blinked, and it returned to that detached calm.

The words were out of my mouth before I could stop them. "Are you sure that you're okay?"

"Of course," Tobias said coolly. His face was serene, but the way the tray shook slightly said otherwise.

He acted like emotions were dangerous, something to be handled and erased. It was unsurprising given how long he had to hide them…and how much he had to lose if he broke.

I let out a soft sigh, fighting the overwhelming urge to take his hand. "You can talk to me, you know."

"I thought we'd already covered this part of the evening."

Tobias's pace quickened. I struggled to keep up as I followed him back up the spiral staircase that brought us here.

"You were never given time to grieve, Tobias." I wasn't sure if it was the statement or me finally using his first name that stopped him in his tracks. His shoulders went rigid as the syringes slid toward him, though they stopped short of touching him. "And you obviously haven't taken time to process what happened to you. It's okay that you need time to settle into things, especially with an entire kingdom that needs you too. But it's past time to face things—"

"If you haven't noticed, we're immortal now, Sagray." My last name was pointedly curt, his voice sharper than I had ever heard it. "Or practically. Let me deal with my own life on my own time."

"You can't expect to get better if you don't at least talk to someone," I continued, undeterred. "I imagine half this realm has post-traumatic stress disorders after the war. But you were Aviel's prisoner for *years*. What he put you through…"

Tobias turned to glare at me, the first real sign of emotion I had seen from him since Eva had collapsed in his arms. "Stop diagnosing me."

I stood my ground, glaring right back. "I just want to help."

His eyes flickered, a flash of light igniting his irises. "Why?"

"You're my friend."

His flinch was nearly imperceptible, but I caught it.

"You're my sister's friend," he said, his words clipped.

It was my turn to flinch as he started to walk away. I followed, taking the steps two at a time to keep up as I snapped, "That's bullshit, and you know it. We were friends before you died—"

A muscle in his jaw jumped. "This isn't the time to talk about this—"

"—and friends during the war, or did you think I spent every day riding next to you on the journey to that freaking mountain because I'm friends with your *sister?* She's also worried about you, if that wasn't obvious."

Tobias walked faster. "What's obvious is that we have more important things to worry about right now."

My voice echoed in the stone stairwell. "I don't know why you decided to push me away after everything we've been through, but I'm sick of it."

We reached the top of the stairs. Tobias came to a stop so quickly I almost ran into him.

His eyes closed like he was in agony. "Maybe I realized you're better off without me."

The tray trembled, metal clattering against metal, and I reached out to steady it. My hands closed around his unthinkingly. Tobias's eyes flew open, staring at where we touched. He looked furious, not at me, but at himself.

"Well, I disagree." My lower lip trembled despite the anger still tinging my words. I was on edge, scared out of my mind for my best friend, and feeling the aftereffects of all the wine at dinner. While part of me knew that tears would be cathartic, I didn't have the luxury of allowing myself to break down just yet.

"I wouldn't expect anything less," Tobias drawled defensively. His eyes still seemed to glow like they were lit from within—a hint of the magic I only now realized I hadn't seen him use in forever. "But that doesn't mean I'm wrong."

"Doesn't mean you're right, either," I said sullenly. I should've waited to confront him about this until we were both in a better mindset to do so. In fact, I had promised myself I wouldn't mention it again until after Eva's wedding…when we could team up on him together. But it was too late to take the words back now that I had finally let them out.

"Who else will you talk to?" I demanded, a hint of pleading entering my voice. "Who else knows your heart?"

Something like longing crossed his face, too fleeting for me to be certain of it.

Tobias took an abrupt step back, breaking my hold. "My heart has nothing to do with it."

His face hardened, the light in his eyes disappearing like he had closed a door on his power. Even the gold flecks scattered around his irises seemed to darken.

I was starting to hate that look on his face. The cool, collected façade that felt like he had never been freed from the mask he had been forced to wear. The empty, hollow look in his eyes that seemed like he was trying to erase himself entirely.

Tobias cleared his throat. "Let's focus on Eva, shall we? I'm not the one who needs, or wants, your help."

That dismissive tone hurt worse than his words. I tried to bite my tongue against everything that I wanted to say in response, but I couldn't stop myself from throwing out one last lifeline.

"When you change your mind, I'll still be here."

Light flashed in Tobias's gaze. It was the only sign he heard me before he stormed from the stairwell.

My grip tightened on Silvius's notebook, the leather binding slick between them. I could only hope its contents weren't the cause of my best friend's illness—even as something within me whispered that I knew better.

✧

"You think *Silvius* is behind this?"

The rage in his tone turned Bash's words into more of a growl than a question. Shadows roiled down his arms, agitatedly weaving between Eva's fingers. Her hair was damp from her bath, and both she and Bash wore fresh, comfortable clothes. Eva's simple black nightgown was half-hidden under the covers that had been meticulously arranged around her.

Bash must have gone in the bath with her to safely cool her down and wash the blood from her hair. I blinked away the tears that mental image evoked, nodding as my voice failed me.

Bash's shadow-filled gaze found Rivan's, then narrowed. "I thought he disappeared."

"Our rangers followed his trail to Mayim over a month ago before it went cold," Rivan replied. "If there were any updates I would've told you. Though the added security ahead of your bonding ceremony should've made this impossible."

Marin frowned. "Then how do you think he did this to her?"

"There's been an influx of outsiders involved in the preparations," Yael said contemplatively. "And there are plenty of the False King's supporters who bought his lies and could've assisted Silvius."

Rivan crossed his arms. "That's our theory as to how he's evaded us so far, anyway."

Using the rubbing alcohol I found in the lab, I sterilized Eva's arm beneath a temporary tourniquet.

"Everything in that notebook matches her symptoms so far," I said grimly. "Lightheadedness, tiredness, and aggressive nosebleeds…all symptoms that Silvius noted for the incubation period. Then unconsciousness while the magic takes hold." I swallowed, hating the next words out of my mouth. "The research Tobias found shows Silvius was experimenting with weaponized pathology. He was trying to create a targeted magical illness to make his victims more malleable."

Bash winced as I carefully inserted a syringe into Eva's inner arm. His fists clenched and unclenched as he watched the steady drip of her blood into the syringe, like he was actively reminding himself I wasn't a threat. I undid the tourniquet, turning my attention back to my task. Bash ran his hand through his already mussed hair, the way his auburn strands stuck up in every direction telling me it hadn't been the first time tonight.

Worry shrouded Yael's expression. "I don't like how that sounds."

Carefully, I switched out a fresh syringe, wishing I had blood collection tubes instead. I crooked my finger at Tobias, placing the used one back on the tray when he complied with the silent ask. He might be skittish around needles, but the others' deep-seated fears still made him the best choice to assist me.

"I don't see how he would have gotten close enough to Eva to infect her with this," Rivan added, his eyes locked on the full syringes. His repulsed fascination was clear as day, though I was grateful he held his tongue.

"*He* wouldn't need to," Tobias said darkly, staring down at the tray in his hands. "With the wedding preparations, would anyone have noticed an extra server in the kitchens put something in Eva's food?"

Rivan shook his head. "There are safeguards in place against that sort of foul play—"

"Then he was able to coerce someone with access to her," Tobias interrupted, his tone flat but certain. "Whoever it was, they did their job. I doubt they stuck around afterwards."

Stuck…something needled at me in the back of my mind, begging for me to get there.

I gasped aloud as it hit me. "The seamstress. Eva said she was here earlier today…and that she pricked her with a pin when Eva couldn't stay still."

It was the perfect cover, really. Something that might have gone entirely overlooked otherwise.

Bash looked murderous. "I want her found and questioned."

Yael and Rivan exchanged a look, then stood in almost perfect unison.

"Our rangers are already questioning anyone who got anywhere near Eva's food or drink tonight," Rivan said evenly. "I'll have them track down the seamstress."

Bash nodded. "I don't need to tell you that finding Silvius is now our top priority." His hands clenched, shadows ominously streaming between his fingers. "We need him alive…and preferably holding a cure for whatever he gave her."

"We'll leave for Mayim straightaway," Rivan said gravely. "If Silvius has the answers she needs, we'll find him."

Yael pressed a quick kiss on Marin's forehead in a chaste goodbye. "If there's any change, let us know."

She and Rivan were already discussing their next steps as they raced out of the door.

With the final syringe filled, I withdrew the needle and pressed a clean cloth against the puncture to staunch the bleeding. Then I neatly wrapped a bandage around Eva's arm to hold it in place, my movements automatic as my mind whirred. If I had interpreted Silvius's notes correctly from my brief review, this was more than a poison…this was a *virus*. Thankfully it didn't seem easily transmittable—not if he had needed someone to inject it for him.

Unfortunately, with magic involved, this would be far from a simple fix. I had known that from the second my own magic had been rebuffed by whatever Silvius had wrought.

Bash broke the loaded silence, his speech strained. "You said this illness makes its victims more malleable. What exactly do you mean by that? And is it…" His voice broke. "Can you heal her?"

Marin looked up from where she was scouring the notebook, seeming to come back to herself at her brother's attention. "The good news is that the aim of Silvius's research wasn't to kill the target."

Bash's jaw clenched. "And the bad news?"

Before Marin could respond, Eva's eyes fluttered open.

CHAPTER 9
TOBIAS

It took me a moment to figure out what was different. A cloudiness had settled in Eva's eyes, nearly obscuring the golden crown around her pupils. It had been strange to see her irises swirl with those golden flecks ever since she had become High Queen in an echo of the crown she could now summon at will. Now, seeing their stillness was far more unsettling.

"Eva," Bash breathed, every ounce of his concern condensed into those two syllables. He quickly walked back over to her, taking one of her hands in his. "You're awake."

"Bash?" Eva's voice was sleep clogged and raspy, but I could hear the relief in it.

Bash quickly brought a glass of water to her lips, supporting the back of her head. His every muscle was tense as he watched her take a sip, his eyes tracking each swallow.

His voice was hoarse as he asked, "Do you remember what happened?"

Eva blinked, then shook her head.

"You collapsed at dinner," Bash continued softly. "You had a nosebleed and now a fever, though there's a chance there's more to it—"

"Dinner?" Eva's voice was strained, a hint of panic creeping into her tone. "I don't understand."

She let out a gasping sort of breath. Her hand flew to her neck, and I recoiled as she reached for the pale scar that banded around her throat as if expecting something to be there. Her lower lip trembled as her hand flattened against her skin, rubbing it nervously. "My magic. There's something wrong. Why can't I…"

"Try to stay calm," Bash said evenly, though his hand shook as he reached for hers. "We think it has something to do with the virus itself." He glanced away, and I could hear the words he didn't say—namely, who was behind it. "We'll figure this out, hellion. I'm just glad you're awake—"

Eva gasped again, cutting him off. Her eyes went almost comically wide, though I wasn't laughing.

Because my sister was staring at me like she had seen a ghost.

"How…*how* did you escape?"

A cold weight settled in my chest. I opened my mouth, then closed it again.

The room seemed to freeze as Eva glanced between us all, her face paling as she noticed Quinn. "You're here, in Agadot. I thought you might be…" She swallowed hard, turning back to me. "How did you escape A-Aviel?"

Fuck.

Shadows flared from Bash's arms, curling around Eva protectively, though my sister's *anima* seemed to have turned to stone from how still he was standing.

"You saved me, Eva," I offered weakly. I looked at Quinn like she might be able to fix this. "And Quinn followed you here."

Quinn glanced between us, before softly asking, "What's the last thing you remember?"

If Eva knew I was alive but thought I was still imprisoned, that narrowed it down to a matter of days—a brief window that occurred months ago. Fear wrapped its fingers around my throat. Whatever this was, Silvius was indeed behind this. From the look Quinn gave me, she knew it too.

But it wasn't fear on her face. No, her features had hardened in steely determination.

Eva winced, rubbing her temples. "I'm not sure. My head…it feels cloudy, like looking through a fog."

"Our bond feels the same," Bash added with a shudder. "I can feel you, but it's tenuous. I thought it was the fever while you were unconscious, but it's almost like your magic's being blocked by the band again."

I couldn't help my flinch as Eva's hand slipped back to her neck to reconfirm her freedom. Quinn and Marin exchanged a look, though neither looked surprised.

"It's not exactly a regular fever, it's magically induced," Marin said grimly. "Silvius may have found a way to create a similar blocker through blood magic. And if it affected your memories..." She got to her feet, walking toward Eva. "Let me try something."

Eva's eyes widened at Silvius's name. The worried look she gave Bash seemed to snap him to attention, his thumb rubbing a gentle circle along the top of her hand. At least she still remembered who he was to her.

Marin's fingertips glowed with the faint green of her healing magic as she pressed them to Eva's forehead. "I'm going to try to...clear the fog. I could feel it there earlier, like a strange sort of barrier. I hoped it might be the magic of the land protecting your mind from the fever. I should've realized sooner that it was something more insidious."

My breath caught in my throat as Eva's eyes squeezed shut, barely breathing as Marin worked. Marin grimaced, a trickle of sweat beading at her brow.

Eva's eyes flew open.

"Oh," she breathed, the sound a sigh of relief.

Bash's chest heaved, as if he had finally allowed himself to breathe when she did. "Eva?"

"*Oh,*" Eva said again, this time sounding stricken.

The virus had made her lose *months*. She looked like the world had shifted, blinking again and again as her eyes filled with tears. Bash held her closer, his face deadly with rage.

Marin swayed on her feet. Quinn hurried forward, helping her onto a chair.

"Were you able to get rid of it?"

With a sigh, Marin shook her head. She sagged against her chair looking utterly exhausted. "I pushed it back, for now...but it's only a temporary solution. A way to treat the symptoms, not a cure."

Eva's chest rose, then stilled as she held her breath. I mimicked her breathing almost unconsciously, my counted exhale matching hers as my father's deep voice echoed in my ears.

"Hey sis," I said after the next inhale, forcing my voice to remain even. "What's the last thing you remember now?"

Her voice trembled as she whispered, "I...I think I remember dinner. You and Quinn were dancing." I couldn't help my glance at Quinn—keeping my expression carefully blank despite the warmth I could feel on my cheeks. "And then...nothing." She drew in a shaky breath. "Why does it feel like that was a lifetime ago?"

Marin leaned forward. "So, you remember all of us? You remember defeating Aviel and his army at Adronix?"

"Every time I reach for a memory, it feels like I'm fighting for it." Eva rubbed her temples, looking pained. "Like there's a barrier between the present and the past that's getting stronger."

"Silvius is behind this," I said quietly. "The research in his lab all but confirmed it."

Eva shuddered. She closed her eyes, and I watched her chest rise again, holding her breath before she carefully exhaled. "If he wanted to kill me, there are better ways."

"I-I think his goal is control," I said, willing my voice to stay steady. Whether or not it scared her, Eva deserved to know all the information. "The research mentioned making the infected malleable. Though I can only guess at his motivations."

I didn't have to say the reasons Aviel would have wanted to use this on Eva specifically. Nor was I the only one who had guessed why Silvius had created this virus in the first place. The way Bash's shadows sharpened like they were ready to strike told me we were both thinking it. If Aviel was alive, forcing Eva to bend to his will would've made sense, though the reason why turned my stomach. But what was Silvius's goal now beyond revenge?

Eva nodded woodenly. "I wish this was something I could fight with swords and fists. Something tangible, something real."

"Fighting a disease is a physical and mental battle," Quinn said gently. "It's a quiet sort of war, waged in the body and soul. But it's one we'll fight together."

Bash's voice was firm, certain. "And one we'll win, hellion."

My own assurances caught in my throat, trapped behind the hard knot of fear lodged there. Eva squeezed Bash's hand, looking pale but determined.

Quinn's nod held a confidence I ached to borrow. She turned to Marin.

"If you can push back the fog with magic, do you think we could get rid of it with more help?"

Marin shook her head. "It was like holding back the tide. I may have stemmed the flow, but eventually it'll break through the dam."

"Keep that up and I'll find that cure," Quinn said, and I found myself relaxing slightly at the sheer determination shining in her eyes as she looked back at my sister. "We have his research and your blood. You're going to be okay, Eva. We just need time and for you not to lose hope."

"Here I thought I was due for some time off from nearly dying," Eva said with a shaky laugh. Bash smiled in response, though it didn't touch the worry in his eyes. "But…my blood?"

"I took your blood to test it," Quinn said hesitantly. "I'll likely need more, too."

Eva winced but nodded. "Do what you need to do."

Quinn glanced at the tray beside the notebook that held the full syringes. I had set it down as soon as I could, unable to stomach the sight of them.

How many times did Silvius use those syringes on me?

I crossed my arms, trying not to think about the needle marks that had accumulated on my inner arms during my stay below this castle, though they had long since faded. Eva closed her eyes, trembling faintly, and I knew the sight of the syringe brought back similar memories. Barely contained fury darkened Bash's expression, but he gently took Eva's hand, his fingers blanching as she squeezed him tight.

Quinn sidestepped in front of the tray, hiding the syringes from view. "Hopefully more won't be needed." She paused, wearing a look I knew all too well—the one that meant the gears in her head were grinding toward something. "After what Marin did, can you reach the power of the land? Use its healing magic like you did under the mountain?"

I held my breath as I watched Eva's lips press in a thin line, her eyes fluttering closed in concentration. Her every muscle tensed, the room silent in anticipation.

Finally, Eva blew out a frustrated breath. "I…I don't think so. My head is still…" Pain flickered across her face, betraying its depth for a split second. "It feels like I can barely think."

Marin nodded like she had expected it wouldn't be that easy. "What about your darkness?"

Bash's shadows flitted from his hands, moving around Eva's fingers in swirling loops like they were trying to coax her magic out to play.

Eva closed her eyes again. Her hands trembled, her fingers extending until her joints locked. Then her shoulders slumped in defeat. "I'm sorry."

"From Silvius's notes, the virus is calibrated using the intended victim's own blood in order to block their magic," Marin said apologetically. "I didn't expect you to be able to, but I wanted to be sure."

Perhaps this had been Silvius's plan all along if he still had some of Eva's blood to use against her. When he vanished after Aviel's death, I hadn't considered what he might have taken with him. I was only grateful he was gone, though the knowledge he was still out there lingered like a shadow, darkening my thoughts whenever my mind strayed.

"There's nothing to apologize for," Bash assured Eva, taking her chin between his thumb and forefinger. "This isn't your fault."

"Here I thought you couldn't feel my emotions easily," Eva grumbled.

"I happen to spend an inordinate amount of time studying your face, hellion," Bash said, his mouth quirking in a faint smirk. "Just because I can't feel it doesn't mean I haven't memorized what every purse of those perfect lips means."

Eva's eyes softened. "A shame I'm not exactly up to what I'm currently thinking then."

Bash's smirk became a full grin. It quickly slipped away as Eva's expression twisted in pain.

She sucked in a breath through clenched teeth. "My head…"

"You need rest." Bash gently replaced the damp towel on Eva's forehead. "Try not to worry, okay? You just focus on feeling better."

Eva let her eyes fall shut, tilting her head to rest against Bash's hand. It flattened against her cheek, and she let out a weary sigh.

Her tone was wry as she asked, "Because you're worrying enough for the both of us?"

"Something like that," Bash admitted.

Eva sighed. "Well at least that tracks."

She ran her tongue over her chapped bottom lip. Bash immediately reached for her water glass. She intercepted it before he could lift it to her mouth, taking a large gulp. "What does Silvius's notebook say?"

"Based on the dates he wrote, this was in the works long before Aviel's death," Marin answered. "It's meant to target your mind, cutting you off from your memories so you'd be reliant on whomever you were with. And it went after your magic—or rather, your access to it. Aviel likely had this made to ensure those opposed him would bend the knee, whether they wanted to or not, though he would've needed their blood."

Eva grimaced. "So why now?"

"Destabilization, maybe," Bash said grimly. "Delaying the bonding ceremony to make you look weak, especially given the propaganda Aviel spread during the war about your legitimacy. Or perhaps it's a form of leverage if Silvius has a cure to barter. After all, he's been hunted for months now."

"Or revenge."

I immediately regretted saying it out loud. Because if Silvius was only out for revenge, then Eva was in far more danger. After all, we only hoped that Silvius had a cure. Eva's face fell, a flicker of fear flashing in her eyes before she shut them.

Quinn glared at me, her gaze full of reproach.

Eva's voice wavered as she asked, "So what can I do to help?"

She was putting on a brave face like she always did, but it wasn't hard to see how scared she was beneath it. I was going to tear Silvius limb from limb.

"The fever…that means your body's fighting it," Quinn said softly. "Your job is to keep up your strength. And to trust we'll find a way to fix it."

"And keep fighting, hellion," Bash added hoarsely. "Until we find a cure."

Eva swallowed hard, then nodded like she was too exhausted to formulate a response. Her skin looked sallow despite the flush to her cheeks, shadows stark beneath her glassy stare. Even her eyes looked terrifyingly lifeless without the flurry of gold flecks swirling around her irises.

For a second, I thought I could see a white fog reflected in her pupils. She blinked, and it was gone.

Bash tucked Eva's blanket beneath both arms, his shadows smoothing it as he did so. "Do you think you're up to eating something?"

"Maybe later," Eva sighed, sinking back into the pillows.

She was far too drained, too quickly. It was more of an effort than usual to keep the fear off my face.

My sister was many things, but weak was never one of them.

Yet the worry in her eyes, the sluggish, careful way she moved…not only was she afraid, but she was also in pain, and failing to hide it. The way Bash tracked her every movement, the tension lining his forehead, told me he felt it too.

"Rest if you can," Marin said softly. "We'll be here when you wake up."

Eva closed her eyes. We would be here, racing against time to save her. The real question was, would she remember us when she opened them?

CHAPTER 10
QUINN

Silvius's lab seemed more sinister now that I was alone. The sterile countertops gleamed dully in the moonlight as I stared into my blurred reflection, unable to shake the thought that he had engineered the virus stealing her memories in this very room.

After Eva had fallen asleep, I quickly excused myself, bringing the samples of her blood down here despite the late hour. It wasn't like I would get any sleep tonight anyways. The sight of my best friend so weakened after mere hours of fighting this cursed virus had my palms itching to get to work and see what I could find out.

If this research wasn't threatening her life, I might have welcomed it. After all, this was exactly the sort of thing I was uniquely qualified to solve—a challenge that was the perfect mix of science, magic, and medicine. While I enjoyed helping with the day-to-day needs in Soleara, I was looking forward to when things settled down and my passion for healing felt less like a hobby. I had been meaning to visit Mayim for a while now to learn from the influx of healers there.

Marin had even put me in contact with one of the head healers of the Enclave, Dolion. The Enclave was both a hospital and a research lab all situated by Queen Sariyah's castle—and Dolion was one of the Enclave's head researchers. He had been instrumental in helping set up my personal lab in a world that didn't run on electricity. I had come to cherish our correspondence, especially when I found myself stuck on a problem.

There were so few people that thought like me—that truly cared about the science as well as the magic of this realm—but Dolion was one of them.

As I walked to the centrifuge, I marveled yet again at the modifications that had been made to power it with magic. Yael had brought it here, looking perplexed as I set it up, before she returned to help with Eva.

My hands trembled as I portioned the blood sample I had taken from my best friend. Then nearly jumped out of my skin as a low voice behind me asked, "How can I help?"

I glared at Tobias over my shoulder, then set the syringe aside. "Maybe by *not* scaring me while I'm holding a glass vial of your sister's blood?"

He had the presence of mind to look properly chastened. "Sorry, Sagray."

I should've known he would follow. After all, I wasn't the only one dying to fix this as soon as possible. There were circles under his eyes, though there always seemed to be nowadays. I didn't remember him being a night owl, but every time I passed his door, light streamed through the crack no matter how late.

"Knock next time."

Though I had been so lost in thought as I thought through the tests I needed to run that I doubted I would have noticed if the False King himself rose from the dead and decided to follow me down here.

Tobias leaned sideways, rapping twice on the metal counter. "Now...how can I help?"

To anyone else he would have looked utterly indifferent, but I knew him better than that. The casual lean against the counter was for show. I had seen how his hands slipped into his pockets to hide their shaking; the worry he was trying to hide. I didn't have it in me to rehash my frustrations with him, especially not when that had achieved nothing in the stairwell earlier.

I had more important things to deal with for now.

My teeth sank into my lower lip as I gathered my thoughts. Tobias cocked his head, waiting.

"I need to separate the blood's components in a centrifuge," I said, thinking aloud. "Then we can prep the plasma to view the virus under magnification."

Tobias nodded, though he looked confused. "What can I do?"

"There's a drawer with what we'll need over there," I said, pointing to the opposite side of the lab. "I can talk you through how to use the negative stains in order to see the virus under the microscope."

I looked back at the blood samples, glad I had thought to ask Yael for the magically impermeable gloves from my lab. They were a gift from Dolion that had been tucked into one of his missives after I had complained about running low on disposable gloves from the human realm. If Silvius's notes were misleading—if the virus was transmittable without an injection—then we were all already exposed. But coming into contact with blood laden with the virus was another risk entirely.

"First, you need to stop shaking," Tobias said firmly. He stepped closer—close enough that I was forced to look up at him. Even when we were kids, I had always been the shortest of the three of us, but the difference felt so much more pronounced now that he had grown into his frame. His shoulders were broad and sturdy, the muscles of his arms and chest shifting as he reached for me.

Wordlessly, Tobias took my hands in his. I jumped slightly at the immediate static. He gently removed my gloves—one hand easily holding both of mine before the other came to join it.

"Big breath in," he started, before breathing in through his nose.

"Count each second," I continued impatiently.

He gave me an exasperated look, one eyebrow arching.

I shrugged. "Your dad taught me too, remember?"

"Prove it then," Tobias grumbled before pointedly sucking in a breath through his nose.

"Sorry." I closed my eyes, breathing in for a steady four count—listening as Tobias matched me. Only when he exhaled did I do the same, our timing perfectly in sync. As we inhaled together, I couldn't help but breathe him in—the earthy, slightly smoky scent almost hypnotic.

"There," Tobias murmured, his voice noticeably deeper.

I opened my eyes to find him already staring at me. "Hmm?"

The space between us had all but disappeared. I was suddenly very conscious that I could count each golden speck in his irises. A long moment passed as his eyes traced my face, his gaze as heavy as a touch. My heart skipped a beat as his gaze lowered to my lips.

Tobias was still holding my hands, his thumbs brushing back and forth across the backs of them in soothing strokes. He looked like he was bracing himself—like there was something suspended in this moment that one wrong move could scare away.

"You know, my mom always told me to ground myself in the details when I was feeling overwhelmed," I said quietly. "To make a list."

His thumb paused. "A list?"

"Five things I could hear, four things I could see, three things I could touch, two things I could smell, and one thing I could taste. A mental list to bring myself back to the present."

"I'll have to remember that." Tobias's eyes searched mine like they were looking for something I didn't know I lost.

Then he dropped my hands, stepping away so abruptly I nearly fell forward. "You're not shaking anymore, Sagray. So, let's get to it."

✧

I squinted at the centrifuge, making sure it was balanced one last time before turning it on. Then I returned to the microscope with a sigh. Silvius had installed the equivalent of an electron microscope in his lab, one powerful enough to see the virus on the slides Tobias helped me painstakingly create.

Stifling my yawn, I leaned forward. My tiredness seemed to melt away as I focused on the helical viruses clustered around Eva's blood cells, the capsids encasing the viral genetic material clearly visible. I blinked as the virus shimmered strangely.

Tobias cleared his throat, and I jumped.

"Sorry," he murmured.

Maybe it would help to talk it through. The later it got, the harder it was to focus. All the information was there, slowly coalescing, even as the answers I wanted remained frustratingly out of reach. I often found that talking through what I knew helped me find things I missed.

"Actually, come here." I ushered Tobias forward with one bent finger, stepping aside so he could look into the microscope. "Do you see the smaller clusters?"

Hesitantly, he bent so he could peer through the magnifier. "I see a lot of wiggling things."

"The spiral shapes are the virus. But even looking at a regular blood smear…" I pointed at the smaller microscope beside it and Tobias dutifully moved over. "Look there."

A pause. "At…?"

"The donut-like shapes are red blood cells," I explained impatiently.

Tobias made a small sound that might have been a laugh. "Donut-like?"

I rolled my eyes though he couldn't see me. "Would saying biconcave discs been easier for you to understand?"

"Fair point." He frowned into the microscope. "Why are the spirals so… shiny? Are they usually like that?"

"I think it's the magic involved," I said eagerly. "The infected blood cells have that sheen after the virus attaches itself to them. If it wasn't trying to kill my best friend, I would be impressed. The research that must have gone into creating this…"

Tobias pulled back, staring at me inquisitively. "Does your magic tell you more about it?"

I blinked slowly, barely stopping myself from hitting my palm against my forehead. To say it had been a long night was an understatement. While I had used my magic to try to heal Eva, I hadn't considered what it could tell me about the sample itself—not when I had been too focused on identifying it.

Tobias's eyes narrowed. "Don't tell me that wasn't the first thing you tried."

"Okay, I won't tell you," I muttered as I pushed past him.

His hand fastened around my upper arm, stopping me before I could reach the microscope. "Unless you think the magic can somehow infect you if you do. Is it safe for you to be messing with it?"

I shrugged, and he immediately released his hold. "Considering Silvius's notes detail how the victim's blood is used to target the virus, I don't think so. This was made specifically for her. Otherwise, I would've quarantined everyone here tonight."

Tobias still looked uneasy. "Are you sure?"

"No," I admitted. "But since Eva was most likely injected with the virus, I doubt it's a risk. It may not even be bloodborne."

"Or magic-borne?"

I leaned over the microscope, letting my magic gently seep into the sample. "I'll let you know in a second."

The bluish glow of my magic lit up the slide. I winced, closing my eyes.

"Sagray?" If I didn't know any better, I would have thought Tobias sounded panicked. "Are you okay?"

"Let me focus, Maris," I chided. "A little light won't hurt me."

He swore under his breath, his voice closer than before. At least he hadn't tried to hold me back again.

My magic engulfed the sample, the blue flooding the red as I focused on the virus itself. It felt as though it was repelling me—like it sensed an intruder trying to separate it from its host.

"It feels like the bands," I whispered, shuddering as I realized why it felt familiar. "Like Silvius somehow warped it. This magic feels similar."

"That makes sense considering it's blocking her magic." Tobias sounded carefully detached. "Is it even curable?"

As I pulled back, I nearly collided with Tobias. Goosebumps rose along my skin with the sudden awareness of his nearness. He stared at me intently from where he stood inches away.

"Of course," I said quickly. "It has to be."

"You've always been painfully optimistic," he said flatly.

I shrugged. "And you've always expected disaster."

Tobias simply arched an eyebrow at me, as if to say, *Was I wrong?*

I met his unblinking gaze, noting the way the ice seemed to thaw behind his eyes the longer he watched me. A shiver ran through me as that stare dipped again to my lips.

He glanced down at where goosebumps had multiplied on my arms. "You're cold."

It wasn't a question. I was still in the dress I wore for dinner, and the sterile room had grown colder as the night progressed.

Tobias backed away, retrieving his jacket from the back of a chair. My mouth parted in surprise as he stalked back toward me.

"Here." He draped the jacket over me without waiting for me to respond. It hung loose on my shoulders, the length of the sleeves almost comically long.

I wrapped it around me, breathing that comforting scent of him in as I did. "Thanks."

He looked away, absentmindedly rolling up the sleeves of his shirt. I didn't let my eyes linger on the scars that circled his wrists, their bands layered over each other. Not because I thought there was something ugly about them—far from it. Like Eva's, they were a mark of his survival. But I knew how self-conscious he would be if he caught me staring.

His gaze rested on where the bottom of his jacket reached nearly mid-thigh. "I take it you aren't going to sleep anytime soon?"

"It wouldn't be my first all-nighter," I said, tracing the embroidery on the jacket's lapels.

Tobias followed the path of my fingers, his jaw flexing. "What's next?"

I stifled a yawn. "If you want to go to bed, you don't need to—"

"Don't insult me by finishing that sentence." Tobias fixed me with a glare, daring me to continue. "Tell me what else we can do."

I rolled my eyes at his dramatics, though the corner of my mouth betrayed my smile. "We test for antibodies in the plasma. We're lucky she's fae or it would take longer for her immune system to react adaptively."

"And after that?"

I looked over at the bookshelf behind Silvius's desk. Tobias followed my gaze.

"More research?"

I paused, considering how to phrase this. "I need to understand more about the blood magic Silvius used to create the bands, since it seems to be the premise of how Silvius bound a virus to her blood. Most books that have anything to do with blood magic have been destroyed…from what I understand, at least." My cheeks warmed, though Tobias didn't show any reaction to my interest in the subject. "If I could understand the theory… maybe find more information about how Aviel managed to create the bloodbond between him and Eva. Anything could be helpful," I added quickly. "I'm guessing that's easier said than done with how cagey everyone is about me simply drawing her blood."

"You think that'll be in a book?"

"Aviel was a siphon, but the dark magic was learned," I said with more surety than I felt. "And Silvius is a scientist, which means there should be notes somewhere unless he took them with him."

A muscle twitched in Tobias's jaw. "Or you c-can just ask me."

He was avoiding looking at me, the slight flush on his cheeks either from my attention or a reaction to the stutter I was careful to ignore. It was obvious it bothered him, though it only happened intermittently now. It seemed to have gotten much better the longer it had been since he was freed of the mask that silenced him.

"I'm sorry, I didn't think—"

"No need to be sorry." Tobias's tone sent a chill down my spine, the blank look on his face worse than anger. It scared me how easily he blocked his emotions out, though I was certain it was how he had survived all those years in Morehaven's dungeon.

It had likely taken more courage than I realized for him to even come down here.

"I'm not sure about the process of making the bands, only that it was blood magic that locked it," Tobias said, his voice clipped. "But Aviel...he spent four years stealing my blood along with my magic. He must have siphoned someone with the magic needed to create the bloodbond." I stiffened, but Tobias kept talking, his words tumbling out as though, now that he had begun, he couldn't lock them back in.

"From what I could tell, the process was simply intention and magic, just like most of the magic in this realm—along with a red glow at his fingertips when he touched my blood." It was my turn to school my face into that false calm. "I'm sure he would have been more careful about what he did in front of me if he thought I'd ever escape."

Four *years*. I had been in college with his sister, going on dates, getting drunk at parties...and he had been tortured in ways it made me nauseous to think about. How often had he assumed he would die in that dungeon? How long had he held out hope he would be rescued, only for it to dim each day he remained trapped and utterly alone?

"Was he planning on killing you?" I couldn't keep the horror from my voice. "I thought he needed you...not only for finding Eva, but to siphon your magic to maintain the charade he was Celestial."

"Oh, he told me when my death would be," Tobias said so matter-of-factly my skin crawled. "When he used Eva to go through the Choosing and stole the power of the land as his own, there wouldn't be a use for me anymore. I'm the one who hoped he might slip sooner..." He abruptly stopped talking, running a hand over his face. "S-sorry. It's been a long night."

I had the overwhelming urge to wrap my arms around him. Either that or scream into the void at a world that refused to stop taking from that boy with an easy smile until he was hollowed out and broken.

But he hadn't broken, had he? He survived the king that murdered his parents as well as mine. He found a way to stay strong—and sane—all those years, even as they took his blood along with his magic.

All it had cost him was the light in his eyes—the spark that had nothing to do with his power.

I knew better than to give in to the urge to comfort him. He would likely take it as pity. Or worse, push me away yet again. I wouldn't risk that happening now that we were finally working together, even if he was only doing it out of necessity and obligation.

If only he knew the way I felt was the furthest thing from pity. What burned inside me was rage—raw and unbridled, raging for release. Rage that was laced with sorrow and threaded through with guilt that not only hadn't I known to save him from what Aviel put him through, but I was still failing to help him now.

Red filled my vision. I quickly turned away, shoving my hands into the pockets of his jacket to hide the power building there. This wasn't the time to explain, especially not after what Tobias had shared.

At least it was a start in the right direction. Maybe one day he would feel comfortable enough not to shut away his fears, his torment, and face everything that had been taken from him. Maybe one day, he would find a way to remove the mask that had long since been destroyed.

Maybe one day, I would remove mine and we could scream together.

CHAPTER 11
TOBIAS

I recounted everything I could about blood magic as Quinn worked and I sorted through Silvius's library. Despite her frequent yawning, Quinn adamantly kept at it until it was so late it was early, the first rays of dawn cutting through the dark. She hadn't wanted to stop working even then, not when every minute counted. I barely managed to convince her that some rest and food was an important part of our cure-finding strategy, as it was entirely reliant upon her brain.

It was a relief to escape to a different wing of the castle. I doubted I could sleep no matter how bone-deep my exhaustion. Not here.

Once, I had dreamed of a warm, cozy bed…and now that I wasn't forced to sleep on a cold cot atop unyielding stone, I found myself tossing and turning, unable to get comfortable when the bed felt so soft it might swallow me whole. But sleep eluded me, even after I dragged the blanket to the floor.

Perhaps it was a mercy. Even if I did fall asleep, visiting that cell in my dreams felt inevitable. After all, I had spent the night in the laboratory that had spawned my worst torments, so close to the dungeon where my nightmares had been carved into me.

I hastily changed out of the fine, albeit rumpled clothes I had worn all night, then stepped into the shower, turning the knob so it was nearly scalding. Eva's blood had soaked through my shirt, its presence masked by the dark shade even as it dried against my skin. It left a stain on my arm that I scrubbed until my skin was raw, then kept scrubbing like I could erase the memory of her unconscious and bleeding along with the stain.

By the time I fell back into my overly pillowed bed, it was light enough outside that the sun's glow seeped against my eyelids, my vision turning blood-red.

There was a knock on the door. My eyes flew open.

"Tobias?"

From the way the sunlight had strengthened, I knew I had managed to sleep, though it felt like a mere moment.

"Be there in a minute, Sagray," I called out, rolling out of bed. It took me a moment to hunt down a pair of pants. I opened the door as I pulled a shirt over my head.

Quinn's eyes lingered on my exposed stomach, meeting my eyes as I yanked the hem down. "Did you sleep?"

I nodded. Not a lie for once. Little did she know that this amount of sleep was a common occurrence. I hadn't gotten used to feeling safe enough to sleep—often startling awake at the slightest sound, even months later.

Quinn's hair was pulled back into a no-nonsense bun, though a few curls were already escaping. She wore casual clothes, but the jeweled dagger I gave her rested on her hip, the diamond on its grip glinting with purpose.

A delicious smell wafted toward me. "Did you bring something to eat?"

Quinn held up a satchel. "I brought *us* something to eat. Breakfast burritos...or at least something like it. It took a bit to explain the concept to my friend in the kitchens." She looked at me knowingly. "They used to be your favorite, right?"

Whatever remained of my heart tugged painfully in my chest. I hesitated, unsure how to respond. The teenager who used to make a version of these nearly every morning existed a lifetime ago.

Quinn gave me an exaggerated wink. "You need your energy too if you plan to keep up with me."

"Don't I know it," I muttered, turning away to grab my belt. I fastened my dagger to it, though I left Duskbane, the matching sword that had once been my mother's, where it lay across the desk. "Straight to the lab?"

She shook her head. "I want to check on Eva before we head down."

"Let's eat while we walk," I said, then added at Quinn's affronted look, "Don't worry, I know a pretty good healer if I choke."

She let out an unamused huff before passing me my burrito, but I didn't miss the twitch of her lips as she started to unwrap her own. Quinn glanced at me, and I quickly buried the smile that threatened to surface with a hasty bite of my breakfast. The silence felt comfortable as we walked down the hallway even as the arched white ceilings sent a shiver down my spine.

Quinn's arm brushed my elbow as we turned around a corner. The glancing contact of her skin against mine sent a jolt of awareness through me that nearly singed my food as my magic reached for her. But my shoulders relaxed, her nearness banishing any sense of unease.

It was dangerous, falling into old habits. Letting her in again would end badly for both of us, even if it felt as natural as breathing to do so.

I needed to put some distance back between us, but my sister's life depended on Quinn succeeding. I couldn't walk away now. And Quinn needed someone too, someone who could help her bear the burden.

I was far too selfish to let that someone be anybody else.

✧

Marin opened the door to Eva and Bash's room, looking as tired as I felt. Bash barely glanced at us from where he sat next to the head of Eva's bed, softly stroking her hair as she slept. With her chestnut hair spread out behind her and the feverish flush to her cheeks, Eva reminded me of a princess in one of the fairytales we used to read together long after we should have been asleep.

Nevermind the fact that she was a queen, not a princess, and a dubiously consensual kiss wasn't the cure we needed.

Marin raised her finger to her lips in a shushing motion as she ushered us back, leading us to the small seating area outside Eva's room.

Quinn stared at Eva through the doorway for a long moment before she followed. "Any change?"

"She hasn't woken since you saw her," Marin said, keeping her voice low. "And her fever hasn't broken—which I can only hope means her body is fighting the virus as hard as I am. The fog..." She let out a short sigh. "It's resisting my magic. Any luck downstairs?"

"We're making progress," Quinn replied, mimicking her tone. "The magic involved is a variable I still don't completely understand. Though it's probably a good thing he bound it to Eva's blood or else we'd risk the virus spreading."

Marin shuddered. "Yael, Rivan, and Pari left for Mayim first thing this morning to ramp up the search for Silvius along with some of our rangers. Queen Sariyah is sending a few of her most trusted healers to provide some assistance keeping Eva stable. She also offered the resources of her healer's enclave should you need help with your research."

"I keep meaning to take the time to visit the Enclave," Quinn said wistfully. "That's not a bad idea."

Marin spoke through her yawn. "Did you ever reach out about the experiments you've been running?"

"There's a healer there I've been in correspondence with..." Quinn looked thoughtful. "I should've asked him for his help sooner."

Something dark slithered in my stomach, curling around my gut. I was not about to be jealous of Quinn's pen pal. Yet the thought of her writing letters to some fae scientist who was probably as brilliant as she was rankled.

After all, it wasn't like I had any claim on her...

"Do you want me to throw that away?"

Marin's question cut into my thoughts, and I realized I was strangling the napkin that had been wrapped around my breakfast. I cleared my throat, avoiding her knowing gaze. "I've got it."

I reached out, plucking Quinn's napkin carefully from her hand, careful not to brush my fingers against her palm.

Quinn gave me a grateful look before asking Marin, "Have you eaten?"

"Yes," Marin assured her. "Well, I ate. Then I force-fed my brother. I'll send for some warm broth and toast when Eva's awake again."

I turned away, waiting until I was above the trash can before opening my hand. My napkin was visibly charred, five dark fingerprints marking where my fingers dug in. I swiftly dropped it into the bin, dusting off the few burnt flecks where they were stuck to my palm.

Feeling conspicuous, I glanced behind me. Bash stood by the doorway, looking dead on his feet. I tensed, but he only blinked tiredly.

"You should sleep when she does," Quinn said softly. "Take shifts to monitor her."

He grimaced. "I slept a little last night, trying to see if I could dreamwalk to her…not that I had any luck. I can barely feel her through our bond, and the fog keeping her from me is getting stronger despite Marin's best efforts."

My head snapped to Marin. "I thought you were able to hold it back?"

Marin flinched slightly, and Quinn less-than-discreetly elbowed me in the side.

"Sorry," I muttered. "I just meant—"

"I'm trying," Marin said flatly. "It's progressing too fast. I'm hoping Queen Sariyah's healers have some fresh ideas on how to keep it from getting worse until Quinn can work out a cure."

Quinn's lips tightened, the only sign of the pressure she had to be feeling.

"But it's f-fixable, right?" I gritted my teeth before trying again. "She was able to remember what she forgot after you removed the fog last night. So the effects won't last once she's cured?"

"I don't know," Marin said tiredly. "The stronger it gets, the more challenging it is to push back. This is all speculation and hypothesis until we get answers from Silvius. Unless you found a notebook down there with the answers?"

It was advancing into her mind—and the longer we let it, the more damage it could cause. We needed time to find the cure, if there even was one. *Time* to read and research and test. Time to hunt down Silvius and rip those answers from his throat.

Time that Eva didn't have.

The question was out before I could stop it. "You're saying this—her magic, her memory loss…it could be p-permanent?"

Quinn whirled so quickly her curls whipped against her face. "Don't you start thinking that way, Maris." She pointed one finger at me, then pressed it firmly into my chest. "I won't allow it, especially when she could hear you."

I glanced toward my sister's lifeless form, then back to Quinn's furious face.

"I-I'm sorry."

I let her see the truth of those words on my face, just for a moment. Quinn remained silent for a beat, no doubt weighing my apology.

"I'll be optimistic enough for the both of us, Maris," she said finally. "I'm used to it by now."

Her shoulders slumped, and her hand dropped to her side, though the pressure from her finger remained in an ache above my heart. It was an effort not to reach for that hand as she closed her eyes, taking a deep, stabilizing breath. We were all terrified for Eva, but Quinn had the added strain of not only her best friend's life but the fate of the realm resting on her shoulders.

And here I was making things harder for her.

"I'm sorry," I said again, knowing it was nowhere near enough.

"I know." The disappointment in her voice hurt like a physical blow. Quinn didn't even look at me before she walked over to Eva.

It took more effort than usual to hide my fears away—to bind them with iron chains inside the cells where they belonged. When I was sure my face was impassive, I glanced over at my sister. "Should we get back to—"

"Quinn?"

Eva's voice was a dry rasp, barely loud enough to hear. Bash rushed toward her, but Quinn placed a steadying hand on his arm as she passed him to reach Eva's side.

"Hey there," Quinn said softly. She lifted a glass of water from Eva's bedside table and brought it to her lips. "How are you feeling?"

"I'm—" Eva swallowed thickly, then took a large gulp of water. The room was so silent I could hear each swallow. "I'm okay. Just thirsty."

She took one more sip, then shook her head slightly. Quinn set the water back down.

"I can get you something to eat too now that you're..."

Quinn trailed off as Eva blinked, staring up at Bash with bewilderment. The fog whitening the irises of her eyes had gotten worse, like a winter frost creeping across a windowpane. Her breathing accelerated as those eyes searched his.

"I don't understand."

Bash reached for her. "I'm here, hellion. It's going to be okay—"

Eva reared back. Bash immediately pulled his hand away as the surprise in his expression turned to pained understanding. I winced. Whatever my issues with my sister's betrothed, it was obvious how deeply he loved her.

Eva looked around in confusion before refocusing on Bash. Her eyes were wide as they scanned his face.

He had gone utterly still, like the smallest movement might spook her. Even his shadows retreated, wrapping around his forearms like a snake.

Her brow furrowed, her tone halting as she murmured, "I feel like I know you."

The room seemed to freeze at the confirmation that all our fears had been right, the evidence like a dagger in my gut. I was glad I was mostly out of sight in the other room, especially as I shifted behind Marin. If Eva didn't know Bash, I didn't want the shock of my return from the dead to drain her further.

Quinn had been her constant, not me.

The flash of heartbreak across Bash's face was there and gone in an instant. "You do."

"Hellion..." Eva whispered, her voice tinged with confusion. "Is that supposed to be a nickname?"

The shadows in the corners of the room surged forward like a storm of night, swirling agitatedly around the bed just outside Eva's view. Their master remained perfectly still.

"It's not any worse than 'freckles'." Bash's tone was forcibly light though I could hear the underlying strain. His throat bobbed. "But you can call me Bash."

"Bash," Eva repeated. Her tongue darted across her chapped upper lip. "I feel like I...like I should..."

Her face crumpled. Bash started to reach for her, before resting his hand on her pillow. His fingers curled in a fist, trembling with tension—the sole betrayal of his composure. A single strand of shadow slipped past his hold to weave within the tangles of her hair.

Eva stared at Bash, confusion knitting her brows. "Why do I feel like this?"

Bash's mouth parted but no sound came out. He blinked rapidly though it did nothing to dispel the sudden sheen in his eyes.

"You have a fever," Quinn said evenly. "One that's affecting your memory."

"When you feel better, I'll explain everything, I promise." Bash's voice had gone hoarse, worn thin with emotion, but he managed a strained smile. "Right now, food and rest are the best cures."

"No," Eva whispered. "That's not what I mean. Why do I feel like you're..."

She tilted her head, the question hanging in the air. The hope in Bash's eyes may have broken what was left of my heart.

"I'm whatever you need me to be, Eva," Bash said, his tone unwavering. "Your nurse, currently. Your protector, though you rarely need it. Your friend, though Quinn might fight me for the title of 'best'. Your *anima*, though that's a term better saved for another time. There's no me without you, and I never want there to be."

The cloudiness in Eva's irises seemed to clear for a moment. "Tell me something..."

"Anything," Bash prompted, his shadows stilling in anticipation.

Her voice was hesitant but clear. "Tell me something...true."

Bash jolted slightly, his wide eyes darting to Quinn before quickly returning to Eva. His voice was miraculously steady as he asked, "Something real?"

Eva's lips curved in a small smile.

"I love you." Bash's voice broke, just slightly.

A line formed between Eva's brows, and I found myself holding my breath as a hint of that familiar gold flickered behind the unnatural cloudiness in her eyes.

"I feel like I'm lost," Eva whispered. "Like there's something I need to remember. But I know that I love you too."

The shadows faded back to their corners, except for the few still trailing around Bash's arms. His voice shook as he vowed, "We're going to fix this, Eva."

He glanced at Quinn, who went still at the pleading in his gaze before nodding. Her jaw set with resolved determination, though I could see the doubt behind her eyes. It was all I could do not to step between them.

Didn't he realize the pressure wasn't helping?

Marin sidled up next to Eva, a steaming bowl of broth in her hands. "Let's get some food in you while you're up, okay?"

Eva's eyes immediately darted to Quinn. Marin gave Quinn a tight smile as she passed her the bowl, then added another pillow behind Eva's head. She was so weak that Quinn helped her bring the spoon to her lips while Bash's hand supported the back of her neck.

Quinn already knew what was at stake. She had been carrying the weight of it since the moment Eva had first fallen sick. After all, she had taken responsibility for my sister long before that. Following my supposed death, our parents, and Quinn's, it had been just the two of them for years—the only family either of them had left, at least to their knowledge. And while I was sure Eva looked after Quinn in return, Quinn had been the only one to know the whole truth—and thus the one to bear the burden alone.

I owed her far more than I could ever repay for all she had done to keep Eva safe, both mentally and physically—and I would do anything I could to ease her burden now. But the weight of this? I knew without a doubt that if Eva didn't survive this, Bash wasn't the only one it would ruin.

Quinn helped Eva to the bathroom, only our joint helplessness filling the silence as we waited. When they returned, Bash gently lifted Eva onto the bed.

"I trust you," Eva said sleepily, her words slurring together as she let out a yawn.

Bash carefully arranged the blankets around her, his fingers trembling as he lifted a glass of water to her lips. He waited for her to swallow before asking, "Do you need anything else?"

Eva's eyelashes fluttered slowly, fighting a losing battle to remain open. "Will you stay with me?"

"Of course," Bash said softly. "Rest now. You'll need your strength to fight this."

Shadows pulled the covers higher, fluffing Eva's pillow as she sank back against them. Her eyes shut instantly as if she lacked the strength to keep them open.

They should have gotten married today. They should've been happy—laughing at their ceremony, dancing under the starlight, and being celebrated by their friends and subjects alike. Instead, Bash was barely holding himself together, and my twin was fighting for her life in this godsforsaken castle once more.

"If I forget when I wake up, remind me again..." Eva let out a sigh, her next words so quiet I almost missed them. "That I love you."

Bash's chest rose sharply as he swiped the back of his hand across his eyes.

His voice cracked as he promised, "Always."

CHAPTER 12
QUINN

I looked up from my work to find the laboratory empty, although I had no idea when Tobias slipped away. He was unnaturally quiet on his feet. We barely said two words to each other after visiting Eva this morning outside of my instructions on how to assist me in the lab and a few brief questions.

I caught him watching me more than once. He hadn't said anything about the extent of Eva's decline, like he knew that bringing it up or breaking my concentration would add to my already overwhelming anxiety. My nerves buzzed like static beneath my skin, the weight of a thousand what-ifs pressing down on my shoulders.

Closing my eyes, I sucked in a steadying breath. A reddish glint flashed through the crack in my eyelids. It took me a long moment to realize that a missive had appeared in front of me, that flash of light from the magical method of its arrival. Before the note could hit the ground, I snatched it from the air, immediately recognizing the distinctive letterhead of the Enclave.

I had been corresponding with Dolion long enough to recognize his handwriting, though it looked more cramped than usual—different, like he wrote it in a hurry. With everything going on, I almost forgot that I had sent him a rundown of Eva's ailment, as well as my thoughts on an approach to a cure.

Dolion reminded me of many medical researchers I knew back in the human realm: kindhearted but clinical to the point of detachment. When I started to share my research into medicine and magic with him, I had expected some opposition to my methodology—after all, I was trained in the human realm, where practices and principles differed greatly from those of this world. Instead of considering my research radical, Dolion had written back almost immediately to share his thoughts on my initial experiments, an entire dissertation about his own research, and to formally offer me a position at the Enclave.

It had been a relief to realize there was an entire group of people in this realm who shared my interests; however, I had politely declined. Soleara was my true home, and I wasn't ready to leave it just yet. Not when it, Eva, and a certain broody king needed me.

I hadn't stopped my personal research, nor my messages to Dolion keeping him updated. Though our letters had grown sporadic, especially lately, it was fascinating to discover how this realm's healers compared to the doctors and researchers I studied with in the human world. It reminded me of my life before the mirror, of the researchers more at home in their labs than the outside world even as they unraveled the secrets of its microscopic wonders. Dolion helpfully sent several tomes about how to use magic for diagnosis and detection, though fae ailments were considerably rarer.

His postscript often contained a reminder that his offer to join him in his research remained open should I change my mind.

Today's dispatch was much briefer than most. Dolion's message about Eva's condition was edged with concern, his tone short even for him. It was obvious he didn't think I could do this without help—*his* help, if I read between the lines. He was likely right, considering his knowledge of fae viruses. If he were to assist me effectively, he would need access to Eva's bloodwork, not just copies of my findings.

Dolion had been fascinated by the human methods of using blood for diagnosis and treatment, though he too had warned me to be careful who I shared my methodology with due to the dark associations with blood magic. It hadn't stopped him from writing though, even as I guiltily skirted around the subject in my responses. It also hadn't stopped his regular invitations to visit the Enclave. While I had always planned to go once things in Soleara had settled down, I wished it would finally happen under better circumstances.

I blinked at the clock ticking on the wall. It was late for him to be writing to me. I had worked right through dinner, based on how dark it was outside.

Maybe Tobias had left to find something to eat or get some sleep after last night's marathon.

As if thinking his name had summoned him, the door swung open. Tobias stood there, holding a tray full of food that made me immediately ravenous.

I was already shaking my head. "You can't bring that in here. You'll contaminate the lab."

"Then come have a quick snack before you continue working yourself to the bone." Tobias tilted the tray slightly to show off its contents, looking slightly abashed as he added, "…or a full dinner. I got a few of your favorites."

He had—and not just my favorites from childhood. There were creamy noodles with extra grated cheese and toasted garlic bread, a salad made of roasted beets, goat cheese, and sliced citrus, and an assortment of fruit alongside chocolate tarts I recognized as Rivan's mother's recipe. Last but not least was a Solearan dish I had grown fond of: strawberries wrapped in sweet dough and steamed like dumplings.

When had he even noticed?

My stomach grumbled loudly enough that Tobias's lips twitched.

"Thank you," I said, hoping the exhaustion in my voice didn't diminish my sincerity. "Let me finish something up and then I will."

"Can I help?"

I smiled as I shook my head. Tobias had been saying those three words all day. It was more than that though—it wasn't just that he listened to what I needed, he paid attention. He had been my shadow in the lab, fetching anything I needed, taking measurements, and preparing samples. His notes were immaculate, he never had to be asked for something twice, and when I explained how to do something, he jotted down the answer so that I didn't have to repeat myself. Best of all, he was able to anticipate the next step based on what we had already done, figuring out what needed to happen next without me asking.

Like bringing me dinner before I even mentioned I was hungry.

"It won't take long, I promise. As much as I want to keep working, tired eyes make mistakes." It was a phrase one of my professors was fond of back in college. "And we don't have room for those right now."

Taking a dinner break is exactly what I needed. Leaning over the counter, I quickly finished updating my notes, though Tobias had already filled in the majority of it. I would send a copy to Dolion in the morning.

My task completed, I gave Tobias a nod, stifling a yawn. We walked in silence up the stairwell, finding a quiet spot near the kitchen. Tobias ignored the long wooden table in the center of the room, though it was empty at this hour, instead crossing the room to where a small, two-person table was half hidden in an alcove.

Setting down the tray, Tobias made a gesture for me to dig in before disappearing into the kitchen. When he returned, it was with a steaming pot of tea and two porcelain mugs. He looked far too serious as he drizzled some honey into each cup as he waited for the tea to steep, wholly focused on his task.

Tobias's guard was down for once. His face was still, softer somehow, stripped of the defenses that usually rose from my attention. I studied the lines around his mouth, the faint scar by his temple, the shadows under his eyes—details I usually didn't dare to linger on. It made me realize how much effort he spent holding himself together in front of me, as if any vulnerability was a weakness he couldn't afford

He looked up, and I bit into a strawberry dumpling a bit too eagerly. An explosion of sweet liquid only partially made it into my mouth. Tobias started pouring the tea as I happily sucked the strawberry juice off my fingers.

"These are heavenly," I gushed. "You have to try one."

"Hmm?" Tobias's eyes flicked up from where they were fixed on my lips, a hint of his light sparking in their depths. Then he swore under his breath as the cup he was filling overflowed, the tea scalding his fingers. "Sorry, what did you—"

I pushed the bowl toward him in a wordless offer. We used to share snacks after school beneath the giant oak tree behind his house. Sometimes we would climb it, and I would drop pieces of popcorn or orange slices down from my branch to his, Eva and I cheering if he caught it in his mouth.

He shook his head. "That's for you."

"You brought more than enough for both of us." I pouted at him, refusing to be deterred. "Don't make me eat alone."

Tobias sighed as he gave in, somehow eating the doughy strawberry without getting it all over himself. I didn't miss his soft moan of appreciation, or the way my skin pebbled in response.

"You're good at this," I said, quickly clarifying, "The research, that is."

"You're a good teacher," Tobias said, his tongue darting out to lick a drop of strawberry juice from his bottom lip. "*You're* the one who's good at this. I'm just lucky enough to learn from you."

Realizing I was the one now staring at his lips, I quickly refocused my gaze upward. Plenty of the people I dated—mostly the men—had been intimidated by my career and ambition. The way Tobias looked at me, the pride and genuine appreciation in his tone, made me realize how rare it was for that respect to be given so easily. He knew I knew more than him and hadn't once considered being threatened by it.

Not that we were dating.

My mouth quirked. "Given my magic, it would be unfortunate if I wasn't good at it."

"No," he said firmly. "It's more than that. There are plenty of people with skills they aren't patient enough to teach or who lack the understanding to explain things in a way that's easy to understand."

"When you were..." I hesitated, my voice catching slightly. "...gone. I was working on my doctorate in biomedical sciences and molecular medicine. Plenty of time spent in labs with lots of professors and researchers. Some were brilliant but short-tempered...and some were smart and kind and inspiring. I was fortunate to have a few good examples to learn from." I smiled, thinking of a mentor who had taken me under her wing when I was new and unsure of myself, who I had instinctively modeled my teaching style from. "Not just how best to teach. She reminded me to look deeper, to ask why, to not settle for surface answers."

Tobias leaned closer. "It's no wonder your magic is healing. It must have been a relief when you could finally wield it."

I blushed at the compliment even as part of me cringed away from the double edge of that sword—the one he didn't even know he was wielding.

"Thanks," I said weakly. "Healing...it's art and magic, knowledge and passion, power and patience." It was, in short, everything I loved. "It's one thing to have power, it's another thing entirely to run your magic through another being. To let it beat in their heart and breathe into their lungs. To mend with a mere impulse. To be able to save someone's life just by willing it." Tobias watched me intently though his expression remained unreadable. "And of course, there's something special about helping those who need it. I'm glad healing is a more common magic, especially since I have more to learn." I picked up my mug, taking a sip. Tobias had added the perfect amount of honey. "I'm babbling. I must be more tired than I thought…and there's still more I need to do tonight."

"Don't apologize." He frowned at me, albeit fleetingly. "It's honestly amazing."

I tilted my head in question. "What is?"

"Your utter lack of ego." Tobias's gaze was sharp and unblinking, as if he was dissecting me with his eyes. "You make it sound like your abilities fell into your lap, but while you may have been given your magic, you've obviously worked hard for the knowledge that makes you so good at it. And though healing magic might be common, the way you use it—working into the night on your projects after spending your days helping everyone else with whatever they need—*isn't*." He leaned closer, and smoke and cedar filled my nose. His voice lowered as he drawled, "Have you ever done something purely for yourself, Sagray?"

"I'm plenty selfish, Maris," I retorted, unsure why I suddenly felt so defensive. "Though I can't afford to be right now."

Tobias took a bite of an apple, swallowing before he said, "I'll believe it when I see it."

"I'm doing what anyone would do in my situation, and with my skills," I argued, still feeling vaguely put out.

"The fact that you think that anyone would put their life on hold to save someone else is admirable in itself, if a bit naïve." Tobias topped off my tea before pouring himself another cup. "After all, we both know you'd do this for anyone, not just Eva."

I hated how cynical he sounded. How certain he seemed that good people were the exception and not the rule.

"If I'm naïve, then you're jaded."

He shrugged. "We're a product of our experiences. I have a right to be. What confuses me is that you aren't."

Something dark roiled inside my veins, begging to be released. "Maybe I don't feel the need to let my trauma define me."

Light whited out Tobias's pupils. It faded so quickly I almost thought I imagined it.

"Maybe," he replied noncommittally. But his pulse jumped just below his jawline, giving his game away.

I downed the rest of my tea in a gulp that burned the back of my throat.

"We should get back to it," I said, biting back my annoyance. "That is, if you're done telling me the way the world works?"

If only he knew not to put me on a pedestal. His opinion of me—that I was some sort of martyr, apparently—would vanish the second he knew what I was really capable of, especially after what he had been forced to endure.

"Sagray, I didn't mean to offend—"

I got to my feet, refusing to meet his eye. "You didn't."

The words tasted bitter in my throat, like the tea had steeped too long.

Tobias quickly stood, sliding his hands into his pockets. "I-I just meant…"

"I don't need this from you too right now," I snapped.

He jerked back so abruptly it was if I had slapped him.

Don't you dare cry, I told myself even as I felt a sharp prick behind my eyes. I needed to get out of here before my frustration turned into tears. "I don't have time to have tea with you while Eva's suffering. I don't have time for any of this."

I spun on a heel and stomped down the hallway. The hurt on his face followed me down the spiral staircase along with his footsteps—though I knew if I turned back around, he would already have locked it away.

CHAPTER 13
TOBIAS

The sound of glass breaking woke me with a start. I hadn't realized I had fallen asleep while watching Quinn work, but apparently my lack of it had finally caught up with me. A bit of drool smudged the notes I had been copying.

Quinn's back was to me—as it had been since our fight two days ago. A vial of Eva's blood had fallen to the floor next to her, shattering on the stone. I blinked blearily as I watched the blood spread out from its shards in a small pool, a single drop dripping from the largest piece of glass to join the rest.

A sob tore from Quinn's throat. I was on my feet in a second, rushing over. She only stared at the blood creeping towards her feet in an expanding puddle.

"Don't move," I ordered. "The glass...I don't want you to get hurt."

Quinn finally looked at me, her amber eyes brimming with unshed tears.

It was all I could do not to pull her into my arms. "We can get more. I'll see if Marin is up to drawing it this time, so you don't have to stop what you're working on. And then—"

Quinn's answering laugh was hysterical. "It's not that."

"Okay," I said, fighting for calm even as it escaped me, my fear slipping through the bars I tried to cage it behind. "Then what is it?"

She sucked in a shaky breath. "I can *see* the virus. The second I use my magic on the slide it lights up like it wants to be found. We even have the godsdamn blueprints written by the psychopath who created it. And…I have no idea how to stop it." A tear slid down her cheek, then another. "All I can see is her blood. Dripping from the needles she hates as I stick them into her arm. I see it in microscopic detail as her body tries to fight against an invasion. I feel it staining my hands in my dreams every time I fall asleep." Her lower lip quivered. "But it's not as bad as the hope on all their faces every time they look at me for a progress update. Or the fear in her eyes every single time she remembers how much she's forgetting."

"No one's expecting you to find an immediate fix." I took a step closer, glass crunching beneath my boot. "No one expects you to get it all right."

"I do," Quinn snapped. "When it comes to magic and medicine…this is exactly the sort of thing I should get right."

"I think you need some sleep," I murmured, not wanting to push too hard when she was obviously already at her limit.

Another humorless laugh. "What's wrong, Maris? Haven't you seen someone have a mental breakdown because they're their best's friend's only hope and they're *failing*?"

I inched forward, careful to avoid the largest shards of blood-covered glass. "You are not—"

Quinn swiped her arm across the counter, sending a beaker careening against the nearest wall. It shattered into a million pieces, the clear liquid inside spraying across the wall. A fine shimmer of glittering dust hung in the air for a moment before drifting to the floor.

For a long moment, neither of us spoke. Quinn looked angrier than I had ever seen her as she glared at the broken glass like it had personally aggrieved her.

"Aren't you going to tell me to get a grip and keep going?" The disgust in her voice made me flinch. "That your twin sister's life hangs in the balance while I quite literally throw myself a pity party? Or remind me that breaking down now isn't going to help anyone?"

She glared at me, the red in her cheeks matching the fire in her words. The fury in her eyes after days of seeing them so dull and clouded with worry may have been the most beautiful thing I had ever seen.

I shook my head. "Break anything you like. Break everything if that's what you need."

If it's what kept her from breaking, I'd let her break me too.

"You might want to save the vials." I continued as I walked nonchalantly to one of the cabinets. I could feel her eyes on me as I opened it, then removed a large glass sphere I had noticed during our initial search of the room. "But I can't imagine we'll need this."

Her eyes widened as she took in my meaning. I held it out to her in offering.

She shook her head. "You first."

My surprise must have shown on my face because her eyes gleamed with satisfaction.

I shrugged. I wouldn't let her bear this alone.

My grip tightened on the sphere. Then I hurled it as hard as I could at the wall. Quinn's eyes went wide as it exploded into a sparkling mist of fine shards, the larger fragments cracking as they hit the floor. My gaze quickly returned to hers, taking in the flash of delight that was quickly masked by self-condemnation. Before she could say anything, I strode to the cabinet, then casually tossed her an oblong bowl.

She caught it reflexively then scowled. "What if I'd dropped it?"

I rolled my eyes. "I know you better than that, Sagray. Now throw."

Quinn's eyes narrowed. A sudden gleam of red flickered in them, gone as quickly as it came. For a second I thought she might fling the bowl right back at me. Then she threw it against the wall, grunting with the effort. A smile curved her lips, the shatter of glass glimmering in the corner of my eye.

"Another?"

I didn't wait for an answer as I found a decanter in the cabinet behind Silvius's desk. The faint hint of alcohol stung my nose. He was never outwardly drunk, not like many of the guards. But that scent…

His breath was heavy and sour as he bent over me to take my blood. Aviel had drained my magic, leaving me so weak I couldn't do anything but instinctively cringe away from the needle. The syringe pierced my already battered vein anyway.

I wanted to scream, though I knew I couldn't. I wanted to fight, but there was nothing I could do to stop this...stop him. My next breath was laced with something bitter and stale as Silvius leaned closer.

"So docile today," Silvius sneered. "We'll make you bow before your king soon enough."

"Tobias?"

My eyes found hers, something fragile passing between us before I dragged that memory back where it belonged. Walking over to Quinn, I wrapped my fingers around her wrist to lift her hand. A shock traveled up my arm, the spark a dire reminder I was alive.

I let go the second she grasped the handle.

"Again."

My demand was low, almost insidious.

Quinn shook her head. "Your turn."

I tilted my head to the side consideringly, then gave her a slight bow. Leaving the decanter in her hold, I retrieved the accompanying crystal goblets and raised them for her appraisal. I nearly dropped both at the smile she rewarded me with.

Drawing my arm back like I was about to throw a baseball, I hurled the first goblet at the wall, then launched the second in quick succession. They exploded with two sharp, crystalline cracks followed by a spray of glass, each piece catching the light like tiny, jagged stars.

Quinn mockingly lifted her leg like she was winding up for a pitch before she threw. The burst of laughter that escaped her when it shattered was real and lovely and far too perfect.

It faded too soon. The second it did, she seemed to deflate, backing away from the mess we made together. She slumped against the counter behind her, staring at the broken aftermath scattered across the floor.

An overpowering urge drew me closer—something inexorable, something dangerous. I placed one hand on either side of her, my fingers dipping into the metal countertop as I trapped her in place. She stared up at me with a mix of defiance laced with something fragile. Being this near felt excruciatingly intimate, though I couldn't bring myself to walk away.

I leaned closer, unable to stop the urge to breathe her in. My voice was low, almost a growl, as I asked, "Better?"

Her throat rose and fell with a swallow. "Surprisingly, yes."

"Good."

A lump rose in my throat at the way she looked at me. That trust…I didn't deserve it.

I backed away, putting some necessary distance between us even as every instinct screamed at me to go back to her.

"Back to monosyllables again, are we?" Quinn let out a resigned sounding sigh. "Here I thought we were making progress."

I would take that hint of teasing in her tone, the levity despite her obvious exhaustion. Especially if it meant the hopelessness had faded from her voice.

"For you, I'll suffer through full sentences."

Her smile was brief before it fell away. "I'm sorry, I shouldn't have brought that up. I know after the mask..." She trailed off, wincing, like even the word might set me off.

"There's nothing to apologize for," I said tightly. "You don't have to tiptoe around it. It took some time to remember that speaking aloud won't...hurt. Th-that speaking at all..." I winced at the stutter that flared to life as if to declare exactly what the prolonged cost of those years in the mask had done to me.

I knew the exact number of years down to the days, hours, and endless minutes I had spent in silence, letting the mask's magic train me into submission. Sometimes I wondered if the scratches I clawed into the stone of my cell still tallied each excruciating day.

"There's no need to be embarrassed around me, you know." Quinn took a cautious step closer like she was afraid I might run from her. "I don't think any less of you, and I never could. After what you went through, keeping Eva and me safe...your refusal to give in to him..." She swallowed hard. "You should be proud of your resilience."

Something felt like it was breaking in my chest at the acknowledgement, even as the cell I shoved those memories into rattled like they wanted out. Gritting my teeth, I closed my eyes, trying not to let them overwhelm me.

Quinn didn't seem to expect a response. When I finally opened my eyes, she had returned to her notes, flipping through the work we had done today.

She smiled sadly as she caught me watching her. "How is it that you never seem scared of anything? You'll have to show me how you do it one day."

Is that what she thought? That I wasn't afraid? I had spent every day for four years being terrified, every second certain that I would let something slip and lead Aviel to Eva...and to Quinn.

And now, I was always afraid. Of space, of the open sky. Of waking up one day and finding myself back in my cell, entombed for eternity as I realized that this was all a dream.

Quinn looked away. I opened my mouth, trying to find the words to voice the fact that she was mistaken. That my fears might have been suppressed, but I spend every day adding to the prison that held them, guarding them as they fought to break free. Even now, I could hear the rattling chains, the clanking of iron bars. The incessant dripping…

With effort, I shoved those memories back where they belonged. A key turned in a lock and that familiar numbness slid through me, taking the place of my panic.

Quinn crossed something out, her pen scratching against the notebook as she added an addendum.

"I'll clean up," I muttered, wondering where I was going to find a broom. Or would the magic that kept the castle clean beat me to it?

"No need," Quinn said with a sigh. "As I said, I may have identified the virus that's causing this, but I don't know enough about the magic needed to counteract it."

"Maybe Marin…"

Quinn was already shaking her head. "It's time to visit Mayim. Like Marin said, they have the resources we need at the Enclave." She nodded as if deciding something. "My healer friend there has been pushing for me to bring my research to Mayim anyway. Now that we know what we need to counteract, it's time to take a trip through the mirror together."

Together.

Despite everything, the word made my reckless heart clench. It didn't help that she was looking at me like she needed me as much as I needed her.

She had no idea the depths of my selfish longing. And she had no clue how much her presence was chipping away at my control while forcing me to acknowledge exactly how disconnected I had become. But giving in and admitting my feelings wasn't what was best for her, even if the thought didn't terrify me.

Quinn deserved someone whole—not this shattered version of me.

I bowed slightly to avoid her gaze, sweeping one hand out in invitation. "Lead the way, Sagray."

CHAPTER 14
TOBIAS

Bash looked haggard as he answered Eva's door, his stubble was overgrown and the circles under his eyes matched the shadows that swirled within them. His clothes were rumpled as though he had slept in them, though from his drawn expression, it hadn't been for very long.

"Is she—"

"Still breathing," Marin whispered from where she stood by Eva's bedside. My sister's eyes were closed, her hair lovingly spread out against her pillow. Marin's hand rested on her forehead, a steady trickle of green light streaming from her fingertips to Eva's temples.

I reared back, my heart lodging in my throat. "Was that ever an issue?"

"Yes." Bash's voice cracked on the word. "She took a turn for the worst last night."

Light crackled at my fingertips. I clasped my hands together, letting the latent energy snuff out against my skin. The burn of my magic barely registered as I fixated on the gentle rise and fall of Eva's chest. There was a roaring in my ears, my entire body trembling with barely controlled fury at the thought that I had almost lost her and hadn't even known it.

My father was murdered before I even realized his last words were a goodbye. He had gone to hold Aviel off to give us time to flee, taking on the False King and his fire wielders without hesitation. Sometimes, in my darkest moments, I wondered how exactly it happened. If Aviel had stolen my father's darkness first, or if they had simply burned him alive.

I couldn't do anything but watch when my mother sacrificed herself for us. All I could do was beg her to come with me before she forced me through the mirror with the same light as my own. I could still hear her final scream before Aviel killed her, too.

But I had made my mother a promise that night as the flames burned our house down around us: that I would keep my sister safe.

I wouldn't lose Eva too.

Quinn looked as furious as I felt as she snapped, "And you didn't tell me?"

"It wasn't anything I couldn't handle," Marin said sharply. "Especially now that I have other healers helping me. We need you focused. Nothing else matters more than you finding a cure."

Quinn's shoulders tensed, blinking hard as worry clouded her features, and I felt my magic rise again in response. I swiftly shoved it back down, letting my light die in the dark prison of my mind.

"I told the healers Queen Sariyah sent to rest while she's stable," Marin said, crossing her arms as if preparing to defend her decisions. "Ondine and Esme are both well trained. They both studied at the Enclave."

Quinn sighed heavily. "I was hoping to talk with them. We need to take a visit to—"

A soft knock on the door interrupted her mid-sentence. I swiftly crossed the room, to find Rivan and Yael looking travelworn and exhausted in the hall. They both wore lightweight linen tunics and pants and smelled faintly of salt—like they had spent time at the sea. Reinforced, hardened leather covered their shoulders and chests, though neither looked any worse for wear.

They didn't have Silvius in custody, that much was obvious.

Shadows exploded from Bash's hands, lacing around his arms like a curl of a whip as he demanded, "Did you find him?"

Yael grimaced. "We saw Silvius yesterday not far from Queen Sariyah's castle. We're here to get reinforcements now that we've confirmed he's there."

My voice was dangerously soft. "You found him, and you *lost* him?"

"Our rangers got waylaid." Yael sounded strained, her shoulders rigid. "By the time we dispersed the crowd, Silvius disappeared."

"We questioned some of those who were with him without any luck," Rivan said cagily. Even he seemed off, his normally unflappable composure rattled.

There was something they weren't saying. Something they probably felt they were protecting us from.

I crossed my arms. "Was the crowd helping him?"

Rivan and Yael exchanged a pointed glance. Bash's bloodshot eyes narrowed at them in a wordless order.

Yael let out a deep sigh, her shoulders slumping. "There's been some unrest since the news of Eva's illness got out. We couldn't hide it: too many people knew about the bonding ceremony not to speculate on why it was delayed. Some of the crowd was…" She paused, looking faintly nauseous. "…celebrating. Aviel's supporters, the ones that hid in plain sight…they were shouting that the magic of the land turned on Eva since she stole their so-called 'True King's' crown."

My magic flared, the burn so sudden I flinched.

"There were plenty of people protesting on our side too," Rivan quickly added. "This was just a small but vocal minority. Fighting broke out. That's why Silvius was able to get away."

I wanted to scream. If I had been there…

You would've what? A cruel voice mocked. *Cowered under the weight of the open sky and ran to find shelter?*

"We'll find him," Rivan said with a confidence I wished I possessed. "And then force him to make a cure." Rivan looked at Quinn. "Unless you figured out an alternative?"

Quinn's face fell, guilt flashing across her features.

Bristling, I stepped in front of her, squaring my shoulders like I could shield her from it. "Quinn's doing everything she can to find a cure. Which is why when you return to Mayim, we're going with you."

I expected an argument. Instead, Rivan simply nodded. The exhaustion was plain on his face, worry etched into every line. If I were a better person, I might have figured out something to say to comfort him, but I was barely holding it together myself.

Rivan looked over my shoulder at Quinn, letting out a heavy sigh. "If that's what's best for Eva, you won't get an argument from me. But you need to be careful who you tell that you're experimenting with her blood, especially with Silvius in the same city."

Quinn gave a quick dip of her head to accept his apology. I jerked to attention as she gestured between us, explaining. "We need help if we're going to figure this out quickly and the Enclave's the best place to get it."

We, she said. Like I had any right to be included when this was all her genius.

"I already wrote ahead to let Dolion know of our plan," Quinn continued, moving beside me. "He's caught up on our work so far, and has discussed it with Queen Sariyah, so I don't expect an issue. I'll make sure it's a closed lab—just the three of us."

"The healers at the Enclave are the best in the realm." Marin said it like she was trying to reassure herself, the mix of hope and fear in her voice almost painful. "Their hospital is second to none, and their research wards are full of everything you should need. Hopefully their resources can assist you with—" Marin cut herself off with a yawn.

Yael's gaze flicked over to Marin, then her eyes narrowed. With a few quick steps she crossed the room, one hand sliding to the nape of Marin's neck and directing her gaze up with a firm tug. "You're draining yourself. You need to rest too, my love."

Marin might have ensured her team was resting, but it was obvious she hadn't heeded her own advice. She stubbornly shook her head before tiredly laying it against her *anima*'s arm. "I'm needed right here."

"*Marin.*" Yael rubbed her hand down Marin's back. "I know better than to argue with you, but..."

"Then don't," Marin interrupted, her smile sliding from her face. "You have enough to worry about considering you're essentially running two kingdoms right now."

Rivan strode up beside them, crossing his arms across his chest. "Take an hour to close your eyes, Marin. I'll keep Eva steady until we depart. Tobias and Quinn will need the time to pack up anyway."

Marin's hesitated but she nodded, waiting for Rivan's hands to slide into place above Eva's temples before she slowly released her magic. Her shoulders dropped, eyes closing as the faint green of Rivan's power replaced hers. Its color was more gray than Marin's, like the stones I knew Rivan favored.

"My turn to help save you," Rivan murmured to Eva, a sad smile on his lips. "Not that we'll ever be even."

Bash's elbows dug into the mattress as he took Eva's opposite hand, bowing his head as if silently praying to any gods who might be listening. I wanted to scream at him to wipe that defeated look from his face—not when there was a chance my sister could feel his despair.

Quinn solemn voice broke the silence. "Can you still feel her?"

"Faintly," Bash replied. "I know I should try to sleep, to find her in my dreams. Last night, I could feel the battle raging within her…her confusion and her terror at what's happening to her and the realization that she's slowly losing her mind. It's like her spirit is withering right in front of me, and there's nothing I can do to stop it."

His throat bobbed, his shadow-dark eyes glassy with unshed tears.

"You don't have to leave her to sleep," Quinn coaxed. "There's plenty of room on that bed for you to lay down and rest while still holding her hand."

She was just as drained as Bash was—likely more so with the amount of magic she was using—and here she was offering him strength and empathy. It left me humbled.

Rivan nodded encouragingly and promised, "I'll wake you if there's any change."

Bash looked between us but didn't budge from Eva's side.

"I need to be doing…something," Bash said hoarsely. "I can't just sleep while she's hurting and in pain and…" His hands trembled so hard that Eva's started to too. "She needs me, and I can't help her."

Quinn shook her head. "You're exactly where you need to be. Keep trying to reach her through your bond. Even if she doesn't know *you*, she can feel your soul—and deep down, she recognizes what you are to her. We'll keep her breathing until we have a way to save her."

Bash nodded, looking numb as he brushed a tangled strand of hair behind Eva's ear.

Animas rarely survived the death of the other. I hated myself for even thinking it.

"Marin?" Pari peeked through the open doorway, panting like she ran here. She too wore lighter clothes suited to warmer weather, her short, silvery hair pulled back in a bun. "I'm sorry to barge in. Queen Sariyah gave me the information you asked for, and I heard you were here."

Rivan bristled, squaring his shoulders like he was preparing for battle. "I thought we weren't there yet."

Feeling slightly betrayed Quinn hadn't mentioned whatever this was to me sooner, I looked first at her then at Pari, before demanding, "What's that supposed to mean?"

Pari raised a brow, her smirk crinkling her dark brown eyes. "Nice to see you too, Your Majesty."

I didn't let myself react to the sarcasm in her voice or the title that made me shift on my feet as I waited for the answer.

"It's the process on how to induce a magical coma," Marin admitted, a hint of defeat in her tone. "I thought it might give us more time to find a cure."

Bash whirled on her, his voice harsh as he asked, "And you just thought to mention this?"

"It's not easily done," Marin continued tiredly. "And it's meant as a last resort. Eva will need some form of magical anchor to stay stable while comatose, and with *animas* that usually means—"

"What do I need to do?"

Bash's voice was steady, his jaw set. Despite my less than spectacular first impression of my sister's *anima*, this was exactly why he had won me over in the end. His love for her was all-encompassing. Even if it would cost him his life, he wouldn't hesitate to do whatever was necessary to save hers.

"You'll both be incapacitated."

Bash waved his hand dismissively. "My brilliant *anima* set up a system of representatives, all of whom I have full faith in."

"It's more complicated than that," Marin argued. "If this doesn't work—"

Bash was already shaking his head. "Nothing else matters. Nothing matters more than her, not to me."

We may have had our differences, but I had to respect Bash's devotion to my twin. She deserved someone who would risk everything for her, whose heart would always find its way back to hers, no matter the cost. My eyes found Quinn almost instinctively, and I watched as she restlessly tucked a stray curl behind her ear.

Eva wasn't the only one who deserved that level of devotion.

"I still need to review the process," Marin grumbled. "But from what Esme explained, we'd need to put both of you into a joint sort of stasis. Your bond will keep you there together while Bash's magic will keep it powered and stable. If done right, it should protect her brain from the effects of the virus and pause its progress by keeping you both in a state where the virus can't multiply."

Quinn looked hopeful as she murmured, "Like a sort of magical life-support."

"With the mental fog as it stands, I can't tell what's reversible," Marin continued. She looked over at Quinn and me. "If you're able to find a cure and force the fog to recede, then we can see what the damage is to those pathways and focus on healing them."

The pity in Marin's eyes hit me like a slap. My jaw clenched, biting back my retort.

"When," Quinn corrected her. "*When* I find a cure, not if."

Quinn lifted her chin, as if daring fate to contradict her. The fierce light in her eyes, the stubborn tilt of her lips—she looked every bit the force of nature she was, and it nearly brought me to my knees in awe.

Marin nodded solemnly. "When you find a way to clear the fog, then we can figure out what she remembers."

The muscles of my neck seemed to freeze in place as I tried to mimic Quinn's nod, like even that passive agreement might jinx us.

"What matters is keeping her alive until she's cured, by any means necessary. When she's better, I don't care how many times I have to make her fall in love with me," Bash said with a hint of his usual charm. "But we'll cross that bridge when we get to it."

Yael reached across the bed to lay a comforting hand on Bash's shoulder. I found myself meeting Quinn's gaze, though I quickly looked away.

Bash's thumb brushed across Eva's cheek. "If we're in statis together, will I be able to dreamwalk to her?"

"There's no guarantee of anything," Marin said carefully. "But from what I understand, it's likely."

Bash straightened. "I could talk to her? Find her on the other side of the barrier?"

"I'm not making any promises." Marin sighed. "If it goes as expected though, the hope is that you'd be able to…reach through the fog."

"Do it," he ordered.

"Bash…" Marin started.

He cut her off. "If it's the only way for me to reach her—"

"It's also highly probable that a virus that magically targets the mind could be transmitted in that state," Marin snapped. "Not to mention what would happen if she took a turn while you're linked like that. It's why I waited to bring it up—it's a last resort. We can't risk losing both of you."

Bash's smile held a shadow of pain. "You say that like losing her isn't tantamount to losing me anyways." He extended his hand to his sister in a silent appeal. "Please, Marin. We both know if it was Yael in this bed, you wouldn't give it a second thought."

Marin stared back at him, her gaze glassy. Bash's lips pressed together, waiting.

I bit my tongue, knowing Marin was only coming from a place of keeping her brother safe. If our situations were reversed, I would've said the same. If there was anything I could do to ensure Eva's safety—if I could trade places with her right now—I would do so in a heartbeat. Between the two of us, I knew who I needed to live.

But Bash could be trusted to put Eva first. Whatever silent conversation passed between the siblings ended with Marin letting out a weary groan.

"Fine," she sighed. "Give me an hour to finish reviewing this." She shot a look at Yael, who looked ready to argue. "Time is of the essence here. I'll sleep once it's done."

Quinn gave her a grateful look. "This is exactly what we need. More time to give me—give *us*—a chance to find a cure." Quinn glanced at me like said cure wouldn't be entirely her doing.

Maybe it was more than sharing credit where credit wasn't due though. Maybe she needed someone to share the burden.

I met her gaze and managed a slow nod—a silent promise. Wherever this road led, I would be at her side. I wouldn't let her walk it alone.

Bash looked between us, his eyes an endless, swirling gray. The plea in them was unmistakable.

My voice was low but steady. "Keep her alive, and we'll find a way to save her."

Marin rubbed the bridge of her nose. "If it doesn't work, I'll bring you out of it. I'll be monitoring you both closely, so it'll be easy to tell if she deteriorates."

Shadows curled around Bash's arms as if bracing him. "It won't hurt her, right?"

"No," Marin confirmed as she used her free hand to cover a yawn. Her magic had to be drained from keeping the virus at bay. I felt a twinge of guilt that I had yet to thank her for keeping my sister alive. "But this sort of magic doesn't come without risk. If she dies—"

"Then I don't care what happens to me," Bash interjected, his tone leaving no room for argument. "If it gives her a fighting chance…if it gives us time…" He lifted Eva's limp hand, intertwining their fingers together. "Then it's worth it."

Looking uneasy, Marin gave a small nod. "I'll make the preparations. We'll do this tonight."

I turned back towards Quinn in time to see the light in her eyes dim as she watched the slow, fragile rise and fall of Eva's chest. When her lower lip trembled, I made myself a vow—

This time, I wouldn't fail them.

CHAPTER 15
QUINN

It is a special kind of hell watching someone you love slowly forget you.

Bash's shadows hovered around Eva like a dark fog, swirling in agitation as I drew more of her blood to bring with me. Their master silently stared at her flushed but peaceful face, holding her hand like a lifeline.

As I switched out a vial for a fresh one, I prayed to whatever gods were listening that this was reversible. Whether it was with magic, or simply her own inner strength, I knew Eva would fight the sickness with everything she had—clinging to who she was with all she had to give.

After throwing a few outfits into a bag, I had changed into a simple green eyelet dress suited for warmer weather. My pack waited with the carefully packaged research down in the laboratory. I was thankful for my seemingly bottomless bag and the easy delivery system through the mirror, since I refused to let just anyone handle Eva's blood.

Tobias was packing a few final necessities while I visited Eva. Better he wasn't here for this. In the quiet of the lab, it had been easy to hear that intentional four count of Tobias's breathing as I gathered the syringes. I wondered if he noticed the way I matched each exhale.

It was enlightening seeing what made that indifferent mask slip, even as the growing list of Tobias's triggers made my blood boil at all he had endured.

Eva's breath stuttered, and I reached for a fresh cloth, dipping it into the bowl of cold water on her bedside before carefully wringing it out. I let my magic flow into her as I pressed it gently against her forehead. This fever was designed to make her body's defenses so focused on eradicating the virus's effects that she didn't have any energy left to fight the fog enshrouding her mind.

Putting her in a medically induced coma was a stroke of genius. Selfishly, I was glad it would give me the time I needed to work on a cure. Not that it wouldn't be paired with the constant fear of failing her.

"Always forward," I murmured as I pushed back the fog. I gritted my teeth as the magical barrier only solidified against my magic, each attempt more difficult than the last. "Remember when it was just the two of us? We were lost and alone together, and we somehow made it through. You found your way here to your true home, you found your soulmate…and you better believe I won't let you leave behind the life you've built or the home you've created."

I swore under my breath at the effort it took to push the mist back. Every time I felt it give, it pressed forward somewhere else. It was no wonder Marin looked so exhausted. This was a losing battle—and it was up to me to win the war.

Eva stirred slightly, her eyelids fluttering. I kept talking in case she could hear me, refusing to be cowed into silence from the anxiety of sharing my memories aloud. Bash was clearly not paying attention, his focus narrowed on the syringe plunged beneath Eva's skin.

"Remember in college when we would pick a destination for the weekend and just drive?" My voice shook. "You'd always make me camp under the stars somewhere woodsy and teach me about constellations. And I'd take you to find sand and sea and sunshine…"

When my voice finally gave out, Bash filled the silence. He sounded painfully hopeful as he spoke, as if the sound of his voice might bring her back when all else had failed.

If I had any doubt about Bash's love for my best friend, the intimacy of his words would have convinced me. He told her about the moment they met in the mortal realm and the way he had fallen more deeply for her day by day during their journey through the Faewilds. He spoke about their shared joy at finally admitting what they were to each other, and the way that love had grown ever since. He spent far too long describing that one perfect dimple that taunted him with her every smile, unabashedly sharing all the ways he loved her while promising her everything and anything if she would just open her eyes.

It wasn't until he finished that I realized these were his vows—the words he might have said on their wedding day, now choked with tears.

"I'm coming for you, Eva," Bash said hoarsely. "I always will." His throat worked as he stroked her flushed cheek with the pad of his thumb. "I'll find you in our dreams until you wake up safe in my arms."

I quickly wiped my face on my sleeve when the door swung open. Marin strode in, determination in every step despite the frown on her face. She was flanked by Yael, Rivan, and the two healers that must be Ondine and Esme. With a deep sigh, I released my magic, feeling the fog replace it as the blue glow faded into Eva's skin. Marin quickly took my place, the steady stream of her magic flowing into Eva's temple.

"Please keep us updated," I said to her. "And good luck."

She surprised me by pulling me into a one-armed hug. "Right back at you."

As a scientist, I was trained to rely on data, to find patterns, and to trust only evidence. But I also knew that even the smallest variables could tip the balance. We needed far more than luck, but I clung to the hope it offered.

Yael turned to Rivan. "I'll make sure things are in place here, then join you four in Soleara as soon as I can." She gave Marin one last lingering kiss. "Unless you need me here longer?"

Marin shook her head. "I have help. And Imyr is being taken care of in our absence. Just focus on hunting down Silvius so this nightmare can be over."

It was an effort to suppress the shudder that worked its way down my spine at the mention of that bastard's name. I had passed far too much time buried in Silvius's research, reading the details of the people he had tortured for his own experimentation. Tobias had spent years as one of those unwilling participants—and the only one who had survived.

Nightmare was putting it mildly.

"We're a mirror away if you change your mind," Rivan said gently. "Good luck."

"You too," Marin replied. "Now get going. Ondine, Esme, and I will need all our focus for this to work." The glow of their healing magics were already rising to their fingertips as Marin waved us away.

It would be a short trip through the mirror to reach the southern kingdom. I wondered if the city Silvius had found refuge in would genuinely be safe or merely waiting for our guard to slip. Not that I had any intention of letting my guard so much as waver.

I caught Bash's eye. "Say hello for me when you see her, okay?"

He nodded, his jaw clenched so tightly I could see the muscles work through his unkempt auburn beard.

The vials of Eva's blood weighed heavily in my satchel as I walked away. Turning, I took one last look as I reached the doorway. The three healers worked in unison, whispering shared instructions. Bash pressed a gentle kiss to Eva's forehead, threading their hands together as he lay down beside her.

Her face remained serene, like a princess from a fairytale doomed to eternal slumber. If only it was as simple as true love's kiss to wake her up from this nightmare.

If love were enough—if devotion could mend what was broken and loyalty could cure what ailed her—they would have long since earned their happily ever after.

"Fight for me, hellion," Bash whispered as he closed his eyes. "Please…" He sucked in a shuddering breath I could feel in my soul. "Remember that I love you."

CHAPTER 16
TOBIAS

My heart stopped before lurching back to life, pounding erratically as my eyes adjusted to the bright light. The world was a kaleidoscope of blues and greens, the sunshine blinding.

We were inside, but barely. The mirror we had walked through still rippled, the glass embedded into an enormous coral wall studded with seashells and precious stones. A gilded doorway stood opposite us, gleaming in the sunlight, as did the castle behind it. Its pale stone walls were softened by centuries of salt and sun and veined with gold. Arched open air windows exposed us to the sea air and endless blue waters of the Namaris—the ocean that surrounded Mayim.

The city had been built atop a series of canals, the waterways serving as the streets upon which small boats floated beneath the pedestrian-covered bridges. Water poured endlessly from a carved creature's mouth into the canal below, each drop sparkling in the sunlight.

Everything was too loud, too bright, too much. I sucked in a ragged breath, then another, each more shallow than the last. The heated air only scorched my throat.

My panic fought back the more I attempted to push it away, trying to break free before I could cage it again. Clenching my fists around the straps of my bag hard enough to indent the cording into my palms, I used the limestone floors beneath my feet to ground myself in the knowledge that I was inside, even as I felt completely exposed.

The oppressive heat bore down on me, the sun unrelenting. I squeezed my eyes shut against my body's reminder that light meant pain…especially mine.

My sword felt too heavy on my back, the metal heating against my skin. My brain screamed for me to run back to the mirror and back to the sanctuary of Soleara. My hand reached for Duskbane's hilt of its own accord —though there was nothing to fight, no foe to vanquish except the fear searing my soul.

Familiar footsteps came up beside me. I opened my eyes, already knowing it was Quinn.

Her eyes were wide with concern. "Are you okay?"

Apparently, my panic wasn't as inconspicuous as I had hoped. At least Rivan and Pari had walked through the entryway ahead of us, the heavy door still swinging. I opened my mouth to reply to her, but only a choked, stunted sound came out.

"No, you're not okay," Quinn whispered softly, almost to herself. "What just happened?"

My muscles were locked so tight my entire body tremored. Sweat dripped down my back. I tried once more to form an answer—or even to *breathe*—and only managed a loud gasp for air. The scar around my neck tightened as I tried to regain control, spots forming in my vision as my mental prison evaded my grasp.

Quinn moved in front of me, her amber eyes filled with alarm. I could feel my magic rise in response, reaching toward her as steadily as I wished I would.

"Breathe, Tobias," she pleaded.

She took my hand, her touch immediately grounding, and breathed in for a careful four count. I zeroed in on the sound of her exhale, forcing myself to match it. When she breathed in again, I sucked in a gulp of air along with the sweet, floral scent of her—immediately relaxing as I held it in my lungs.

I couldn't help but focus on the way her thumb rubbed against the back of my hand as we breathed in tandem. My every thought narrowed to the heat of her palm. How easy it would be to tug her closer…

Reluctantly, I pulled away, putting some much-needed distance between us. "I don't need you to—"

"Don't bother lying to me, Maris."

Before I could put together a reply, she stomped away. I found myself hypnotized by the sway of her hips as I followed.

Quinn heaved the large doors open, and a bright smile spread across her face as she curtseyed. "Nice to see you again, Queen Sariyah."

I bowed my head as I recognized Mayim's queen through the doorway, then quickly followed Quinn inside with our bags. Pari looked at me quizzically from where she stood next to an impatient-looking Rivan, likely concerned about our delay in following them. I pointedly avoided her gaze, keeping my eyes fixed on the queen.

Queen Sariyah offered me a matching tilt of her head—a sign of respect from one ruler to another. She looked ageless, though I knew she had to have at least a few hundred years on me. Her sea-green gown exposed large diamonds of dark brown skin around her waistline, the long slits in her skirt revealing her legs as she walked. Her black hair was braided atop her head, surrounded by a sapphire crown.

Her almost equally regal companion bowed at her side. He had an aristocratic air to him, a certain refined look about his expression. The deep vee of his blue shirt revealed the olive skin of his chest and jet-black hair brushed against his shoulders, half of it tied up in a sleek bun. Piercing gray eyes met mine. There was something familiar about them despite my certainty we hadn't yet met.

"Thank you for hosting us," I managed, my tone coming out curt in my efforts to keep my voice steady.

Being marked as rude was better than allowing the stutter I couldn't seem to shake garner the pitying looks that only made it worse. Not that either was the best trait for a ruler who needed some semblance of diplomacy. It was one of the many reasons I was in Quinn's debt after she took on so many of my public duties.

"It's the least I can do for our High Queen," Queen Sariyah insisted. The soft consonants and rounded syllables of her accent had an effortless elegance to it, refined and musical. Her wise turquoise eyes took me in, her irises the same shade as the ocean peeking through the domed structures and colorful facades of the buildings that surrounded this palace. When she turned that stare on Pari and Rivan, it was a relief to be released from her gaze. "I trust there was no change from your last update?"

Rivan held up a piece of paper that must have arrived while we were still outside. "Marin says the statis worked, and Eva seems to have stabilized. Thank you again for sending the healers to help her. As far as Silvius…the Imyrian rangers we sent to search for him have a few potential new leads," Rivan added in a low voice, as if careful not to be overheard. "Which I'm told they already shared with your city guard."

He didn't sound happy about that development. Mayim had been overrun by the False King's supporters during the war, zealots who embraced Aviel's tyrannical vision of the mortal realm kneeling before fae they didn't even realize existed. It wasn't hard to see why Silvius had hidden here. And now we had proof they remained—and were likely sheltering him.

I wasn't about to stick to social niceties, especially when it pertained to my sister's life. "Are we sure those involved can be trusted with that information? After all, Silvius managed to get away once already."

Rivan sighed, but the twitch of Quinn's mouth seemed amused if not approving of my lack of diplomacy.

Queen Sariyah's gaze turned steely as her eyes flicked back to me. "My guard are as trustworthy as your rangers."

"We kept the circle of those in the know small," Rivan cut in smoothly. "Just to be safe."

"Though if there is a leak, this will be a good test," Pari muttered loud enough for me to hear.

From the look on Queen Sariyah's face, she hadn't missed it either, though she chose to ignore it. She glanced at her companion, then gave us a practiced smile. "This is Dolion, the head of the Enclave's research ward. He'll personally help you search for a cure, as I'm told you've already discussed. You'll find that my healers are the best in all of Agadot and my researchers second to none. I have no doubt we'll be able to find the cure you're looking for."

Dolion gave a short bow, his eyes fixed on Quinn. "Lovely to meet you, my dear."

I stiffened, resisting the primal urge to step in front of her. His expression might be mild but the look in his eyes made me scowl in a blatant lapse of control.

"Oh!" Quinn exclaimed happily. "You're the one I've been writing to about my research."

I inwardly bristled at the excitement in her voice. For some reason, I had been picturing someone a little less handsome. He seemed young to be the head of anything. If he were human, I would have guessed late-thirties, though I knew he was likely much older than that.

"The same," Dolion simpered. I straightened as he stepped forward, my entire body tensing as he lifted Quinn's hand to his lips. "It's a pleasure to finally meet face-to-face. As I hope I've already expressed, you are most welcome here. I'm looking forward to continuing our conversations...and examining the samples you've brought with you, of course."

Power surged to my fingertips, angry and burning. I clenched my fists against the light that tried to escape me, letting the sparks sear into my palms. The pain was a welcome reminder to ground myself. A reminder that I had no right to Quinn, or to the jealousy now crowding my chest.

I cleared my throat, walking closer. Dolion had the good sense to release Quinn's hand as I stepped between them.

"I'll be accompanying Quinn while Pari and Rivan see about tracking down Silvius." I raised both bags—magically light despite their contents and far smaller than they should be for what they contained. "Let's get started, shall we?"

✧

The Enclave was the most lavish hospital I had ever seen, if I could even call it that, all whites and blues and gilded accents. Gold veined the polished limestone, stunning stained-glass windows adding to the vibrant exterior. Sunlight streamed in through pointed archways and large, diamond-paned windows. Gold-leaf patterns glimmered like vines throughout the interiors.

The Enclave was an extension of the ornate castle Queen Sariyah called home. A covered bridge connected the two, the octagonal windows built into the marble allowing a picturesque view of the boats passing through the canal below. As we walked, Dolion launched into a long-winded description about its history and setup like we had come for some casual tour. Patients occupied the lower floors, while the upper floors were dedicated to research. A separate wing housed students and faculty.

Quinn hung off Dolion's every word, fascinated by his explanations. They moved on to rapidly discussing Quinn's progress as I followed close behind, trying not to char the leather handles of our luggage in my jealousy.

On the one hand, I appreciated being able to blend into the background as I tried to acclimatize myself to my new surroundings. On the other, Dolion was standing far too close to Quinn. When he stepped closer still and placed a hand on her lower back to guide her through the correct hallway, a growl caught in my throat.

He looked back at me with a smile that was more of a leer. "Given the nature of our work, I've closed the laboratory to anyone else," Dolion said loftily. "Especially as Quinn and I move into the next phase of her experiments. I know you said you would join us...but perhaps your talents would be of better use assisting your other companions?"

I had no intention of leaving Quinn. Not with this stranger, even if she seemed to trust him. Not in this place, when there was a high chance it could be compromised. Was this sense of foreboding due to my general anxiety at being in a new location, the fact that my sister was in mortal peril, or were my instincts warning me about something darker?

No matter what, I wasn't about to let this bastard run me off.

"I'll stay where I'm needed," I said dismissively, brushing past him. "Quinn and I have worked pretty well together so far." I bit my tongue to avoid adding *without you*. "And I'm not taking any chances with her safety."

Quinn looked between us, a line forming between her brows.

Dolion's disgruntled look was quickly replaced by a smile that didn't meet his eyes, his voice edged in accusation as he asked, "Were you expecting a known fugitive to break into my laboratory?"

There was something about the way he talked that made the hair rise on the back of my neck. Something familiar about his tone...or maybe it was the way he looked down his nose at me, like he found me lacking. Maybe it was simply the desire to wipe that smarmy look from his face.

"That known fugitive has apparently been hiding in your kingdom since the war's end." I let my derision for his so-called security creep into my voice. "Not only is Silvius a psychopath with a god complex, but he also managed to infect my sister with this virus...and she's arguably the most protected person in this entire realm. There's no telling how many people are working with him, especially in a city that was nearly overthrown by the False King's supporters. I trust our people to find him, but in the meantime, I have no intention of letting my guard down."

Especially not where Quinn was concerned.

Dolion's dark eyes gleamed. "You speak as though you know him."

A cage in my mind I kept firmly shut rattled as I fought to keep my cool. Merely saying his name was enough to dredge up a few memories from the dark that were best left buried. Their sharp edges dragged through me like broken glass, fighting to be freed.

My voice was tight as I replied, "You could say that."

"Oh, that's right," Dolion drawled with faux apology. "You're the Solearan prince that was trapped in the False King's dungeon. How fortunate you survived a fate so many didn't return from."

I held his gaze, even as I shoved the images those words evoked back behind bars, dampening the screams of those long-since dead. My heart thundered loudly in my ears like it alone could block out the sound.

"We're lucky he did," Quinn gently interjected, her gaze flicking between us as her frown deepened.

Dolion's calculating gaze however was fixed on my neck...no, on the white scar that encircled it. I slipped my hands into my pockets, resisting the urge to block the scar that suddenly felt tighter.

Pursing his lips, Dolion turned away and walked up to a large, iron door. With a practiced movement, he twisted the scrolling metal latch that barred it.

"The iron is, of course, a precaution against any experiments reaching the castle."

A clang of metal against metal echoed through the corridor as the door swung open. I jerked back, a flood of icy terror nearly drowning me.

Dolion crooked his fingers, gesturing for us to follow—but my feet were frozen in place.

Every time that iron door opened it meant pain.

My breath quickened as the hallway dimmed, going slightly out of focus. The light leeched away; that incessant dripping filling my ears. The corridor seemed to narrow as the walls pressed in around me. A familiar, cold iron mask slid into place, as though I had never been freed....

The only way to survive was to feel nothing at all.

"Tobias?"

Quinn came up next to me, her hand close enough I could feel the warmth of it along the side of mine. I avoided her gaze, locking my true feelings back in their cage, even as her stare bore a hole into the side of my face.

Then her hand intentionally brushed against my own.

That invisible charge jumped between us—hot and sharp like lightning. It melted through the cold in an instant, banishing the chill that had invaded my blood. My head snapped to hers, startled at its intensity.

Quinn's eyes were wide as she met mine. Her mouth had dropped opened, the soft 'O' of her lips so inviting I found myself leaning closer—

Dolion cleared his throat, watching us with a curious expression. "Is something wrong?"

With a heave, I mentally swung those iron rungs shut, sealing away my memories—and the weakness that came with them—and forcing my feelings back into the cell where they belonged.

"No," I said shortly as I hurried through the doorway. My magic, usually bursting to get out, cringed away from the iron like a kicked animal.

I resisted the urge to do the same.

Quinn followed, looking frustrated as she caught up with me. I couldn't blame her—not after I had nearly fallen apart twice before we even began.

That icy calm settled deeper as I avoided her knowing gaze. It was nice feeling nothing. Easier, certainly. Though some part of me whispered it couldn't last—at least not while she stood so close to me.

"Just this way," Dolion said as we reached a large white doorway. Silvery writing that shone so brightly I was forced to squint arched above the door. Fleetingly, I wondered if doctors in this realm were also made to take oaths to do no harm.

"If you'll press your hand to the side of the door, there's a unique bit of magic that will recognize your magical signatures," Dolion explained. "It will allow you access going forward. Given that there are those who would like to see our efforts fail, I thought it best to add some additional security."

I hadn't even noticed the rectangular pad that blended into the stone. There was a hum of magic as I warily pressed my hand against it. Quinn followed my lead, looking visibly intrigued.

She reached for the door handle just as I did. I jerked back before our fingers touched, turning my hand over in a wordless, *after you*.

Quinn paused, exhaling in a quiet huff before shoving the door open.

Dolion's laboratory reminded me far too much of Silvius's lair with its dull metal countertops, though I was sure that was the norm. The laboratory was bright and sterile, the air tinged with the faint scent of reagents. Refrigerated units took up the entire back wall, a neat bit of magic that I knew involved imbuing ice magic, a rarer form of water wielding, into the structure. I wondered if it required regular maintenance or if it could be powered by the magic of the land after the initial imbuing.

The question died on my tongue as Dolion took Quinn's arm to walk her through each station. My jaw flexed as her hand covered his, squeezing it in thanks.

It was an effort not to glare at him, or at this place that looked like we never left the depths of Morehaven save for the view. A decanter even sat atop the desk.

My lips twitched as I imagined Dolion's reaction if I were to throw it against the wall.

"As you know, we have many instruments similar to those you've used in the human realm, though of course they're powered by magic…"

As Dolion continued the tour, I set our bags down, then paced around the circumference of the room to look for potential weaknesses. A solitary door stood behind his desk. I reached for the knob, only for it to refuse to turn.

"That's locked," Dolion said sharply from behind me.

"I can see that," I replied dryly. "Any reason why?"

"Storage for some dangerous components I don't want accessible to just anyone." From the scorn in Dolion's voice, I was absolutely on that list. "If we need something from there, I'll retrieve it myself."

I crossed my arms as I turned around, catching the flicker of tension in Dolion's posture. So much for the warm welcome he was attempting to show Quinn—clearly, he didn't appreciate me questioning him.

"The labs are all individually warded to contain any potential leaks, either viral or magical," Dolion continued, his attention fixed solely on Quinn. "You can't work through the night. There's cleansing magic that triggers to clean the room and sanitize any used beakers or vials at sundown. Any samples will need to be transferred to the refrigeration units…" He gestured at the back of the lab. "Since the heat treatment used for decontamination will result in sample inactivation. It also happens to be at a temperature no one can survive. A good reminder that your brain needs rest to function as well, though it can sometimes be ill-timed."

Quinn nodded though she looked somewhat put out. I, however, felt a tinge of relief despite my efforts to lock it away. Quinn needed the rest now that Eva's condition was stable. While keeping Eva in a magical coma wouldn't work forever, Quinn had spent far too many nights staying up through the sunrise. It wouldn't help either of them if she was too exhausted to continue.

"I made sure everything was ready for you," Dolion simpered, "but let me know if there's anything else you need. Due to the nature of your research, and the stigmas around blood and magic, no one besides us knows the exact nature of our work. I, of course, will assist you with anything you need."

I didn't like the way he looked at her. Like he was thinking about far more than simply working together.

"She has me for that," I said before I could stop myself.

So much for control.

"I meant as a fellow healer." Dolion eyed me dismissively. "As I said, perhaps your expertise would be best used elsewhere. I'm sure the brutes searching for Silvius could use the assistance—"

"If you two are done posturing, I'd like to get to work," Quinn cut in, her tone unusually acerbic.

My cheeks grew hot as I turned to face her. She briskly unpacked the first bag, avoiding my gaze as she removed the samples of the virus she had painstakingly worked to extract. When she finally looked up, her eyes were ablaze with pure determination.

"We don't have time to waste," Quinn reminded us in a quiet voice that was no less powerful. "*Eva* doesn't have time for us to waste."

My stomach sank like a stone, any response dying on my tongue—shriveling against the sheer force of her reprimand. I nodded in mute agreement.

Whether or not this magical statis was working, my sister was still sick. As much as I hoped that she and Bash were happy in whatever dreamland they were in, there was no way of knowing until they woke up. And for that to happen...we needed a cure.

"Of course," Dolion said smoothly. "Let's get to it then."

I hurried over to the other bag, hesitantly reaching for our supply of syringes. Quinn passed me Eva's blood samples before I could grab them with a muttered, "Can you refrigerate these?"

Taking them, I did as she asked. The three of us carefully unloaded the rest in silence.

"Right." Quinn let out a quiet sigh that made my gut twist. "First, I'd like to talk over the way it targeted her by using her blood, and the implications that has on its genetic makeup..."

She spread Silvius's research on the table, as well as her own meticulous notes. Jealousy flared through me as Dolion took up my usual place beside her. He leaned close as she tersely walked him through what we had already completed, the work so thorough that I marveled at what she had managed in mere days.

It was a different kind of magic to watch the way her mind worked: how she made sense of that which seemed impossible. She was able to understand a different layer of the world—comprehend it on a microscopic and biologic level—and make connections that anyone else would be oblivious to.

Dolion watched Quinn almost covetously as she spoke, occasionally interrupting her to ask questions. Her answers only seemed to impress him more.

My magic rose to my fingertips and I curled my hands into fists—welcoming the distraction of its burn.

Quinn was extraordinary. Kind without losing her strength of character, smart without being arrogant about it, and beautiful without even trying. No wonder Dolion was looking at her with a mix of surprise and reverence.

She was everything.

He might be some brilliant fae scientist, but if we discovered the cure, there would be no 'we' about it. Quinn had gotten us this far, and I had no doubt she would be the reason why Eva survived this.

Had they exchanged more than scientific musings in their correspondence? It was an effort not to bristle as he moved closer to her, turned a page in Silvius's journal, then didn't bother to step back.

When she mentioned writing to a friend in Mayim, I had pictured an older professor type. Not that Dolion was necessarily close to our age. The aging process slowed significantly for fae after their Seventeenth and the claiming of our magic. He looked to be in his early thirties, which meant he was likely closer to a hundred or more—especially given his position in the Enclave.

Was this the sort of person Quinn dated back in the mortal realm? Highly educated, ambitious, and with a mind for science...someone that could keep up with her brilliance?

I didn't deserve her, but he certainly didn't either. Maybe no one did.

"We should probably draw his blood."

I jerked back to attention as I realized they were both staring at me. Quinn looked thoughtful; Dolion shrewd. As I realized what he said, I took an unintended step backwards.

Quinn raised a hand in protest, her eyes flaring with concern. "If we have Eva's, then we don't necessarily need his—"

"Given your familial link, your blood might shed some insight into the biological nature of the virus." Dolion explained. "Studying it could help us understand potential transmission, not to mention how the virus targets its host."

I far preferred his pointed disregard to the way he now surveyed me like a test subject.

"Like a control group of one," Quinn added hesitantly. "A baseline for comparison."

My jaw clenched as I tried not to let the memories slip through the bars of their cage. It was a long moment before I could get my voice to work.

"If you need my blood to help her, I'll do it," I muttered to Quinn. "T-take whatever you need."

"Excellent," Dolion said briskly. He brushed off his sleeves, then made his way toward the iron door. "Given the sensitivities of blood drawing and the potential magical implications, syringes are not as common in this realm, so I'm glad to see you brought some with you." He paused in the doorway. "I need to grab a few additional supplies. I'll return shortly."

The door closed behind him with a clang that made me shudder. I let out the breath I was holding, letting my lungs empty completely before sucking air back in. This was to help Eva. It wasn't Aviel, or Silvius, or someone that would use my blood to hurt the people I loved. After all, I trusted Quinn, and if she trusted the need for it...

"You don't have to," Quinn said quietly.

When had she walked over to me? My next inhale carried that faint floral scent that immediately calmed my nerves. Unable to meet her eyes as

I tried to wrangle my fear, I stared at the sunflower amulet she always wore. All I wanted to do was wrap my arms around her, pull her close and let her touch ground me again.

My hands clenched at my sides. "I told you, I'm here to help. If that means letting *Dolion*," I injected as much derision into the syllables of his name as I could, "draw my blood, then that's what I'll do."

What was it about him that had made my hackles rise? It was hard not to feel protective about Quinn, though I knew I had no real claim to her.

"I can do it, if you prefer." A smile flirted at her lips. "Though you realize Dolion's here to help us, right?"

"I don't think that's all he wants from you," I muttered darkly. The way he watched her, like he had any right to, made me want to wipe the look from his face with my fist.

To my surprise, Quinn laughed. "Could you *be* more overbearing?"

I shrugged indolently. Little did she know there was no limit to what I would do to keep her safe.

"I could certainly try," I deadpanned.

She rolled her eyes, even as I watched her fail to stifle her smile.

The sound of the iron door opening sent a spike of fear down my spine. Quinn frowned slightly, and I cursed myself for letting down my guard, even for a moment. Dolion glanced between us from the doorway, clearly trying to decipher whatever he had walked in on, before his mouth curved in the faintest of sneers. It was gone before Quinn looked his way.

"You've done well to move as fast as you have identifying the virus," Dolion said to her as he walked over to our supplies, opening the familiar carrying case that held the syringes. "Reading your research was truly enlightening. The technology you brought with you from your realm mixed with the magic of ours yielded impressive results."

I quickly looked away from the syringe. "You forgot to mention that it's also the result of pure stubbornness, perseverance, and determination," I added admiringly. "All of which Quinn has in spades."

Dolion sniffed, as if affronted I had jumped in on his moment of praise. He came forward, the needle of the syringe glinting ominously in his hand. "This will only take a second."

Closing my eyes only brought on a barrage of memory; a sick slideshow of every time Silvius had done the same thing to me, only without my consent. Sucking in a breath through my nose, I pictured my cell—the iron bars, the musty, freezing floors—trying to push those memories back where they belonged.

I refused to fall apart again. But the footsteps coming closer sent fractures through my calm with the sound of each step. My eyes flew open, immediately finding Quinn's.

In an instant, she was beside me.

"Let me."

It wasn't a question. Dolion raised an eyebrow but relinquished the syringe to her outstretched hand.

"Just breathe," Quinn murmured. Her hand brushed against my arm as she raised my sleeve. Was it my magic that caused that shock as it built beneath my skin? It's not like I had touched anyone else enough to test it. Her fingers glowed with the blue of her magic as she prepped a small area on my inner arm.

My inhale was audible, my exhale far too fast.

Quinn stepped closer, her bare legs brushing against my knees. "Look at me, okay?"

I obeyed. A line formed between her brows as she focused on her task. I couldn't help but drink in the details of her face, the long, sleek line of her neck. She bent forward to wrap a tourniquet around my arm, and my eyes dropped unbidden to the ample curve of her cleavage.

"Quick pinch," Quinn murmured, tapping a vein by my elbow. "Your eyes look especially golden today."

Was it my imagination or was she intentionally pressing her breasts together?

"What?"

Was she *flirting* with me?

The needle pierced my skin before I realized what happened. My heart raced, pounding in my ears.

"Must be the sunlight," Quinn mused as the tube started to fill. "I'm looking forward to summer in Soleara. We're overdue for some time to enjoy ourselves. Maybe when Eva's better, we can come back here for a vacation. I wouldn't mind a swim together. Do fae wear bathing suits?"

"I-I don't know."

It was a distraction. It was working.

"Eva mentioned skinny dipping on her journey to Imyr," Quinn said, her voice teasing. "Which I'm not opposed to."

My mouth went dry. "I imagine we'll have a few things to take care of once this is all over."

Quinn sighed exaggeratedly, switching out the vial for another. I barely noticed as she leaned closer. Our foreheads nearly touched. Her gaze was downcast, focused on her work.

A small mercy. If she were to lift her chin, I might get lost in those amber eyes forever.

"Live a little, Maris," she said a little sadly as she pulled away. "After all, this is your second chance at it."

I swallowed against the sudden knot in the back of my throat. My rebirth from that dungeon had come at too great a cost for me to be squandering it. I might not be who I was before, but I owed it to everyone who sacrificed for me to do better. To at least try.

"You're right," I admitted.

Quinn released the tourniquet, neatly wrapping a bandage around my arm. "Of course I am." Her smile was dazzling. "That wasn't so hard, was it?"

My mouth dropped open as I realized she had finished the blood draw without me noticing...and without needing to sedate me for it. She passed the samples to Dolion. My stomach lurched at the sight of the needle, and I looked back at her.

"Thank you," I whispered.

She shook her head. "You don't need to thank me for that."

There was an edge to her voice as she stared down at my arm—not at the bandage she tied there, but at the scars around my wrist. I had never stopped struggling against those shackles, never gotten used to the way their icy grip bit into my skin. The metal's natural anti-magical properties had ensured those scars would never fade.

I hadn't been afraid of needles once. Hadn't been this broken version of myself.

And I couldn't stand the pity in her gaze.

"I'll get us some food," I blurted out, swiftly rising to my feet. Dolion had pointed out the cafeteria on our way in, if the beautiful, sunny food hall could be called that. "I assume you don't want to break for a full lunch."

Quinn lips formed a tight line. "Do you want me to come with you?"

No, I needed a second to compose myself. To wrangle the emotions that she drew out of me so easily. To chain them back into the cells I had never really escaped from.

She was maddeningly adept at destroying my carefully crafted control.

"I think I can manage," I drawled, trying for nonchalance but falling short.

Quinn only sighed, crossing her arms across her chest. I would have been able to hide my true feelings from anyone else, but she had always been able to see straight through me.

My tone was curt as I ordered, "Don't leave this room."

Her eyes narrowed. "I happen to be able to take care of myself, as you well know."

"That's not—" I let out an exasperated breath. "We don't know who you can trust."

Quinn crossed her arms. "Maybe you shouldn't be wandering the halls alone then. I'm the one safe behind a biometrically locked door."

"I'll be fine," I growled, feeling my light rising to her challenge. The familiar heat of it warmed my blood even as I shied away from that particular part of my power.

"So will I," Quinn said staunchly.

If anything happened to her, it wasn't just my sister's fate she would irrevocably alter. I knew without a doubt it would shatter me completely.

Somehow the space between us had vanished, as though we had been drawn together. She glowered up at me, lips parted, her chest rising and falling. The defiance in her amber gaze sparked something deep inside me straining to break free.

"Besides," Dolion cut in. "She won't be alone."

I gritted my teeth so hard my jaw popped. I had almost forgotten he was there.

Quinn crossed her arms. "See? We'll be fine without you. As I said, I can—"

"I know you can take care of yourself," I hissed under my breath. "But will you just let me take care of you too?"

Heat rose to my cheeks. Quinn stepped back, shock coloring her face.

"I'll be right back," I exclaimed loudly, my eyes briefly meeting Dolion's across the lab. The threat in them, however, was clear.

If anything happened to her while I was gone, I would make him pay.

I didn't dare look back at Quinn before I all but ran from the room.

CHAPTER 17
TOBIAS

The sun had almost set into the sea, sinking beneath the horizon as darkness encroached upon the last rays of daylight. Rivan and Pari found us walking back to our rooms after what sounded like a sweaty, fruitless search that had ultimately led them to a dead end. I tuned out their bickering as a young healer brought us to a wing of guest rooms. They were all attached to a shared living room, leaving me with far less privacy than I liked.

Definitely not enough space to easily hide away from their company. I eyed the door of the nearest bedroom. I was lucky the circumstances of my nightmares, and the mask that waited for me, meant that I rarely screamed.

A coral-colored dining table on the outdoor balcony was laden with a small feast. My stomach rumbled at the delicious smell wafting through the windows. After so many consecutive nights working until dawn, it felt decadent to stop for a warm meal and somewhere to shut my eyes, though I doubted the night would be restful. At least Queen Sariyah hadn't expected us to dine with her. Amid the research and the ongoing hunt, maybe she knew none of us were up to the usual song and dance. Though from what Dolion told us, the Queen was a healer in her own right and regularly spent her nights attending to patients in the hospital wing.

My breathing quickened as I neared the glass double doors that would lead to the balcony. I hadn't eaten anything since I brought Quinn lunch, but as my focus fixed on the sky, my stomach twisted into too many knots to be hungry anymore. I abruptly veered away, ignoring everyone else and a call that might have been my name as I fled to the farthest room.

I rushed into the attached bathroom and gripped the sides of the pearlescent sink, feeling the cold stone beneath my fingers as I panted, trying to get my rising panic back under control.

My reflection in the mirror peered back at me. The seemingly permanent shadows beneath my eyes had deepened. My face looked sickly from the lack of sun and sleep, my pallor even more pronounced than usual. I grimaced at the bright glow of light that overtook the hazel and gold of my irises—a sure sign of my loss of control.

I might be able to pretend I merely wanted to wash up before dinner, but if I took much longer pulling myself together, Quinn was sure to come looking for me. Sucking in a careful four count breath, I closed my eyes, picturing those cells. Painstakingly, I locked away my fear, and that light, behind those bars where I had been broken, so I wouldn't break again.

It took more effort than usual to find that faux sense of calm. And it felt like forever before I managed to shut everything away, numbing myself enough to do something as banal as walk back outside and eat dinner. Even then, my mask slipped far too easily lately.

Was it worth the endless effort that it took to simply exist?

Sometimes I wasn't sure.

My fingers had lost feeling from squeezing the sink by the time my icy mask was firmly back in place. I splashed some cold water on my face I barely felt, washing away the sweat of the day before I forced myself to leave my room and go back to my companions…back to her.

Despite everything, I closed my eyes as I crossed the threshold—resisting the urge to grab onto the glass doors and refuse to let go.

When I opened them, my gaze went straight to her, as it always did, subconsciously drawn to her despite my best efforts to stay away.

Quinn was laughing with Rivan on the opposite side of the table, their heads ducked together in a way that made a feral need rise in me to walk over and sit between them. I shoved the thought away before I did something unhinged.

Feeling nothing was far better than the alternative. There was too much I refused to face, too much fear and pain to ever truly escape it. Yet I couldn't seem to compartmentalize the flicker of jealousy at the easy way she laughed at whatever Rivan just said. The pure joy in it made my heart ache like the organ refused to be silenced with the rest of me.

Pari sat beside me, giving me a knowing look I ignored. When I had returned to Soleara, Akeno and Thorin had given me space, obviously realizing I wasn't the same person I used to be. Pari hadn't given up so easily. She had been the one to extend invitation after invitation to rejoin their circle, and when those had failed, make sure I was looped in on the goings-on of the Solearan Senate. And not brief missives, but detailed play by plays of exactly what I needed to know to make informed decisions.

She deserved to be led by a king who wasn't afraid to leave his own castle. The best I could currently manage was to faithfully follow my mother's outline to let our people govern themselves and leave me to my duties behind the scenes. Pari, Akeno, and Thorin had been keeping Soleara safe long before I fell through the mirror and found myself there. And they had continued to do so during my capture. If anyone deserved to lead, it was those who had held Soleara together in my family's absence—not its withdrawn farce of a king.

Maybe it would have been better had I never escaped that dungeon.

Pari reached over, breaking me from my internal musings as she placed a platter of roasted fish next to my plate, quipping, "Did you know that food generally requires you to eat it in order for you to get the benefits?"

A sigh broke past my lips but I obediently added some of the offering to my empty plate. My stomach felt too tight to even contemplate eating, though it did look appealing. I kept my focus on my plate, staring at the crisp basil leaves atop the fish and not the rapidly darkening sky that made it hard to breathe, let alone consider taking a bite.

"It sounds like Akeno and Thorin have everything under control in Soleara," Pari pronounced as I added a few grilled vegetables to my plate.

I frowned. "I haven't heard anything from them."

She shrugged. "They know better than to contact you for anything less than an emergency."

Inwardly, I winced. I was fully to blame for that dynamic, after months of hiding away. After how hard they searched for me, it had to be a slap in the face that I had essentially become a ghost since my return, haunting the bronze castle I grew up in.

Maybe it was the resigned formality of her tone, like we were nothing but strangers, that shamed me. Or maybe it was fear—that, like Eva, something would happen to her before I could mend the gap between the friendship we once shared and what we were now. But I knew I needed to try.

"Thank you, Pari," I murmured, hoping she knew how much I meant it. "Not just for taking charge without me even needing to ask. I owe you much more than a thank you for all you've done for your kingdom and her people."

Pari's eyes went wide. Was my praise *that* unexpected? I knew I had hurt her with my refusal to confide in her as I once did, but that didn't mean I didn't still care or notice everything she had taken on in my stead.

"I appreciate it, Your Majesty," Pari remarked coolly.

"Tobias," I corrected her. Though I no longer deserved her familiarity, I wanted it anyway. "My coronation doesn't change anything. We were friends first, after all."

Pari looked me over, as if appraising me. "Are we, still?"

She had never been one to mince words. My eyes dropped to the fish I had been steadily mutilating with my fork. My mental cages rattled.

I drew in a deep breath and looked her in the eye. "I'm sorry. I know I've been distant since my return. And I'm…" I chanced a glance at Quinn. "I'm trying."

It was something, if not nearly enough. I owed her far more than an apology for my seclusion, for turning my back on our friendship, and for my failure to live up to the crown that had been entrusted to my family, figurehead or no.

Pari watched me appraisingly, the silence between us stretching unbearably. Then a smile lifted her lips at whatever she saw. "It's about time, Tobias. Glad to have you back."

I gaped at her.

Had it really been that easy?

"I don't know about back," I muttered. "But I'm physically here, at least."

I shoved my full fork into my mouth if only to keep myself from saying anything else, and was surprised to find the light, flakey fish both flavorful and utterly delicious. The knot in my stomach loosened, yielding to my hunger. I neatly finished off the rest of it before reaching for seconds.

"How did today go?" Pari sounded uncertain, like she was out of practice making small talk with me. "Research run smoothly?"

I made an assenting sound as I chewed. A glint in the corner of my eye caught my attention, and I turned to see Quinn unsheathing my dagger. Something swelled in my chest at the sight. She hadn't taken it off except to sleep since I had given it to her months ago. The diamond in the pommel caught the fading light, the engraved patterns on its hilt bringing me back to the day my mother had placed it in my hands.

It looked right in hers.

Quinn flipped it end over end, the move so expertly done it looked casual, and I suppressed a smirk.

Rivan glanced at me, his brow furrowing. "Isn't that the match to Eva's?"

Quinn nodded. "Tobias lent it to me on the way to Adronix."

"Gave it to you," I corrected quietly. "I have no intention of taking it back." My hand slid to the hilt of my own dagger, feeling the hum of energy as my magic tried to intertwine with the blade. I had left the matching sword in my room but kept the smaller blade attached to my belt, just in case. "Duskbane came as a set. Besides, Quinn has always been deadly with a dagger. I have no doubt it's in good hands."

Rivan's fingertips brushed Quinn's as he took the dagger from her. That corrosive jealousy heated my veins. He held it up, examining the details carved into the hilt…but Quinn's eyes were on me.

A heated flush darkened her cheeks. She opened her mouth as if trying to figure out what to say, then closed it again. Rivan handed the dagger back to her, hilt first. But Quinn held my eyes a second longer, then let out a nervous laugh when she realized Rivan was waiting, releasing me from her gaze.

Pari snorted softly. I forced myself to look away from Quinn, then grumbled, "Something to say, Pari?"

"You're, um…sparking," she muttered under her breath.

I blinked, then glanced down to where my hands rested on my lap. Sparks flared at my fingertips, dropping to the ground like fallen stars before sizzling out on the stone. I clenched my hands into fists, blowing out a breath as I attempted to force that emotion into the cage I was failing to keep closed.

"Be careful the next time you're on carpet," Pari said with a loud laugh.

"You're not helping," I muttered sullenly as the embers died against my palm. The redness would be gone by morning, the pain a fleeting distraction from my apparently noticeable jealousy. Here I thought my biggest challenge during this meal would be my agoraphobia.

Though I had been doing just fine, for a moment.

Quinn looked over at us, glancing between the two of us with a frown. But it was Rivan's reaction that piqued my interest. The usually lackadaisical warrior stared me down with a challenge in his eyes, his jaw so tight it could cut glass.

I leaned closer to Pari, whispering just loud enough for her to hear, "Looks like I'm not the only one who's jealous."

She looked at Rivan, whose lavender gaze dropped to his plate. He aggressively cut into a grilled asparagus.

Pari rolled her eyes. "He's not…"

"Keep telling yourself that," I drawled.

She scowled, but her immediate flush only confirmed my suspicions.

I speared another bite of fish, then raised my voice to include the rest of the table. "So, what's the plan for tomorrow?"

"We stop searching the same spots we've already covered and go down the lists of Silvius's potential conspirators," Pari said, fixing Rivan with a glare.

His jaw flexed as he reached for the bread, ripping a chunk from the rest of the loaf with more force than necessary. "Silvius had just as much of a chance of being there—"

"I told you it didn't match his pattern," Pari interrupted, her eyes flashing. "He must be hiding in one of the homes of those who supported the False King or were at least suspected of it. We have a list of those spotted either at the last demonstration or who have vocally supported Aviel in the past."

"All of whom both Queen Sariyah's guard and our rangers have already visited and searched. Silvius was spotted—"

"Weeks ago," Pari gritted out. "And by starting there, we risk leading him straight to Quinn and her research to stop him."

Quinn raised a hand, as if asking a question in school. "Spotted where?"

"At the Enclave," Rivan muttered mutinously. "We spent most of yesterday interviewing staff for any leads. A healer saw someone matching Silvius's description sneaking into a lower level not long before Eva fell ill, though she lost him soon after. It's safe to assume he has someone helping him within the Enclave's ranks, maybe even someone who helped him create or transport the virus. And we can't risk him creating more supply, if he hasn't already."

My eyes snapped to Quinn. I hadn't let her out of my sight today, but my sister's blood, as well as my own, was behind that iron door in the research wing. If Silvius still had a way in…

"Don't worry," Quinn said, though she twisted her cloth napkin around in her hands. "Dolion assured me our research is well warded."

It was an effort not to bristle at his name on her lips. "Well, if *Dolion* said so." I turned to Pari. "If we're looking to find a mole, then perhaps what's needed is a trap. Too many people already know we're here to keep our research quiet, and it doesn't take a genius to guess what Quinn's working on. What better way to flush Silvius out than, I don't know, loudly discussing how close she is to finding a cure the next time we're walking into the Enclave?"

Rivan tipped his head to the side. "A good plan, though I hope our targets tomorrow yield results. Though maybe a few of our rangers should join you two to make sure you're safe."

For once, I consciously let my magic flicker at my fingertips, feeling that familiar heat behind my eyes as my power reflected there. As much as I hated that part of my power—the searing heat that had been used to hurt me and so many others—the thought of Silvius anywhere near Quinn made it ignite with unexpected fervor.

Quinn shook her head. "Catching Silvius is also a priority here. Not only to answer for what he's done to Eva, but before he infects anyone else. I don't want anyone potentially contaminating the lab, and there's no point having guards wait in the hallway when no one can get inside besides Dolion, Tobias, and me."

I nodded in agreement, albeit begrudgingly. "Quinn can take care of herself. But I'll be there to help and make sure there isn't any chance she's caught off guard."

Quinn gave me look so full of gratitude that it made my heart skip a beat.

"We'll stick to our teams then," Pari said decidedly. "Remember, you can ask for help if you need it. This won't work if we don't work together."

The words were pointed—and obviously directly at me.

"I will," I promised.

If we were going to save my sister, I needed to step up and face my fears and my feelings, whether I was ready or not. I couldn't hide from the world anymore, no matter how much I wanted to. I couldn't pretend that silence was safer than speaking up or that distance was easier than connection. And I couldn't let the echoes of my past keep me locked in the cell that once held me, not anymore.

To do so was a disservice to all my friends and family who had risked their lives to bring me back, and an insult to my parents' sacrifice, the last gift they gave to me.

Maybe true strength wasn't the absence of fear but the choice to keep moving despite it. Maybe survival meant learning to live alongside the cracks and broken shards instead of trying to seal them.

I might not ever be the person I had once been, as much as I grieved who that boy could have become. But maybe that mattered less than becoming the person I was meant to be now.

Either way, it was time to try—not just for Eva, but for myself and the fractured future I was finally ready to piece back together.

CHAPTER 18
TOBIAS

Everyone retired immediately after dinner, to my immense relief. We all had early mornings tomorrow and much left to do in the days ahead. And everyone needed a good night's sleep to replenish their magic use today besides me, Quinn especially. She hadn't been able to hide her yawns by the time the sun fully set. Rest wasn't just a necessity; it was required for our survival.

My room was large and luxurious, with colorful seashells adorning the seafoam green wallpaper and sea stars atop each bedpost. The bed's enormous frame and headboard were made of iridescent circles that reminded me of bubbles rising to the surface of the ocean. I spent a full minute tossing the shell-shaped throw pillows from the bed, then threw the suffocatingly heavy quilt on an armchair by the curved bay windows.

At least the soft silk sheets underneath looked inviting.

I closed the blinds with a sharp yank, shutting off the peaceful view of the moonlight shimmering off the dark ocean waves. Stripping off my shirt and pants, I pulled on a light pair of sleep shorts before falling into bed. I stared dully at the seashell light on my bedside, wondering how long it would take tonight until I was huddled and shaking on the floor.

Maybe after today's excitement I would actually be able to convince my mind to allow me a longer stretch of sleep. Hopefully I would make it a few hours before my nightmares ripped me from my rest, and I inevitably spent the rest of the night staring balefully up at the ceiling—wishing the darkness would swallow me whole.

Soft footsteps stopped outside my door. I instantly recognized it as her. The was a long pause like she was contemplating whether to knock.

I held my breath, Quinn's name trapped on the tip of my tongue as I waited for her decision.

Two hesitant raps on the door made me jolt straight up.

"Maris, are you still awake?" Quinn's voice was quiet, but the uncertainty in it made my stomach drop.

"Come in," I called out hoarsely.

The door creaked open, even that movement hesitant.

"I—" Quinn started, then froze with one foot inside the doorway.

Her eyes leisurely trailed down my bare chest, then back up again, taking her time as she did so. I may have flexed, just a little, as her perusal paused on my abdominals. My blood heated at the way her breathing quickened.

It started to boil as I took her in. The long, green silk robe that tied around her middle, begging for me to unwrap her. But it was her unbound hair that made my mouth go dry. She so rarely wore it down—always tying it back when she was working on something, which was pretty much always.

I wanted to feel those wild curls between my fingers. I wanted to wrap them around my fist and make her moan my name.

But it didn't matter what I wanted. Not when she was owed so much more than I could offer.

"I'm sorry, I saw the light on, and I thought—" Quinn started to say.

I quickly cut her off. "I wasn't asleep yet…just thinking."

"Can I join you?" Quinn lingered by the doorway, her hand still on the doorknob as if my answer wasn't obvious. "I needed someone to bounce some theories off of, and I wasn't sure where else to go." She shifted her weight side to side clearly feeling unsure. "I can't sleep with my mind whirring like this, no matter how tired I am…"

I understood that better than she could ever know. As exhausted as I was, sleep would be a long time coming no matter how hard I tried to turn my brain off. The more I shoved my feelings and fears away during the day, the more I found myself facing them at night. When my mind was tired and the world was quiet, and I had nowhere left to hide.

"Get in here already," I demanded.

If she needed me, there was never a question about what my answer would be. But maybe she didn't know that.

Quinn's answering smile left me breathless. She softly shut the door behind her, then came toward me. I found myself entranced by the gentle sway of her hips. Utterly mesmerized by the way her legs peeked through the slit in her robe as her bare feet padded silently across the carpet.

My tongue tied as she crawled on the bed beside me. My heart caught in my throat as the bottom of her robe spread open, the lace of the matching slip beneath riding up her tawny thighs. Speech abandoned me entirely as she slid beneath the covers.

Suddenly, I was very happy I hadn't gotten up to greet Quinn as thoughts of her tangled in my sheets, spread out on *my* bed, forced me to rearrange the covers on my lap. I looked away, distracting myself by pouring some water for her from the pitcher on my bedside table.

"Make yourself at home," I drawled as I passed her the glass.

Quinn flushed. "Sorry, I can—"

My hand darted out, my fingers fastening around her wrist as she made to move away. "Joking, Sagray. The bed's plenty big."

Was it my imagination or had her eyes darkened at the way my much larger grip encircled her dainty wrist? She relaxed, pliant in my hold.

It took me a long moment before I made myself let her go.

I was *not* going to think about the implications of sharing this bed with her—about how perfect she looked next to me, like she belonged here. Or obsess about the way her breath had caught when I had my hand wrapped around her wrist.

Did she like that, having me restrain her? It made me wonder what else she liked. And if her cheeks would be the same perfect shade of pink when she came on my tongue.

"Isolating the virus was only the first step," Quinn stated, all business despite the way her flush lingered. "Now that I have an understanding of its biology, I can figure out what targets are unique to the virus and essential for its survival."

She said it so simply, like it wasn't utterly amazing she had been able to do so much in such a short time. I shoved aside my desire, forcing my drifting thoughts back to what she actually needed from me.

"I'm following so far," I confirmed. "Though please do remember I never finished high school bio, let alone your level of education."

Her face dropped, likely remembering the reason I hadn't finished high school, and I immediately regretted opening my mouth. Eva told me they had held a funeral for me. I hadn't known what to say as I pictured her mourning over the empty grave. She had buried me next to my parents' with Quinn at her side.

Eva had given a eulogy, but had Quinn said anything? Suddenly, I wished I had asked Eva questions instead of rushing to apologize again.

"Luckily, I have a good teacher," I added softly.

Quinn's tongue darted out to moisten her lips before she continued, and I bit back a groan. She repositioned her pillow, then burrowed further into the bed, tucking the sheets beneath her arms. I mimicked her on my side of the bed, unable to help myself.

"Dolion agrees with my hypothesis that in order to reverse the effects, we'll need a magical and medicinal cure." Quinn started talking so quickly it took a second for my tired brain to refocus. "Basically, we need to create a magical antiviral. Something that controls the spread while eradicating the symptoms…"

She didn't so much as take a breath as she continued. I could listen to her explain this all night. The excitement in her voice, the genuine curiosity. She was brilliant and obviously in her element, and watching the way her brain worked was utterly fascinating. For once I was thankful for my inability to fall asleep—and that I was the one she wanted to talk these things through with.

"And for those of us that didn't go to medical school…how do we do that?" I coaxed, as she finally paused to breathe.

Quinn turned on her side, facing me. Once again, I followed her lead. I was utterly aware of how close she was to me; that I could tuck the errant curl that lay across her cheek behind her ear with barely a movement. Yet the space between us might as well have been a chasm for how impassable it was.

No matter how comfortable this felt, or how dangerously easy it was to fall into old habits, I knew better than to believe I deserved to have her here with me.

Quinn remained oblivious to my internal struggle as she delved into her response. She snuggled into my pillow like she was sharing a bedtime story rather than a mini medical seminar.

"Antivirals target the processes that viruses use to replicate and spread within the body," Quinn explained patiently. "Unlike antibiotics, which target bacteria, they're specifically designed to interfere with viral life cycles. If we can imbue that with an element of magical healing, one that can travel to the host cells and undo the damage, I'm hopeful that the fog will disappear, and Eva will regain control of her mind and memories."

"Sounds simple enough," I said dryly.

She let out a breathy sigh as she burrowed further beneath the covers. I had a feeling it would play on repeat in my brain from now until the end of time.

"Developing antiviral medications is challenging because viruses rely on host cells for replication, making it difficult to target the virus without affecting the host. I have a few ideas on what we should try to target. From there, we'll work to identify the best compounds to bind to the target and inhibit its activity. That's where the Enclave's research and magical screening processes will really come in handy."

I nodded slowly as I tried to commit each step to memory. "And the imbuing process? What do you have to do for that?"

"It's easier than it sounds," Quinn replied, her amber eyes lighting up in a way that made my heart pound. It was impossible not to get swept up in her excitement. "A lot of simple, everyday magic in this realm is imbued, like a hairdryer using air magic. The imbued power basically creates a magical battery. Most medicine used in this realm or 'cures' are essentially antivirals anyway—they work indirectly by strengthening the body's immune response to fight off the virus."

"I don't understand why the magic alone isn't enough," I said before quickly backtracking. "Not that I don't think that your magic, what you're doing isn't..."

Quinn laughed as my words tripped over each other. "I know what you mean. I wish it were as easy as knitting together a wound, or willing it to stop attacking her. But this virus was purposely created to block healing magic from working—so we have to attack it from the inside out."

The last few words were said mid-yawn, and I found it was contagious as I covered my own.

"I was hoping the fever was a sign of the magic of the land burning the virus away for us," I admitted, thinking back to the blur of terror after realizing Eva's newfound magic wouldn't be able to save her. "It makes sense that with the magic-blocking element, you need to fight the virus directly."

Quinn nodded sleepily. "Heat can kill viruses. That's exactly why the body's natural response is to raise its temperature. But the effectiveness depends on the virus, the duration, and how hot you can get without killing the host along with it. In this case, for it to succeed, the temperature needed would also boil Eva's blood."

I winced. "How lucky we have options then."

My eyelids were getting heavy, but I fought to keep my eyes open so that I could memorize this moment—the way her curls fell perfectly around her heart-shaped face, the glow of her light brown skin in the low light, the soft, open look in her eyes. She yawned again, and again I echoed it.

If she wasn't going to mention the late hour or the need to return to her own bed, I wasn't going to say anything that might scare her away. Though the sweet torture of my sheets smelling like her when she left might be the death of me.

"So, this magical antiviral…" I prodded, eager to keep her here. "I assume you'll need to test it?"

"Mmhmm," Quinn murmured. "We'll run initial trials on Eva's blood, but before I give it to her, I want to be sure it won't have any adverse reactions…"

My eyes closed, just for a moment, as I let her voice wash over me. Her exhaustion seeped into every elongated vowel as I blinked again, slower this time.

The soft smile on her face was the last thing I saw before I succumbed to sleep.

✧

The morning light always felt like a breath of relief. It meant I had survived the night.

I blinked blearily, feeling strangely peaceful. I couldn't remember the last time I had slept until sunrise…let alone the last time I hadn't jerked awake from a nightmare. Yet for some reason, I had managed to do both last night.

The warm weight on top of me let out a soft sigh.

I went still as the sudden realization swept over me—of where I was, and more importantly, *who* was still with me. Not only had I fallen asleep with Quinn in my bed, but she had stayed—and was now sprawled across me. Her face pressed against my chest, her breath warm against my bare skin. That green robe had fallen down her arms in the night, her shoulders now bare except for two thin straps.

One leg draped across my hips, her thigh dangerously close to the rigid part of me that had obviously noticed her nearness before I did. My arms were securely wrapped around her, holding her against me like I was guarding something sacred.

I needed to try to extricate myself before she woke. Instead, I found myself unable to do anything but breathe her in. The bright, floral scent of her made every cell in my body relax into a sense of calm I barely recognized. No wonder I had been able to sleep for once.

The gentle cadence of her breathing matched my own. For one achingly perfect minute, I let myself treasure this stolen moment, my fingers gently flexing against her skin to make sure this wasn't a dream.

Gods, I wanted her.

Just once, I allowed myself to admit it. I wanted her so desperately I wondered how it was possible she couldn't see it in my eyes—couldn't feel it radiating out of my soul. But no matter how natural this felt, how instinctively my heart reached for her, the person that might have been worthy of her died in that cell.

It didn't matter what I wanted. What mattered was what she needed—and it could never be me.

Gathering my composure, I loosened my hold just slightly, shifting so her leg slipped down my thigh—

"Tobias?"

Quinn's voice was groggy, and more than a little confused. I stifled a groan as she stretched, her hips swiveling against my side.

"I didn't mean to fall asleep on you," I said quickly. "I just closed my eyes for a second..."

Quinn laughed under her breath. "I mean, I'm the one who's *on* you."

The sound of her laugh left me winded. I was almost jealous of how nonchalant she was; her complete lack of awkwardness that we had accidentally spent the night together. For an endless heartbeat we stayed as we were—with her smiling up at me as I held her in my arms. Then I let my hands fall down to the bed. Quinn pulled away a second later.

I hated the way her expression turned troubled, like she was worried *she* was the one who crossed a line. That my abruptness had chased away that smile and turned it into hesitancy.

With a sigh, I pushed myself upright, leaning against the headboard like it might steady me. She swung her legs off the side of the bed, then paused, looking back at me over her shoulder. The sunlight framed her curls so angelically she didn't seem real.

She was art, each strand of her hair outlined by brushstrokes in gold leaf as soft sunlight leaked past the blinds. Her lips alone were a masterpiece, her eyes a study in amber no painter could ever hope to replicate.

It took me a moment to realize that her mouth was moving.

"—so we'd better hurry up and get to the lab," she was saying. "I can't remember the last time I slept that well."

"I can't remember the last time I slept," I muttered, too caught off guard to think through what I was saying.

Quinn cocked her head at me appraisingly. "Me neither."

Her eyes were soft as she gave me one last lingering look. My mouth went dry, my throat closing. Before I could think of what to say, she had already disappeared through the door.

I ran my hand across the bedding where she had been, like a dream dissipating into the daylight. Her warmth faded away, leaving me with a profound sense of loss—though I knew it was the absence of something that had never been mine to lose.

CHAPTER 19
QUINN

Tobias was waiting for me outside my door by the time I got ready, two steaming mugs in hand. He silently gave me one, his face so impassive I wondered if this morning had been a dream. I took a small sip, then let out a hum of satisfaction that brought a flush to his cheeks.

At least the Tobias I knew was still in there, somewhere, no matter how hard he tried to hide himself away.

Black tea, honey, and a splash of cream. Maybe I should have been surprised he knew exactly how I liked my morning tea, but I wasn't. Instead, I was thankful the blush that tinged his tanned skin couldn't be hidden behind his mask.

"Thanks," I breathed. "This is exactly how I take it."

He lifted a shoulder in a small shrug. "Anyone who's paying attention would know."

"And you were paying attention."

It wasn't a question. That blush deepened.

I took pity on him and walked past him to the joint living space. Rivan's and Pari's doors were ajar, as well as a third that had been readied for Yael. The bed was unmade—she must have arrived late last night. All three were already gone. I wondered idly if any of them had noticed my unused bed… or heard me tiptoe from Tobias's room to my own before they left.

Tobias took a gulp of his own tea before finally saying, "I figured you wouldn't want to waste any time this morning."

"You thought right," I confirmed as I took a seat at the dining table.

Two warm croissants sat in a basket on the table next to a bowl of fruit and a plate piled high with steaming eggs. I set my mug beside me before scarfing down the croissant. It was delicious, but I didn't have time to savor it.

The lab would open soon, and getting there even a minute late wasn't happening. Not when Eva needed me. If it wasn't for the cleaning cycle and the need to recuperate my magic, I doubted even Tobias would have been able to drag me away for the night.

My fingertips turned a familiar blue, as if my magic, too, was raring to go.

Tobias sat next to me, swallowing a bite of breakfast before drawling, "You know, if you choke, we won't get to the lab any faster."

"You'll save me," I said dismissively.

A smile curved his lips—gone so quickly I might have imagined it.

As I started on the eggs, Tobias passed me the seahorse-shaped pepper shaker before I could ask. We ate in a comfortable, albeit hurried silence.

I took him in as I ate. It was strange seeing him clothed in something other than his usual black, though the hint of color hardly softened him. To my utter delight, our hosts had provided us both with closets full of weather-appropriate attire. The tan linen of his short-sleeved shirt hugged the bulge of his biceps, its threads straining to contain his muscles as he reached for some fruit. I was used to the severe long-sleeved shirts he favored in Soleara, but the vee of his borrowed shirt exposed a tantalizing glimpse of his chest hair that I was far too grateful for.

My eyes snagged on the stark white lines encircling his wrists, darting away before he could notice my attention. Was that the reason he usually wore sleeves? I hadn't thought about it, not when Eva bore matching marks, but there was a quiet vulnerability in this simple change of attire.

A brown belt wrapped around his narrow waist, his dagger already affixed to the soft leather. His pants showed off the powerful muscle of his thighs, especially with the way one ankle rested on the opposite knee.

I glanced back up guilty as I realized I was openly ogling him.

But when I did, I found it was Tobias who was watching me—his stare tracing the lines of my legs where they were exposed through a slit in my skirt. My skin grew hotter where his eyes touched, the openness on his face startling in comparison to his usual purposefully blank expression.

My outfit today was cute but comfortable, the short, sleeveless top revealing a sliver of skin over the matching skirt. Subtle embroidery decorated the scalloped edges of my neckline as well as the entire length of the skirt. It may be going under a lab coat soon, but I couldn't resist the pale yellow—it perfectly matched the sunflower amulet resting just above the dip of my sweetheart neckline.

Tobias's eyes rose slowly, his tongue darting out to lick a crumb off his lower lip. My breath caught in my throat as our gazes finally met. He immediately looked away, but that telltale blush darkened his cheeks as he got to his feet.

I palmed an orange from the bowl, then tossed a second to Tobias as I stood. He caught it without looking.

"Let's get to it then," I said as I dropped mine into my satchel.

Tobias let out an unintelligible grumble but beat me to the door to open it. After dating my share of men in the human realm, it was refreshing to remember gentlemen still existed…or whatever the fae version of that was. I smiled up at him as I passed through the threshold, trying to coax a smile in return, though without any luck.

We walked side by side down the hallway. I noticed Tobias kept a careful distance from me, except whenever we passed someone else. Though most were dressed in the thin robes the healers all wore, this realm's version of scrubs or lab coats, Tobias eyed them all like they might attack at any moment. It didn't go unnoticed that he casually placed himself in between everyone else and me like my own personal bodyguard.

Nor did the way he tensed when he saw the iron door leading to the lab. His face showed nothing, but his body went so taut he could have been made of stone. The light faded from his eyes until they were as closed off as the rest of him.

And it was this utter lack of emotion, the way his expression shuttered like he was reliving a moment so awful he couldn't allow it to escape, that made me take his hand.

Tobias's gaze jerked to mine as soon as our skin touched. A flurry of emotions played across his face in rapid succession—fear and anger, grief and rage, heartbreak, and something like longing. My hand squeezed his, only for my magic to flare to attention as he winced in response.

I turned his hand over. Four circular red marks were burned into his palm. Horrified realization crashed into me as I stared at the burns.

He had inflicted these on himself. The blue glow of my healing magic washed over the marks like a wave.

"What the hell, Maris?" My sharp voice echoed down the hallway, but I was too worried to care if anyone else overheard. "Were you *trying* to hurt yourself?"

Tobias slid his hands into his pockets as if to hide the evidence. "My magic tends to try to find a way out. Better than b-burning the carpet," he stuttered before a look of distaste flitted across his features.

For a split second, I saw red at the callous dismissal of his own pain. In what universe did he think his discomfort mattered so little? That any level of pain was an acceptable alternative?

I could feel myself shaking, as I asked, more softly this time, "Does this happen a lot?"

He wouldn't meet my eyes, though his silence was answer enough.

"With more powerful magics, I've read that it can help to release it more frequently." I took a deep breath, thinking through the texts I had read on Celestial magic. "When you use your light, is it always heated?"

He let out a sound between a laugh and a scoff. "Of course you would have an answer from a book. It's fine, Sagray."

"It's not," I protested. But then it struck me…

When was the last time I saw him use magic?

He used it to fight beside me in Adronix, but ever since…

I hadn't seen him consciously use it once. Not in Soleara, not in Morehaven despite Silvius's underground laboratory and the shadowy stairway to get there. Not here in Mayim though we had been together day and night.

Why hadn't he...

"I'll be more careful." The words were clipped and completely unfeeling. "You don't have to worry."

"Don't placate me," I snapped. "And please, don't lie to my face. I know you—"

"No, you *knew* me."

It might've hurt less if he had slapped me.

"What's the matter, Tobias?" The anger in my voice was palpable. "Did you realize that you were finally letting someone in and got scared?"

After last night, I thought we had reached a place where he felt safe being open with me. That maybe he was starting to trust me again.

Apparently, I was wrong.

Tobias sucked in a breath like he was about to speak—

Dolion opened the iron door, and Tobias's mouth snapped shut.

I scowled at him, making sure Tobias knew we weren't done. But he had retreated so far into himself it was like glaring at a statue.

Dolion gestured for us to enter. "Let's get started. My time is valuable, you know."

We had gotten here right on time…though we had spent the extra minute arguing outside the door. My shoulders slumped slightly at the rebuke. I was well aware of Dolion's type—the scientist so sure of their brilliance and so focused on their work that they lacked a certain social decorum. Though from the warmth of his letters, I hadn't expected it from him.

I also didn't miss the way he pointedly ignored Tobias as he gestured at me to follow.

"Tobias and I were talking about antiviral options last night." I glanced at my stone-faced companion before I looked back to Dolion. "If we're going to target the structural proteins, I have a few mortal methods that might help. But I wanted to talk to you more about the magical component before we get started."

"Magically imbuing a treatment tends to work best when the antiviral compounds are derived from natural sources," Dolion said, his tone clinical. "For example, we keep a store of water taken directly from the Source itself—and yes, the current supply is low, since it was last restocked by Queen Amerie. Perhaps if it's able to save the High Queen, she'll be able to visit the site of the Choosing for a fresh supply." There was a strange look on his face as he turned around. "The virus really is quite genius, given that her own healing abilities can't save her."

"That's not exactly the word I would use," Tobias said, his words so low they were almost a growl.

While I understood Dolion was only talking about the science, his phrasing was callous if not cruel, intentional or not. If Dolion wasn't careful, Tobias might finally lose control.

After all, his magic had laid bare the truth beneath his composure—the tension crackling under the surface, threatening to scorch his restraint. As much as I wanted to be there when that particular dam broke, this wasn't the time or place.

"There is a certain irony to it," Dolion continued as though he hadn't heard him. "That the very magic she needs to save herself is being blocked from her use. There's a certain forethought in his creation that I'm forced to admire purely from a medical point of view."

Tobias's face hardened, but it was the light intensifying in his eyes that made me step in between them. My hands rested on my hips. "Let's see what we can do to ruin all his hard work then."

Tobias's jaw flexed but he stepped back, rolling his shoulders. His lips pressed in a tight line as he turned away.

Dolion launched into a long-winded explanation of the common elements we would work through today. I nodded along, already setting up my station. He had brought a range of known compounds to test for effectiveness, though we both knew the virus Silvius created was far too unique. We would have to design something new—though with luck, we could build on an existing compound to save time.

Our first step was to prepare test tube samples for each compound, diluting the virus I had isolated to a concentration suitable for controlled testing.

The monotonous task left far too much time to think.

Rivan had promised me last night that he would share updates, especially if they were successful in their search for Silvius. The fact that Silvius had been *here,* in the Enclave, sent a shudder through me that had nothing to do with the temperature control of the lab.

The thought that someone here might be helping him made me want to hit something.

How could Aviel's followers be foolish enough to continue helping Silvius? Were they so bent on revenge for their so-called True King that they refused to see that Aviel had only ever cared about himself?

He hadn't spared a second thought for his followers other than what they could do for his own power, that much was obvious in how expendable they were to him. Now Silvius was drawing on the same fanaticism that had kept those supporters willfully blind to the monster they had anointed their savior.

A knock shattered the silence. I swore under my breath as I nearly dropped the compound I was working with.

Dolion hurried to the door, opening it a crack.

"The queen requests a consult," said a male voice.

Dolion bristled with annoyance. "I'll be back shortly."

The moment the door closed, I walked over to Dolion's workstation like my feet were being drawn there. Everything was as we discussed. And yet, there was something in the back of my mind that made me pause, a truth my subconscious was begging me to piece together.

Tobias's blood was being used as a control of sorts, a test of its targeting and transmutability. Something deep and long suppressed clawed its way to my fingertips, reaching for his blood. I closed my eyes, instinctively pushing the impulse away even as warning bells blared in my head for an entirely different reason.

It was so, so dangerous, what we were doing here. Worse, there would be no one to blame but myself if his or Eva's blood fell into the wrong hands.

If Silvius stole it, Tobias could be infected, or worse. I couldn't help but think of how Aviel had taken Tobias's blood to forge a bloodlink—the forbidden blood magic allowing him to haunt Eva's dreams. And he had stolen Tobias's magic for years to keep up the pretense of a Celestial prince. I knew from Eva how agonizing that process was, and Aviel hadn't drained her magic nearly as often as her brother.

That thought stopped me dead in my tracks.

Was that why Tobias didn't want to use his magic? Because of how it had been used against him?

There was a soft footfall behind me—the sound of someone who knew how to be silent letting me know he was there. I kept my back to him, not wanting him to see the horror on my face as I thought my hypothesis through to its inevitable conclusion.

Tobias had spent years in that dungeon having his magic torn from him, then forced to silently watch behind his mask as Aviel used it to kill others. And he had been tortured repeatedly by the same burning light he now seemed reluctant to use.

No, not just reluctant. He was *afraid*.

My blood boiled in my veins, my sudden fury blinding me. My vision turned red as something inside me fought to be unleashed.

"What are you thinking?" Tobias's wary voice broke into my thoughts. I tensed as he came to my side.

I kept my eyes downcast, knowing exactly what he would see in them. "It...it doesn't matter."

"Don't tell me it's nothing," Tobias said dismissively. "I saw your face when you walked over. I've known you too long not to recognize the look you get when you have an idea."

I kept my gaze fixed on the vials in front of me, trying to stifle the proof of my fury—and praying he wouldn't look too closely. "And what look is that?"

"Your lips press together, and you get that little line between your brows as your eyes go far away. Then you start to smile as you figure it out..." Tobias's mouth snapped shut, like he had said more than he had meant to. Out of the corner of my eye, I saw his hand reach up to scratch the back of his neck in a rare show of discomfort. "Since you're not smiling yet, how about you let me help?"

So much for not looking too closely.

"I was actually thinking I could use some lunch," I lied. "Would you mind bringing me back something again?"

What I needed was him to leave before I either confronted him or revealed something far worse. What I *needed* was to stop having to hide from him. But he could never know—not if I wanted him to trust me.

Silence stretched between us before he cooly replied, "Of course."

I walked back to my workstation and picked up a random test tube, trying to look busy.

"Just knock when you're back." Was it my imagination, or did my voice sound higher pitched than usual? "I can eat in the hallway so we can waste as little time as possible."

His gaze scorched a path across the side of my face before he walked away. I let out an audible sigh of relief when the iron door closed.

Tobias wasn't the only one who imminently needed to expel unwanted power.

CHAPTER 20
TOBIAS

We walked silently back to our rooms. Quinn seemed more tired than usual as the lab closed for its magical sterilization cycle. I knew she had slept well, having spent the night beside her. Maybe she had used more magic than I realized...though the imbuing process hadn't started yet. She hadn't even tried to grill me about our conversation this morning.

I knew she hadn't forgotten—not with the way she frowned at my palm all day.

Part of me hoped this was her way of granting me a brief reprieve. The other part knew there must be more to it.

Rivan was waiting for us when we reached our shared living room. He wore his fighting leathers and the grime on him suggested he hadn't bothered to wash up in his urgency to talk to us. The look on his face was bone-weary yet full of apprehension.

Was it Eva?

Suddenly my throat was too tight to ask the question.

Quinn had no such issue, demanding, "What's wrong?"

"Eva's unchanged," Rivan hurried to say, as if realizing the source of my alarm. I let out a breath I hadn't realized I was holding.

Quinn, however, was nonplused. "I assumed so, or you wouldn't have waited to find me." She crossed her arms impatiently. "But I take it you're not here with good news?"

Rivan let out a short sigh. "Yael and Pari went to update Queen Sariyah while I waited to tell you two. We found a gathering of Aviel supporters, some of the ones we tracked from their initial meetup. It wasn't anything we couldn't handle, but we did have to fight our way out."

Quinn sucked in a breath, her magic softly glowing at her fingertips. With the amount she apparently exerted today, I was surprised at its strength. Rivan took a step back, shaking his head.

"We're in a castle full of healers," he said with a wan smile. "I've already been well taken care of, I assure you."

My voice was flat to the point of sounding disinterested as I asked, "I take it Silvius wasn't apprehended?"

Rivan shook his head again, his frustration leaking into his voice. "He was there recently, but we missed him. We're questioning a few of his cohorts in hopes they'll give up his current whereabouts."

Quinn's mouth pursed in disapproval. She might not like the idea of torturing Silvius's allies for information, but I had no qualms doing so if it meant ensuring my sister's survival.

"Trust me, they're not worth your concern," Rivan said to her. "They were guarding…" He trailed off, looking faintly nauseous. "We found a few of Silvius's…test subjects." The hair rose on the back of my neck. Something told me I didn't want to know what he meant as he continued. "He's testing the virus on them."

The blood drained from my face. Silvius had created a new dungeon. Another torture chamber full of those forced to participate in his experiments.

The sudden onslaught of dark memories was almost enough to bring me to my knees. It took a long second before I managed to wrangle my past into submission, fighting to stay in the present. Even then, my heart pounded so hard I could hear it.

Quinn's voice wavered as she asked, "Are you sure?"

"Dolion confirmed it when we brought them in," Rivan said grimly.

Quinn and I exchanged a glance. Apparently, that was why Dolion left for his consult earlier.

"How did he infect them?" Quinn sounded calm, but I could hear the underlying strain.

It was one thing to have a single patient, no matter how important she was to us. It was another thing entirely to have to deal with an epidemic.

"The same way as Eva, from what the ones who were conscious could tell us." Rivan's deep voice vibrated with barely contained rage. "But Dolion said he's likely trying to—"

"Make it viral," Quinn finished. She swayed on her feet, and I grabbed her elbow to steady her reflexively, my thumb brushing against the lace of her sleeve.

Her eyes met mine, a hint of red reflecting against their usual amber. It only took a heartbeat for my defenses to shatter in the face of her outright fear, the feelings I caged slipping through the bars that held them.

"If he succeeds at that, there's no telling how many could be infected," Quinn whispered.

My grip on her tightened. "Then we won't let that happen."

It wasn't a promise I could make, but the way her expression shifted from dread to resolve was worth it.

Rivan cleared his throat. "From the notes left behind, it's not slaughter he wants." He gestured behind him at a leather notebook open on the dining table. "It's control. Though whether he wants that for leverage or revenge is yet to be determined."

Quinn hurried over. I didn't have to look any closer to recognize Silvius's handwriting, not after reading every word of the stacks of matching notebooks in his lab.

"We took those affected to the Enclave once we were sure they weren't contagious," Rivan continued.

Quinn thumbed through the first few pages before asking, "How many?"

"Four are in the infirmary," Rivan said heavily. "Only one was conscious when we found them."

I wondered if Quinn noticed the way he cut himself off. If she saw the swallow that lodged in his throat, the subtle shift of his eyes that told me exactly which number he decided not to include.

Silvius had never cared about survivors. Only results.

Quinn only nodded, her tone turning businesslike. "I assume Dolion already took care of it, but we'll need samples of their blood in order to cure them too."

Rivan's shoulders slumped. "The people he took, they're unattached. People that wouldn't be missed, whose disappearances weren't noticed right away. The ones still…well, they're all much farther along than Eva. They're empty shells." Revulsion laced each word. "Utterly open to suggestion. They're being closely watched."

Still *alive.*

The word he didn't say echoed in my ears, tying my tongue. Though death might be a mercy if we couldn't cure this.

"We won't know if the cure will work on them until we try," Quinn said, her tone leaving no room for argument. But her voice faltered as she added, "How many did he kill?"

It had been foolish to think she hadn't come to the same realization, probably before I did.

Rivan closed his eyes, bowing his head. "Eleven. Silvius didn't even bother to wipe the blood off their faces before they succumbed to the virus."

He never seemed to notice or care that his subjects were people. Their screams had only ever seemed to annoy him, unlike Aviel who had basked in the sounds of suffering.

For Silvius, their lives were simply a means to an end. And without his master alive to hold his leash, there was no telling his endgame.

"He has to be stopped." Quinn's voice was soft but determined. "I can cure this, I know I can. But the longer he's free, the more people he'll hurt."

Rivan nodded in staunch agreement. "We'll get him."

"And make him pay for what he's done," I added, my words a promise.

Maybe I would even give him a taste of his own medicine.

Quinn didn't lift her gaze from the notebook in front of her as she started to sit down. I quickly pushed the chair behind her forward with my foot before she missed the seat. Rivan raised an eyebrow, but Quinn seemed none the wiser.

Taking a pen from behind her ear, she tapped it against her mouth with a faraway look I had long since come to recognize. Eva and I used to tease her about the way she focused so intensely that everything else ceased to exist. It was like she slipped away into a pocket of her mind where nothing else mattered. When her concentration finally broke, it was like watching someone coming up for air after being underwater too long—blinking, and not entirely sure the world above was the same as she had left it.

When Pari and Yael strode in, both looking grim and battle worn, the clang of the door opening made Quinn startle so badly her pen dropped to the notebook. Her gaze immediately found mine, looking dazed as she reintegrated herself from wherever she was lost.

It was instinct to step closer, my mouth twitching in a slight smile at the surprise on her face. Quinn gave me a sheepish grin.

Rivan, however, immediately rushed over to Pari. "Are you…" He cleared his throat, then pointedly looked over her head at Yael. "Are you both okay?"

Pari looked like she was trying not to roll her eyes. "With the way you kept taking down anyone who tried to get close to me, I didn't have the chance to get injured. Unlike *you*." The annoyance on her face slipped away as she scanned him for injury. "The healers fixed that gash on your arm before you came here, right?"

My gaze trained on the dried blood on Rivan's arm directly beneath an ugly looking tear in his leathers, though without any alarm. Quinn would've noticed had it not been mended.

Rivan didn't take his eyes off Pari. "Of course."

"Good." Pari took two swift steps toward him, then smacked him directly above the injury.

Yael let out a guffaw before muffling her mirth with her hand. Rivan swore loudly.

"What the—"

"Next time, try to remember that you wouldn't have gotten hurt if you hadn't got in my way," Pari hissed. "In fact, if you ever want me to fight by your side again, do me a favor and remember I'm just as capable as you and *just* as good in a fight, if not better. The only reason your blood is drying on your leathers right now is because you didn't trust my ability to protect myself."

Rivan's face had gone ashen. "Pari…"

She held up a hand, silencing him. "I don't want your apology. I don't even want an explanation. Do better, or next time I'm leaving you behind."

Rivan's mouth fell open, wordless. Pari turned on a heel before disappearing into her room, no doubt to wash off the battle.

Yael crossed her arms, staring at Rivan. "You have to admit she has a point. Is there some reason you decided she couldn't defend herself?"

"I wasn't…"

"You absolutely were."

Rivan gave Yael a look of pure betrayal. "She…it's just…there were so many of them." He stopped himself, exhaling. "It's not because I don't think she can protect herself. I *know* she can protect herself."

Yael's voice was carefully neutral. "But you didn't want her to get hurt?"

"Something like that," Rivan admitted.

He dragged a hand down his face, leaving a dark trail in the dust that covered him. Yael exchanged a look with Quinn, whose mouth curved into a knowing smile.

"Anyways..." Yael sat down next to Quinn. "Walk me through what you're working on, Quinn. Maybe I can help."

As Quinn rifled through her notes, Yael gave Rivan a pointed stare over her shoulder. Her shoulders relaxed as Rivan dipped his head in a barely there nod.

Subtly, Rivan tilted his head in a *follow me* motion. He pushed the door open to his room, looking behind him to make sure Quinn was still occupied as I followed him inside. His room was the same as mine, though his bed was made, its coral headboard inlaid with pink pearls. Rivan closed the door behind me. Quinn's voice was muffled as I listened through the door, Yael's lower tone occasionally interjecting, their words too quiet to decipher.

I stayed silent, waiting for Rivan to speak. Obviously, he needed to tell me something that he wanted to keep from Quinn.

He leaned against the desk by the window, his shoulders slumping in obvious exhaustion. With one finger, he gestured for me to come closer, his eyes darting to the door.

"I wasn't sure if it was best to share this with Quinn considering the strain she's under right now..." His voice was so low that I could barely hear it.

My response was immediate. "I won't keep secrets from her."

"I'm not asking you to," Rivan said defensively.

I kept my face neutral, even as my impatience crept into my tone. "Then what exactly are you asking?"

"You need to keep an eye on her." The gravity in his voice made it obvious this wasn't a trivial matter. "I know you already are but...you can't let her out of your sight."

Dread curled in my gut. "Why?"

"There was a note on one of the bodies," Rivan said tightly. "When I saw her, I thought..." He swallowed hard. "The victim's complexion was lighter, but she had Quinn's curls. And she was in healers' robes, despite us confirming she wasn't one. There was a note pinned to her chest."

A roar filled my ears. My magic blistered my palms, trying to fight its way out—desperate to destroy any threat against her. "What did it say?"

"'Stop or she'll be next.'"

CHAPTER 21
QUINN

Tobias was pacing—no, prowling. His long strides ate up the length of the laboratory. He had been withdrawn all morning and quieter than usual. Whatever inner turmoil was eating at him had surfaced today in a swell of frenetic energy that practically radiated from him. Only when I set aside what I was working on and came toward him did he stop, positioning himself in between me and the door.

I glared at him. "Are you going to move?"

"Only since you asked so nicely."

He gracefully stepped to one side, his eyes hooded as he watched me retrieve the tea I had forgotten while I worked. It was disappointingly cold, the leaves now bitter.

It was just the two of us today, our usual rapport replaced by strained silence. Dolion had left me a note about gathering samples from the additional infected and had yet to return. Pari had sent a missive to Tobias, sharing that Queen Sariyah had been doing her best to treat her people, along with her best healers. Unfortunately, they were having no more success at holding the fog at bay.

I took another sip of tea, grateful for the caffeine even as the stale taste lingered on my tongue. It was distracting how intently Tobias watched me as I returned to my workstation. A flicker of power lit up his eyes as they darted between me and the exits.

He had been strangely attentive all morning. I had woken up to him already standing outside my door, a mug of tea in hand that he needed more than I did based on the circles beneath his eyes. Not to mention he had been acting like every shadow was about to attack us.

There was something off. Something he wasn't telling me.

I didn't have time to be distracted, or the patience to needle it out of him. Looking him in the eye, I demanded, "What's wrong?"

"Plenty," Tobias drawled. "Though we don't have time for me to list them all."

I finished my tea with a gulp, grimacing. "Try me."

For a second, I thought he might refuse. Then he let out an exasperated huff. "My sister's in a coma and this city is teeming with the False King's former supporters who happen to be actively working against us, Silvius is coming after...all of us, and despite being on the run still manages to be two steps ahead. And you think there needs to be something else wrong?"

It was more than enough to worry about, and all of it was true. And yet I couldn't shake the feeling Tobias was hiding something.

"And that's all?" I demanded.

Tobias stilled, that mask slipping across his features—but not before I glimpsed the dread in his eyes before his icy calm façade deadened it.

"Hmm?"

His attempt at nonchalance pushed me over the edge.

"Don't," I spat as I took a step toward him, lifting my chin to stare him down despite our height difference. "I told you not to lie to me."

At least Tobias had the wisdom not to test my patience. He immediately folded. "I was going to tell you later, I swear. Rivan mentioned there was a message left behind yesterday."

"And?" My frustration seeped into the single word.

Tobias blew out a breath. "It told us to stop hunting him or you'll be the next infected."

I barely stopped myself from rolling my eyes. "An original threat at least. Though to infect me, he would need my..."

A thought ripped through me, and I froze at the implications.

His hand gripped my chin, raising my eyes to meet his. "Breathe."

It was a command—one I couldn't help but obey as his urgency cut through the faint buzzing in my ears. His irises glinted with that unnatural light, but his fingers didn't burn—only comforting warmth sank into my skin.

"I'm not going to let anything happen to you," he said, the words a promise.

"It's not me I'm worried about," I exclaimed. "He doesn't have my blood, but if Silvius had Eva's…then he also has yours."

There was no hint of surprise on his face, not that I had expected any. What I didn't expect was for him to say, "I wish I wasn't surprised at how quickly you put that together."

Of course, he already knew. He had been there, bound but conscious, every time those needles were stabbed into his skin.

"You need to get somewhere safe," I begged, even as I knew he wouldn't.

Tobias shook his head. His hand fell from my face. I seized it before he could pull away, desperate to keep him close.

"You're the one he threatened, Sagray, not me," he sighed. "I've known the risk, the probability of him still having my blood, since the beginning." He looked down at where our fingers were laced together, his voice a gentle caress. "Besides, I'm exactly where I need to be."

My heart caught in my throat even as something deep and fiercely protective stirred within me. "If he comes for you, he'll have to go through me first."

"I'm not the one I'm worried about," Tobias said, looking troubled. "He may have my blood, but his obsession is with you. Maybe he knows how close you are to curing this before he can weaponize it. Maybe he recognizes a mind that can rival his—gods know that must terrify him."

"Then I must be on the right track."

Tobias's eyes narrowed. "Sagray…"

"Do you think me so easily cowed that one threatening note would scare me off?" I forced a smile. "You should know me better than that, Maris."

Tobias only raised an eyebrow. "Then you should know I have no intention of leaving your side until he's dead."

Fair enough.

"Whatever helps you sleep at night," I said with a saccharine smile. "Now can you please stop pacing and help me work? We need to finish the imbuing process before we test the candidate…the cure. If it inhibits the virus's ability to infect and replicate…"

"Then we can try it on Eva?"

I shook my head. "Not yet. We still need to evaluate the compound's effectiveness before moving to dosage, not to mention assess any potential side effects for a living organism. But, hopefully, soon."

By the time Dolion returned to help us, we were well on our way. We carefully helped him unload the vials of blood samples he had taken from our new patients.

It didn't take long to confirm that these samples had also been targeted using the victim's own blood—something Dolion and I would need to consider once we figured out dosing. I could only hope the cure wouldn't need to be individually calibrated.

As we worked, my mind kept returning to the note and what Tobias had told me. For Silvius to target me, he had to have eyes on me. He was too hunted to try something himself, especially out in the open.

But maybe I could force his hand.

Suddenly, I knew the best way to lure Silvius out. With my overprotective companion glued to the side, the only question now was how I was going to pull it off.

✧

It was well into the afternoon before we had created enough test tube samples to test the compounds. Multiple concentrations of each compound would be evaluated, along with control samples to compare effects. Dolion and I had imbued each and every one of them with healing magic—a process that took far more magic than I realized.

I nearly sank to the floor in exhaustion now that I was finally done. Even Dolion had excused himself after we finished the last compound, his gray eyes dull with exhaustion.

Tonight, I would write to Marin and update her about our progress, and the potential for a preliminary treatment soon. There would need to be more tests before administering it to Eva or any of the others, of course. But the rate at which we were progressing was unheard of, at least for someone trained in the human realm. Preclinical studies there would take months even at an accelerated pace, while most took years. With magic, we had cut that process down so significantly I could scarcely believe it.

However, the next step was to wait and see what worked. And while I wanted to sink into an extremely hot bath and then pass out for a nap, there was something else I had to do.

"I could use a few moments outside," I said to Tobias, keeping my tone light. "My eyes are crossing after being in the lab this many days in a row. I feel like I haven't seen the sun for days."

Tobias hesitated, his brow furrowing. He drew in a deep breath, seemingly steeling his resolve before saying, "I-I can go with you."

I shrugged as if it didn't matter one way or another.

"Actually, could you finish transferring those notes from earlier? I was hoping to review them all together before moving on." I gave him a weak smile, hoping he didn't see right through me. He had been painstakingly taking notes while I worked all day so I wouldn't be slowed down by writing them myself…but I had purposefully left some in shorthand for exactly this reason. "I won't be long, and I won't go too far. I'm not stupid enough to let my guard down with an active threat against my life. Besides, we both know I'm perfectly capable of protecting myself if need be."

It wasn't a complete lie. I *did* plan to go outside, though not where he was thinking. And I certainly planned to protect myself.

If he hadn't realized during the battle of Adronix exactly what I could do, if pressed, I wasn't about to tell him now.

I didn't think I could handle him looking at me differently…and he would.

A muscle flexed in Tobias's jaw like he was about to argue, but I beat him to it. "There's a nice sunny section by the cafeteria."

One that I still planned to visit, though not today.

Tobias eyed me appraisingly, and I tried not to fidget. "You have your dagger?"

"You mean *your* dagger?" I removed it from my belt, flipping it end over end without breaking eye contact. I didn't hide my smirk as I caught the familiar hilt, running my thumb along the etchings in the silver.

Tobias's eyes darkened as I threw it upward a second time—only for him to snag it midair. He was so fast that I reached out for the blade before I realized he already had it in his grasp.

"No, I mean *your* dagger." My heartbeat skittered as his hand came to my waist, two fingers sliding beneath the leather belt that normally held it. With a tug, he yanked me closer.

Time seemed to stand still as we stared at each other. My breathing quickened, though Tobias seemed to have stopped breathing entirely, his body hard and still against me. Slowly, he slid my dagger back into its sheath, his eyes never leaving my face. He was so close I could feel the whisper of his words against my lips as he muttered, "Try not to lose it a second time."

I sucked in a breath, feeling lightheaded as he backed away.

"I—" I could feel the blush rising on my cheeks. "Thank you for letting me keep it. For the gift."

Tobias brushed his hair out of his face with a shrug as he stepped back. "Don't mention it."

"Your mother gave it to you," I continued, refusing to be deterred. "I owe you—"

"You don't owe me anything," Tobias said sharply. "You...you were there for Eva when I wasn't. You kept her alive and kept her from breaking when it was just the two of you left. Even when you lost your parents, you still didn't stray from your mission or your friendship. I don't think I've thanked you for everything you did for her. I know it couldn't have been easy after I left."

The admiration in his gaze made my heart ache from the weight of truly being seen.

"You're leaving out the part where a golem tried to kidnap her and then Bash took her straight to Aviel."

"And you came for her, traveling back to Soleara solo and leaving behind the life you created for yourself," Tobias continued, undeterred. "You stood by her through it all. I'm glad you had each other, but I'm thankful every day that she had you." His expression softened, and I stilled, like the slightest movement might chase the emotion from his face. "Besides, my mom would've wanted you to have it. *I* want you to have it."

His eyes flickered with the warm light of his magic. His voice was so earnest it reminded me of the boy I once knew. That kindhearted kid might have been hidden away, but he was still in there. Just that glimpse of him made me want to burst into tears.

And here I was, lying to him.

"I'll use it well," I promised, looking away.

"I know you will." Tobias blew out a breath. "Just…keep your guard up, okay?"

It was an effort not to let my guilt ruin my plan. "Always."

CHAPTER 22
QUINN

It was easier than I thought it would be to find my way out of the Enclave. I walked right out the front door, smiling at the healers crowding the ornate atrium at the entryway, all easily identifiable in their matching robes. The enormous limestone archway that led outside was covered in floral carvings that made me reach for my necklace, the points of the sunflower pressing comfortingly against my palm. There was a phrase in a language I didn't recognize emblazoned across the top.

I was letting myself be seen. Practically painting a sign on myself in neon letters that screamed, 'Come and get me'.

"Excuse me," I said to a nearby healer, my voice loud enough to be overheard. "Do you happen to know what the lettering means?"

She smiled. "Art is long, life is short. Which is to say…even with the longevity of fae lives, the skill, the technique, the enduring nature of medical knowledge will outlast us all."

The phrase sounded familiar. I wondered if this was another thing to traverse realms.

"Thank you," I said sincerely.

Maybe it was only my imagination, but I thought I felt more than just her eyes on me as I walked away. My heartbeat picked up as another outpaced it.

The late afternoon sun momentarily blinded me as I stepped outside. I closed my eyes against the glare even as I savored the warmth on my cheeks, the slight saltiness in the air. After so long stuck in a lab, it was glorious to escape.

Not for the first time, I hoped I would have the chance to return to Mayim under better circumstances. The city was an awe-inspiring maze of staircases and bridges, the marble and lustrous limestone structures bisected by waterways. Blue accents mirrored the water almost everywhere I looked, their shade an almost identical hue to my healing magic. I paused at the end of an empty bridge to admire the swirling brass work of the railings and the brightly tiled bridgeway.

While I had some idea of where I wanted to wander, based on where Silvius had been sighted near the Enclave, the most important piece of my plan was to position myself somewhere I could be found.

If we were correct about Silvius's allies infiltrating the Enclave, then I had essentially painted a giant target on my back simply by walking out the front doors. But he possessed Eva's and Tobias's blood, and was a threat to their lives, as well as everyone else I loved.

It was worth the risk if it meant finding him.

We might be quickly working toward a cure, but the longer Silvius stayed free, the higher the chance he would create a viral version—a plague able to wipe out both magic and memory that would not be so easily stopped. Once viral, there was no telling who it would strike or how it would mutate.

And who better to drive him out of hiding than the person actively working to make his efforts useless?

It wasn't as reckless as Tobias would think. My only worry was that I was wasting time not being in the lab. I would need to return soon, once the samples were set. Marin's updates assured me daily that Eva's condition remained the same, yet every day it took me to create a cure made my anxiety rise.

We had no guarantees that her memory loss wouldn't be permanent. She may not be getting any worse, but even this brief interlude was time she didn't have.

The street was deserted, but I could sense someone near. Little did they know, I could feel their faint but steady pulse—the one that had been stalking me since I first left the Enclave—quickening as they got closer. My fingers curled, ready to strike first—

A familiar drawl cut through my thoughts. "Where, exactly, do you think *you're* going?"

Crap.

My dagger—*his* dagger—was already in my hand, the move instinctual despite knowing I wouldn't need to use it. Tobias leaned against the limestone wall of the alleyway, his arms crossed over his chest. His tendons stood out starkly against his tan skin, his jaw clenched so hard it could cut glass. And his face…

I could practically see the mask he wore, shimmering like a mirage in the heat.

"I told you," I said as nonchalantly as I could manage. "I needed to get out of the lab for a bit."

Tobias's eyes narrowed. "And what's your excuse for not telling me you were leaving the Enclave entirely?"

His voice was carefully neutral, but there was an edge to it that sounded suspiciously like hurt.

I winced. "I…I didn't think that you'd want to come."

Tobias abruptly pushed off the wall, closing the distance between us in an instant. Light flared from his irises, his entire demeanor transforming in a rare display of anger. In a low voice that shivered down my spine, he murmured, "You're a terrible liar, Sagray. Always were."

Well, I knew he would follow. I did, however, underestimate how quickly he would find me.

I lifted my chin. Time to try a different tack, even if I wasn't sure I could convince Tobias to adjust his sails. At the end of the day, we were in the same boat, whether he wanted to be or not.

"I'm here to get the answers we need to save your sister," I quickly explained, willing him to understand. "Given the mixed allegiances in this city, the near certainty that Silvius has spies in the Enclave, and the threat he made on my life…me walking out the front door alone seems like the perfect time for him to show his hand."

A muscle quivered in Tobias's jaw, like he was fighting for control. "So you're hoping someone will try to capture or kill you?" His tone dripped with derision. "Or were you expecting Silvius to find you himself?"

"If I'm lucky."

I didn't dare look around. There was still time left for this to work if I could get Tobias to leave.

"*Lucky*," Tobias repeated flatly.

"So, if you don't mind heading back…" I ventured, though I already knew it was a lost cause.

His expression darkened. "Don't play games with me. I'm not in the mood."

"As opposed to your usual happy-go-lucky self?"

He swore under his breath, running a hand through his hair. A tousled lock fell back into his eyes and light flared between its strands.

"You're going to be the death of me," Tobias growled. "Just because you can take care of yourself doesn't mean you're invincible."

"Of course it doesn't." I gave him an imploring look. "But the risk is worth the reward."

His lips pressed into a thin line. "And you didn't think to tell anyone about this half-cocked plan of yours?"

"It's not as reckless as it seems," I muttered uncomfortably. "Having you following me around is exactly what I wanted to avoid."

Tobias's hands closed around the railing behind me, one arm on either side, boxing me in. He was close enough for me to feel the tension rippling from him, though he was careful not to touch me. I stared up at him, desperate to change his mind before time ran out.

"If you think I'm leaving you alone here, especially after this stunt, then you don't know me at all." His knuckles had gone white where he gripped the railing. "You don't know him like I do."

I flinched at the casual reminder of the years he spent under Silvius's control.

"I know he wants to stop me, considering how close I am to beating him."

My magic surged in response to the unseen threat, roaring to be used.

"Not stop you," Tobias snarled, the sudden force in his voice catching me off guard. "He wants to *kill* you. The only question is if he'll try to take you alive to use your blood to experiment with or simply attempt to murder you. Not that he'd be brave enough to do the latter himself."

"Silvius has the answers we need, and our friends have been playing a game of cat and mouse with him that I'm not entirely sure they're the feline in," I hissed. "If he sends someone after me, they can lead us to him, which is exactly what I'm hoping for."

"Without a single person knowing where you are if your plan fails,"

Tobias snapped, the anger in his voice palpable. "What happens to Eva if you get captured? What happens to all those poor souls Silvius infects after he kills you?"

I chewed on my lower lip, debating if it was worth explaining why he didn't need to worry. If, even then, he would be willing to leave me behind.

I would never forget the way Pari's expression changed from curiosity to suspicion when the truth came out, her interest turning to outright fear. It was like the trust we had built had been eradicated with one short sentence.

Tobias may not have been brought up with the same preconceptions as those raised in this realm, but he had more reason than anyone to hate what I was…and I wasn't ready for him to stop looking at me like I was his safe place.

But he didn't deserve me lying to him, even by omission.

I swallowed against my suddenly dry mouth. "If I show you why…"

"Why what?" Tobias prompted, as my voice failed me.

"Why you don't have to worry about me," I said in a hurry. I only needed him to back off for a few minutes, if that. "Will it change things?"

Tobias's eyes moved between mine as if he could find the truth there. Then he crossed his arms, his face unreadable.

"Try me."

He won't push you away, I told myself even as I felt my heart start to race—and mine wasn't the only one. *This won't change things.*

My dagger quivered in my hand as I tried not to think about the alternative. Tobias only watched me, his face unreadable.

I nervously dug my fingers into the grip, keeping it at the ready. "If I show you why I'll be safe, you'll leave me to my plan?""

"No."

I recoiled. "And if that wasn't a request?"

"I'm not asking either, Maris," Tobias bit out, his voice unwavering. I wondered if he realized sparks were dropping from his fingertips like fallen stars. "If I need to throw you over my shoulder and carry you back to that castle, I will. Silvius has already attacked my sister. If you think I'm letting him, or anyone working for him, get anywhere near you—"

A heartbeat spiked in a split-second warning. I turned my head just as a blade whizzed past my face—so close I felt a whisper of it against my skin. My magic moved before I did, my vision turning red as my focus narrowed to that throbbing pulse, the blood pumping through his heart. I threw my dagger a heartbeat before Tobias dragged me behind him, sending the silver blade straight at my attacker.

The burly male bellowed as it stuck his shoulder and dropped the second dagger he had been about to throw. Light swallowed my vision, blinding me. When it receded, bands of light pinned my attacker to the stone wall behind him. One blistering loop sunk through his healer's robes, the scent of burned flesh turning my stomach.

"Are you okay?"

The question was urgent, laced with panic. Tobias spun me around, gripping my shoulders as his gaze fixed on my face. I sensed the blood on my cheek before I felt the sting of pain. His thumb brushed against my cheekbone, and I grimaced.

"Your eyes," he whispered.

Reflexively I looked down, knowing the red would fade quickly into innocuous amber.

"What the hell was that Sagray?"

The answer shriveled on my tongue even as something inside me told me it was past time to tell him. His thumb and forefinger gripped my chin, making me face him. "Don't make me ask you again."

I jerked my head back. "I told you. I can take care of myself."

"Said the person who was nearly—" He sucked in a furious breath. "This is exactly why you can't wander off alone."

It was an effort not to roll my eyes. "Says who? I'm perfectly fine—"

"You were almost stabbed," he growled.

The key word being *almost*.

I glared at him. "I grew up training just as hard as you did, Maris. You should know by now that I am my own protector."

"I know that," he insisted, "but—"

"Besides, now we have someone to question," I said smugly, a smile rising to my lips at the success of my plan.

My attacker let out a pained gasp as he fought against his bonds.

Tobias had gone completely still. "You knew you were being followed."

"All the way from the Enclave." I shrugged indolently. "At least you didn't scare him away."

With a smirk, I stepped around Tobias and walked toward my still struggling assailant. He hissed as those bands of light cut through his sleeves, biting into his skin.

"Clever," Tobias said, the admiration in his voice making my stomach flip concerningly. "Dangerous and idiotic. But clever."

I placed my hands on my hips, glancing at him over my shoulder. "I told you. I have this handled."

Tobias's gaze moved from me to the blade still sticking out of our attacker's shoulder. One corner of his mouth quirked. "I stand corrected, Sagray."

I was starting to hate that one-sided dimple, even if I had missed its appearance.

Tobias stalked forward, every footfall echoing with ill intent. I sucked in a breath as light curved from his right hand like a scythe. It sliced the front of my attacker's jacket open, and he let out a bloodcurdling scream…but the small pack I hadn't noticed hidden beneath his tunic fell to the ground.

Tobias knelt, his expression darkening as he opened it. His hand shook as he handed it to me.

Inside there were two carefully packed syringes. One was filled with a red-tinged liquid, the other empty. The shorter needle and its larger gauge left no doubt it was intended to draw my blood.

Tobias's mouth curved into a ruthless smile. It was one I had never seen on his face before, made even more sinister by the magic sparking in his irises like lightning in a storm. He lifted his dagger slowly, turning it almost lazily in front of the male's face. Then he pressed it against my assailant's throat. I gasped as it drew a thin line of blood.

The male's eyes bulged. "You won't kill me."

From the soft, rounded vowels of his accent, there was no doubt he was from here.

"Won't I?" Tobias shrugged, sheathing his dagger. "Maybe you're right. I won't kill you…not yet at least."

Tobias grabbed the blade still embedded in the male's shoulder with his other hand and twisted. His cry echoed so loudly I was certain someone would come running.

My objection burst from me. "Tobias, stop!"

He looked back at me, his face utterly devoid of emotion, his eyes so cold I took a step back. The fear on my face must have gotten through to him because he let go. The male slumped forward as much at the bands of light holding him would allow.

Tobias tutted. "Let's try this again. Starting with a name."

"Thibault," he wheezed, then cried out as a band of light moved under his chin, bringing his fearful face back up.

"See, that wasn't so hard, Thibault." Tobias's tone was almost kind. It was the expression on his face that scared me—the frozen indifference was so much worse than before. "If you keep answering my questions, I'll even consider letting you live."

Thibault shrank back like he might escape through the solid stone wall. "He'll kill me—"

"No, *I'll* kill you." Tobias's voice was startlingly matter of fact. "But not before I make you wish you were dead."

He brushed a finger against the diamond embedded into the pommel of my dagger, and Thibault yelped.

"Where is Silvius?" His voice was barely over a whisper, the demand in it deadly. "And who else is he working with?"

"I…I don't know," Thibault said pleadingly.

Tobias pressed my dagger downward, and Thibault let out a panicked cry.

"*Tobias*," I protested as my stomach rolled. My healing magic flared at my fingertips.

My attacker's eyes darted downward.

"You're a healer," Thibault gasped. "You…you won't kill me."

"She won't need to," Tobias said calmly. "Not when she has me."

He pressed the blade in further. Thibault scream turned into a sob, just as I yelled, "That's *enough*."

A muscle in Tobias's jaw flexed, the only sign he heard me. "Where's Silvius? What's in that syringe?" His voice was unrecognizable—more unfeeling than I had ever heard it and laced with cruelty. "This is your last chance to tell me before I remove that dagger and let you slowly bleed to death. It would be such a shame if I were to nick an artery on the way out."

"Please don't let him do this," Thibault said, still staring at me. "*Please*."

"You're smart to ask her," Tobias said coldly. "Mercy isn't a weakness I possess. Not anymore."

He pushed the blade against Thibault's neck in slightly, and I gasped as blood flowed from the wound. I knew I could heal it, despite the rate at which Thibault's blood spread down his shirt. It was the calculating wrath in Tobias's eyes that made my heart spasm. This version of him was vengeance incarnate—the spawn of all those years in that dark dungeon finally unleashed.

"I don't know where Silvius is." Thibault nearly tripped over his tongue in his rush to save his own skin. "All I know is my priority was to retrieve her blood, if possible, and use the second syringe on you if I got the chance."

My eyes widened. "To infect him?"

Thibault's fearful eyes turned on me. Tobias shifted his grip on his blade.

"Don't you dare look at her," Tobias spat, and Thibault squeezed his eyes shut.

I didn't need Thibault's broken yes to confirm it. It was exactly as I had feared.

Tobias merely blinked at the confirmation, the detached look in his eyes so unsettling I suppressed a shudder.

Though if that was truly a syringe full of the live virus, then this might be a blessing in disguise—the very thing we needed to finish a viable cure. Hope rose within me, despite my attempts to temper it. Dolion and I could break down its components and reverse engineer them to be certain our treatment would be successful. This was exactly the breakthrough we needed to reduce our margin of error and shorten the time required to test our cure before dispersing it.

"Please." Thibault was trembling so much that Tobias had to move his dagger back slightly or risk decapitating him. "*Please*, that's all I know."

Tobias ignored him, almost sounding bored as he asked, "When and where are you supposed to report back to Silvius if you were successful?"

Thibault hesitated for a second too long. Those bands of light dug in, cauterizing Thibault's wounds even as they cut into him. My stomach turned at the smell of charred flesh.

"I-I don't know," Thibault sobbed. "As a loyal follower of the True King, I simply offered my services. I received Silvius's messages, but we never met face to face."

"That's not what I asked." Tobias arched an eyebrow. "I asked—" Thibault's scream cut him off as he reached for the knife in Thibault's shoulder and twisted, a fresh gush a blood staining his shirt "—*where* you were supposed to bring her blood."

It was a good question. And yet, all I could think about was that, while Silvius had failed to get my blood, the proof that he had Tobias's was inside that first syringe.

"A bar near the Enclave," Thibault whimpered. "I was supposed to meet someone tonight right before last call. The directions are in my back pocket. I don't know anything else, I swear…"

He fell silent with a terrified sob. Tobias's fingers twitched against his blade.

"That's enough," I demanded sharply.

He stared at me, his expression almost incredulous. The coldness on his face gave way to icy rage as he focused on my face…no, on the blood dripping down my cheek.

"He made you bleed," Tobias said as if that was a reasonable explanation.

"This isn't you." I stepped closer, lifting my hand to his face. His eyes closed as my thumb grazed his cheek. "Let's just bring him back to the castle and see what Queen Sariyah wants to do with him."

Tobias's eyes softened as they met mine, the light giving way to the hazel and gold I knew so well. To my utter relief, he lowered his dagger.

"No, no, *no*," Thibault screeched, struggling anew. "If you do that, you sign my death sentence."

Before I realized what was happening, he wrenched a hand from his flickering bonds. Then he yanked my dagger from his shoulder with a yell.

Tobias moved quicker than I could track. In one swift motion, he slashed his dagger across Thibault's throat. Thibault fell to his knees as those bands of light vanished entirely. He clutched at the blood streaming between his fingers, mouth gaping soundlessly before he collapsed to the ground.

My magic came to my fingertips in flares of blue light, even as something else within me reached forward, feeling the final beat of his heart.

Tobias took my hand, his voice gentle. "There's no need for that, Sagray. It's too late to help him now."

He was right. Thibault's blood had settled without his heart working to pump it, his circulation ceasing entirely. Tobias knelt, seemingly unaffected as he checked Thibault's bloodstained pockets. He pulled out a rectangular piece of paper that had to be the directions to the meeting place before retrieving my silver dagger. He wiped the blood on the back of Thibault's tunic, then extended the blade to me hilt first.

The silence stretched as we stared at each other. I didn't reach for it.

Tobias let out a sigh as he got to his feet. "I told you not to lose it a second time."

"You didn't have to kill him," I exclaimed, my voice a little too loud.

His mask slid firmly back into place. "Would you have preferred I let him kill you first?"

"Well, you didn't have to torture him," I snapped, ignoring the outstretched blade Tobias used to do so.

"I did, actually." His tone might have been cold, but his eyes were burning. "If you haven't noticed, he tried to kill you. Not to mention his purpose here was to obtain a *vial of your blood*. We both know why Silvius wants that." His jaw tightened, a swallow working its way down his throat. "I'm not going to let anyone hurt you."

The deadly edge in his voice sent a shiver down my spine, even as the possessiveness in his words made me wonder if it was for an entirely inappropriate reason.

This time, when he offered me my dagger, I took it.

"Come on," Tobias said gruffly. "We need to get back. You need to confirm what's in that syringe. And I could use a shower."

I grimaced as I took in the blood on him, the splattered droplets irrevocably staining the light fabric. But I stood my ground.

"We can't just…leave him." My hand shook as I gestured at the body behind me.

Tobias pointedly looked around at the empty area. I didn't miss the way he shuddered slightly as he looked skyward.

"If any guards were around, they would have made themselves known when he started screaming." He let out a heavy sigh. "I'll alert the first one we see. It's not like he's going anywhere."

His hand flattened on my lower back, a spark jolting up my spine at the touch as he led me away from the bloody scene. My adrenaline faded, the urge to lean against him almost overwhelming.

Slowly, so as to give him enough time to react, I stepped closer into his body, letting myself relax against him. He stiffened, and I immediately started to retreat. Then his arm snaked around my waist, holding me there.

I ran my tongue across my lips. "Is this okay?"

"It's helping, actually," Tobias muttered. I opened my mouth to ask what he meant, but he cleared his throat, then leveled a pointed look at me. "Before we were interrupted, you were about to tell me why your eyes, well, *changed*. Don't think I forgot."

"I was kind of hoping you had," I said, aiming for teasing but not quite getting there.

He frowned. "I hope you know that you can trust me to keep your secrets."

Here was the Tobias I knew. Not some hardened warrior demanding answers from me, but my friend, my confidant, concerned and asking.

I blew out a breath, rallying my nerve. "During the final battle, when we were trying to fight our way across the room to get to that mirror before Aviel did…I tried something by accident. Well, more like on instinct."

I glanced up, trying to read Tobias's expression, but it was as closed off as ever.

"And?"

"The way my healing magic works…I can sense what's wrong with someone the second my magic reaches for them," I said hesitantly. "But it's more than that. It's feeling the nervous system and the way each neuron communicates with another. It's feeling each muscle, each bone, the circulatory system, and how they all work together."

"I understand the concept." Tobias caught my hand where it twisted my skirt so tightly I trapped my fingers. "But that's not what you're scared to tell me."

I drew in a shaky breath. "I never realized how unusual it is that I can sense someone's heartbeat without physically touching them…until I found a book in Soleara's library about magics that are considered dark and forbidden. Most are bodily magics, though obviously healing isn't among them despite the way it could be used. There's siphoning, like Aviel. Shapeshifting, though that's even more rare. And blood magic."

Tobias stiffened. I forced myself to keep going.

"Blood wielding is considered the worst of all, for reasons I'm sure you understand." My voice wavered. "Because of the way blood can be used against the fae it came from, any form of blood magic is restricted. There was a time that those able to wield it were systematically eradicated for the good of the realm. Their books of knowledge on how to control others by wielding their blood were burned to stop others from mimicking it…not that they were successful, considering how Aviel used its teachings."

Tobias's hand spasmed, his fingers digging into my side. It was an effort to say the next words aloud.

"I didn't realize what it was until the battle in the mountain," I whispered. "But to me…it's a natural extension of what I can already do. It makes me a better healer, too. It's why I was able to sense Thibault following me. And it's the darkest form of magic known to this realm."

There was something fragile in the silence, something delicate as freshly blown glass as I waited for his next words to shatter me.

Tobias hadn't been raised prejudiced against blood magic like those brought up in Agadot. No, he had been subjected to it, though the puncture marks along his veins had long since faded..

He had every right to hate what I was.

Tobias tilted his head, watching me carefully. I held my breath, bracing myself for his inevitable disgust. The knowledge and ability to exert control over another fae using their blood existed because of my kind. Those with blood magic had experimented in ways to bend blood to their will, even for those without that ability.

When Pari found out, she begged me to never use that part of my magic again, not only because of what it could do but for fear it would corrupt my soul. She was the one who explained that it wasn't just dangerous, it was taboo. The stigma surrounding blood magic, and the belief that those who wielded it carried a bloodlust for power, would have made me a pariah among my people. Our friendship felt altered ever since, like she was holding her breath around me—waiting for my magic to turn me into a monster.

It was why I hadn't told anyone else. After Aviel used Eva's blood to bind their lives, nearly costing her hers, I even hid that piece of myself from my closest friend. She had been through enough. But the truth was, I couldn't bear it if she looked at me differently too.

I couldn't risk her trust. But here I was, risking his.

When Tobias spoke, the judgement I expected was entirely absent. In fact, his tone was vaguely vindicated as he grumbled, "It's about time, Sagray."

It took a long second to understand his meaning. Then my sense of gravity shifted beneath my feet. "You…you *knew*? That I was…that I have blood magic?"

"I suspected." Tobias sounded so unbothered his words were nearly flippant. "I saw the way your eyes turned red as we fought against those impossible odds in that chamber in Adronix. Not their normal shade of amber, but that deep, blood red I saw again today." His gaze bore into me, and I found myself unable to look away. "I saw how outnumbered we were. And when Eva ran toward the Seeing Mirror, I saw the way Aviel's soldiers suddenly froze at the wrong moment or ran into a waiting blade. Bash's magic was exhausted by the time we reached the top, and against those odds…" He gave a soft shake of his head, a hint of something like admiration in his voice. "Well, he might have been too focused on saving Eva to notice it was too easy…but I was fighting right next to you the whole time." The look he gave me was almost incredulous. "I've known you since my first breath, Sagray. And I know exactly who saved us."

All this time. He had known all this time what I was...but was that part of why he had avoided me ever since?

I swallowed against my dry mouth. "And you didn't bring it up until now?"

Tobias shrugged. "I wasn't about to confront you about it, but I was curious. From there, it was as simple as spending time in my parents' library and researching uncommon forms of magic much like you did. It didn't take me long. I found a whole book on bodily magics, blood magic, and the so-called corruption of the healing arts." He raised a single brow. "You might want to borrow it when this is over. Though it got into how blood magic has been used for evil, it also included excerpts from some ancient texts. Did you know those who could wield blood like water used to be renowned healers a few millennia ago?"

"Until some fae used those teachings to steal the blood of those they wanted to control, and the practice of all blood magic was banned after their reign of terror," I recited, then made a derisive sound. "Did you think you outresearched me, Maris?"

Tobias's answering smile was bright, if fleeting. "You'd be surprised. I spend most of my time reading lately, learning about the magic of this realm. Learning about everything I missed, really."

"Then you'll know that those with my power didn't use it to heal," I said darkly. "They used it to make this world worse, and they were eradicated for it. Not just killed but entirely drained of their blood to be certain there was no coming back." My laugh was forced. "There is no cure for me."

"You don't need to be *cured* of your magic, Sagray," Tobias said with a flicker of outrage. "It's part of you."

It was the exact opposite of what I had expected. I had been so certain this would be the breaking point, the moment everything fell apart. And yet, instead of shattering our fragile friendship like glass, it was like a fog clearing from a mirror—showing me what had been there all along.

"And you don't..." I swallowed hard. "You don't hate me for using the very magic that—"

"There's nothing that could ever make me hate you, Sagray." The finality in his voice was almost wistful—as if he had tried and knew the futility of it. "You comparing the magic that saved us to how Aviel perverted it is the real travesty here. Maybe blood magic is considered evil by association because of what it had been used to do, but that doesn't mean I think that magic itself is inherently wrong. And in your hands?" His voice dropped, low and deliberate. "I'd love to see you unleashed."

He crooked his finger beneath my chin, lifting gently. My mouth closed with a snap, my knees nearly buckling beneath me.

"I'm glad you finally felt comfortable enough to tell me though," Tobias continued, effortlessly nonchalant. "Have you been using blood magic to help your research?"

It took a second before I could respond. "Yes. It's not much different manipulating the blood in someone's body versus the blood in a test tube. But with the stigma against it...the expectation it will be used for evil...I didn't even tell Eva."

He tilted his head inquisitively, the gold flecks in his eyes glinting in the midday sun. "You didn't tell *anyone*?"

"I told Pari," I conceded. "She saw what I was reading and...well, she's the one who told me not to mention it to anyone else. That doing so could reflect badly upon me, and the work we've done in Soleara." I cringed at the memory. "You should've seen her face when I told her, like she was worried I could be the next False King."

Even months later, I could still picture it—and the wave of shame I felt at her judgement. In a single sentence, I had been reduced to that solitary part of me, despite all that time we had spent working together side by side. "I've been meaning to tell Eva, but it never seemed like the right time to bring back the trauma of what blood and magic can do. Now, I wish I hadn't been such a coward."

There had always been an excuse not to tell her, especially with Eva perpetually busy in her new role as High Queen. She was exhausted from the rebuilding efforts, then her bonding ceremony, and didn't need me to add to her stress. And she would've told Bash, who I could only assume had his own prejudices against blood magic.

Most of all, I hadn't wanted it to change anything between us. The longer I took to tell her, the harder it became to do so.

Eva had lived through some of the worst of what blood magic could do. And here I was, able to literally control the blood in her veins.

"You're many things, but never that, Sagray," Tobias gently admonished me. "You can tell Eva how you used it to save her when she wakes up if you need to balance the scales. But I have a feeling our High Queen will be able to tell the difference in intent rather than condemning you for a magic you were born with. Knowing her, she'll go on a campaign to change the rest of this realm's minds about blood magic too."

He was probably right. I could practically picture Eva's outrage that I hadn't told her sooner, and her reaction to anyone who thought less of me for it. If I ever wanted to know her actual reaction though, it was past time for me to get back to her cure.

"You're right," I said simply. "I should've given her…given you both more credit. I'm sorry."

"If you feel the need to make it up to me, I'll take a promise that you won't wander off without me again." His tone was almost cavalier, but I could hear the underlying worry. "That you'll wait for me next time."

My laugh was barely more than a loud exhale.

"Deal," I whispered.

Leaning my head against Tobias's shoulder, I let him lead us through the sunny streets, feeling safe in his arms.

CHAPTER 23
QUINN

I tore off my blood splattered clothes, then quickly showered in my hurry to return to work. My chest felt tight at the time wasted in the lab, despite knowing I had been successful. No matter how many times I scrubbed my hands and face they still didn't feel clean. The sense of that blood staining me lingered as I slipped out of our rooms and hurried to the lab without Tobias.

No doubt he had more blood to wash off than me.

I couldn't stop replaying the detachment in Tobias's face while he tortured my assailant as I shut myself in the lab. Nor could I forget the way Thibault's heartbeat had slowed to a stop as my magics reached for him—both useless in the end.

Closing my eyes, I made myself focus on that mental list. What I could hear, what I could see, what I could touch, what I could smell…by the time I reached taste, it felt like I could breathe again.

Even so, it felt good to get my mind off everything that happened as I got to work determining what was in the syringe.

It didn't take long to confirm what I suspected: That this virus was the same as Eva's except keyed to Tobias's blood. My magic alone had been able to sense the similarities without molecular confirmation. This virus had been created to enslave him, to make him malleable after all those years in captivity hadn't managed to break him.

My hand shook, not with fear but with a rage so primal my vision turned red, and I set the vial down on the counter. Silvius may be after me, but Tobias was in more danger. I was looking at incontrovertible proof that Silvius was not only in possession of Tobias's blood but that he carried a grudge he intended to act on.

At least today's risk had been worth it. Thibault may not have led us directly to Silvius, but the meetup we had uncovered held promise—a concrete lead I could place my hopes on. More importantly, having the live virus in hand would be endlessly helpful in determining how to reverse it. I would have to ask Tobias for more of his blood in order to break down the exact components used, though I loathed the idea of putting him through that again.

Dolion must have used up the blood I had already drawn from Tobias, unless he had stored it somewhere else for safekeeping. I glanced at the locked door behind his desk. He had already left for the day for some urgent business he had to attend to, though he hadn't specified what. He was likely helping Queen Sariyah treat the other infected.

I shuddered as I carefully stored the vial, trying not to picture what would have happened to Tobias if Thibault had succeeded. He had already been through so much. I needed to get rid of the syringe before Tobias found me and—

As if my thoughts had summoned him, Tobias stormed in, his hair still damp from his shower. He crossed the room to me in a few long strides.

"What part of 'wait for me' didn't you understand?"

He sounded furious. He *looked* furious, I realized with a start. For once, he wasn't able to hide behind that mask of his.

Just this once, he looked as scared as I was.

"I didn't realize that extended to the lab," I said waspishly even as guilt overwhelmed me. I hadn't thought about my promise, only that I needed to get back to work as soon as possible. Today's adventure may have been worth it, but I didn't want to lose any more time.

Tobias gritted his teeth. "We just confirmed that Silvius's spies are hiding among the healers, and you *didn't realize* the hallways aren't safe for you?"

I turned my back on him, covering my wince. We were both too on edge from today's events to be able to discuss this calmly. "I have work to do, Maris."

"You've got to be kidding me." He let out an incredulous laugh. "You're being hunted by a monster with a biological weapon so horrific that it wipes your mind along with your magic. Worse, he *knows* you're the only one who can stop him. And you couldn't wait a few extra minutes for me to escort you here?"

"I'm not in the mood for a lecture," I snapped, spinning around to face him. Today had wrung me dry, and I still had more to do before I could be done. "I thought you understood by now that I"—I jabbed my finger into the hard muscle of his chest to emphasize my point—"can take care of myself."

"So can my sister," Tobias hissed. "And she's in a coma right now in case you forgot."

My hand moved before my mind caught up, slapping him hard.

I sucked in a breath as I took in the angry red handprint on his cheek. My magic flared bright blue at my fingertips, urging me to heal the damage I had caused.

Tobias wrapped a hand around my still raised wrist before I could. That strange current passed between us—restless, reaching—as something buried deep inside me stirred. I stepped back, but he followed, crowding me back against the counter. His eyes darkened as they scoured my face, lingering on my lips, his gaze so intense I felt my cheeks burn.

The look on his face stole the air from my lungs after so long of nothing. I knew I didn't misunderstand that quiet, unspoken want. Hope and longing and something more—something that might sear my very soul if I wasn't careful.

His breath brushed against my lips, and they parted in response. My eyes fluttered closed…

The heat of him vanished. My eyes flew open as he abruptly moved away.

His absence echoed like heartbreak. The question burst from my lips before I could stop myself. "Why did you stop?"

Tobias was watching me so wistfully, I could feel my heart breaking. "Because Sagray…we only get our first kiss once. I have no intention of ruining it a second time."

So he did *remember.*

The ground tilted beneath my feet. He wanted this…wanted *me*. And yet, once again, he was walking away.

My heart pounded in my ears, all my pent-up frustration breaking loose at once. I was tired of waiting; tired of fighting this. So, so tired of ignoring the feelings beating in my heart, not now that our timing was finally right.

"And if I were to kiss you?"

Tobias's eyes snapped to mine, his gaze heating. "You shouldn't."

It was my turn to close the distance between us. To feel his slow, shuddering exhale against my lips. To hear his sharp inhale as I wove my fingers into his hair, bringing his face down to mine.

I pressed myself against him until our mouths were barely a breath apart, each shared breath shallow—the anticipation so heady I almost didn't want it to end.

"Why not?" I breathed against his lips. "Or do you think I'll 'ruin' it?"

Slowly, I brushed my lips against his in a whisper of a kiss. Gone before it had even begun and yet the world itself seemed to shift. He let out a soft sound that might have been a plea.

"No," Tobias said shakily. "I think you'll ruin *me*."

Then he yanked my face to his, his lips meeting mine.

With a muffled gasp I kissed him back. Tobias groaned into my mouth, his tongue darting against the seam of my lips. A question I already knew the answer to.

My lips parted with a moan. Then he was kissing me so thoroughly I saw stars.

This kiss—*this kiss*—was a collision of desire and overdue regret, urgent and inevitable. It was everything we had held back, a yearning that bordered on desperation, and years of wanting all at once in a claiming too long denied. It was something I couldn't think about just yet, not when my every thought disappeared except the need for *more*.

The way he kissed was hungry—no, ravenous. Like he had been longing to taste me for far longer than I had realized. Like he had always wanted this, wanted *me*, perhaps even longer than I had wanted him.

My knees buckled. His arms wrapped around me, holding me up even as he pulled me closer. My hands bunched in his hair, tugging at the wild strands—wordlessly begging him to continue.

I gasped as he hitched my legs up and around his waist, effortlessly lifting me. I barely registered the cool metal countertop beneath me as he set me atop it, sweeping my notes to one side. He took full advantage of my willingness, his hands sliding down my body in a worshipful caress. My back arched, my legs widening in response to allow him better access…

His hand dropped away. Something solidified in my gut as he took two steps back, raking that hand through his hair. The cold of the countertop seeped into my bare thighs where my dress had ridden up, chasing away the warmth from where his body had been a moment before. I could still feel the grip of his hands on my hips, the absence of them even more glaring because of it.

"Tobias?"

That hand dragged lower, covering his face.

"Just once." He sounded utterly defeated. "I had to, just once."

Tobias looked off-balance yet composed in a way I had grown used to over the last few months, his restraint completely at odds with the intensity that rolled off him.

His voice was full of self-loathing as he rasped, "I shouldn't have...I'm sorry."

I couldn't hide my hurt as I snapped, "You shouldn't be."

Sliding off the countertop, I angrily tugged my clothes back in place. Here I was thinking he would push me away because of my magic. I should've known it would be because I got too close.

"Don't you get it?" Tobias squeezed his eyes shut. "This...*we* could never work."

"Why not?" I demanded. "Because you're too scared?"

His lips pressed into a thin line, like he was silencing his response.

A heaviness pressed in on my chest as I tried to swallow the lump in my throat. "I kissed *you*, remember? And I have no regrets at all."

His gaze flinched toward me, his hands tightening into fists as he took one step backward, then another. With a choked sound, he fled from the room.

CHAPTER 24
TOBIAS

I hadn't gotten far. Despite the need to get away from her—and from the flood of emotions that had come rushing back all at once—I wouldn't let my feelings compromise her safety. Staying away from her was an exercise in futility when set against the almost primal urge to protect her. So I paced outside that iron door, wishing I could hear her through it, even as I shoved that kiss into a cell and chained my longing for her beside it.

There was something unspeakably precious about what we had. The friendship we built long ago had literally come back to life. I couldn't risk upsetting it, or worse, having her only to lose her when she saw how damaged I truly was. Even if this dance I was doing—trying to be around her without letting her see too much—threatened to destroy me, along with our fragile equilibrium.

By the time she finished for the night, I was numb and so cut off from the turmoil I had locked away that I barely felt like a person anymore. Quinn's obvious disappointment barely stung as she silently took in my detachment before walking away. I trailed after her, staying alert for threats until we reached her room.

She paused in the doorway, not looking back at me. "And the meetup?"

I nearly tripped over my own feet. "The others should be back soon, let's decide what to do together. I don't want to risk sending a message that might get intercepted."

The muscles in her back tensed above the curve of her neckline. Her loud sigh echoed in my ears as she shut the door in my face.

It didn't take long for the others to return, their voices echoing on the other side of my door. I waited for the sound of Quinn's door opening before leaving my room. Quinn didn't look at me as we joined the others for dinner on the outdoor terrace.

Tonight's spread looked delicious. The table was covered in a variety of fresh fish and aromatic yellow rice, along with a mango salsa I immediately knew Quinn would love. Fried plantains sat next to a basket of flat bread covered in garlic.

Too bad no one was eating it.

Rivan paced back and forth, his long strides eating up the balcony. "If you hadn't decided to intervene, we'd have them in custody already."

Pari threw up her hands. "I was trying to help—"

He rounded on her, his lavender eyes flashing. "I don't need your help."

"*Rivan,*" Yael chided. "We're all trying—"

"And yet, without me, you would've been stabbed in the back," Pari gritted out. Her cheeks were flushed, the scar that slashed across her cheekbone stark in contrast. "You're welcome, by the way."

Rivan turned away, his braids whipping over his shoulder with the force of it. I didn't think I had ever seen him so frustrated, let alone outwardly rude. He was generally the epitome of calm. Pari was more outspoken but rarely this worked up—like she was teetering on the edge of control. The way they glared at each other told me there was something I was missing.

Quinn raised an eyebrow at me, looking similarly taken aback before seeming to remember she wasn't acknowledging my presence. My chest panged, even as I reminded myself this was for the best.

It wasn't pride…it was fear. The aversion to being hurt. Of giving her some part of me that she could break when I was already so broken, despite her attempts to convince me otherwise.

It was better for both of us, in the end. I knew I couldn't be the person she needed, even if I wanted to be. When this was over, Quinn would return to Soleara where she was safe, and I would no longer have a good excuse to be around her. She would go back to her life, and I would lock myself behind the walls I built before she breached them. With time, I could go back to pretending my solitude was a choice and not a shield.

I had no doubt she would find someone better than me. Light seared my palms, though the pain felt far away.

Yael looked vaguely amused as she walked between Rivan and Pari, despite the shadows under her eyes. "If you two don't knock whatever this is off, I'm going to lock you in a room together until you figure it out. We don't have time to fight with each other, not when we have enemies to face."

Rivan's mouth opened in outrage while Pari made a sputter of indignation.

"This is the second time we've had him only for him to disappear," Rivan grumbled.

"There has to be a mole among Queen Sariyah's guards," Pari said tightly. "There's no way Silvius keeps getting away right before we arrive without someone warning him ahead of time. We need to find a way to keep our next lead to ourselves."

Rivan was already shaking his head. "It would look suspicious after Queen Sariyah integrated our rangers into their ranks for the search. I don't trust her people not to leak our intel to Silvius either, but if we remove ours for a side mission, it might cause a diplomatic incident we can't afford right now. Not to mention tip them off."

"I think Eva's life trumps diplomacy—" Pari said sharply.

"If you think I'm not thinking of her—" Rivan cut in, talking over her.

Quinn loudly cleared her throat, silencing them both. "This seems like a good time to bring up some time sensitive intelligence." She lifted her chin, smugly adding, "I may have done my own reconnaissance earlier."

Rivan gave me an affronted look. "I take it that no one decided to listen to my warnings today."

"We intercepted a message with a location and a time from one of Silvius's followers," I said, ignoring him. After all, I already blamed myself enough for the both of us. "We don't know who the bearer was meant to meet with, but given that he tried to steal Quinn's blood, it's safe to say they're working for Silvius."

Nevermind the syringe meant for me.

The room seemed to freeze at the news, then ignite with the flurry of voices asking questions.

"We're fine," Quinn exclaimed, cutting them all off.

Rivan didn't look convinced. "And the person who tried to steal your blood?"

"No longer breathing," I said grimly. "But that's not what we need to discuss."

I pulled the folded piece of paper from my pocket, laying the crude map on the table. There was one word scrawled along the top: *Seawater*.

Yael leaned over it. "That bar's not far from the Enclave. When's this meetup?"

"Tonight," I said shortly. "Before last call. Which doesn't give us much time."

Pari looked thoughtful. "If there's a mole among the guard, they'll be watching us."

I didn't like the expression on Quinn's face. I knew that look—it meant she had a plan.

"*We* could go." Quinn gestured between us, and I jerked to attention. "The rest of you just need to act like all is usual so the mole won't suspect anything. If there's a mole among the healers, they won't know to follow us based on our pattern. With the way we've been trading between the lab and sleep, no one will expect Tobias and me to be there…let alone Silvius."

"No, he's just trying to steal your blood in order to infect you," I drawled. "Which is why you're not going anywhere near that place."

"Don't tell me what I can and cannot do, Maris," Quinn said coldly.

I matched her tone. "I'm serious, Sagray."

"I know," she said so snidely I reared back. "You're always serious."

"You say that like it's a bad thing."

Quinn shrugged. "You didn't used to be."

My response caught in my throat.

Quinn turned to the others. "We'll keep our hoods up and find a shadowy corner. We just need to be careful not to be seen leaving the Enclave. You three"—she gestured at Rivan, Yael, and Pari—"can make a scene to distract anyone who might follow us."

I hated the thought of leaving this place to go outdoors at all. It had cost me when I had followed Quinn into the city earlier, even if my fear for her outweighed the fear of what I was doing.

But I hated the thought of Quinn going without me more.

"The two of you are already his targets," Yael argued, though she sounded more contemplative than concerned—likely swayed by the necessity of Quinn's plan. "You'll need to be on your guard."

With Quinn's blood magic, she would be able to tell if someone was following us. This plan wasn't quite as rash as it seemed—not that I could explain that to Rivan or Yael. Pari, however, looked like she had come to the same conclusion.

"We're all his targets," Pari countered. "And Quinn's right. They'll be watching us three, but they won't expect Tobias and Quinn to leave the castle, especially not after their outing earlier. If we want this to succeed, then they're our best shot."

Quinn nodded. My attention fixed on the curl that had escaped her braid as it bounced against her cheek like a caress.

"We won't fight anyone if we can help it," Quinn said, her tone conciliatory. "We'll just follow them and report back."

It wouldn't be without risk, especially if they caught onto their tail. But I knew that look in Quinn's eyes: pure stubbornness mixed with determination. Arguing with her would only end up with me being left behind—which wasn't a fucking option. Just the thought of it made my throat close.

Yael bit her lip. "It could work. They won't expect you to leave the Enclave for the night, and you can wear healers' robes, so you don't look out of place."

Rivan looked thoughtful. "And your research?"

"We can't do anything overnight anyway," I said reluctantly. The thought of putting Quinn in danger again when she had already been attacked today was the last thing I wanted. But if I didn't play along, I knew Quinn would find someone else to bring along. "Recon only?"

Pari nodded. "Send a message once you identify them. Follow but don't engage."

"I could go with Yael or Pari if we're staying hooded," Quinn mused. "If we're relying on a diversion anyways..."

"No," I growled. Like hell was she going anywhere without me to protect her, whether or not it meant venturing outside for a second time today.

I could bear it if it meant staying by her side.

Quinn bristled, turning to glare at me. I swore I saw Pari and Yael exchange a smirk out of the corner of my eye.

"We need all three of you at the Enclave to make it seem like there's nothing going on if we want this to work," I said quickly. "If Silvius has a mole among the guard, we don't want to give them a reason to suspect anything—and if Yael or Pari go missing, they will. You and I will be far less obvious."

It was good reasoning, but it wasn't the real reason.

I would keep her safe or die trying. And I didn't trust that job to anyone but myself.

Quinn's head tilted in the same way it did when she was trying to figure out a problem in the lab. Those amber eyes studied me far too intently. I hastily looked away, painstakingly forcing my fear for her back into its cell along with everything else.

The bars trembled so violently I thought they might tear off their hinges.

"Fine," Quinn murmured. "We'll leave when it's darker to get a sense of the layout."

I nodded, keeping my face detached as I silently tried to prepare myself. Not only would she likely be in danger, but I had willingly offered to venture outside. Quinn's lips formed a tight line as she saw the look on my face—or rather, the lack of it.

Didn't she realize that mask was the only thing holding me together?

With a deep sigh, Quinn asked Yael. "Any update from Marin? How's Eva?"

"Marin says she's the same," Yael replied with an unusual trace of melancholy. "As is Bash. No change, not for the better or the worse...but I guess that's the best we can hope for." It was a struggle to think about Eva being stuck in that stasis, though she was right—it was far better than the alternative. "I've been sending her daily updates along with yours. Marin promised she wouldn't let anything happen to them in the meantime." A hint of a smile lifted her lips. "She moved a cot into their room and sleeps with both daggers."

Pari raised an eyebrow. "How many does she normally sleep with?"

That hint turned into a full grin. "Just the one under her pillow." She shrugged. "A compromise. The other sits within reach on her nightstand."

Quinn smiled, and I found myself incapable of looking away. I had kissed those perfect lips today. I had wanted to do much more than that before I came to my senses and pushed her away. It had been a herculean effort not to give in to that desire and take her exactly how I wanted to.

"Tobias?"

It took a second to realize Pari was talking to me, my name hesitant. Quinn's smile melted away as she found me looking at her. It was an effort not to flinch at the echo of hurt in her eyes.

I slid my hands into my pockets. "Yes?"

"It might be worth getting some dinner in before you go." She gestured at the food spread across the table, her lips twitching as she fought her smile. "Especially if you're going to get a drink to keep your cover."

I fixed her with a glare. "Are you calling your king a lightweight, Pari?"

It had been a long time since I had been on the receiving end of one of Pari's laughs. "If the shoe fits, Your Majesty."

CHAPTER 25
QUINN

The crowded bar smelled like salt and seawater, likely due to the number of sailors in attendance. Even their fae features looked wind chilled and leathery after decades of baking in the sun. I could only hope that the bar was dubbed Seawater due to the livelihoods of its denizens and not the flavor of its drinks.

It had been simple to sneak out of the Enclave given my talents at sensing the heartbeat of anyone close enough to catch us. Rivan, Yael, and Pari had gone to find Queen Sariyah, who apparently spent most nights tending to her people in the hospital wing. Tobias and I had donned the freshly pressed healer's robes Yael had somehow obtained, then blended into the crowd of them leaving for the day. We weren't the only ones in a hurry, nor the only ones heading to nearby bars, though most were likely rushing to get home.

I doubted any of them had been forced to double back as often as Tobias had made us, nor needed to ditch their robes in an alley. An additional precaution Tobias had insisted on, as he handed me one of the lightweight cloaks he carried beneath his arm. Despite my reassurances that I would have sensed anyone following us from the telltale pounding of their hearts, Tobias insisted we stick to the shadows the entire way here. In return, I made him promise we wouldn't forget to return our borrowed robes when we were done.

The mood at the bar was lively, raucous even, though there was an undercurrent to it like a livewire about to spark. I tensed as I heard someone loudly mention the "High Queen's ailment" among the chatter of voices. Another replied he heard she was already dead. My head snapped his way as he started going on about how "the truth was being hidden" and would be "until The Choosing took place in secret", even as loud jeers overtook the rest of his sentence.

Tobias's hand fastened around my upper arm, leading me forward as he muttered, "So brave of him to be so confidently wrong in public."

It hadn't taken long for news of the severity of Eva's sickness to spread. Not that I expected otherwise.

"Keep your head down and your hood up." His hand moved to my lower back as we pressed through the throng, and an unbidden flutter stirred low in my stomach. "If Thibault recognized us, whoever he was supposed to meet likely will as well."

We hadn't worked so hard to sneak out of the castle undetected to get caught now. I tugged my hood lower, shading more of my face despite the heat of the room, but draped the attached cape open for some relief. Beneath it, I wore a sleeveless black tank, a triangle of skin exposed at the base of my collarbone. My wrap skirt concealed the dagger attached to my leg, though we were hardly the only ones armed at this establishment. Tobias wore his usual black on black, his own hood keeping his face hidden. The sleeves of his shirt were rolled above his elbows, exposing the taut veins of his forearms as he ushered me forward. I knew his dagger hung on his belt beneath his cloak, ready if needed.

"I'm not the one he—" I was careful to avoid saying Silvius's name, despite the miniscule chance we could be overheard. "I'm not the one *he* has a ready-made virus for."

Tobias walked us over to an empty booth in the back. "Like the alternative's any better."

Reminding him what was at stake should we be discovered wasn't my brightest idea. My fingers drummed on the table. "Won't it look more suspicious if we're just sitting here and waiting?"

A grimace flickered across his face. "I'll get us drinks. Stay here where I can see you, okay?"

He waited for me to nod before pushing his way back through the crowd. I had to admit that Tobias had chosen our table well. The booth not only faced the entrance, but it was slightly raised so we could easily look over the heads of everyone crowding the bar. Even in the dim lighting, we could see everything except some shadowy corners.

More than one person noticed me looking around the room and gave me appraising looks in return. They were no doubt in search of any warm body, considering all they could see of me was the vague curve of my figure beneath my cloak. I ignored them and continued my perusal, but I didn't see anyone who immediately aroused my suspicion, only those looking to unwind.

A lone figure walked towards me. My hand automatically found my dagger. He shuffled slightly as he walked, likely a few drinks in. His arms were bare and muscled from what I assumed was a life at sea based on the fishy smell emanating from him.

He gave me a smarmy grin. "What are you drinking?"

"I'm not looking for company," I said dismissively.

He snorted, then slid into Tobias's empty seat. I could smell the alcohol on his breath as he leaned in. "Give me a chance, darling. It's a drink, not an *anima* bond."

"My friend is taking care of it," I said impatiently, scanning the room for Tobias. I hated using him as an excuse—like me asking for this asshole to leave didn't count unless I had a male companion superseding his advances—but it was better than causing a scene. "Last chance to leave me alone. I won't ask you again."

I could easily fight him and win, but that would draw attention we couldn't afford. If this drunkard didn't leave on his own though, I would happily teach him a lesson about what happened when he didn't listen to the word 'no'.

His eyes fixed on my cleavage. My hand twitched on my dagger, ready to draw it and point it at the bastard's balls.

"How about I keep you company until your friend gets back." His words slurred together. "Wouldn't want you to be lonely…"

"*Move.*" Tobias's voice was a low growl, the threat in it unmistakable.

My interloper blanched, jerking back. His eyes widened as he took in Tobias standing over him, the muscles of his arms testing the stretch of his sleeves as his hands curled into fists.

"We were just talking," the sailor mumbled drunkenly.

"The lady said no." Tobias set two frothy mugs in front of me. His face remained impassive, but I swore I saw a flash of his light gleam around his pupils. "Now get out of my seat."

The stranger swayed as he got to his feet. "She didn't say she was taken—"

"She's not," Tobias said sharply, his eyes narrowing. "That doesn't mean you have a right to her time or attention."

"But I—"

"Owe her an apology." Tobias leaned forward, the move only serving to demonstrate how much larger he was. "Unless you'd prefer to settle this outside."

With a grumbled apology, the male quickly disappeared into the crowd.

Tobias crossed his arms. "I was barely gone a minute and still had to conduct a rescue mission."

"I don't need rescuing," I said flatly.

His lips twitched. "You misunderstand...I was rescuing *him*." Tobias glanced down at my hand, which still rested on my dagger. "It was a mercy, really...I thought I'd let him leave with his balls intact."

Despite the awkwardness of our situation, I couldn't help my snicker.

"Well, thanks for coming back when you did." I clinked my beer against his a little too exuberantly. A bit of foam sluiced down the cold glass onto my fingertips.

Tobias shook his head. "Don't thank me for that. You would've handled it just fine without me."

"Well then, for the beer," I said with a grin. As much as I wanted to take him to task for running away earlier, now wasn't the time. Besides, it had been a long time since we had a beer together.

Tobias's eyes softened, a small smile curving his lips. He picked up his mug, taking a large sip and promptly gagged.

I eyed my own drink suspiciously. "Poisoned?"

"I watched him pour it from the tap into two fresh glasses right in front of me." Tobias looked affronted as he took another sip, like the first one might have been a fluke. "I swear I didn't order a sour ale."

I took a drink of my own, my cheeks sucking together as the taste hit my tongue. "I don't mind a tart beer, but this is..."

My next swallow was more measured, but Tobias braved a larger gulp. I slapped a hand over my mouth at the expression on his face, trying not to spit my drink out laughing.

"Sorry," Tobias muttered, a blush spreading across his cheeks. "I ordered something on draft that looked popular." He looked vaguely dejected at his failure to return with something I liked. "Maybe it's an acquired taste?"

I gamely drank another sip, struggling to hide my revulsion. "It's growing on me."

My tongue darted out to lick the foam from my upper lip. Something vaguely predatory reflected in his eyes as that gaze fixed on my lips, and my entire body heated. We might both be pretending right now—clinging to some fragile truce—but he was kidding himself if he thought I couldn't see right through him.

The noisy bar faded to a dull hum as he leaned closer…Almost as close as he had been earlier when he had me in his arms, my fingers tangling into his hair as he—

A glass shattered. Voices rang out, and we both looked away, the spell broken. I could feel my heartbeat in my throat. Tobias took a large gulp of his beer.

"I'd offer to get the next round, but we're not here to get drunk, Maris," I teased him under my breath. "It's almost last call, and we need to…"

I trailed off as I noticed the hooded figure filling the doorway. He wore healers' robes, the uniform out of place in this seafaring crowd. And the fact that he hadn't removed his hood…

Could this be the mole?

I watched his progress over the rim of my mug as he weaved through the bar, no longer tasting the beer as I brought it to my lips. Tobias had gone utterly motionless next to me, only his eyes moving as he tracked our suspect's progress. I angled my body toward him, gesticulating like I was saying something as the figure scanned the room, looking right past us. He tapped the bar three times—a signal, I realized, as a second male got to his feet from where he sat at the end of the bar.

I reached for Tobias's arm, the contact sending a jolt through my entire body. Thibault wasn't the only one who was told to meet here. Tobias gave me a subtle nod as our suspects started moving through the crowd in unison.

They were heading toward the back door.

Suddenly I was glad we had scoped out the exits before we came in. "Let's go out the side door."

Tobias slid across the booth so he sat next to me, likely to get a better view.

"Wait until they leave, so they don't notice their tail," he murmured into my ear. A shiver ran through me despite the heat.

The two reached the back entrance, their heads ducked together.

Tobias's whisper brushed against my earlobe, his deep voice eliciting another quiver as he asked, "Ready?"

I was on my feet before the door closed, Tobias close behind. My heart was pounding by the time we reached the side exit even as I tried to zero in on our suspects' unique heartbeats. There were too many people around for it to work. Carefully, I pushed the door open just enough to slip through. Tobias shut the door behind us and the noisy bar faded to a low buzz through the thick wooden door.

It had started raining while we were inside. A sandstone archway that was barely visible through the winding vine that covered it blocked us from the raindrops.

With a quick look to make sure the coast was clear, I started forward. Tobias's hand fastened around my wrist, tugging me back against him. Two distinct voices were coming toward us along with two sets of footsteps. The downpour made it hard to hear what they were saying, even with my fae hearing, but they would reach us soon if they continued this way.

I turned in Tobias's arms. We were so close that I could count the gold flecks in his eyes as they widened. He retreated a step, then stopped as his back hit the stone. His face shuttered like he was trying to wipe any trace of feeling from it.

"Kiss me," I demanded quietly.

Pure shock overtook his efforts as he whispered, "*What*?"

"We need a reason to be out here, especially if the one waiting inside noticed us casing the place," I hissed. "If we go back in, we'll lose them. More importantly, if they get close enough, I can track their heartbeats so we can easily tail them." There was no way I would be able to focus my magic enough to do so with them getting closer, especially with a bar full of distractions. "No one will think twice about a couple finding a quiet corner outside after a few drinks."

Tobias's throat bobbed. "Quinn…"

"You already kissed me once, Maris," I said, unable to help the hurt that edged my tone.

A muscle flickered in his jaw. "That was a mistake."

"Don't I know it," I murmured, flinching at the sting of his words.

I knew I was setting myself up for another disappointment, but the footsteps were getting closer. I stared up at him imploringly. "It doesn't have to be real." This wasn't the time to discuss it, but I couldn't help but add, "I know it isn't…that you don't want me…"

His expression darkened. "Is *that* what you think?"

In one quick movement, Tobias pulled me against him then spun us around, pressing me flush against the archway. His hand slid behind my head, cushioning it. I wrapped my arms around his neck on instinct. My breath caught at how perfectly we fit together even as I tried not to let myself hope. Tobias's eyes sparked as a hint of his light burned away the gold in his eyes.

"*Shh*," he whispered against the shell of my ear. I knew he could feel the way my body responded, arching against him. "Just listen. This is enough for now."

It wasn't nearly enough. But I froze as the voices finally got loud enough to hear over the rain.

"I don't know why we had to meet here first," the first voice said in a low grumble.

The second voice sounded exasperated. "I told you already. You can't get in alone. And he doesn't meet with anyone who hasn't proven themselves loyal to the cause."

"Sounds like he should be less picky about his help considering how badly the first one botched today's attempt. Did you see that they tortured that poor sod and then left him behind for the guards to pick up?"

There was a grunt of assent. My hand tightened on the nape of Tobias's neck, the memory of his earlier callousness clashing with the heat rising between us now.

"Public displays of affection make people uncomfortable," I breathed into his ear. "We need them to look past us, or our cover's blown. But if you don't want to, there's still time to slip back inside."

Tobias groaned deep in his throat. "Does it feel like I don't want to? That I don't want *you*?"

He rolled his hips, and my eyes went wide as the hard length of him pressed against me. My core went loose and tight all at once, the primal need to get closer nearly making me forget our precarious situation.

I wanted to climb him like a tree. I wanted to wrap my legs around him and let him take me hard against this doorway. I wanted…so much more than I was willing to admit, even to myself.

"Then what's the problem, Maris?" I fluttered my eyelashes at him, letting my bravado bury my fear of what came next. "Afraid I'll bite? Or are you into that sort of thing?"

My breath caught as his finger crooked beneath my chin, lifting my face up to his. The world seemed to hold its breath along with me, even the rain fading to a murmur as he leaned in.

"Fuck it," Tobias breathed against my lips. Then his mouth met mine, swift and hard and claiming. His arm tightened around my waist, lifting me onto my tiptoes. For a split second, I could feel his heartbeat as it raced in time to mine, my magic reaching for him as assuredly as I did.

"His orders are clear," the first voice said, far too close now. "He wants her alive, but I can't imagine for long."

It took my brain an extra second to realize that they were talking about me. The muscles in Tobias's back went taut beneath my hands. His kiss became urgent, like he couldn't get me close enough.

The second voice snickered. Then they fell silent, their footsteps pausing as they reached us.

My fingers twisted in Tobias's hair, his hand covering my cheek either to hide my face or to tilt it exactly how he wanted me. I nearly forgot my task as his tongue delved into my mouth just as his hips moved against me so deliciously that I moaned into his mouth.

When exactly had I straddled his thigh?

I didn't want this to end, but my blood magic was already waiting—the need to use it unexpectedly insistent. Tunneling into it felt easy despite how long I had kept it leashed. It was as simple as focusing on the pump of their blood, the path it took through their veins to their heart; each cell coming to attention as my magic jumped between them.

If they got closer, I could stop their hearts with a thought.

I shoved the intrusive thought away, feeling shaken. That wasn't our mission…and I hadn't let myself give in to that urge since Adronix. I could still remember the looks on those soldiers' faces as my magic took control of their sword arms, bending each blood cell to my will. It was foolish to think Tobias hadn't noticed his opponents suddenly giving him the perfect opening to kill them.

Even then, I hadn't stopped the blood flowing from their hearts—hadn't realized I *could*—until one soldier stabbed Tobias in his side. Then it had been far too easy to stop his heart between one beat and the next. Tobias's sword had passed through his opponent's chest a second later, destroying all evidence of what I had done.

It was no wonder Pari looked at me like I might be a monster. Maybe that much power, and the moment I had given into it, had corrupted me more than I realized.

The footsteps continued, passing us without incident. But now I could feel their heartbeats, both nervously accelerating as they hurried down the alleyway.

Tobias let out a soft sigh against my lips. "How close do you need to be?"

"I haven't really tried this before," I admitted nervously. "My magic can sense their heartbeats, but I think I'll lose them if they get too far away, or they walk into a crowd. We won't have to keep them in our sights to follow them…but we can't let them get too far ahead."

"Then let's get going."

With a smile, I inclined my head, looking pointedly down at where Tobias still pinned me against the wall. A flush rose to his cheeks, barely visible in the glow of the streetlights. He set me back down on my feet so gently my heart skipped a beat, his hands holding me for a moment longer to make sure I was steady before finally letting me go.

I closed my eyes, focusing on the pair of heartbeats. They were growing fainter as the distance between us stretched. Thankfully the streets had emptied to the point that the trail was clear.

Taking Tobias's hand, I led him into the warm rain.

CHAPTER 26
TOBIAS

That kiss.

I needed to focus on the fae we were following to Silvius. I needed to focus on anything but the feel of her hand in mine as she led me down the empty, dark streets, and the ghost of that earth shattering kiss bruising my lips. But I couldn't bring myself to let her go, not when I was just starting to get used to the way her touch grounded me in something that felt like safety.

My need for her had broken right through the bars I tried to cage it in. It was all I could do not to let the rest of the dungeon crumble in her wake.

The rain was too heavy now to see through, the summer storm soaking me to the bone. At least the water was warm and muffled our footsteps as we tracked our prey. Quinn's curls had lost their usual bounce, her braid now plastered against her chest along with the thin fabric of her shirt. My gaze lingered a moment longer at how the fabric revealed the curve of her breast, hoping she didn't notice the way my heartbeat thundered.

I dragged my focus back to our task. This was our best chance of finding Silvius, and a dark part of me was glad that Rivan, Yael, and Pari hadn't tracked him down first. I wanted to give him a taste of the pain he had put me through. He was no warrior. I doubted he would keep his secrets safe for long, especially when I had him alone in a cell. If he did have a cure for this virus, I planned to be the one to extract it.

And if he didn't? It would be my pleasure to make him pay.

Quinn stopped short, and I nearly ran into her. We had reached the corner of a stone building near the end of an empty street. Quinn gestured past it, wordlessly letting me know they were around the corner as water dripped down her face.

I wanted to yank her behind me, but I knew she wouldn't stand for it. Silvius wanted her alive, which meant he needed her for something. Whether that was to learn what Quinn had discovered in her attempts to find a cure or because he wanted to use her for his own ends before he killed her, I wasn't sure.

Either way, the bastard thought he could take her from me. He would pay for that. The thought of him near her made my blood boil, though I was careful to keep my magic carefully contained, not risking it rising with her hand in mine.

Quinn gasped, then ran forward, dragging me around the corner with her. The alleyway was empty.

I scanned the sides of the stone buildings and the cobblestone wall ahead. There were no doorways, no rope, no low windows to disappear into or a mirror secured to the stone. "Where did they—"

"I can still feel them," Quinn whispered. "They're close."

I knew that look, the furrow between her brows. She was solving the problem before I even had the chance to be confused.

She walked toward the wall ahead as though in a trance as I followed close behind. "There has to be a way through."

Carefully, I placed my hands against the slick rock, feeling for anything out of the ordinary. I half expected a trap door to open if I pressed my hand against the right stone. Quinn joined me, silently starting on the other side of the alley.

The rain had gotten worse, ricocheting off the wall at me as my fingers scraped against each stone. It wasn't until I touched the far corner that my hand disappeared into the rock. A glamour, I realized, as I held back my gasp. Some sort of secret passage through the city, likely shown to Silvius by his Mayimite allies.

My stomach bottomed out as I pictured what was waiting for us, the damp stone sure the stir my memories. But if she was descending into the darkness, there was no question that I would go down with her.

"Here." I waved Quinn over, hoping I wasn't leading her into an ambush. "How close are they?"

"Far enough that they won't notice us behind them." She started to reach for the glamour, then stopped. "We should tell the others."

I stuck my hand in my pocket, realizing too late what I would find in my sopping clothes. The paper I brought with me had partially disintegrated, what remained now formed into a wet clump. Quinn swore under her breath as she realized the flaw in our plan.

"You head back to the castle to update everyone," I said quickly. "I'll follow our new friends."

Quinn was already shaking her head. "I'm the one who can track them. So unless you want to play messenger…"

"Absolutely not."

"We go together, Maris." She reached for my hand, a stubborn glint in her eye. "You're not getting rid of me that easily."

"If it's a trap—"

"Then you'll need backup," Quinn cut in, completely undeterred. "I'm not leaving you. Now, do you want to keep wasting time until I lose their trail entirely?"

I may not like it, but I knew she was right. With a short sigh, I turned my hand over in invitation.

A spark leapt between us as she took it.

With a deep breath in through my nose, I pulled her behind me into solid stone. It parted around us like a dense fog, each rock sliding unnervingly along my skin. For a heartbeat, the wall pulsed around me, digging in as if unsure whether to let us pass.

Then we were through.

Cold horror froze me in place. It was like I had been transported back in time, the darkness so suffocating I thought I might drown in it. A visceral pain set every scar on my back on fire. My hands flew to my face, clawing against my cheeks as I felt that mask press against my skin—

Quinn's whisper broke through the silence. "What is it?"

I was trapped. And worst of all, I brought her here with me.

That endless dripping sound filled my ears. The walls of the cell seemed to close in around me, that band tightening around my neck like it would finally suffocate me.

I can't breathe. I can't—

Quinn's voice was more forceful as she pressed, "Are you okay?"

My lips formed her name, but I couldn't push the sound past my throat.

She was stuck in here with me, in some cruel echo of my worst nightmare. Trapped underground where no one would ever find us.

And I couldn't save her.

"Tobias."

I only realized I sank to my knees as they hit the stone with a splash, a hollow echo of pain radiating up my thighs. My lungs spasmed as I struggled to draw in a breath.

There wasn't any air.

"*Breathe*, Tobias," Quinn demanded sharply. Then her hands were on my face, somehow finding me in the darkness. I hadn't realized how hard I was shaking until her hands started trembling too.

Her voice trembled slightly. "I'll count, okay?"

There was only darkness, no difference between my eyes open or closed. I tried to focus on the sound of her voice.

"You're safe, do you hear me? I'm with you." Her hands moved down from my neck to my shoulders, shaking me slightly when I didn't reply. "Please, Tobias. Breathe for me."

My gasp of air filled my ears, unable to ignore her plea. It felt far too quiet down here after the rush of the rain. Each breath was so loud it echoed around me as I attempted to draw another.

"There you go," Quinn murmured. "Now do it again, slower this time."

Utterly at her command, I obeyed, shaking as she led me through the boxed breathing my dad taught us both long ago. Her voice was calm and soothing, but she held me so tightly her fingernails bit into my skin.

Quinn's voice was soft as she asked, "Do you think you can use your magic?"

My magic was blocked. My magic...

My jolt of surprise was quickly followed by a crushing wave of shame. I had the means to fix this the whole time...and I had panicked. Worse, I had frozen, useless to help myself, let alone her. Had this been an ambush, she would have been on her own as I gaped like a fish flung ashore.

I welcomed the burn of my magic as it came to my fingertips; that searing light pricking my skin as I held it there. When I finally released it, it blossomed from my fingertips as if reaching for her, balls of light rising around her like tiny stars.

Quinn's eyes were blood red from her power and wide with worry as I got to my feet. With a flick of my fingers, I let the balls of light roam free. They flew to the rounded corners of the tunnels, illuminating the grime that had built up over the centuries as they cast the room in a warm glow.

"Tobias, are you—"

"I'm f-fine, Sagray," I said curtly.

It was obviously a lie.

She was silent for a long moment as I attempted to push that overwhelming fear back into its box, picturing the cell doors opening and closing—

"Don't," Quinn said suddenly.

My eyes snapped to hers. "Don't what?"

"Don't block it out," Quinn pleaded, coming toward me. "Let yourself feel it. Maybe it'll be overwhelming for a bit...but blocking it out is only delaying the inevitable."

"The inevitable what? My inevitable breakdown?" I hated the cruelty in my voice, the way she flinched at my tone, but I couldn't make myself stop. "We don't have time for me to be useless. In case you didn't notice, our best chance at finding Silvius is getting further away as we speak."

"There's never a good time," Quinn said softly. "But if you don't do the work, you're never going to escape that cell."

I jerked back like she had slapped me again. She couldn't know about the prison I had created for myself, the cells in my mind in which I trapped each memory, each feeling—the place I had hidden *her.*

"Leave it alone, Sagray."

I sucked a breath through my nose, trying to push away the fear and anger into a place where it couldn't reach me. Needing to ensure my panic wouldn't endanger her again.

"Tobias..."

The cell I conjured seemed to disintegrate into midair, pale yellow sunlight streaming into the dusky prison as that one whispered word broke through my attempt at control. Quinn looked resigned, the sadness in her eyes breaking through my final vestiges of restraint.

I took a short, gasping breath before my lips curled in a snarl. "I told you to leave me alone."

The hurt on her face felt worse than if she had stabbed me. Then her eyes narrowed. "If our places were reversed, would you let me continue like this? Would you let me suffer when you could do something?"

She wrung her hands, glancing down the tunnel.

She didn't have to say it. We needed to go before she lost the ability to track them.

"We need to start moving," I said tonelessly. "If we lose them..."

"Then answer me," she hissed.

"Our places being reversed was *exactly* what I feared every day for four fucking years," I snapped, unable to hold it in any longer. "I was willing to give my life to prevent you from being in that dungeon along with me. So no, Sagray," I bit out. "Your suffering isn't something I can stand."

I stormed down the tunnel, the water dragging me back with every step. Quinn sloshed behind me, swearing under her breath as she tried to catch up. She let out a gasp. I turned the second her foot slipped.

My hand closed around her upper arm, the other encircling her wrist as I yanked her against me. For a second, the feel of her pressed against me made me wish we had never left that alcove.

Her pulse beat wildly beneath my thumb. Each beat was a reminder of what I needed to protect—and what I had to lose. My light drew closer, spinning around us like it needed to touch her as badly as I did.

"I'd say thank you if I wasn't so furious with you," Quinn said crossly. My mouth quirked despite myself, then I let out a soft sigh.

"I'm the one who owes you a thank you, and an apology," I admitted. "If I'd gone in alone..."

Not only would I have lost them, but I would likely still be frozen in the darkness, despite the light I had entirely forgotten was at my command.

Quinn scrunched her nose. "Was that supposed to be an apology or just a promise of one?"

The hand I wasn't holding in a death grip reached up to graze my cheek. Her thumb pressed into the corner of my lips where my nearly forgotten dimple must have made a fleeting appearance. My light reflected in her eyes, a tiny ball of it swooping between the curls of her hair as she smiled back.

"I'm sorry." I whispered. "I'm okay. Thanks to you."

"And you wanted to leave me behind." She tried for teasing, but I could hear how shaken she was—how much I had scared her.

"As always, you were right, Sagray."

She shivered, and I cursed myself for not having any dry clothes to give her. I reluctantly loosened my hold on her as she pulled away.

"We need to hurry," she said, determination sharpening her tone.

I gave her a solemn nod. "Let's go catch a rat."

It was my turn to take her hand and lead her down the passageway. There was something about her touch that loosened the knot in my chest, letting my light bloom there instead. Or maybe it was simply something about her.

Two balls of light soared ahead, another illuminating the stones at our feet as it skimmed above the standing water. These tunnels had to be ancient based on the layers of muck and their general air of disuse. As we turned a corner, a raised pathway jutted from the water, its rounded edges worn down by water and time. The footsteps in the thick mud were unmistakable—and from more than just the two fae up ahead, though theirs were the freshest.

The steady drip of moisture down the walls was getting to me more than I wanted to admit. I held Quinn's hand tighter as the damp scent of stone tried to drag me back to that dungeon. And for once it was the squeeze of her hand in return that made it easier to breathe rather than locking that memory back into its cell.

I was careful not to let my light stray too far as we continued onward.

"Let me know when they're close," I said quietly.

My light danced around us like it was showing off for her.

"Those are useful," Quinn whispered, her eyes bright as one of the balls of light circled close to her face. "If you can figure out how to enclose them, they would be a nice nightlight."

I looked at her askance. "I'm not sure if they could be...enclosed."

My light flew around me in agitated circles, like the thought of being caged unsettled it as much as it did me.

"You know, when lightning hits sand in the desert it creates glass," Quinn mused. "The heat's so intense it melts the silica in the sand, creating these tube-like structures called fulgurites." A playful smile spread across her face, nearly making me stumble as it caught far too much of my attention. "I was picturing what it would be like if they glowed."

Not a cage, I realized. *Art and magic and warmth combining into something both functional and beautiful.*

It had been a long time since I thought of my magic as anything other than a source of pain and destruction. After all those years of having that power used against me, creating something with it sounded like a balm for my soul.

It was simple to follow the path of the footsteps as we reached a fork in the tunnel, even though Quinn murmured directions. The walls grew brighter as light bled in from ahead, the limestone familiar.

The realization hit me like a blow. We weren't simply near the Enclave... we were underneath it.

Inwardly cursing myself for not keeping better track of our whereabouts, I looked over at Quinn. She held a finger to her lips, nodding at the expression on my face. Obviously, she had beaten me to the same conclusion.

Quinn sidled closer, murmuring in my ear. "They stopped up ahead. This must be how Silvius was able to get in."

I grimaced as I let my light fade, wishing I brought my sword with me. It had seemed too ostentatious for the bar when we were trying to keep a low profile. I would have to make do with my dagger and my magic.

As if reading my mind, Quinn drew her dagger. She crept slowly forward, careful to keep her steps silent against the stone. I followed her lead, my own dagger in hand.

Voices echoed off the walls, and I strained to decipher them. I had no doubt I would recognize Silvius's reedy tone. But if he were there to meet our quarry, his voice was lost among the discord.

The voices suddenly went silent. Quinn's eyes flared wide.

"They're gone," she said at full volume.

I stared at her. "Another glamour?"

She ran forward, no longer hiding the thuds of her footfalls. It didn't take long to understand how they disappeared.

A brass mirror stood at the end of the hall, its surface still rippling.

CHAPTER 27
QUINN

I didn't stop running until I reached the mirror. Its oval frame was surrounded by eight twisted points, the adornment vaguely reminding me of the star amulet my sister always wore. The top and bottom points stretched from floor to ceiling, gleaming in the light of the sconces surrounding it. It had been angled slightly upward—its surface reflecting the distorted ceiling above it in whorls of white stone.

The ripples had moved to its outer edges, already fading. We didn't have time to delay in case they closed the gate behind them.

If we went through, it would mean a fight, whether or not Silvius was waiting on the other side. But if we didn't go through and lost him again…

Fear twisted low in my spine. My grip tightened on my dagger.

"We need to follow them," I said with more conviction than I felt. "We at least need to see where this goes."

The center of the mirror rippled as if sensing the intent behind my words.

Tobias stepped closer—not in front of me this time, but to my side. I could tell by the set of his jaw how little he wanted to put me in danger. But here he was, letting me decide.

Light crackled around his pupils. "If Silvius is there, then we—"

"We're not attempting to murder him," I cut in quickly.

He looked almost incredulous. "You have so little faith in me. After what he's done? It wouldn't be an attempt."

It was an effort not to roll my eyes. "What I meant is we need him alive."

Tobias stared at the dying ripples in the mirror. He shook his head with a sigh.

"No one knows where we are, and there's no guarantee there are only the two we followed on the other side." He lowered his dagger but didn't sheathe it. "I don't like it either, and I don't trust Silvius not to have a contingency for intruders…The two of us walking in there might be exactly what he wants."

"I know," I said, gritting my teeth.

Of course I knew that. But the thought of being so close to finding him and just walking away…

All I needed was a few seconds—long enough for my magic to immobilize him, slither into his blood, and force him to be as malleable as he wanted us to be. With Tobias at my side to help take down the others, it felt worth the risk to try.

"We could wait for them to come out…" Tobias started walking along the walls, running a hand against them like we had for the glamour in the alleyway. "Though our best bet is to figure out how Silvius is getting from here to the upper levels of the Enclave. Then we can lead the others back here without wasting time walking through the tunnels."

He was right. Even if I had a way to send a message, I had no idea how I would direct anyone here, let alone manage to draw a map of the tunnel system from memory.

"Silvius could be *right there*." The words came out sharper than I intended, frustration lacing every syllable. "Along with the knowledge to save your sister and everyone else he infected."

The muscles in Tobias's jaw went taut as he continued surveying the wall. "I'm not happy about waiting either, Sagray. But I'm not going to take risks when it comes to you. We don't know where that mirror leads or what could be lying in wait for us there. It's not closing, not yet, so we have time to think this through."

I blew out a frustrated breath, turning away from the mirror to face him. "You're right. We should hurry before our friends worry." They no doubt already were. "We should've checked in by now—"

An arm wrapped around my throat, cutting off my scream. My hands reached up instinctively, clawing at the arm as I struggled against its hold.

"*Quinn*," Tobias roared.

The last thing I saw was Tobias's wild eyes as they met mine before I was dragged through the mirror.

CHAPTER 28
TOBIAS

I had been here once before, racing toward a mirror with someone I loved on the other side, only to be a heartbeat too late. My imprisonment, and the circumstance under which I had been forced into that hellhole, made me brutally aware that life didn't allow do-overs, no matter how much I wanted to.

This time, I wouldn't fail.

This time, I didn't hesitate.

Dagger in hand, I dove into the mirror.

I didn't care if two of them were waiting for me or twenty. They would all die for daring to lay a finger on her.

It felt like an eternity and a blink before I was through. My gaze found her the instant my body broke through the other side of the mirror. Quinn struggled in the arms of the hooded figure from the bar, his companion leering at her in a way that made me want to tear him apart with my bare hands. The first had her pinned against his chest, his meaty forearm pressed firmly against her throat and his other hand tight around her wrist so she couldn't use her dagger. I reached for my power, my fury so potent it alone might sear them to the bone—

There was nothing.

My whole body seized as my magic was ripped from my hold, the effect so violent I almost fell to my knees.

"You can't use magic here," the second one sneered as he came toward me.

No wonder their hearts were still beating.

I twisted just in time, barely dodging the ax he swung at me. My attacker was small and quicker on his feet than I expected. Dangerous, especially with the way my head swam as my memories threatened to overwhelm me —the loss of my magic worse than any blow.

But I couldn't be distracted, couldn't let that weakness win. Not when I had to save her.

I slammed those mental cell doors closed, shutting everything out until I was nothing but violence, vengeance, and one all-encompassing thought:

She needed me.

Quinn gasped out a warning. I drove my dagger upward in time to block my opponent's next wild swing. She used the distraction to launch her own attack, clawing at the arm around her throat, kicking backward—trying desperately to find leverage as her face turned purple.

Rage ripped through me, electric and blinding, like a lightning bolt cleaving the sky. I ducked underneath my opponent's ax, turning into him before I threw my head back into his face. His scream was wet as his nose crunched against my skull, his weapon thudding to the floor. I spun, slicing my dagger across his throat. His body fell with a dull thump as I turned to Quinn.

My eyes met hers as I raised my dagger. Quinn's heel slammed into her kidnapper's kneecap. He howled, his grip on her slackening.

It was all the distraction I needed. My thrown dagger lodged into his eye with deadly accuracy, his other eye flaring wide before the life left it.

He deserved a slower death for hurting her...but it would have to do.

I lunged forward, grabbing Quinn before he took her down with him. Blood splattered her cheeks, and I reached up, wiping it away from her cheekbone with my thumb. She coughed loudly as her hand flew to her throat, rubbing the area as she gasped for air.

We needed to get out of here so she could heal herself. My eyes ran over her, checking for any injuries I missed as I demanded, "Besides your throat, are you okay?"

She nodded, her chest heaving as she croaked, "Thank you."

I yanked her into my arms, closing my eyes at the sense of relief that left me trembling. "No need to thank me for that either."

"Where—where are we?"

My eyes flew open. I hadn't taken much notice of our surroundings for once—not when my every thought had been consumed with saving her.

We were in another laboratory. Sterile and eerily familiar.

Quinn let out a small gasp. But no—we weren't in Morehaven. This was an almost exact replica of Silvius's lab there: silver counters and white walls, the same furnishings down to the decanter on the desk. There were no doors; not even a window to give us an idea of where we were. I couldn't even tell if we were still in Mayim.

And in the back of the room was a single cell. Iron bars. Hooks where shackles could be affixed to the stone.

My stomach bottomed out, my entire body shaking. A phantom band tightened around my neck.

"We need to get out of here," Quinn murmured. Her gaze was on the hand I had unknowingly wrapped around my opposite wrist, twisting it against my scars. I dropped it to my side. "If Silvius can somehow block our magic here, there's no telling what else he has up his sleeve. We need to tell the others what happened and quickly."

It took a moment for me to find my voice. "The second he sees the bodies, he'll know he's been compromised." I looked around like Silvius might be lurking beneath one of the ominously bubbling beakers, no doubt brewing whatever fresh nightmare he had planned. "All he has to do is close off the mirror and we'll never find this place again."

I turned to look over at the mirror we traveled through. The frame on this side was embellished with twisting vines that cut into the sides of the glass in repeating loops. Large flowers decorated the vines, each so intricate they looked like real flowers had been coated in gold and affixed to it, never to return to the sunlight. It was smaller than most—the glass itself barely tall enough for me to walk through without ducking my head.

"He could be here any minute if he was supposed to meet them," Quinn retorted, glancing at the mirror.

The mirror rippled faintly as I stepped closer. "I'm going to hazard a guess that this mirror isn't connected to the one in the castle. Which means our only option is going back through the tunnels or finding a glamour."

Quinn glanced around, a scowl pursing her lips as she realized I was right.

I clasped Quinn's hands in mine. My magic warmed my fingertips as it reached for her too. "You go. Find the others and bring them back through the tunnels. I'll wait for Silvius and do my best to keep the gate open."

Quinn glared at me. "Don't you dare even suggest that. I'm not leaving you."

As much as I abhorred the thought of splitting up, she had to survive this, and not just because she was the key to saving everyone else.

"One of us needs to stay—" I tried to persuade her.

"Then you go," she shouted, her suddenly blood-red eyes wild.

It was so unlike her it took me a second to respond.

"I'm not the one who can figure out the cure, Sagray." I glanced at the door, knowing Silvius could return any minute. "We both know who should stay, and it isn't you."

"Then we both leave," she said adamantly, her fingers threading through mine.

I shook my head. "We don't have time to argue."

"Then stop arguing, Maris."

Quinn's chest heaved, that stubborn look on her face nearly bringing a smile to mine. For a moment, all I could think was how beautiful she looked when she was angry, all fire and challenge.

"Quinn, I—" I cut off the words I wanted to say, weakly adding. "I'll come back."

Her eyes went wide. Her nails dug into the back of my hands, her voice going taut as she gasped, "We need to get out of here."

"I just told you—"

"Look."

Quinn pointed behind me, her gaze fixed above my head. A thick cloud of white gas leaked in from a vent on the ceiling, billowing right at us.

I pushed Quinn ahead of me towards the mirror, both of us immediately starting to run. The undoubtably noxious gas expanded toward us like a silent explosion, white tendrils grasping for us with deadly fingers.

Quinn reached back, her hand searching for mine as we neared the mirror without breaking her stride. I took it the moment before we collided with the glass.

Between one ripple and the next, we were gone.

CHAPTER 29
QUINN

Tobias looked furious as we stumbled back into the tunnels. The second I was steady, I immediately placed a hand over his chest. My magic permeated his lungs in a wave of blue, searching for any sign the gas affected him.

"Of course it was a trap," he hissed as lightning flashed across his irises.

I raised my hand against my own chest after I was convinced Tobias was safe, double checking I hadn't inhaled anything dangerous. Then I moved to the bruising around my throat, healing it enough so I could breathe without it hurting me. "He knew, somehow. Our attackers didn't trigger it…we did."

Tobias was shaking—with rage or fear, I couldn't tell. He walked away from me, fists clenched tightly against his sides.

I internally kicked myself for being stupid enough to get captured in the first place. "We need to go get backup."

"By the time we get back through the tunnels, it won't matter." Tobias's shoulders slumped. He drew in a fortifying breath that I found myself mimicking. When he turned around, I nearly flinched at the lack of emotion on his face. "Though we don't have a better choice."

I wanted to hit something…preferably a certain scientist with a god complex and an uncanny ability to stay one step ahead. "Maybe we'll be able to get back through the mirror once the gas is gone…"

Tobias merely jerked his head at the mirror. The edges of the glass had already hardened, like a lake freezing over, its entire surface dimming as the stillness swept inward. We had seconds until it would be impossible to pass through…and no way to stop it.

"We don't even know where that room is." Tobias's toneless voice grated on my already fraying nerves. "There were no windows, no hint that we were still in this city…" He nodded at the tunnel that brought us here. "We should go back before our friends worry."

It was definitely too late for that.

"We should check for a passage through to the Enclave first," I argued, unwilling to give up yet. "If we can at least figure out how he's sneaking in, this won't entirely be a loss."

"If we get backup, it'll be faster than only the two of us searching," Tobias countered stonily. "Besides, Silvius likely knows exactly where we are right now. We need to leave before we're ambushed again."

I hated this. Absolutely hated going back empty-handed almost as much as I hated the emptiness in his voice. We had been so close to finding Silvius, so *close* to everything not resting on my ability to produce a cure.

We could have finished this tonight.

My voice broke as I whispered, "I can't just…give up."

Tobias's eyes softened, the mask he was hiding behind cracking enough to glimpse a flicker of something real. "We tried, Sagray. Sometimes things don't go our way, but that doesn't mean we give up. Far from it."

I wanted to scream, or cry, or both. Instead, I trudged back down the tunnel. Tobias's light footsteps barely echoed behind me, but I knew he was close enough that if I reached back, I could grab his hand.

The light started to fade the further we walked away from the mirror. My clothes, sopping wet from the downpour earlier, were freezing by the time we reached the stagnant water in the tunnels, its level noticeably higher than before. Only darkness lay ahead.

Tobias's magic danced around me as if he had sensed my thoughts, those familiar balls of light bobbing next to my face. They spiraled almost excitedly around my arms and torso before leading the way forward.

I didn't look back.

✧

. . .

We trudged through the water in silence. I had long since started to shiver, the warm rain a distant memory. The steady drip of water had become more urgent, the summer storm bringing the unpleasant smell of brackish water along with it.

I was so lost in thought—caught between self-condemnation and replaying every single thing I could have done differently—that I nearly jumped out of my skin when Tobias took my hand.

"Are you okay—"

His hand clasped over my mouth, pulling me back against his chest with a small splash, just as his lights went out. Only one faint ball of light lingered between us, barely enough to cast Tobias's face in shadow.

"Shh," he breathed against the shell of my ear. "I don't think we're alone."

He was right. The low murmur of voices ahead were barely audible above the sound of the rushing water, but whoever it was blocked our path. They were too far away for me to feel their heartbeats, but I doubted their appearance now was a coincidence.

We had three turns left if I remembered correctly. Three more turns until I could get out of these damn tunnels, walk home in the rain, and wash off the grime and defeat of today. Anyone standing between me and a warm bath were about to find themselves regretting every one of the decisions that put them in my way.

Tobias removed his hand from my mouth, moving it to my waist now that I had gone quiet. The warmth of his fingers against my lips seemed to linger.

Low voices echoed down the tunnel, louder now. Tobias squeezed me more tightly against him.

"We need to get closer," I said under my breath. Close enough for me to determine how many of them there were and then incapacitate them. Maybe we could still get some of the answers we came here for.

Tobias silently drew his dagger. His other hand dropped down to clasp mine tightly as we prowled forward as silently as we could manage. I tensed at every slosh of water, the runoff from the storm now rising over my knees as I reached out with my blood magic…

There were only two of them. I pressed two fingers into Tobias's palm, knowing he would understand my meaning.

They would be easy enough to subdue, even without using my magic. Either Silvius had gravely underestimated us, or they simply had unfortunate timing.

No matter what, I couldn't let them get close to Tobias. If they had a virus meant for him, there was still a chance they could administer it mid-fight—which meant I needed to keep them as far from him as possible. My blood pounded in my ears at the thought of Tobias losing his memory like his sister—except without an *anima* bond to keep his mind safe. The roaring got louder, its crescendo breaking into my dark thoughts as I realized it wasn't inside my own head.

Tobias had gone utterly still beside me. "Quinn..."

The wave of water hit us before I could draw another breath.

CHAPTER 30
TOBIAS

My mind narrowed to a single, desperate thought as we tumbled through the dark water:

Don't let go.

We were helpless as it dragged us back the way we came. There was no sense of up or down. No way to tell when my next breath would be.

I yanked Quinn's hand, pulling close enough to wrap my arms around her. Using my body as a shield as the water battered us against the stone, I fought the merciless pull of the flood as it tried to wrench her away from me. The fear of losing her threatened to drag me under as surely as the water trying to drown us.

Something rammed into my back, pushing the last of the air from my lungs in a brutal crack that sent pain racing through me. I needed to breathe. I needed—

My magic surged from me in my panic, lighting up the raging waters.

There.

One hand released Quinn, and I grabbed at the metal ladder. My fingers wrapped around a rung a moment before we were swept away. I held in my scream as my arm wrenched in its socket. The water pounded against me, trying to tear us apart.

My lungs burned, my bicep straining as I tried to brace myself against the wall, desperately searching for a foothold. Quinn wasn't moving. I realized with dawning horror, her body a dead weight as I kept her afloat. My foot slipped, then caught on a lower rung.

With a final burst of strength, I moved Quinn between me and the bars, then yanked us both upward, gasping in a breath as my face breached the surface. A single ball of my light hovered between us, circling around her like a crazed crown.

"Q-Quinn?" Quinn's head lolled against me, and I fought my terror. It wouldn't help her. "*Quinn.*"

She wasn't breathing. She wasn't *breathing.*

I wedged one arm around the metal rung, then slammed my other hand against her back, once, then again. Tilting her head back against my shoulder to open her airway, I pinched her nose with my opposite hand before sealing my mouth over hers. Her chest rose and fell as I delivered two slow breaths.

The water rushed around us with a vigor I knew wasn't natural, but I couldn't focus on that now. Not when every cell in my body cared only about keeping her alive. Fighting the rising tide and my racing heart, I pounded my hand against her back again.

She had to live. If I lost her...

Quinn coughed so hard she convulsed, spewing water in my face before another cough wracked her frame. The relief flooding through me felt like I was the one finally able to draw in air.

I thumped my hand against her back, trying to help expel the water as I croaked, "Breathe for me, sweetheart."

She sucked in a gasping breath, then another, audible even over the sound of the torrent. I propped her on a higher rung of the ladder as the water rose. Her head almost bumped against the ceiling as I held her there, shielding her with my body.

"I'm okay," Quinn rasped against my ear.

She almost drowned in my arms. I had almost lost her. Neither of us were okay.

I would make them pay for it.

"We need to get out of here," I yelled. The water now reached my chest, its roaring nearly deafening. "There must be an Elemental controlling the flood."

If I could get to them, they would already be dead for hurting her. My light roiled within me, searching for an outlet. Its searing power would only be extinguished by the flood, and lightning would only make this worse.

Quinn closed her eyes. When they opened again, their usual amber had darkened into a dangerous blood red.

She shook her head. "We aren't close enough. I'm having trouble reaching them."

The rushing water tore past me so violently I could barely keep my grip on the ladder, let alone her. But I wouldn't allow myself to be separated from her, even if it broke me in the process.

Perhaps I could blind them. With enough light…

"I can try to—"

"No," Quinn gritted out. "I can do this."

Her red eyes went distant with concentration right before my mouth dipped below the surface. My arms trembled, my muscles screaming for relief, but I wouldn't let go until death released my grip for me.

If this didn't work…

No, I chastised myself. *It would, if only because Quinn didn't know how to fail.*

My arms tightened around her waist, lifting her higher as I took one last deep breath. The current surged, enveloping me entirely—

The water receded so suddenly I nearly fell into the trickle that was left.

Keeping Quinn in my arms, I climbed down the ladder into the flooded tunnel, ignoring the way my shoulders burned as I gripped each rung one-handed. I wanted to collapse on the ground. But I wanted to get out of this fucking deathtrap first.

Quinn silently wrapped her arms around her middle as her feet hit the water, now barely over her ankles. My light circled around her, as terrified for her as I was.

"Are they—"

"Dead." Her tone was so flat a chill went down my spine. For once, Quinn was the emotionless one. "I didn't know which one was doing it…so I killed them both."

She trembled as I held her closer, softly pressing a kiss against her sodden curls. Letting out a shaky breath, she relaxed into my arms.

"You saved us." I held her tighter like my warmth was enough to stop her shivering. "If you hadn't done that, we would've died today."

If I could've done it for her, and kept her from breaking the oath I knew she must have taken in the mortal realm that pledged to do no harm, I would have without a second thought.

"I told myself I would never do that again," Quinn whispered, her anguish starting to crack through. "The reason that type of blood magic is forbidden is because it can corrupt the soul. The stories I read about blood magic said ancient fae would take control of other people's bodies. At first it was used to protect, to stop infighting, and for the greater good. But the more those fae used it, the more that they got used to controlling others..." Her voice shook. "That's when their magic took over their empathy, their understanding of right and wrong. That's when it corrupted their souls. Blood magic wasn't forbidden because of what they could do, but what it did to those who used it. And when they started to stop hearts out of spite, and use it to steal power and murder anyone who stood in their way..." She sucked in a gasping sort of breath. "Tobias, it was so easy to kill them."

I had my power stolen over and over, so many times I was sure the pain alone would kill me. I had looked evil in the face and stared into his tortured, corrupted soul. And I knew, without the shadow of a doubt, that no matter what power she wielded, that fate could never be hers.

"You're the least corruptible person I know." My voice was firm, my confidence in her unshakable. "There's a big difference between using your magic to hurt someone and using it in self-defense. I have no doubt about your strength of heart or the quality of your soul." Shifting her in my arms, I brushed her hair away from her face so that she could see my sincerity. "I know exactly who you are, Quinn Sagray, and nothing will ever change that."

A tear slipped from the corner of her eye, mixing with the wetness on her cheek. She had to be exhausted; her magic spent after days of nonstop work in the lab and harnessing a power she had never really trained.

It was instinct to carry her as I started back toward the entrance. I held her tightly, high above water like she wasn't already soaked through.

Quinn laid her head against my chest as I trudged down the tunnel, ignoring the way my muscles protested. I was thankful her eyes were closed as I turned a corner to find two lifeless bodies floating face down.

She already knew what she had done—had felt the exact moment their hearts stopped—but I walked faster, keeping my body angled away from them in case she opened her eyes. This, at least, I could carry for her.

When I ducked through the glamoured wall back out into the empty streets, the rain had slowed to a sprinkle.

"I can walk," she whispered wearily, making no move to extricate herself from my arms.

"You can," I agreed as I continued holding her against me. "But you don't have to."

Just let me hold you, I wanted to say, but the words stuck on my tongue.

Quinn seemed to hear them anyway. Her arms wrapped tightly around my neck, a soft sigh brushing against the damp skin at the base of my throat as she relaxed against me. I wondered if she could hear the way my heartbeat pounded—slamming against my ribs like it was trying to reach her.

The water in my shoes squished with every step as I carried her back to the castle. I may as well have been cradling my own heart in my hands.

CHAPTER 31
QUINN

I closed my eyes for a moment, lulled by the sound of Tobias's heartbeat under my ear and the swaying motion of each step. Everything hurt after being knocked around in that tunnel, the pain in my chest growing worse even as I gave in to my exhaustion.

All I wanted was some sleep and for him to never let me go.

"Quinn?" Tobias's voice cut through my muddled thoughts. "*Quinn*!"

The panic in his voice made me fight to open my eyes. I couldn't remember ever hearing him sound so frightened.

It was all I could do to cling to consciousness as he broke into a run, his arms almost painfully tight as his footsteps pounded in a frantic rhythm. My chest hurt worse with each jostling movement. I wanted to say something, anything—but I couldn't speak, could barely breathe.

Then came an order: *"Help her."* Not just a plea but a command.

A warm hand touched my collarbone, green light shining through my eyelids. The knot in my chest immediately eased, and a violent cough wracked my body, every hack excruciating. Then came a loud and very concerned, "What the hell happened?"

Tobias's familiar scent wrapped around me as securely as his arms. His voice shook as he whispered, so quietly it might have been to himself, "Oh gods, sweetheart…I thought I lost you."

The endearment struck me square in the chest. It wasn't just the word, but the way he had said it, tinged with affection like it was something he had called me for years.

I strained to open my eyes. We were just outside the Atrium, the sky dark but no longer stormy. Rivan looked down at me, his healing magic still glowing at his fingertips. Yael and Pari lingered just behind him, their expressions etched with concern.

Their presence barely registered. Not as Tobias's gaze desperately searched my face, the raw, unguarded expression on it leaving me breathless. Fear and pure, unadulterated relief, all tangled with a possessive look in his eyes that made my heart skip concerningly.

"You had water in your lungs," Rivan said grimly. "Something you might have noticed if you hadn't completely burned yourself out." He tilted his head at Tobias. "You're lucky he got you here when he did."

"I'm okay," I said just as a yawn overtook me. "A little waterlogged."

Tobias stared at me, incredulous. "A *little*?"

"We've been searching for you two," Yael said breathlessly. "What happened to sending a message?"

Pari let out a scoff. "What happened to *not* engaging?"

Tobias brushed past them, still holding me as he brought us inside the inner atrium of the Enclave. "We said we would try. In a world of magic, you would think having something dry to write on wouldn't be an issue. And yet..."

I looked over his shoulder, blearily taking in the watery trail we had left behind us, each of Tobias's steps marked with its own puddle. A few healers looked at us curiously, probably about to direct us to the hospital wing.

"You can put me down now," I said tiredly.

He had the audacity to roll his eyes. "We've been over this, Sagray. Now, do I need to get the Queen herself to take a look at your lungs or are you certain you're okay?"

I closed my eyes, letting the dregs of my magic delve into my chest. Whatever water had remained in my lungs was gone now.

"I'm fine, I promise," I said with a reassuring smile. "Thanks to both of you."

Rivan folded his arms across his chest. "Do either one of you want to explain why you're half-drowned?"

"Trust me, it's much better than the alternative," I mumbled. With a sigh, I gave them an abbreviated version of what happened as Tobias carried me to our rooms, though I left out any mention of my blood magic. Tobias interjected only to clarify the directions to the alleyway and the path we had taken through the tunnels.

"We'll send our people to the mirror straight away," Pari said. "We can see if we can figure out the path Silvius used to get into the Enclave and if there are any clues as to where that mirror led."

Tobias's fingers dug into my thigh and upper arm at the mention of Silvius's name. There was something entirely overprotective about the way he held on to me—something I didn't mind in the least.

"I doubt he'll be stupid enough to reopen that mirror." Tobias's voice was full of self-recrimination at the missed opportunity. "But if there is a way up to the Enclave, it's worth continuing the search to see who else he's working with."

I lifted my hand unthinkingly, stroking the stubble on his cheek. "We did our best. Just because we didn't find him doesn't mean this is a defeat. We're close to curing this even without Silvius's confession."

Light warmed his eyes, his expression softening. There was a long pause…and I realized everyone was staring at us. My face heated as my hand fell away.

"Not to add any pressure," Yael said hesitantly. "But do you have a timeline for when this cure might be ready? Marin hasn't mentioned any change…but, reading between the lines, she seems worried about the effects of keeping Eva and Bash in that state for too long."

"We'll see how the compounds we're testing do first thing in the morning," I said, mentally crossing my fingers at least one of them worked. "I'll send her an update as soon as we do."

"Quinn's close," Tobias added. "If it's not this round, it will be soon."

"*We're* close," I corrected him.

He glanced skyward, wearily conceding, "I'm just glad I can feel like I helped somehow."

I frowned at him. "Are you kidding me, Maris? This wouldn't have been possible without you." I shifted in his arms to better face him. "You're the one who found Silvius's notes after Eva fell ill, and you've been there every step of the way since. You've been there every day in the lab assisting me in more ways than I can count." Tobias opened his mouth to object, but I wasn't done. "You saved me from drowning and from my own self-doubt. We wouldn't just have a potential cure without you…I wouldn't be *alive* without you." The words tumbled out, needing to be said. "You didn't just help, you idiot. You're extraordinary."

He looked at me askance, his expression unreadable. Then his eyes softened, and a full, real smile lifted his lips—one I hadn't seen in a long time. It was so heart-stopping that I nearly forgot how to breathe.

I didn't miss the glance Yael exchanged with Pari as Rivan darted around us to open the door to our shared living space. With a sigh, I weakly pushed against Tobias's chest. Tobias seemed as reluctant to let me go as I was to let him, but he lowered me to my feet without further comment. I hadn't realized the top buttons of his shirt had been ripped away at some point, leaving a smattering of dark chest hair exposed. The wet fabric clung to his pectorals beneath my hand. I forced my eyes away from the tantalizing sight and back up to his face.

His fingers tightened against my waist, making sure I was steady, but he didn't let go. A smile quirked my lips as I raised an eyebrow in question.

A blush tinged his cheeks as his hand dropped to his side.

"Hopefully the mirror wasn't washed away," I muttered as I walked toward my bedroom. I needed the warmest shower possible before I went to sleep. There were scant hours left before the lab opened, and I refused to waste a single second when it came to finding my best friend's cure.

"Gates are more fragile when they're closed," Pari said from behind me. "It's the only time the glass can be broken. Hopefully the water didn't get that far, but we'll know soon enough."

I faintly remembered reading that somewhere. Usually, the mirror's magic meant they barely showed sign of wear. It made sense, especially after the Seeing Mirror's lack of rust after so long entombed in Adronix. I hadn't considered what conditions would be necessary to break one.

If I had been raised here, these would be facts I would know by rote. Sometimes it bothered me that I had spent so many years in the mortal realm and missed out on so many formative moments here. However, considering the medical prowess I earned there was going to save my best friend, I could never regret my upbringing.

Tobias stumbled towards his room, his feet dragging with every step. Hadn't he been reading about the magic behind the mirror gateways before we left for Morehaven? I wasn't the only one who had been reintroduced to this realm, or trying to make up for lost time…

"Wait," I pleaded.

He stopped immediately, pivoting back towards me with a puzzled tilt of his head. The tension in his posture seemed to ease as I came closer.

"I never checked your lungs," I said, quickly raising my hand. My healing magic felt as sluggish as I did, though my fingertips turned a familiar blue. "Can I?"

Tobias frowned. "Are you sure you're up to it?"

Rivan opened his mouth, likely to volunteer, then shut it as I shot him a glare. Drained or not, I needed to be sure Tobias was safe myself.

He inhaled sharply as my hand flattened against his bare chest. Part of me felt vindicated that he was just as affected as me, the other part was too tired to think about what that meant—not just what we were to each other, but what I wanted us to be. Instead, I focused on my magic, letting it flow from his trachea into each bronchus, filling both lungs to ensure he hadn't inhaled any water.

I looked up at him as my magic faded away. His eyes crinkled slightly around the edges, the gold flecks in his irises glistening in the light.

His voice was low as he drawled, "So?"

I blinked up at him, dropping my hand. "You—you're okay. Nothing to be concerned about."

Biting my lower lip, I stepped back, swaying slightly. He reached for my hand, tugging me back against him.

A muscle ticked in his jaw. "*You're* not."

"I'm fine," I muttered. "Just wiped out. It's nothing a warm shower and a good night's sleep can't fix."

Pari stepped up next to me, and I nearly started in surprise. I forgot we had an audience.

"I'll make sure you don't fall asleep in the shower," Pari chuckled, taking my arm.

Tobias relinquished his hold, a flicker of disappointment crossing his face. With a knowing smile, Pari led me into my room, then closed the door behind us.

"You don't actually have to stay," I mumbled as I walked into my bathroom, stripping as I went. I didn't care about propriety, especially since nudity was far less scandalous in this realm, and I had no qualms about Pari seeing me naked. I kicked the soggy, mud-coated garments into a pile. There was no chance they could be salvaged.

"I figured I would give Tobias the chance to bathe rather than wait outside your door to make sure you made it from the shower to the bed," Pari said, a smile in her voice as she turned on the shower. "It's nice seeing him out and about again, despite the circumstances."

My sigh of relief echoed through the bathroom as I stepped behind the turquoise tinted glass and into the hot shower. I let the water run down my face and chest, thankful for the magic that meant I didn't have to wait for it to warm up, though my extremities felt like they were burning.

I spent far too long scrubbing myself clean, washing my hair more than once before I rinsed off the suds. By the time I toweled off, Pari had placed a glass of water on my bedside table and laid a simple black nightgown on the bed.

"Thank you," I said as I slipped it on. "I think I can handle it from here though."

Pari nodded but stayed where she was. "Actually…I wanted to apologize to you."

"For what?"

She shifted on her feet, brushing her silver hair behind her ear. I couldn't remember ever seeing Pari nervous in all the time I had known her—but something was obviously bothering her.

"It's been different between us, since you told me about your magic."

Part of me wanted to ask her whose fault that was. A bigger part of me knew the courage it had taken to bring it up. With a deep sigh, I slipped between my seafoam green sheets.

"I understand that there are well-founded fears about blood magic in this realm," I said softly. "Especially seeing how Eva's blood was stolen and used against her. I don't blame you for your concern."

Pari surveyed me, then rubbed the back of her neck with a sigh. "*You've* only used your magic to help people," she said at last. "…even when you used it to kill."

I blinked at her, unsure how to respond. Pari smirked in an echo of her usual self.

"Did you think I didn't read between the lines?" She looked almost disappointed in me. "You and Tobias were trapped in the tunnel, flood waters rising and no way out. It wasn't hard to figure out how you killed them."

"It was the only way." I sank back into my pillow, suddenly feeling too heavy to stay sitting up. "I haven't used that power since we were under Adronix. I didn't want to…but I had to save him."

Pari sat on the edge of the bed. "Maybe that's the difference."

Maybe it was. Maybe my intention mattered more than my methods. Or maybe the actions of a few had irrevocably tainted the image of a rare magic—the true harm not in the power itself but in those who didn't deserve to wield it.

Pari cleared her throat. "When we get back to Soleara, I'll see what I can do to help you research more about it—maybe we can even find others who haven't told anyone about their gifts for fear of being ostracized." She got to her feet. "But I wanted to make sure you knew I'm working on my preconceptions, and the prejudice that came with them. I won't leave you to figure it out on your own again, my friend."

"Thank you," I said quietly. "I appreciate that more than you know."

Pari gave me a grateful smile. I returned it fleetingly before it split into a wide yawn.

"I'll let you get some rest now," Pari said. "Thank *you* for being more gracious than I would've been in your place."

She flicked off the lights before closing the door behind her.

I stared at the space where she had stood, wondering if it had really been that easy. If maybe hiding this part of who I was had never been as dire as it seemed.

What would my blood magic be like if I were to train it rather than hide it away? What if I used it—not to control anyone, but to help others, like any other facet of my healing magic?

Maybe the fear of what I was told I would become had kept me from being everything I could be.

Between one breath and the next, I drifted off to sleep.

CHAPTER 32
TOBIAS

There were circles under Quinn's eyes as she worked, but she didn't let on how exhausted she was—with the blatant exception of drinking three extra cups of tea in addition to the one I greeted her with this morning. I made sure to add some extra honey after seeing the way she added more to the first, then spooned a more reasonable amount into my own. The loose-leaf black tea was spiced with cardamom and cloves, a single star anise escaping the strainer into Quinn's cup. When I tried to fish it out with a spoon, Quinn shooed me away.

She smiled down at how its eight points whirled in wild circles every time I handed her a refill. The sight of her smile made my chest twist with something I refused to identify, even as I made a mental note to include another spinning star tomorrow.

I tried not to groan at the new rows of test tubes—the reminder that the original batch of potential antiviral compounds hadn't worked. It was hard not to feel discouraged, though Quinn had assured me that finding out what didn't work was a crucial step in narrowing down what did. Quinn finished imbuing the next round of compounds as I watched, wishing I could do more to help.

She seemed unusually melancholy today, and far quieter. Perhaps it was the events of last night weighing on her…or she was simply too tired from our ordeal in the tunnels to have her regular amount of cheer.

Even Dolion poured an extra cup of tea for himself as he helped add different compounds to Eva's infected cells. His skin looked sallow, a tinge of gray to his hair I hadn't noticed before. He sneered when he caught me watching him—though the second Quinn glanced over at us, he abruptly looked away.

His tone took on a simpering quality I hated more every time I heard him talk to her. It was an effort not to stand between them and pick my nails with my dagger as they discussed the most promising compounds based on their last round, and what they would try next should they fail.

Something about his smile made me the hair rise on the back of my neck. Quinn, however, didn't seem to find anything amiss. She ran the tip of her pen across the seam of her lips as they went through the list together, snagging my attention more with each pass. The unconscious but sensual movement heated my blood. I turned to make a fresh pot of tea to distract myself…and so I wouldn't get caught staring.

After I left her door last night, sleep eluded me despite my exhaustion. Every time I closed my eyes, all I could see were her waterlogged curls plastered to her face, her chest unmoving as I begged her to breathe. Every time I looked her way, all I could feel was her limp body in my arms as I pleaded with her to come back to me.

I had stared at the ceiling for most of the night, too scared to visit my nightmares about what could've happened instead.

Despite my best efforts, I drifted off sometime before sunrise. I woke sweaty and gasping, even though I had moved to the cold floor, the image of her drowning burned into my brain.

It had taken every bit of my concentration to push that narrowly subverted fate into the prison I had created.

There was a flash out of the corner of my eye, the glare bright enough that I stopped and stared. Quinn and Dolion were deep in conversation by his desk. Neither seemed to notice the sudden change in the sample they had been working on.

I cleared my throat. "Is it…supposed to do that?"

Quinn's head whipped around, her eyes immediately finding the test tube. Her smile was so bright it rivaled the light coming from it.

Dolion merely arched an eyebrow. "It seems we have a viable compound. The light is a marker we use to show if a trial is successful." He cleared his throat, like our joy was unbecoming. "Of course, we'll have to confirm that the treatment inhibits viral replication without harming healthy cells before moving on to the next round of testing."

"Of course," I said wryly.

Quinn's gaze was glassy as she stared at the fading light. I wanted to pick her up and twirl her around. To shout from the nearest window that her brilliance might have saved us all.

Instead, I crossed the room and took both of her hands in mine, holding them tightly. "You did it," I whispered, my voice full of awe.

Smiling, she shook her head. "No, *we* did this, Maris."

"I hope you realize it's impossible to give you too much credit," I quipped, though I meant every word.

Quinn's smile grew. "As long as you realize I couldn't have done it without—"

Dolion cleared his throat, his voice brusque as he grumbled, "As touching as this is, this is far from a cure. While the nature of magical compounds and the imbuing process generally rules out cytotoxicity—"

"—we still need to make sure it's not harmful to healthy cells and tissues," Quinn finished. Her excitement was tangible as she turned to me, explaining, "Next step is to make sure our antiviral can target the virus without causing too much damage to the body's normal functions."

I smiled at her, her delight infectious. Quinn's eyes widened, something like hope glimmering in them. She squeezed my hands once before letting go.

"Let's get back to work."

✧

It was late by the time we finished for the day. Quinn was still buzzing with renewed excitement, a wide grin on her face even with her fatigue. She and Dolion had spent the day fine-tuning the potential cure's chemical structure. The draining medical and magical process had her leaning heavily against me as we walked back to our rooms. I kept my arm tightly wrapped around her despite her insistence that I wasn't the only thing holding her upright.

My hand was cramped and aching after a day of writing down the different dosages we were testing, but I barely noticed now that it rested on her waist. Her flowy linen pants and cropped blouse left an inch of skin exposed...and it was all I could do not to drag my thumb against it. The sand-colored set was decorated with a delicate floral pattern, and I contented myself with tracing slow circles around the flower beside my thumb.

Quinn's breath caught as my thumb trailed upward despite myself, a charge dancing between us the moment I touched bare skin.

Even that slight contact made my pulse race. She shivered slightly as I squeezed her hip, drawing her closer as we turned a corner. Suddenly all I could think about was if she would shiver like that if I had her splayed out on the nearest bed, writhing beneath my tongue.

She turned her face to mine, and I leaned in, our noses nearly brushing. She released a shuddering breath against my lips—

"There you two are," Pari said from behind us, and we jumped apart. There was a laugh in her voice as she asked, "Were you planning on going in?"

I was so caught up in watching Quinn's smile that I hadn't realized we had reached our rooms. Pari smirked at me.

"Thinking about it," Quinn said cajolingly.

She reached for the doorknob, and I stepped forward with her, not entirely sure if she would remain standing if I let go of her. A hollow sigh escaped her lips as I half-carried her through the doorway.

A mouthwatering scent hit me the second I did. I could barely remember the last time I felt hungry, let alone this ravenous. Rivan sprang to his feet from where he and Yael sat at the table, concern filled his gaze as he took in Quinn's weary form.

"Quinn may have overdone it," I muttered as she scowled at me.

Rivan's magic glowed at his fingertips as he demanded, "Do you need a healer?"

"I'm fine," Quinn said, sounding exasperated as she stumbled away from me. I remained close as she laboriously sat at the table, pushing her chair in for her. "Nothing food and rest can't fix."

Yael poured Quinn a glass of water. As she gulped it down, I added a few things that I knew she would like to her plate—grilled fish covered in cilantro, yellow mangos and watermelon dusted with spices, and a white fish ceviche—before making one for myself. I was glad that my stomach was again interested in food, but I wished I was back home where every dish wasn't quite so fishy. Quinn gave me a grateful smile as I sat down beside her, pulling my chair closer to hers.

"I'm not going to pass out at the table." The amusement was clear in Quinn's voice as she took in the negligible space between our seats.

"After last night's adventure, you should've spent today in bed," I said crossly.

Quinn blinked at me, then a sly smile crept across her face. "Is that so?"

My cheeks heated as I replayed my own words, and victory danced in her eyes. I leaned closer tilting my head so my lips nearly brushed the shell of her ear, so only she could hear me.

"When this is over," I drawled, my voice dipping low, "I'm going to make sure you get some rest, even if I have to tie you to the bedframe myself."

It was her turn to flush. Her swallow and the heat in her gaze left no doubt about her desire for exactly that. I resisted the urge to throw her over my shoulder, carry her to my room, and make good on that promise now as all the blood in my body rushed south.

Clearing my throat, I sat back upright, muttering, "In the meantime, eat something. You'll need your strength."

Quinn's lip twitched as she whispered, "Yes, sir."

Those two words nearly tipped me over the edge, especially as she did as ordered.

I could feel Yael's and Rivan's attention on us as they kept talking. By their body language alone, I knew their search hadn't been fruitful. Pari let me know this morning that the mirror was intact but closed. It and the entrance to the tunnels remained guarded by a rotating contingent of Imyrian rangers.

"I hope whatever you did today was worth it," Pari said, eyeing the way Quinn was scarfing down food at an alarming rate.

"Actually..." I waited for Quinn to swallow, wanting her to be the one to share the good news. "It was."

Quinn gave me a close-lipped smile before taking a sip of water. "It's too early to say we have a cure. There's still testing to be done to determine if it's safe to try it on Eva..."

Yael leaned forward. "But?"

"We have a strong contender. Which means we're almost there."

Quinn speared a piece of melon with her fork, biting into it with a happy sigh. Her tongue darted out, catching some of the juice that dribbled down her lower lip. I bit back a groan.

Pari chuckled under her breath, smirking at me, and I forced my gaze away.

"Any luck today?" I asked her in a blatant attempt to distract both her and myself.

Pari shook her head as she added some chips to her plate. "Unfortunately, no. If there *is* a glamoured secret passage the leads up to the Enclave, we couldn't locate it." She looked as frustrated as I felt. "We'll keep guard to be sure the mirror doesn't reopen without us knowing."

"We did manage to round up some of Silvius's network though," Yael added as she spooned herself a second serving. "It seems he couldn't get the word out quickly that the tunnel entry was compromised. We took a page out of his book and had a few water elementals lay in wait."

Quinn shuddered, and I barely suppressed my own. The memory of her drowning was far too fresh, the way the water had tried to tear her from my arms...

The room seemed to blur around me as I relived the moment that I almost lost her. My desperation and panic rose inside my chest like it might implode, the spiral of my thoughts dragging me under as surely as that dark water...

I had almost *lost* her.

I had almost lost *her.*

And it would've been all my fault.

I needed to shove these feelings down before someone saw them and used them against me. I needed to cage them off before that panic caged me. I needed—

Quinn took my hand, her voice low as she asked, "Are you alright?"

I couldn't find the breath to speak. The scar around my neck tightened until I thought I might choke. I needed to get out of here before they all saw me break down.

Blue flared from Quinn's hand where our fingers entwined like she might somehow be able to heal me.

"Hey," she said urgently. "Big breath in."

Though, based on the way I could suddenly draw in a full breath…maybe she could.

The table had gone silent, our joint exhale far too loud. Quinn either didn't notice, or more likely, didn't care. She waited for me to breathe in before joining in with me.

Letting my guard down felt a lot like surrender. And yet, with each breath, the need to push my terror down ebbed, no longer something to cage but something I might finally be able to bear.

My hand shook slightly as I squeezed Quinn's in a silent thank you. Unable to look her in the eyes a moment longer, I reached for my water, emptying the glass in three large gulps.

Pari pointedly cleared her throat like she could distract the rest of them from my panic attack…or at least its aftermath. A futile endeavor with everyone's eyes still locked on me, but one I couldn't help but appreciate as Yael and Rivan looked her way.

I refilled my glass as Pari asked, "Are they still questioning them?"

Rivan grimaced. "The Mayimites are trying to get more from them, but I don't think they were trusted with anything more than they already told us. No one could tell us Silvius's whereabouts, or where the mirror leads, at least not yet."

Silvius was still out there, growing more desperate and dangerous the more we hunted him. He was likely behind the order to drown us both—and he was sure to escalate his attacks if he learned a cure was in reach.

"Quinn's too close to finding a cure for him not to strike again," I said grimly. "Especially if his moles get wind of it."

Though only one of the males I killed in Silvius's lab wore healer's robes, I doubted he was the only healer loyal to him, or, more accurately, their dead king.

"Queen Sariyah remains adamant the Enclave is safe from Silvius and his people, despite our evidence to the contrary." Pari closed her eyes as she rubbed her temples. She had no doubt been more diplomatic than I would have been. "If we try to station our own people to guard you two as you work, we risk causing a diplomatic incident. If we ask her to have her people do so…"

"…then we'll end up with guards we can't trust," Rivan finished. "Which is likely worse than none at all."

Whether it risked inciting something or not, my sword was coming with me tomorrow. I already kept my dagger hidden on me, as did Quinn, despite the Enclave's rules otherwise. Even if one of Silvius's supporters caught us off guard in the warded laboratory, there were few who would be able to best my Celestial magic in a fight…or survive Quinn's ability to stop their hearts with a mere thought.

I knew she would use whatever she had to in order to protect us. She made that infinitely clear last night. I also knew how much she would hate herself for doing so.

The thought that Quinn could possibly be corrupted was ludicrous. I had always known exactly who she was—even when we were kids, she had been the kindest of us, born with empathy, a quiet understanding, and an unfailing desire to help. She had been the one to bring the wounded bird home we found on the walk home from school and nurse it back to health. And she had been the one to stand up to high school bullies not by beating them up, though she could, but by befriending them—somehow speaking to their loneliness rather than stoking their anger.

The fact that she feared the possibility at all was enough to make me certain her humanity would remain firmly intact…never mind the semantics that she wasn't human and never had been. Her soul was unassailable, not because she was free of darker impulses, but because her heart refused to yield to it. She was far too steadfast, too empathetic, too good to let the evil she imagined take root.

She was the best person I had ever known. And nothing, not even so-called dark magic, would change that.

"We can handle it," I promised. "You all need to focus on finding him. I'll keep Quinn safe while she finds a cure."

I didn't know when her safety became my top priority, or if it always had been, but somewhere along the way it stopped feeling like a choice.

Quinn reached for a roll, the movement awkward as her hand crossed her body. Only then did I realize her closer hand was still clasped in mine. I made to pull away, but she stopped me with a look. There was a hint of embarrassment in her voice as she muttered, "I may need your help standing once I finish this."

My voice dropped to a near growl. "I'll happily carry you to bed, Sagray."

There was that blush again. She finished off the roll, popping the last bite of it in her mouth, then pushed up from the table.

I hastily got to my feet. "I can help clear—"

Pari shook her head, waving us both off. "Go get some rest. You'll need it for tomorrow."

"Thanks," I said as Yael and Rivan said their goodnights.

Quinn took a step, then stumbled. Without letting myself think too hard about it, I scooped her into my arms. She didn't object as I walked through the threshold to her room and set her gently on the bed. Then I dropped to my knees beside it.

Her sandals had leather ties that laced around her ankles. The knots took me a few seconds to undo before I pulled her shoes off one by one and set them on the ground beside me.

When I looked up, Quinn's mouth had fallen wide open.

Hastily, I got to my feet. "Sorry, I thought you might need some—"

She quickly exclaimed, "I appreciate it—"

"—help considering—"

"—I was just taken by surprise."

The silence stretched between us. I brushed my hand through my hair, the dark tendrils immediately falling back in my eyes.

Those amber eyes softened though her blush remained. A few curly locks had escaped her ponytail, perfectly framing her face. Her blouse had fallen down her shoulder, the slight puff of her sleeve cupping her upper arm, her chest strained against the neckline as her breasts begged to be freed.

For one bold heartbeat, I pictured myself taking her face in my hands and giving in to everything I wanted.

I wanted to hear her moans. I wanted to hear her beg me for more. I wanted to get back on my knees, throw those toned thighs over my shoulders and feel her come apart on my tongue.

Quinn sounded breathless as she asked, "Was there something you still needed?"

You, I almost said. *I always need you.*

Something still held me back, a certainty of my failings that no longer felt absolute. I may never be worthy of her…but denying her? That was a different kind of battle, and one I already knew I would lose.

Maybe I was starting to trust her when she told me I mattered in all this —that I mattered, period—and was somehow essential to finding this cure. Maybe her confidence, and the way she depended on me, had started to change how I measured my self-worth. And when she called me extraordinary?

Maybe I finally wanted to believe it too.

I backed up so quickly my shoulder smacked against the doorframe. Holding in my wince, I awkwardly stepped to the side and pivoted, blindly grasping for the doorknob as I propelled my body through.

"Goodnight," I said, my voice strained as I shut the door behind me.

CHAPTER 33
TOBIAS

The screams were familiar, a daily refrain from which there was no escape. I steeled myself against the terror and pain in the ensuing cries for help, pushing my own feelings down until I couldn't feel my guilt anymore. There was nothing I could do to end the poor soul's suffering.

My inaction never ceased to feel wrong, but throwing myself against the metal bars that caged me had proven no more helpful. So I sat here in silent vigil, waiting for the quiet that meant it was my turn. I had learned the hard way that there was nothing I could do that would change their fate, nor my own.

Aviel's prisoners never lasted long, especially lately. He was using his stolen magic more recklessly, more often. Unlike all the others, he would make sure I survived until he had no more need for my magic, taking me to the edge of death before healing me just enough to live another day.

Not for the first time, I considered giving in to the obvious alternative.

There was a heaviness in my bones, one that warred daily with the voice inside me telling me to keep fighting. That voice had become as muzzled as I was, its strength fading as the days turned to weeks and the months turned to years. It was only a matter of time before the voice failed, and my fight along with it...along with my will to live.

It felt like forever since I had been truly warm. Since sunlight had touched my skin, since the sky had been anything but a memory. Its color had dimmed in my recollection, washed out to the pale, icy blue of Aviel's eyes. Even the memories I clung to in order to keep going weren't safe to dwell on long, in case they could be used against me.

Soleara still stood. Eva was still out there, safe and hidden from the False King despite his search for her. And Quinn...

No, I couldn't let myself think of Quinn...though the flash of warm amber eyes and that brilliant smile felt like a ray of sunshine had found its way into my cell. To do so would loosen the lock on the place deep inside me where I had hidden her away. And if I removed the heart of my secrets, everything I built to contain them threatened to collapse.

The screams had dwindled into a quiet that was somehow far worse. Silence was my constant companion, but this moment of quiet wasn't peace—it echoed with loss, death, and despair.

It also meant I was next.

I was used to pain. Used to the slow mending of injuries, the heated, aching limbs, the days it took for a wound to scab before it fully closed. After so long being tortured mentally and physically, it was second nature to compartmentalize. To push that torment into its own cage, where I couldn't feel it anymore.

All I needed to do was outlast Aviel for one more day before I woke up and did it all over again.

Dread twisted in my stomach as Aviel walked to my cell, commanding Sylvius to unlock it. Over the years, I had tried to fight my way out, to choose my moment—preying on the times when Aviel seemed drained or distracted to attempt to make my escape. Weakened, chained, and magicless as I was, I never managed to get very far, and bore the scars for each attempt.

But delaying the inevitable had always been the plan, by any means necessary.

Aviel hadn't broken me. Not yet. He had broken my bones and spilled my blood too many times to count. He had gloated time and time again about the lives he had stolen, both of my parents topping that list. He drained my magic so often that I barely remembered a time when my own power hadn't been used to hurt me, especially with the band around my neck blocking it from my reach. Torture had become a constant, a horrific, endless routine.

My mind remained the only safe place I had left; my most important memories unreachable in the mental cages I built for them. There was stubbornness, and then there was whatever kept me from letting him in.

From the first time Aviel used his magic to try to pry my secrets from me, I spent each isolated minute here locking my memories away. I pictured the dungeon I was trapped in, staring at the real version in front of me as I did so. To stave off my panic, I focused on recreating each detail: the rough stone stained with grime, the grayish light that cast long shadows at the base of each iron bar. I memorized each cell, down to the condensation on the walls and the musty scent of decay.

Aviel's obsession with my sister had given me one small advantage. By the time he realized that I had been sharing only the most innocuous memories of Eva to distract him during our torture sessions, I had locked the ones that would lead him to her and to Soleara so deep in my mind that not even he could break in.

And every time I heard the screams that had become my constant companions, I would lock them away too before that suffering could break me. I became as cold as the mask that leeched the warmth from my face, its weight a constant source of claustrophobia. Icy like the iron shackles that bound me, and the constrictive band around my neck, though neither were as cold as my heart had become.

For the people I loved to survive him, I couldn't...at least not as the person I used to be. I couldn't let myself feel anymore. Not pain, not anguish, not fear or terror. Not even the slightest glimmer of hope that I would make it through this to see them again.

Honestly, it was better if I didn't. I didn't want them to see me like this, this cold, hard shell of the boy they once loved. But I couldn't do this forever. Every time I erected another stone, another barrier in my mind, Aviel delighted in punishing me for it in his attempts to tear it down.

He had nothing but time. I might endure battle after battle, but this war of attrition was one I couldn't win.

No matter the cost, I intended on making it very, very difficult for him for as long as I could. After all, Aviel couldn't kill me—not while he still needed my magic and my blood. So despite the blades he used to mark me and the earthshattering pain that wracked me every time he stole my magic, I would grit my teeth and bear it...or rather, bury it away. Even as a small part of me hoped he would go too far and kill me this time.

But if he thought I would stop fighting him, he was very fucking mistaken.

Pale eyes met mine. Fear coursed through my body even as I tried to push it away. Sylvius had already boasted about his plan for Aviel to reach Eva through the bloodbond between us. I was certain this new method would be no less painful than Aviel's previous attempts to ascertain my twin's whereabouts.

Part of me was proud that the mental fortress I built had proven so difficult to invade. The rest of me was terrified that I was about to lose—that this was the moment I would fail my twin and the final promise I had made my mother. All because I was too much of a coward to bash my head in against the metal of the mask that was already leeching the life from me.

It was one thing to guard my memories, but how was I supposed to protect the blood that linked us when every inch of this cell had been covered in it?

My breathing picked up as Aviel stalked closer. He hadn't been able to get much of a rise out of me the last few times he ripped my magic away, and the glint in his eyes laid bare his excitement. I barely felt the bands of my stolen light forcing me to the ground until my mask slammed against the stone. My hands trembled, my body expecting the pain now, even as it made me focus.

Whatever came next, I would fight it with everything I had.

Aviel's hand pressed the back of my head down, shoving my face against the cold, hard metal.

"You could simply tell me where she is," he taunted me. "It would save you so much pain."

I braced myself for the onslaught, shoving my feelings, my memories, and my last dregs of hope behind lock and key.

Aviel's laugh was cold and cruel. "Have it your way."

I would keep them safe. I wouldn't fail them. I couldn't—

A scream tore from my throat, the agony so acute that I broke through the magic stifling my voice. I could taste the iron of my blood; the salt of sweat and tears. I vaguely wondered if I had bitten through my tongue again.

"Tobias!"

Quinn.

I screamed again as my stolen light seared me from the inside out. Her name stuck in my throat as I fought to get to her with everything I had.

No, no, no...she couldn't be here. This had to be another trick. If she was here, that meant that not only had I failed her...I failed them all.

Because if they had her, I would tell them anything *to keep her safe.*

"Tobias, please!"

I couldn't let them hurt her. I wasn't strong enough to stand it.

She was who I held on for, who I lived for.

With one final fortifying breath, I summoned the last of my courage. If I gave my life to save her, then it would be a life well spent.

It was always all for her, anyway.

CHAPTER 34
QUINN

I didn't know what was worse, the fact that Tobias was obviously screaming in pain, or that when he did, he barely made a sound. He had thrown the blankets from the bed, his shirtless form twisted in the sheets. Tears streamed down his face; his expression crumpled in an agony so intense, my magic felt like it might burst through my chest.

Before I even realized I had moved, I was at his side, crawling onto his bed. Just as I was about to reach him, his back bowed and a terrifying guttural sound emitted from deep in his throat.

I gripped his face, taking it between my hands as I cried out his name, begging for him to hear me. The sound of my voice only seemed to make him thrash more frantically. A blue glow sank into his skin as my magic reached for him too, trying to heal his terror.

"Wake up," I demanded, my voice desperate. "You're having a nightmare."

"*No*," Tobias choked out, struggling in my grip. "D-don't hurt her."

"Tobias," I pleaded as my thumbs traced his cheek. "Open your eyes. For me."

He reared back, and my hands slid down to his neck. In a blink, two large, tanned hands fastened around my wrists like shackles. The next second, I was underneath him.

My hands were pinned on either side of my head, Tobias's body pressing mine into the bed. His hair fell into his face, something feral behind his eyes as he looked around unseeingly.

"Tobias, please..." I whispered, my fear for him multiplying.

His gaze was glassy, wide, and wild with fear. "I won't let him hurt you."

My heart broke at the look on his face. "I know."

Tobias's unfocused eyes looked back and forth, searching for a threat that wasn't there. A breath shuddered through him, then another. His whole body trembled, shaking so hard he was practically vibrating.

Carefully, I let my magic reach for him again, trying to break him free of this. That familiar blue light raced up his arms before it faded into his veins. Light flashed at his fingertips before melting into mine, our magics coming together like old friends.

I felt the exact moment Tobias came back to himself, the way his muscles relaxed at my magic's urging. His breathing steadied, his bare chest glistened with sweat as it rose and fell at a more regular rhythm. I tried not to think about how intimately we were positioned, but his hold on me stayed firm, his hard body heavy over mine.

His face slackened, his eyes coming into focus before staring deeply into my own. The horror on his face slid into confusion, then a tenuous calm.

"It was just a nightmare," I reassured him, keeping my voice low and soothing.

He shook his head, the movement jerky. "No...it wasn't."

A memory then. Perhaps one that had morphed into a reoccurring nightmare over time. I didn't have to ask to know it was about his years beneath Morehaven.

Tobias blinked down at where his hands were still manacled around my wrists. He released me like he had been burned, scrambling away so quickly my heart caught in my throat. The sheets fell away as he sprang from the bed, turning his back like he couldn't bear to face me.

He was only wearing a thin pair of shorts, the moonlight illuminating every dip in the muscles of his back. A gasp escaped me, far too loud in the silence.

I knew about the scarred white band where the collar had once bound Tobias's magic. I had touched the circular scars on his wrists, each layer a testimony to his mistreatment. But his back...

Cruel white lines slashed down the entire length of it—so many that they crisscrossed atop each other. Scars from old burns interspersed with the patchwork of lines that could have only come from a blade or a whip, so deep they had flayed the skin from muscle and sinew. Older scars faded into the new, each silvery line cutting across his back with heartbreaking precision.

These were more than just intentional. They had been inflicted to hurt him, to *break* him. The cruelty of it made my stomach turn even as pure, undiluted rage rose inside me like a scream.

Tobias's shoulders lifted self-consciously as he realized where my gaze had gone. My magic flared at my fingertips like it could fix what had long since happened. I had known, of course, that Tobias had been Aviel's prisoner...but to see the marks of his torture? I almost wished the False King wasn't dead, so I could inflict the same punishment, the same pain, as though it could ever make things even.

I swung my feet over the edge of the bed, slowly padding over to stand behind him—giving him time to retreat if he needed. On impulse, I splayed my hand against the worst of the scars on his upper back.

Tobias stiffened but didn't move. My healing magic flowed from my hand, seeking out the ingrained pain there. I tenderly traced one scar with my fingertips, then the next, each one glowing softly beneath my touch.

He shuddered slightly as I reached a particularly brutal indent against his spine, though his head still didn't turn. My magic couldn't fix what had already healed, nor could it change what had been done to him—but I could *feel* the suffering, the despair locked within it.

Gently, I pressed into the thick scar tissue as if I could knead it away.

"I'm glad he's dead." My voice was so gravelly I barely recognized it. "I hope it hurt when he burned. I hope everyone who had a part in it pays for what they put you through."

The silence stretched, though there was no rebuke for the distinctly unhealer-like thought. Not that I had expected one from him.

Tobias half-turned my way, his face lost in shadow. "Alette deserved that kill, even if I wanted it. From what I can tell, the prison guards all traveled with Aviel to Adronix since there wasn't anyone left in the prison. I can't be certain, but I like to think they're buried at the bottom of that mountain with no one to mourn them."

The blue of my magic stuttered, a hint of red coming to my fingertips as I whispered, "Good."

Tobias shifted, the muscles of his back rippling under my touch as it turned back to blue. "And Silvius...well, he didn't have to touch me to hurt me."

Gently, I traced my finger around the scar bisecting his neck as I walked around his body until I stood in front of him. His gaze widened, trailing down my form and oh so slowly back up again. I suddenly found myself far too aware that I had rushed into his room in only a thin silk nightgown that barely reached mid-thigh. It might as well have been see-through with how clearly you could see the shape of my nipples beneath it.

Emboldened by his perusal, my hand slipped lower to a cluster of scars that decorated one pectoral. Slowly, I moved down the chiseled line between his abdominals to the scarred remains of a stab wound, which sat just above the deep vee that disappeared into his low-slung shorts.

I forced my gaze back up to his face as I made myself ask, "Do you want to talk about your nightmare?"

Tobias's lips pressed tightly together like he was biting down on his response. Then he stepped away. My hand hovered midair, still reaching for him.

He looked down, avoiding my gaze as he gritted out, "I'm fine, Sagray. You should go back to bed."

I reared back at his clipped tone. When he finally looked back up at me, his expression had turned stony, though his eyes remained mercurial.

For one moment, he had let his guard down. Now it was all too obvious he was trying to build his walls back up.

"Don't lie to me." I shook my head in disbelief, failing to keep the disappointment and anger out of my voice as I added, "You've never been any good at it, anyway."

Tobias let out a dry, humorless laugh. Light sparked within those hazel eyes, begging for an outlet.

"Things change," he said, a hint of sadness creeping into his tone.

I knew why he had learned to lie in the years we were separated—why he walled himself off so entirely that even Aviel hadn't been able to get him to betray our whereabouts. His scars were a testament to everything he had chosen to endure to keep me safe.

Tobias thought he was broken. And yet, he was the one who *hadn't* broke.

I wanted to heal his scars with one magic, and use the other to eradicate everyone that had ever hurt him. I wanted to undo everything he was forced to face and give him back the years he spent scared and alone. I wanted to throw my arms around him and thank him without risking him disappearing further into himself.

It was clear he didn't want me prying past his defenses. And maybe this was another attempt to push me away...but after so many months of this, I wasn't going to let him.

After all he had done for me, I had to try.

"Please don't shut me out," I whispered so my voice didn't break. "Not now that..."

"Now that what?"

I tried not to flinch at the flat, dismissive tone, nearly devoid of all emotion.

Not now that we have a second chance.

"I deserve better than this, Tobias Maris," I snapped, stepping in front of him. "You're not the only one who has suffered, even if you faced the worst of it." I pointed my finger at him, then pressed it into the hard pane of his chest as I moved further into his space. "You're not the only one whose parents were murdered." I pushed harder, hating his lack of response. "You aren't the only person who found themselves lost in another realm, desperately trying to find someone, anyone that could help." My throat burned, and I hated myself for it. "Why won't you let me help you? *Why* won't you let me in?"

Light leaked from the corners of Tobias's eyes, sparks jumping between his eyelashes. "I spent the last few years guarding my every thought. Wondering if today was the day I would die and knowing there was a good chance it could be. Letting you in, giving you that power over me...it goes against everything I was forced to become to keep the ones I loved safe." His voice cracked. "Everyone around me dies or is worse for having known me. I refuse to lose anyone else."

I expected him to pull away. My breath caught as he leaned into my touch instead.

His broad hand covered mine, pressing it flat against his heart. "I refuse to lose *you*."

"Well, I already lost you," I said, my voice breaking. "You died, and I had to keep living." A tear rolled down my cheek, quickly followed by another. "For seven long years, I carried you with me like a hole in my heart. When I realized you were alive...it felt like a piece of myself came back to life. But there was a war left to win, and you were having such a hard time simply existing." Tobias's throat bobbed, struggling to swallow. "For a moment there, in the woods…I thought you were coming back to me. Then we spent months in the same city. *Months* in the same fucking house, and every time I tried to get close to you…" I could feel his heartbeat accelerating beneath my palm. "Why is it that you always try to run from me, even now?"

"Maybe you should be the one running away," Tobias said darkly, though he made no move to release me. "The boy you knew died in that cell."

"No." There was an ache in my chest so acute I barely resisted the urge to try to heal it. "You can't believe that. Not when you came back to me."

"Great argument," Tobias sneered, and I flinched. "You're forgetting the part where I spent four years beneath that damned castle, unable to do anything but scream as they ripped me apart over and over again. I'm not the person you used to know, Sagray. I'm broken, and it's not the sort of broken that you can heal."

The defeat in his tone, the self-loathing, was enough to tear my heart in two.

"But you're right," he continued, the magic in his eyes fading as that damn mask slid back into place. "You do deserve better than me. So how about we do what we need to do and then you can go find someone else to torment."

Anger flared within me, rising to the bait. "*Torment*? Is that really how you feel about the time we've spent together?"

My nails dug into his chest, and I found myself torn between pulling him closer and pushing him away.

Tobias's jaw clenched. "Yes, Sagray. Every second with you is fucking agony. You should take the hint and leave me alone like everybody else."

The air between us felt charged, like the moment before a lightning strike—the electric anticipation of an oncoming storm.

"You don't mean that." I drew out each word, refusing to back down. "After all we've been through, how can you even say that to me?"

"Don't tell me what I mean," Tobias said, his voice nearly a growl. "You have no idea what I'm thinking and yet you—" He inhaled sharply, then blew it out in a furious rush. "Why do you even *care*?"

As though that wasn't completely obvious. My fists clenched as I cried, "Why do you think?"

A muscle flexed in his jaw, lightning jumping between the gold flecks in his irises.

He was too close. And not nearly close enough.

My voice dropped. "I can't do this anymore. I can't stand here, waiting for you to see what's right in front of you, only to watch you bury your feelings again and again." His throat worked, and my eyes burned with the start of furious tears. My voice splintered as I choked out, "Let me know when you find the courage to face me without your mask."

Tobias's chest heaved like he stood at the edge of a cliff, trying to convince himself to leap. I started to turn away, about to storm out of his room and find somewhere that he couldn't hear my heart break. His hand fastened around my wrist, dragging me back.

I opened my mouth to protest when he placed my hand against his heart, its wild rhythm matching my own. But it was the look in his eyes that froze me in place—his gaze so openly raw I couldn't bring myself to look away.

"You don't understand," he whispered. There was something akin to devastation on his face—like that mask had cracked, and he was desperately trying to hold it together. "It's not a lack of courage. I think I always knew what we could be to each other. But I…I didn't want to trap you into it." He sucked in a shuddering breath. "I didn't want to trap you with *me*, not when we both know that you deserve better."

I tried to protest, but Tobias's next words knocked the breath out of me.

"You're my first thought in the morning, my last thought before I fall asleep, and the only thing that gets me through the night," Tobias said so solemnly it felt like a vow. "You're the only thing I seem to be able to think about despite having a sister to save and a kingdom to run…though I'm well aware I couldn't do either without you. You also happen to be kind to a fault, aggravatingly selfless, annoyingly brilliant, though somehow never arrogant about it, and beautiful inside and out without even trying." His eyes were brimming with hope and longing, and something endless that felt like it was pulling me in. "Whether or not I deserve you, you're *mine*, Quinn. You've always been mine, and I don't have the strength to keep pushing you away."

For a second, I thought a trio of stars had fallen through the window before I realized it was his magic, three balls of light swirling around me. "Maris…" I breathed.

"No, please let me finish," Tobias begged, seemingly unaware of the light circling around us even as another glowing orb joined the rest. "You make life worth living, Quinn. And you made me want to live, even when things were darkest." He glanced down, his voice hoarse as he added, "Especially then."

His gaze was soft as he looked back up at me, his expression so unguarded for a change, I felt dizzy. "I can't get you out of my head, and I don't want to. You...you're everything I've ever wanted, for longer than you can imagine. And I've long since realized that I'll never, ever want anyone else."

That last barrier between us crumbled, unable to hold up against the strength of his proclamation. I had the vague sensation that I was floating above my body—like this was a dream, and one false move might make it fade away.

"You're what I want too," I breathed. "I need this to be real. I need...you."

For one endless heartbeat, we stared at each other. Then his mouth crashed into mine in a kiss so forceful that my knees buckled.

And then I was kissing him back, that fear dissipating into pure lust mixed with something more. His arms wrapped around me, holding me against him as he devoured me body and soul.

The world could have exploded around us, and I wouldn't have noticed with the fireworks going off behind my eyelids. It wasn't until I opened my eyes that I realized that the light was coming from him—an entire universe of tiny stars bobbing around us in celebration.

I gasped his name as he started working his way down my throat, nipping and sucking. When he pulled away, I blinked at him in a daze. "Why'd you stop?"

There was something vulnerable in his eyes...something like hope.

"Say it again," he pleaded.

I pressed my hand to my swollen lips, still reeling. "Say...what?"

"My name, Quinn." His voice was nearly a growl. "Say my name."

"Tobias—"

I cut myself off with a gasp as he yanked me up his body by my hips, hitched my legs around his waist, then carried me to the bed. He cradled me almost reverently as he laid me down—his touch so gentle compared to the furious way he had kissed me that my heart skipped a beat. One hand slipped beneath my dress, grabbing a handful of my upper thigh. He ground against me. My answering moan was so loud it took me by surprise, even as I ached for more.

Tobias drew back, panting. His eyes trailed down my face to my chest—

to my breasts, where my nipples pushed against the thin silk, then lower still to where his hips rucked up my nightgown above my thighs. His gaze felt like lightning, heat searing through every part of me it touched.

I needed more.

My eyes followed the muscle of his neck down his defined chest—tracing each abdominal until I reached the vee that disappeared into the waistband of his shorts.

I wanted him so badly, for so long. And here he was, wanting me too.

When I slid my gaze back up to his face, the look in his eyes made my thighs tighten around him. But after so long of wanting this, I didn't want to rush him into anything. He must have seen the hesitation on my face because he went still before I could even whisper, "What do you want, Tobias?"

His expression was both soft and guarded, like he could barely believe this was real. "I want you, Quinn. I've always wanted you."

"You can have me," I quickly assured him. "You already do." My teeth sunk into my lower lip as I tried to clarify. "I meant tonight…what *exactly* do you want to have happen?"

A sensual smirk curved his mouth. "Do you want the honest answer or the polite one?"

"Honesty, always," I said immediately.

His eyes darkened. "I want what I've dreamed about since I was a teenager. I want to bury my head between your thighs and hear the sounds I've imagined over and over again. I want to wrap your gorgeous legs around my waist again and push my way inside you. I want to hear you scream my name until you can't take anymore. And then I want to make you come so many times you lose count before I make you come again."

My mouth went dry. It was all I could do to nod.

"I need to hear you say it, sweetheart." His voice might have been languid if not for the intensity in his eyes. "What do *you* want?"

"You," I breathed. "Yes, I want that. All of it."

A smile flickered on his lips before it disappeared, his expression turning serious. "Are you on the tonic?"

"Have been since I first arrived in Soleara," I said quickly. It had been more for period management and preparation just in case, considering I hadn't been with anyone since before I traveled to this realm. There had been opportunities after the war was won...and yet, none of them had interested me. Not since I learned Tobias was alive.

"Me too." He started to reach for me, then hesitated. A hint of concern crossed his face, his mouth parting like he was trying to figure out what to say.

I tilted my head. "What is it?"

"Even before my imprisonment, I liked a sense of control. And now..." Tobias swallowed hard, a blush staining his cheeks. "If you aren't into that, or you aren't comfortable with the idea, I understand. I just wanted to let you know everything before we—"

"Are you asking to tie me to the headboard, Maris?"

His breath caught, the hard length of him twitching again me, and I knew I had read him correctly.

"Because it wouldn't be the first time," I said, adding a bit breathlessly, "*Sir*."

I had always enjoyed being dominated. Boyfriends, girlfriends...there was something about submission that made the analytical part of my brain turn off, the bliss of ceding control making the pleasure that much better. Maybe it was because I had always been the sort of girl who had basked in earning gold stars on my homework. Or maybe it was simply a chance to stop overthinking everything and just feel...but I wanted this as much as he did.

"Not for our first time...and not until we set some ground rules," Tobias said, his voice dropping so low a shiver coursed down my spine. "But I won't deny the thought hadn't crossed my mind, sweetheart."

His hand trailed down my chest, circling around my breast—his light touch sending a shiver of need through my entire body. He flicked my nipple just hard enough to make me gasp aloud.

"You're going to tell me what you like," Tobias drawled, his tone sinful. "And I'm going to enjoy doing every single one of them to you."

"Yes, please," I breathed, reaching for him. My hand trailed down his chest, then lower. I needed to touch him—to pull down those shorts and see all of him. If the bulge pressing against me was any indication, well...my mouth watered in anticipation.

He caught my hand right as my finger dipped into his waistband, slowly shaking his head in mock disappointment. "First, I'm going to get you off. *Then* you can touch me."

A thrill shot through me at his words. Heat pooled low in my belly, then lower still.

Placing my hand palm down at my side, Tobias reached for me with both hands, fisting the neckline of my nightgown. I gasped as he ripped the gown in half—tearing it straight down the middle in one powerful jerk—the silk pooling beneath me.

I trembled in anticipation, waiting breathlessly. For a seemingly endless moment, he just stared, his hooded eyes drinking in every inch of me.

"Somehow, you look better than every fantasy I've ever had of you," Tobias rasped, each word rough-edged.

I sucked in a breath as he lowered his head to my breast. My back arched encouragingly as he drew my nipple into his mouth, a low whimper escaping my throat.

He had barely touched me, and I was ready to combust.

"So responsive," he murmured. He drew one nipple then the other into his mouth until I was squirming beneath him. My hands fisted the sheets beneath me with the effort not to touch him. He trailed his hands slowly down my stomach, then lower still to follow the curve of my hips, teasingly avoiding the place I needed him most.

"Tobias."

His breath was hot against my nipple as he chuckled deep in his throat. "I could edge you for days, sweetheart. But since we only have until sunrise..."

My entire body jerked as his thumb flicked my clit.

"I want to feel you unravel." His teeth nipped at my ear, his voice low and dominant. "I want to hear if the sounds you make are even better than I imagined. I want you to mark me with your fingernails as they claw up my back. I want to be inside you so badly that I can barely breathe." He dropped a light kiss behind my ear. "I want...I don't want to ever let you go."

Each word he spoke was a spark, and I was already burning.

His middle finger slid downward, pushing inside me as his thumb started to circle. I reflexively bucked my hips against his hand as he added a second finger.

I opened my eyes to find his gaze devouring me. He smirked. "Are you always this wet for me?"

How many nights had I spent down the hall from him, imagining what would happen if he knocked on my door? Just as many as I had gotten myself off, wishing my fingers were his.

His thumb lifted, and I let out a whine of protest.

"Use your words."

"Yes," I admitted, clenching around his fingers. "I'm always…" I gasped as his thumb resumed its ministrations. "*Always* this wet for you."

"Good."

Those two fingers curled inside me. My eyes rolled back in my head, my hips begging him to continue.

"Don't come yet," Tobias demanded. "Not until I get my mouth on you."

I was panting, my body already starting to shake with the start of my orgasm. "But I'm about to…" My eyes flew open as he withdrew his hand entirely. "*Tobias.*"

There was that damned dimple, back to taunt me. He splayed his hands across my inner thighs, spreading me open. His hair fell into his eyes as he leaned forward…

I squealed when his tongue delved inside me, taking his fingers' place. "Oh, *gods.*"

His groan reverberated through me. I curled my fingers tighter into the sheets, dying to run my fingers through his hair. But I could follow his rules if it meant reaping the rewards.

Tobias held me in place as his tongue trailed up to circle my clit, every muscle in my body starting to shake. My building orgasm felt like the tremors before an earthquake—like I was the epicenter, alive with tension, and it wouldn't be long before I fractured.

"Tobias…I need to—"

"Come for me, Quinn."

His mouth closed around me, his teeth trailing against that sensitive nub of nerves. When he thrust his fingers back inside me, my vision blacked out. I cried out as I came apart, my orgasm tearing through me in wave after wave until I thought it might never end. Tobias didn't let up, his tongue dragging me from one orgasm into the next until I was so sensitive I begged him to stop.

Tobias's eyes gleamed with satisfaction as he sat back and licked his lips. "You taste even better than I imagined."

I lay there, staring up at him in blissful contentment. His hard length jutted toward me, straining against his shorts. I pushed myself up onto my elbows.

Tobias must have seen the hunger in my eyes. His fingers grazed my chin, his hand resting against my jaw as he tilted my head up to look at him.

I ran my tongue across my lips, wetting them.

His eyes darkened. "Tell me what you want, Quinn."

"I want those off," I said, my eyes dropping to the only piece of clothing left between us. Then I looked up at him from beneath my lashes. "And then I want to take you in my mouth before you finally fuck me."

Tobias's thumb pressed against my lower lip. "Is that so?"

I nodded, loving the way he was looking at me. So open, so adoring, I wanted to bask in his light after so long in the cold.

"You *are* perfect for me, aren't you, sweetheart."

It wasn't a question, but I found myself nodding. Letting go of my chin, he got off the bed, then glanced down in invitation. But it was my turn to take my time. I let the wreckage of my nightgown fall away as I sat up, enjoying his attention. His breath caught as I slowly crawled across the bed, arching my back so my ass swayed with every movement.

"*Fuck*," he breathed.

Our eyes met, the heat in his making my core clench. Then I reached for him, sliding a finger on either side of his waistband. The hard length of him sprang to attention as I yanked his shorts down, his cock bobbing in front of my face.

My eyes went wide at the sheer size of him. It wasn't just his substantial length, but his veiny girth made the thought of fitting him inside me… challenging. I bit my lip, my brow furrowing as I assessed him.

Tobias looked down at me, every hard line of him radiating smug, masculine arrogance. "You can take it."

"You sure about that?"

I wasn't fully convinced. But I was sure as hell going to try.

Tobias laughed low in his throat. "You have that same look of determination you do when you're trying to solve a problem. I've never seen you give up, and I don't expect you to start now. Besides—" His word turned into a hiss as I wrapped my hand around him, pumping slowly up and down his length. "We're going to make it fit."

Heat rushed through me. I was more than ready for him to try. But first…

I moved closer, my lips barely brushing against him. His length twitched in my hand, his abdominals going taut with anticipation. I wanted to lick every line.

"Tell me what you want," I parroted back at him.

"I want your lips around me," Tobias gritted out as I spat on my hand, then worked him faster. "I want you to take me down your throat." He raised a brow. "But you only get one minute until you're back underneath me, so you'd better make your time count."

His breathing turned uneven as I leaned forward, intent on exactly that. I stretched my tongue out, licking the underside of his cock, loving the way he shuddered as I did. A faint sound escaped his lips as my tongue traced the slit of his engorged head.

Then I closed my mouth around him, sucking hard. Tobias let out a deep groan as I started to move, taking him as far as I could down my throat as my hand stroked the rest of him.

"That's it," Tobias moaned. "You feel so godsdamned good."

He sounded far too in control. And as much as I knew he craved it, something told me that getting him to let go with me was exactly what he needed.

I gripped his hips with both hands, tugging him closer. Tobias caught my chin, holding me in place.

"Are you sure—"

I nodded slightly, my tongue flicking against him impatiently. If he had any doubts about how much I wanted this, they seemed to leave him as I suctioned my mouth around him, urging him deeper. The sound he let out was utterly unlike him—so unrestrained, it was almost feral.

"If you need a break, tap my leg," he panted, his pupils blown wide.

I sucked in a breath through my nose, letting my throat relax as he nudged himself deeper. His hand fisted in my hair as he rocked himself back and forth, sliding further in with each thrust. The sounds coming from my mouth were obscene as he used me, and I didn't want them to end.

"Fuck, sweetheart," Tobias groaned. "You're doing so well."

I hummed deep in my throat at the praise and felt his entire body jerk. He swore under his breath as he pulled himself all the way out with a wet pop.

His thumb brushed against my lower lip, wiping the trail of saliva left behind. With a grin, I lightly nipped his finger. "Why did you stop—"

I squealed as he lifted me, throwing me down on the bed. I laughed as I barely bounced once before he was on top of me, shoving my legs wide and nestling between them.

"Time's up," he murmured against my mouth.

I pouted, only for him to catch my lips in a soft kiss that quickly turned deeper. My arms wrapped around him, my nails digging into his back. His muscles went rigid beneath my touch as my fingers brushed against his scars, but as I started to pull away, he let out a low sound of protest against my lips, kissing me with a new sense of desperation.

By the time we broke apart I was breathless. "So if I'm good, do I get to do that again?"

"Hmm." Tobias lifted his hips and fisted his cock, sliding it against me. I sucked in a breath as his head bumped against my clit, sending a jolt of pleasure through my entire body. "I'll consider it."

I tilted my hips against him, needing him to fill me.

I needed *him*, period.

He did it again, watching as I writhed beneath him.

"I need you inside me," I whispered. "Please."

"Good," Tobias groaned. "Because I'm done waiting."

I tensed as he nudged against my opening. I was already so wet, but the way I immediately needed to stretch around him was almost too much to bear.

"Breathe for me," Tobias ordered, his own breathing shallow. "Relax."

I sucked in a breath, and he slid further inside me, filling me so deliciously my eyes watered.

"Do you know how long I've wanted this?" Tobias panted into the curve of my neck. "Wanted you?"

"I think I have some idea," I murmured, then gasped as he retreated before pushing in another inch.

He shook his head, then pulled back, his features contorting like he was in pain. "Stay still. I don't want to hurt you."

"You won't," I said, innately knowing it was true.

Tobias sank in further. The pain quickly turned into pleasure as he hit a spot inside me with every shallow thrust, filling me so fully my eyes rolled back in my head. Was it possible to come just like this?

He pressed his forehead against mine, both of us losing our breath as he finally slid in to the hilt. I shifted my hips, squeezing around him, and he let out a guttural moan. Sparks twirled in the air between us, tingling as they brushed against my skin.

"Give me a second. You feel—" He swore under his breath. "Gods, you feel like you were made for me."

I stilled beneath him, letting myself adjust too. He swiveled his hips like he was testing the way we fit together.

"Oh," I gasped. My breathing turned ragged as he pulled out to the tip, then pushed all the way back in. That ache was growing fast, the pleasure so sudden it took me by surprise. My gasp turned into a moan as he did it again.

"*Fuck*," Tobias groaned. "I could hear you make that sound every day for the rest of our lives, and it still wouldn't be enough."

The feeling of how he fit inside me might drive me to madness. I closed my eyes, savoring it. I never wanted this to end.

My arms tightened around him, my fingernails digging into his shoulder blades. The next second, my wrists were pinned above my head. My eyes flew open. One of his hands held mine in place, gripping my wrists together.

His eyes searched mine. "Is this alright?"

"Yes," I said quickly. "Don't stop. I want you—" I rolled my hips against him, watching the way his arms flexed as he tried to keep himself in check. "—deeper. I need you to fuck me..." I squeezed my inner muscles and couldn't help my grin as I saw a muscle quiver in his jaw. "*Hard*. Please, Tobias."

Something primal flashed in his eyes. I saw the moment he decided to stop holding back, my pleas severing whatever was left of his control.

"I love hearing you beg."

He drove into me so hard I gasped. His elbow sank into my pillow, holding his weight as the hand not holding my wrists reached between us. I whimpered as his thumb played with my clit with the perfect amount of pressure, each circle in time with his thrusts.

His pace turned relentless. All I could feel was the building heat as I lost myself to the overwhelming sense of friction—the pleasure almost too much. He filled me entirely, each thrust brushing against a spot so sensitive I was almost afraid for the moment I finally let go.

I was going to break apart. I was going to shatter into pieces that would have to re-form around the piece of himself he had irrevocably placed in my heart.

Perhaps it had always been there.

"Say it again," Tobias panted, his thumb lifting.

I blinked up at him through the haze of my pleasure.

A moan tore from my throat as he thrust back into me, sending a tremor through my core. I was close, *so* close…

He stilled, and I nearly cried out in frustration.

"Quinn." His teeth pressed against my throat, trailing along my skin. "Say my name when I make you come."

"Tobias…"

He pushed back inside me, this thumb pressing down on that sensitive nub of nerves, and I broke apart with a sob. It was too much—almost too perfect. One wave of pleasure turned into another as Tobias rocked his hips, my body shaking like I might indeed come apart.

When it finally ebbed, I lay limp against the sheets, satiated and utterly spent. Tobias gently rubbed my wrists as he kissed the pulse point of each one. Then he leaned forward, brushing kisses up my neck and across my cheeks, bringing a different sort of blush to them.

"That's my girl," Tobias murmured against the shell of my ear.

I felt delirious, like that orgasm had wiped everything away except that need for him and the sort of satisfaction I had never felt before. This was something raw and real and undeniable—something we would have to face together in the morning. But for now…

"Here I thought you were going to make me lose count."

I barely had time to appreciate the dimple that appeared before he flipped me over. One hand kneaded my ass cheek appreciatively, as the other spread my thighs apart.

"A promise is a promise, sweetheart." His lips pressed against the top of my spine as he positioned himself between my legs. "I'm not done with you yet."

CHAPTER 35
QUINN

When I woke up, Tobias held me so tightly it seemed like nothing could ever come between us. One strong arm wrapped around my waist, the other draped over my upper arm, and his chin rested protectively atop my hair. His chest gently rose and fell in time to my own breathing.

The white band scarred around his neck greeted me as I opened my eyes, the reminder of what he had been through stark against his skin in the early morning light. It brought a tightness to my chest—a flash of rage mixed with a possessiveness that made my blood run hot.

I contented myself with brushing a light kiss against the center of his throat before leaning back just enough to see his face. While I would have to wake him soon, the clock on the wall showed we had a little time left before the lab opened. We didn't have long before we needed to return to the real world…but I planned on making every minute count.

Besides, it was rare to see him so peaceful, so unguarded.

He looked painfully young like this, his face more relaxed than I had seen it in years. Dark hair fell into his eyes, mixing with long lashes. His mouth twitched slightly, like he might smile in his sleep, a ghost of that dimple forming before it disappeared.

I could happily stay in this bed forever, if it meant keeping him here with me.

His breathing hitched, a frown crossing his face. Tobias didn't open his eyes as he said, his voice husky, "Go back to sleep, Sagray. You need all you can get with how long I kept you up last night."

I started in surprise. "I thought you were asleep."

"I *was*," Tobias grumbled. He pulled me closer, pressing his lips to my forehead.

I happily snuggled into him, breathing him in. He traced a finger down my spine, kneading circles into the dimples on either side of my lower back, and I let out a contented sigh.

There was something here that felt fated, though I knew better than to say the word out loud just yet. He might have given in to the pull between us, but given how long he avoided so much as touching me after what he had been through…

If he didn't realize what we were, he would in time. But I couldn't help but push. "Do you remember that night before your birthday. The one where we almost…"

His fingers paused their lazy paths along my back, his voice a low rumble as he said, "I remember."

For a heartbeat, he'd almost been mine.

We had almost kissed, just that once. On his Seventeenth…right before I thought I lost him forever.

I pulled back, lifting my chin to face him. "I thought I built it up in my head, that moment you leaned in. I closed my eyes…and the next second you were gone."

We spent the day of his seventeenth birthday together, along with Eva. They were both annoyed that they had to go home early for a family dinner on their big day. Eva had gone inside, but Tobias had lingered, all nervous laughter and hopeful smiles. Then he invited me to come back over that night—after the dinner that instead turned into death and disaster.

I could still picture the way his cheeks flushed when he had haltingly added, *"There's no one I'd rather spend my birthday with, Quinn."* Could still see the way he stepped closer—too close to be friendly—intention in every line of his face. My eyes had fluttered closed, waiting…

"That moment has haunted me ever since." Tobias's hand resumed its wandering, stroking down my side with a sweet sort of adoration. "I told myself that I'd kiss you that night, when you came back. That I should wait for the perfect moment, only…" A soft sigh. "Obviously things didn't go to plan."

"Only took almost a decade to remedy."

Tobias leaned in, a slow smile curving his lips. "I don't plan on wasting another second."

My eyes fluttered closed, wanting to live in this moment forever. When he kissed me, it was soft and thorough and almost lazy like we had all the time in the world.

He pulled away, that lopsided smile still on his lips. It brought me back to high school lunchrooms, weekend training sessions, and summer shenanigans swimming in the lake behind my house. All that time spent together, and I knew even then I would never get enough of him.

I wanted to lose myself in him. But as much as I wanted to forget the next words out of my mouth, they were necessary. Reluctantly, I forced myself back to reality. "The lab opens soon, and I could use something to eat after that…workout."

Tobias's smile was pure sex. "I was thinking of something I'd like to eat, too."

I sucked in a breath as he lowered his head, his lips grazing the point of my ear. A shiver ran through me as he breathed against it, before moving lower, nipping at my neck. His hand squeezed my ass, shifting me closer…

Guilt popped that happy bubble like a knife. Eva was comatose and waiting for me to cure her and here I was, thoroughly satiated and in bed with her brother. The weight of everything I still needed to do pressed on my chest, even as reason reminded me that anxiety was useless—not when we couldn't get back into the lab until it opened.

Tobias seemed to sense the change in me. "Was that…I'm sorry if I—"

"It's not that I don't want to," I said quickly, touching his cheek. He nuzzled his head into my hand, his stubble rough against my palm, and I felt my worry recede just slightly. "In fact, it sounds like the perfect way to spend the day once we cure your sister. But we don't have time…she doesn't have time for us to be…" I swallowed, unsure how to define exactly what we were doing. "We should get back to work."

I hated the way the happiness in his eyes dimmed, the breadth of what we had left to do chasing the smile from his face too.

"I know the weight of the world is on your shoulders right now," Tobias murmured. "But you can let me share that burden, Quinn." He looked down, forehead creasing. "I know I haven't been there for you for a while now... but you can trust me to bear whatever it is you need from me." His throat bobbed. "Whatever *this* is can wait until our task is done, if that's what you want."

I searched his face, but it was once again unreadable. "Is that what you want?"

"*No*," he said quickly. "Of course not, you're—"

I cut him off with a kiss. For one precious minute I let myself get lost to it.

He kissed me like it was the last time—slow at first then deepening, the desire and promise of it all-consuming. Our tongues battled for dominance as his hand fisted in my hair. I sucked his lower lip into my mouth before releasing it with a pop.

"Talk it through with me," he said, breathing hard. "Is there something you need to do right now, or do you just feel guilty for letting yourself be happy?"

I blinked at him. "I'm..."

With the progress we made yesterday, there wasn't anything I could do until the lab opened. Even if I got there early, the doors wouldn't open until the cleaning cycle finished. And with a viable cure, all that was left to do was determine dosages and...

Tobias pressed a kiss between my brows, the tenderness of the gesture leaving me winded. "Out loud. I can see your mind working."

"You're right," I said softly. "I'm just...anxious. And feeling more than a little guilty about how happy I am right now."

The real, full smile on Tobias's face took my breath away. "Let's get ready then. Though I can think of something I can do to help with that anxiety, if you're willing."

"I wouldn't mind some company in the shower," I said suggestively. "We do have *some* time before we can get in the lab, after all. Especially if we eat breakfast on the walk over."

I squealed as Tobias scooped me from the bed, letting the sheets fall to the side. He smirked down at me as I wrapped my arms around his neck.

"I can work with that."

✧

. . .

My hair was a wild, untamable mess when we reached the iron door to the lab a minute before it opened. It was hard feeling put out about the lack of time I had to get ready when it had meant one of the best orgasms of my life against the shower wall as Tobias murmured praise into my ear. Yael, Pari, and Rivan were thankfully already gone, the breakfast laid out in our shared space picked over by the time we got dressed. After how loud we had been, I doubted I would've been able to look any of them in the eyes, no matter how thick the walls were.

I needed to focus. And yet, I found myself replaying what we had done to each other amid the steam on repeat as I got to work. My hand wrapped around my throat at the heat rising there. I could still hear Tobias's groan into the curve of my neck drowning out the cascade of water. And feel the slight soreness where he bit down as his release spilled inside me...

"You're blushing," Tobias murmured as he handed me a fresh vial. "Penny for your thoughts?"

That damn dimple flickered in his cheek. If his self-satisfied smirk was anything to go on, he already knew.

Dolion raised an eyebrow at us from where he had been jotting down notes, having arrived not long after us. But he merely asked, "Any luck with tracking down Silvius? I heard there was some activity yesterday."

Tobias's jaw flexed; any hint of levity gone at the reminder. "Another dead end, I'm afraid."

"We did figure out how he was likely entering the Enclave," I said absentmindedly as I focused on a measurement. "The tunnel system below the castle is pretty extensive."

Tobias shot me a warning look that I ignored. He might not trust Dolion, but I did. Whatever Tobias's issue was with him, we wouldn't be where we were in our research without Dolion's help.

"I didn't realize they were sending healers to do reconnaissance now," Dolion said, his tone deceptively mild. "Glad to see you made it back safely. I heard there was an overzealous water wielder?"

I nodded even as I tried not to remember how close I had been to drowning. Strange to think how much had transpired since then

Dolion tutted softly. "I take it that you weren't able to locate Silvius's laboratory?"

"Only for a minute." It pained me to think about how close we had come to ending this once and for all, though I couldn't imagine doing anything differently. "There are guards watching the entryway to the tunnels we used to get there...but I doubt he'll be foolish enough to reopen the mirror that leads there. We had to make a quick exit."

"Though we left two gifts for his return," Tobias added grimly.

There was no mistaking the malice in his tone. I gave him a reproachful look. He stepped closer, leaning in until I could feel the heat of him against my back.

"I have no regrets about killing anyone who hurts you, let alone those in league with Silvius," he breathed against my ear. "In that order."

I nearly dropped the vial. The vengeance in his voice shouldn't have made heat coil in my core, and yet...

Dolion cleared his throat. "Here I thought he wanted Quinn alive, though I assume it's to gather information about what we're doing here. Which means we're all targets."

Tobias's expression turned murderous, no doubt picturing that very prospect.

Concern flooded my voice as I told Dolion, "You need to be careful."

"I was about to tell you the same after your escapades last night." Dolion looked faintly amused. "There's a reason I've kept our research a closely guarded secret. I have no intention of being killed for it. Or for anyone to intrude where they don't belong."

"We appreciate your help," I said, nudging Tobias covertly in the side. The hard muscle didn't move an inch, and I resisted the urge to rub my elbow.

A muscle feathered in his jaw, whatever he wanted to say staying firmly locked away.

"I'm afraid I must step out for a bit," Dolion said apologetically. "Since we don't test cures on living creatures like the humans do, I must retrieve the life essences for our final testing myself." He let out a long-suffering sigh. "I had hoped they would be delivered, given our urgency, but it seems protocol plus the secrecy of our experiments means I must go in person. I'll return before lunch."

I tried to hide my disappointment. "I'll double check the dosages."

Our next step was to test the cures on the life essences by essentially infecting them—a process that would likely take the rest of the day before letting our cure dosages incubate overnight. Which meant another full day before being able to give it to Eva if it was viable.

One more night, I told myself.

If all went to plan, tomorrow would be the day we would get Eva back.

Tomorrow we'll finally have a cure.

Dolion hurriedly gathered his notes, leaving his desk empty before he scurried from the room. I moved to recheck the same vials I had already checked over twice, only to find Tobias looking me up and down.

He looked far too good in his off-white linen button up; the sleeves rolled up around his biceps. I could feel my face heat as I took in the veins that decorated his forearms and the tops of his hands, remembering exactly what those long fingers had done to me last night.

"Bend over the counter."

Every part of me went loose then tight at the dominance in his voice even as I shook my head. "Zero chance I'm going to risk contaminating our workspace, Maris, but save that thought for when we can celebrate a cure. Besides, I need to check the dosing."

"The dosages you already double checked this morning?" He shot me a look so pleading it was almost comical. "What if we only contaminate Dolion's desk? I've been picturing you in that lab coat and *only* that lab coat all morning."

I laughed as he backed me toward the desk even as I emphatically shook my head. "Absolutely not. You can do anything you want to me after we find a cure, but here you're in my domain. So *no* touching."

My lower back bumped against Dolion's desk as Tobias sighed in defeat.

"The second you find this cure and everyone's safe, I'm going to stay inside you for a week straight, Sagray." A slow smirk spread his lips as he backed away, raising both hands in surrender. "But I can't say I mind being under your command in the meantime."

Turning around, I set my hands on Dolion's desk. "I'm looking forward to being under yours...and you, once we do."

Tobias made a choking sound as I leaned forward, hitching up my lab coat and the short dress beneath. His silver dagger peeked out from where I had tied it unobtrusively around my thigh.

"What are you..." He trailed off as I tugged my dress high enough for him to see that I hadn't bothered to put on underwear this morning.

"No touching," I warned, my voice sultry as I looked over my shoulder. "But I thought you should know how ready I am for you when this is over."

Sparks flew from Tobias's hands, reflecting in his eyes. The look on his face was pure, ravenous hunger.

"As if I needed any more incentive," he drawled. "Now get back to work before I lose my godsdamn mind."

I grinned as he adjusted himself, visibly frustrated. As I let my dress fall, my eyes caught on a piece of paper on Dolion's chair, focusing on the scrawled word despite myself. It must have fallen from his notes when he packed up.

Seawater.

Had I mentioned the name of the bar to him? Or had he written it down when Queen Sariyah debriefed him?

"I'll be back with some lunch as soon as I can," Tobias continued, oblivious to my sudden change in demeanor.

"Okay," I murmured as I walked to the sink, needing to wash up again before putting on my gloves. My brain seemed to stutter as I thought back to what I had told Dolion, trying to connect the dots only to find too many missing.

"Don't leave this room." I could hear the smirk in Tobias's voice. "And try not to miss me too much in the meantime."

I spun around to respond, a retort on my tongue about who, exactly, would be missing whom. But he was already gone.

CHAPTER 36
TOBIAS

We reached our rooms hand in hand. I couldn't remember the last time I had felt this whole, this...hopeful. Tomorrow we would have a cure. Tomorrow, we could save Eva, and everyone else who was fighting to survive in the hospital wing.

Quinn was optimistic that once the magic blocking effects of the virus were negated, any damage it caused would be treatable. Her hope was that once that fog was eradicated, those infected would simply remember once their brains had a chance to heal.

Yael smirked as we entered the outdoor dining area. The nightly wards I set around my room should have blocked the noise we made last night, but she wasn't stupid. Especially not when she had no doubt noticed Quinn's empty bed this morning. Rivan and Pari, however, barely reacted—apparently too busy having a staring contest from opposite sides of the balcony. Pari leaned back against the opposite pillar from Rivan, one foot casually propped up against it. The muscles in Rivan's arms flexed, his jaw tightening. Pari's mouth stretched in a languid, catlike smile.

Quinn bounced on the balls of her feet. "Tomorrow we should have a cure."

The effect of her words was instantaneous. All three rushed over to us, Yael lifting Quinn off her feet in her excitement, and I felt a faint tinge of jealousy I hadn't been the one to spin her around instead.

"Assuming there are no unforeseen effects, we should be able to give it to Eva and the rest of the souls being treated in the Enclave tomorrow," Quinn added. "Then Marin should be able to wake both Bash and Eva from their coma." She grinned at Yael. "I already messaged her the good news. I'll administer Eva's myself while Dolion takes care of the others."

For once, I was looking forward to returning to Morehaven. After Eva was safe, maybe this would be my chance to try again and be the king that Soleara deserved, with Quinn at my side.

A crease formed between Rivan's brows as he looked between us. "And you're sure no one else knows about this?"

He was right to be worried, but I nodded. "Dolion only told Queen Sariyah the news, so it should stay contained—and no one has access to his lab except the four of us."

"He said she'll join us tomorrow to help with the Enclave's infected," Quinn said happily, though I heard the slight note of apprehension.

"Once Silvius learns of this, he'll retaliate," Pari said pointedly as she glared at Rivan. "Which means we need to get ahead of him for once."

Rivan crossed his arms. "Your lead is, at best, a distraction…and at worst, a trap."

"Did you have a better idea?" Pari scowled at him. "If you still want to waste time by starting in the buildings nearest to the tunnels we've already checked for clues, we can. In the meantime, I'll find what we need to finish this once and for all."

"We can't just target some of the most prominent names in this city without—"

"—that's exactly why I said I'll—"

Quinn stepped between them. "What exactly is the issue?"

She turned her stare to Yael who raised her hands in a plaintive 'leave me out of it'.

"While Yael and I have been slogging through the underground tunnels, searching for any sign of Silvius, Pari has been visiting the town gossip," Rivan grumbled.

Pari rolled her eyes. "My contact has been compiling a list of everyone who bent the knee to Aviel, and therefore everyone who might be helping Silvius. If I can get proof of who's still loyal to him, and determine who's feeding him information, then we can cut him off at the knees."

I had known Pari long enough to know exactly how clever she was. If Rivan couldn't recognize that, it was his loss.

Giving him a slow once-over to make my allegiance clear, I turned back to her. "And this lead?"

"Someone interested in switching sides," Pari said shortly. "She was led astray by someone she trusted and now she's scared for her children. Once word spread throughout Mayim about the virus and the innocent lives it claimed, she finally understood the threat Silvius posed. I think I can convince her to help us if we promise to keep her children safe from harm."

"Then do it," I said over Rivan's protest. "I trust your instincts. Our top priority is capturing Silvius before he retaliates and hurts anyone else. There's no telling what he'll do once the cure ruins his plans for revenge."

I barely heard Rivan's rebuttal as Quinn smiled at me, murmuring under her breath, "That may be the first time I've ever had to urge to say, 'yes, Your Majesty'."

She snorted at the look on my face.

"Don't you dare," I muttered, careful to keep my voice low as I leaned in, whispering against her ear, "But if you have an urge to get on your knees for me later, I won't complain."

Quinn's blush was so enticing I had to stop myself from leaning in to taste it.

"It's not your intuition I'm concerned about," Rivan said loudly, he and Pari now nose to nose.

"Oh really?" She crossed her arms, glaring up at him. "You're the one who keeps getting in my way during fights like I'm completely unable to fend for myself."

"It—that's not why—" Rivan spluttered.

Pari's eyes flickered with frustration and more than a hint of hurt. "And now you don't even trust my instincts about a solid lead."

"It's not about trust," Rivan said, raising a hand like he was about to reach for her before he thought better of it. "It's about you getting hurt. If this is a trap—"

"Then I'll take care of myself," Pari said coldly. "I've managed this far without you."

I glanced at Quinn, unsure if we should leave and let them argue privately. Pari angrily started loading her plate, stabbing a knife into a boiled potato so hard it split in two. Yael had already started eating, obviously used to their bickering. Quinn looked between Rivan and Quinn with something calculating in her expression.

"Please," Rivan said softly. "This isn't a judgement against you—"

"You judged me and my people during our ride to Adronix, and you're judging me now," Pari hissed. "Or did you think I forgot your insinuation that us Solearans could've stopped Aviel sooner had we not hidden up north?"

Rivan blanched, going completely still. "I'm not sure what you overheard, but if that's why you have a grudge against me—"

"A grudge implies I care about you at all," Pari seethed, squeezing a fresh roll so hard she flattened it.

"If you're referencing the conversation that I think you are from the ride to Adronix, you should know that what I said was rooted in a moment of frustration," Rivan pleaded, his voice desperate. "I'm sorry—"

"Do you think any of us were happy about biding our time in our mountain as Aviel hunted down anyone who tried to speak against him?" My stomach dropped at the raw emotion in Pari's voice. "Do you think we weren't doing all we could while the rest of the realm went about their lives thinking everything was fine? That *I* wasn't risking my life every single day as we tried to find a way to defeat Aviel without breaking apart the magic keeping our entire kingdom and our current High Queen safe from him?"

Rivan looked stricken. "Pari, is that why you never showed up that night? Before the final battle, when I asked you to…" He trailed off, looking around as if he had just remembered he had an audience.

Quinn's mouth dropped wide open. Pari merely shrugged before finishing off her wine.

"I'm going to go get ready, and then I'm chasing down this lead whether you decide to join or not," Pari said dismissively. She glanced at Yael, who got to her feet even as she shoved one last bite of food into her mouth.

Rivan stepped in front of Pari as she started toward her room. "Of course, I'm going with you."

Pari didn't even look at him as she sidestepped him, walked to her room, and slammed the door behind her.

✧

. . .

Rivan didn't say another word, only stared at Pari's closed door before disappearing into his own.

Quinn leaned forward, whispering to Yael, "Did you know?"

Yael shook her head. "Only that something was off, considering neither tends to act like this. I've known Rivan since we were children, and I've only met a handful of people that have been able to get under his skin like her." She glanced over at the closed doors. "They seemed to get along well enough during the ride to Adronix...but I should've realized there was something unfinished between them."

Quinn nodded even as a yawn overtook her. "If you need help tonight..."

Yael thankfully shook her head before I could object. "You need to rest and recuperate for tomorrow. We've got this."

"Time for bed," I agreed, clearing Quinn's plate along with mine. "They'll do their jobs and we'll do ours. And that includes you sleeping enough for the magic you used today to fully regenerate."

Quinn nodded drowsily, her lack of retort telling me exactly how exhausted she really was. I followed her into her room, not caring what Yael thought. We were both too tired to do more than hold each other, anyway, though I nearly forgot that when she slipped into a black lace nightgown that might as well have been a shirt. She crawled onto the bed, revealing the curve of her ass as I hungrily followed her progress.

I wanted to bend her over like she had been earlier and show her exactly how much I needed her.

But she needed sleep, especially after last night. In a battle between what I wanted and what she needed, the war had already been won—I chose her, every time.

Quinn extended her hand to me as she burrowed beneath the covers, the casualness of the gesture winding me. I obeyed the silent summons, drawn like a sailor to a siren's call as I joined her in bed. My mind whirred as she nonchalantly tucked herself into my side, then closed her eyes with a deep sigh.

I needed to tell her exactly what she was to me—and what we were to each other. There was no way she didn't already suspect with how brilliant she was. The way we responded to each other wasn't natural, and the way I needed her? That desire was so all-encompassing that it was all I could do not to act on it again. It was more than lust, more than trust and friendship.

My world revolved around her. It always had.

Whether I deserved her love or not, I owed her my honesty. Especially now that I had finally given in to what felt inevitable. We owed it to each other to talk about if this was something she truly wanted—not when it couldn't be undone. But already, her breathing had slowed into the heavy cadence of sleep.

I held her closer. She was warmth and life and everything that made it worth living. Even in that dungeon, when I had tucked her away like a secret, she had given me the will to live. Then she had breathed life back into me every time I tried to return to the mental cells of my own making.

And it struck me how rarely I had needed to return to that prison of late, the one where I locked away my fears. Not with Quinn reminding me I could face them.

Careful not to wake her, I reached over to turn off the light. She stirred, then settled the moment I returned to her side.

I would tell her tomorrow, once she finally had a chance to breathe.

But I couldn't resist the urge to brush my lips against her brow. She snuggled closer in her sleep, her curls tickling my chin as I whispered, "I love you."

CHAPTER 37
QUINN

The first thing I heard was the steady drip of water. The world seemed to halt as I realized where I was...and who was before me.

Tobias lay on the cell floor, shivering. The metal mask that hid his face no doubt leeched what little warmth he had been able to retain. Blood soaked through the back of his thin tunic, his chestnut hair overgrown and matted like he hadn't been allowed to bathe for some time.

Rage coursed through me, my blood alive with it, my magic clawing for release—demanding someone pay. I hadn't ever been here in person, but I knew without a doubt where we were: the cells beneath Morehaven. Aviel had already paid for this with his life, though Silvius was still out there.

Which meant this had to be a dream...no, a nightmare. I couldn't even see the edges of his cell where they disappeared into a dark fog. But if it was a dream, and I knew it, why wasn't I waking up?

"Tobias?"

It was like an electric shock went through his body. Tobias shot to his feet, his eyes wild as he stared at me. "Quinn...no." Each word sounded like it cost him even as he struggled to continue. "He's...c-coming."

A chill ran down my spine at the abject horror in his voice.

"Tobias, it's okay," I said, even as I knew it was ridiculous to say so. This was a dream, after all, and the emaciated figure before me was a figment of my *imagination. The False King was dead and Tobias was free—though this nightmare had once been all too real.*

There was a telltale screech of metal on metal as a heavy door slid open. Tobias's entire body went taut, his breathing becoming labored. In one quick movement, he pushed me behind him, his head whipping side to side as if to find a way out of the locked cell.

He felt real, his touch sending a spark through me that woke up every one of my nerve endings. My heart clenched at what must be coming as I watched him tremble.

"It's just a dream," I said aloud, needing to reassure him as well as remind myself. This wasn't real, even if there was something different about it. Something I felt like I should recognize, like a word on the tip of my tongue.

"I...won't...let...him...hurt...you," Tobias gritted out.

A crackle of familiar light skittered along the dank stone. I could feel Tobias's flinch even as his grip on me tightened.

This isn't real, *I thought over and over. Except it still felt real to me.*

"He won't," I promised. "He can't hurt you anymore."

He shook his head. "I'm not the one I'm worried about."

I needed to wake up. Tobias would be beside me, asleep and unharmed, if I could only open my eyes.

"It's okay," I repeated even as unease curdled in my stomach. "You'll be safe when I wake up."

"Quinn!"

✧

The garbled sound of my name yanked me from the nightmare. I sat upright in bed, breathing hard.

But the yell that woke me wasn't a part of my dream.

"Tobias?"

He was tangled in the sheets, his neck twisted so his face was half-smothered in his pillow. His body trembled like he had in my nightmare, each gasping breath cutting off like he couldn't get enough air. Then his mouth opened in a silent scream—

I was across the bed before I knew it.

"Wake up," I said urgently. "You're safe, okay?"

"Q-Quinn," he breathed, and my heart stopped. Because he didn't sound relieved. He sounded terrified. "Please...*no*."

"Tobias, *wake up*," I demanded, taking his face in my hands. He felt so cold...

His eyes flew open, light flaring from each fleck of gold. The next second, his hands wrapped around my wrists, tearing mine from his face. His eyes were wild as he scanned the empty room.

"It's me," I said staying completely still so as not to seem like a threat. "It was just a dream."

Tobias blinked, his grip on me loosening. "Quinn?"

He looked more lost than I had ever seen him. His hands covered his face, baring the white scars on his wrists where those shackles had dug in for years.

I knew what he had been through, but seeing it in my nightmare was another thing entirely. That dream may not have been real, but Tobias had lived that reality.

I hadn't even known he was alive to save.

"I'm sorry," Tobias whispered brokenly. "I...I shouldn't have slept here."

"It's okay," I said, repeating the same words from my dream.

Carefully, I covered his hands with my own, gently prying them away from his face.

"No, it's not," Tobias said dully. His eyes remained downcast, his hands trembling as he fought for control. A full body shudder ran through him, then another.

"It was just a dream," I repeated quietly, stroking the back of his hands with my thumbs in soothing circles. I didn't dare call on my magic to help calm him, not when my rage still bubbled too close to the surface to be sure which form it would take.

"No, it *wasn't*," Tobias snapped. His face twisted in unadulterated anguish. "I was trapped in that cell, trapped in that mask, waiting to be tortured and broken. Telling myself that I wasn't afraid and knowing it was a lie." His whole body was tense, ready to snap. "It wasn't a dream; it was a memory that happened so many times I lost count. The same nightmare I always have, except it was so much worse, because I thought—" his voice cracked "—I thought this time you were trapped in that hellhole along with me." A sob ripped from his throat. "It felt so real, Quinn. I-I thought I finally failed you."

The world seemed to slow to a stop as the implications of our shared dream finally hit me. I had dreamwalked to him—and I knew the only way that was possible. If I was being honest with myself, I had suspected this for some time now, though with everything going on I hadn't dared give into that hope. But Tobias was shaking so hard that I pushed that truth from my mind.

He needed me. Everything else could wait.

"Aviel's dead," I said softly. "I'm safe because of you. And you are too."

Slowly, I shifted forward, carefully wrapping my arms around him. Tobias was barely breathing, as if afraid this was still a part of his dream. Then he sagged into my arms.

Silent tears ran down his cheeks onto mine, my heart breaking at the reason why he learned to cry so noiselessly. I held him more tightly even as my own tears overwhelmed me.

Gently I ran my fingers down his arms, circling along his back, like my touch could free him of whatever memory had held him in its grasp. His hands gripped me almost convulsively, before he started moving them up and down my spine. Comforting *me*, I realized, despite his own distress.

I didn't pull away until he did first, his breathing steadier. My voice was barely a whisper as I finally asked the two questions that I hadn't had the courage to voice before now.

"How did you stay sane? And how didn't you break?"

He was silent for so long that I thought he might not answer. My heart clenched at the thought that he may have donned that mask yet again. That after everything, he was still about to shut me out.

When he did speak, his voice was raw—and so soft I had to lean closer.

"There was nothing to do in that cell but be stuck in my own head," Tobias said hoarsely. "Occasionally there were other prisoners, but they never…they didn't last long. When I was in Soleara, Pari taught me the basics of mental shielding to keep my mind safe." He blew out a long breath. "I knew what Aviel wanted to use me for, and why. He wasn't exactly hiding who he was after he locked me away, not when he was trying to extract any information he could from me."

He paused, looking uncertain. The silence stretched so long I wasn't sure he would speak again until he whispered, so softly it felt like a secret, "So I created my own mental prison, recreating each cell I stared at…and spent every waking moment compartmentalizing everything I had to hide behind those bars. Everything that he could possibly use to find you and Eva, the truth about Soleara, and anything that could be used to hurt those I loved was painstakingly hidden, each dangerous thought sealed away where no one could reach it." He stared past me at the wall, but I knew he wasn't seeing it. "At first it was to hide what I knew from Aviel. Then it became a way to put a barrier between myself and the pain until I couldn't feel anything anymore. I learned to bury the thoughts I couldn't escape behind lock and key, learned to stow away my feelings until it was safe. Except it never was…and now I don't know how not to."

My hand tightened on his, but I didn't dare interrupt. To hear him explain why he had been forced to cage his heart stoked an unimaginable fury in my soul, a cry for justice.

His voice hardened. "Every night when…when he was done with me, I fortified those walls. I sealed away my memories and blocked the emotion behind them, knowing they could doom everyone I loved. I let that mask turn me to ice to make sure that I didn't break, even as my body was broken."

I had wanted to see what lived behind the walls Tobias had so carefully built for so long. I should have realized it would break my heart.

"I'm sorry," I whispered.

"I'm not." His thumb stroked my inner wrist, pressing down on my pulse point. He let out a soft sigh, as if the proof of my heartbeat calmed him. "I'd do it all again, if it kept him from finding you."

I sucked in a shaky breath. "If I had known what was happening to you…"

"I'm glad you didn't," Tobias said quietly. "The thought of you in there with me…what he would have done to you, to Eva…" He shuddered. "He told me his plans for Eva in far greater detail than I ever let her know. What he did manage to do pales in comparison."

My stomach knotted itself tight. I had been the one to heal Eva after she escaped Aviel in Soleara. If he had won…well, we were all lucky it hadn't come to that. But the fact that Aviel taunted her brother with how he planned to use her made me want to scream.

A flicker of red glowed at my fingertips. I closed my eyes until that red haze disappeared.

"I still don't understand how you survived it." I squeezed Tobias's hand, a tangible reminder he was safe and here with me. "Let alone kept him from learning anything important."

Tobias gave the slightest of shrugs, his jaw tight. "Everyone has a breaking point."

"Except for you. You didn't break."

Another infuriating shrug. "Aviel didn't have the right leverage."

I scoffed. "If torturing you for years didn't break you, stealing your magic and letting you rot in that cell wasn't enough—"

"I spent years wondering if each day was the day I would die, knowing that there was a very good chance it could be." He lifted my chin, though my gaze was already locked on his. His eyes flickered as they darted between mine. "But when things were at their bleakest, all I could think about was you."

The way he looked at me, the love and pain warring in his gaze, was more than I could bear. My heart caught in my throat, everything I had been about to say slipping into silence.

"It wasn't a happy thought," Tobias said, his tone matter of fact, "considering I never thought I'd see you again. But I wouldn't give in—not when it meant giving you and Eva up. And I couldn't give up either, even when I found myself hoping he would finally kill me...because there was still the faintest chance that I would find you again one day."

His thumb brushed against my cheek, wiping away the tears I hadn't realized were streaming down my face.

"He couldn't break me," Tobias continued hoarsely. "Because to do so he would've had to find what he was torturing me for." He let out a pained laugh, shaking his head. "Don't you get it, Quinn? My breaking point is *you*."

All this time. All this time he loved me, and I mistook distance for indifference.

"If you l—" My voice broke, and I tried again. "If you thought about me like that, why did you spend so long fighting this?"

Tobias's jaw tensed and for a moment I thought he might not answer. His eyes found me again, reluctantly, the light in them fading. "Because I don't deserve you, Quinn. I never will."

"That's not true—"

"I left," Tobias snapped. "I left Eva...and I left you. I thought I was keeping both of you safe by keeping you in the dark. Instead, I learned my decisions can't be trusted and I—" He hung his head like he couldn't bear to look at me. "I couldn't save my mom when Aviel came for her after he killed my dad. I couldn't save Eva from what he did to her. My blood was the reason Aviel was able to find her in the end. And I couldn't even help her when she had to face him in Adronix." His shoulders slumped, and something in my chest fractured at the broken confession. "I fail people. That's what I do. And I…I can't—I *won't*—fail you."

"You didn't," I said, and was rewarded with a quiet scoff. "You didn't fail any of us, Tobias." Tears blurred my vision. "You spent every day in that hell protecting us after we thought we lost you, something I'll never be able to thank you enough for. You aren't to blame for Aviel's actions. And you were only seventeen when your parents died to save you, and they never regretted it."

His head snapped up. "How do you know?"

"How do you *not*?" My voice cracked. "I knew them too, you know. But even if I didn't, I would know without a doubt that they faced their ends at peace, knowing that their sacrifice meant their children would live on."

His lower lip trembled, those gold-flecked eyes glistening with unshed tears.

"When my parents died, I at least had the luxury of saying goodbye." My voice shook at the memory. "They knew there was a good chance they wouldn't return, and yet they still went." Carefully, I took his trembling hand in mine. "So I'll tell you what my mother told me in case something went wrong. It's the same thing I tell myself whenever I miss them." I blinked away my tears, keeping my voice steady. "Tobias…it's not your fault they were taken from this world. You're how they remain in it."

Tears streamed down his face, matching the ones on mine. And I was glad of it—that he finally had the courage to take off that mask and let himself feel. That he trusted me enough not to pretend anymore.

"I lost them not long after I thought I lost you," I whispered. "I barely survived it."

"I'm sorry," Tobias said brokenly. "I wish I hadn't put you through that. Not coming back sooner might be the thing I regret the most." He squeezed my hands. "But there wasn't a day I didn't picture coming home to you. And when I tried to return and ended up captured…you were the only thing that kept me sane."

"My heart's been broken since the day I thought you died," I said softly. "I might have put on a happy face, but it was just as much a mask as yours."

He wiped his tears on the back of his arm in one angry swipe. "You still deserve someone better than me. Someone who isn't broken. Someone—"

"You're an idiot," I snapped, feeling my magic roil as if demanding I reach for him. "Just because I understand why you have the emotional intelligence of a toe doesn't mean I'm going to wait around for you to figure it out, even if I..."

"Even if you what?"

"Love you." I shouted, the words tearing free before I could bite them back. "I love you, Tobias Maris, broken pieces and all." My chest squeezed painfully tight. "I loved you then. But I'm *in* love with you now."

The truth rang in the space between us.

"You..." His hand shook as he brushed my tears away. "Do you remember the night before my birthday?"

I frowned up at him. "You know I do."

"I should have told you then that I loved you." His throat bobbed. "I almost did...and every night in that cell I thought about how I missed my chance. That you thought I was dead, and I never told you what you meant to me. And that I needed to find a way out to fix that one fateful mistake." His light circled around us like tiny stars. "I am hopelessly, irretrievably in love with you, Quinn Sagray. I always have been."

I blinked up at him, startled, as his words sank in. "You knew you were in love with me, even then?"

There was something like hope in those gold-flecked eyes. "I don't remember falling in love with you. I just know I always did."

My breath caught at the emotion in those words. At his shy smile, so reminiscent of the boy I once knew—the one he kept hidden away until it was safe again.

"Do you really want this?" For the first time, Tobias sounded unsure. "Want *me*, scars and all?"

After everything we'd been through together, did he really not think he was deserving of love?

"I want all of you, Tobias Maris," I said adamantly. "Your scars are part of you, and I love everything you are. I love you, too."

His mouth found mine, insistent and claiming. My fingers threaded through his hair, yanking him closer with the same urgency. I had lost him once, his absence like an echo that refused to fade.

I would never lose him again.

My hand flattened against his heart, needing to feel the wild flutter of his pulse. Its every beat matched mine.

He pulled back, gazing at me like he couldn't believe this was real. His lips brushed mine in the barest of kisses. "Somehow, despite all my imaginings, you're even more perfect than I remember."

I kissed the scars on his neck, his wrists. My power came to my fingertips even as his magic swirled around us, lighting up the dark.

"I wish I hadn't given up on you." My voice broke. "I wish I came to this realm sooner. That I was there for you when you needed someone most."

"You were always with me." He caught a single curl of my hair, slowly twisting it around his finger, and I shivered under the intensity of his stare. "I spent every day in that cell picturing you living your life. Picturing *you*… the bounce of your hair, the curve of your lips, the amber of your eyes." His thumb brushed against my cheek, then pressed against my lower lip. "I memorized every part of you, over and over again. Your name was my own personal prayer for salvation, even if I could never say it aloud. Even when I shut it all away so he could never, ever touch you." His gaze slowly trailed down my face, the weight of it like a physical touch. "When everything was darkest, you were the light."

I had given up on wiping away my tears, but Tobias leaned in, kissing the damp corner of each eye.

"When I got back…I didn't want you to see me like that," he continued. "The broken version of the boy you almost kissed. Nevermind that the thought of our first kiss was one of the only things that kept me going." His laugh was dark and humorless. "One of the things I missed most when I was in that dungeon was the sky. It's almost ironic that once I got out, that open space became the thing I feared. But when you stayed next to me on our ride to Adronix, or training with me in Soleara, it felt like…like a deep breath in. Like being with you was how I kept breathing."

A sob burst from my lips. "You kept *me* breathing. You kept us safe when we didn't even know you were alive." I took his face in my hands. My thumb brushed over his dimple, feeling it deepen beneath my touch. "You can take your mask off and lay it down now. You and your heart are safe with me."

CHAPTER 38
TOBIAS

I could feel her love like a balm, gentle yet electrifying and steadying all at once, even as it threatened to unmake me. The weight on my chest seemed to lift, the last chain I hadn't realized I used to bind myself. It seemed too good to be true to be given everything I had ever wanted: her love, her trust. Just her.

The walls I built around my heart were gone, the iron and stone giving way to something terrifyingly alive. There was nowhere left to lock my feelings away, no bars left to keep me from what I had always known. I needed her, and more importantly, she needed me too. After so long pushing her away, it was time to take that leap: To finally claim the life that I had always wanted but never thought I deserved.

Worthy or not, I would spend my life trying to be. And maybe that was enough.

My eyes caught on the window behind her and the darkness beyond, a waning moon perfectly placed between a gap in the curtains. We had only a few hours left until morning, the thought sobering. Wasting even a minute after pushing her away for so long seemed as criminal as it was impossible.

"Just a few hours until dawn breaks," Quinn said wistfully, in an echo of my thoughts.

"Not nearly enough time for everything I want to do to you," I agreed. "Though that list will take at least a few years."

Her smile was fleeting. "We have so much left to do that it feels wrong to be this happy, especially while those we love are waiting on us to save them."

I knew exactly how she felt, just as I knew she was doing everything she could and more. She had always carried the weight of the world on her shoulders. At least now, I would be there to help shoulder the load.

"There's nothing else you can do until the morning," I said gently. "I shouldn't have to tell you that creating a cure in the time you have is nothing short of miraculous, magic or no. You've done everything you can and more." Quinn pursed her lips, still looking unconvinced. "If I weren't so selfish I'd insist you go back to sleep. You could use some rest before you reap the rewards of all your hard work in the morning."

The look she gave me told me exactly how much of a nonstarter that suggestion would be. "This is a forever thing, Tobias Maris, but if you think I'm going to sleep after that, then you don't know me at all. In the morning, we'll save the realm as planned. Tonight, I need you." Her voice became almost painfully hesitant as she added, "but if you aren't ready, we can go back to—"

I snaked my arm around her, dragging her closer. "I loved you before fate tore us apart, Quinn Sagray, and I'll love you long after I take my last breath. When we save Eva and this is finally over, I'm going to keep you in my bed for a month straight and make you mine."

Her breath hitched. "I'm already yours. I think I always have been."

She loved me. *She* loved *me*.

I nearly laughed at the lightness in my chest, the strange sense of happiness I thought was forever lost. Her love had resurrected the self I thought long buried, breathing life into the ghost I had become. It stripped away every doubt, every excuse I had clung to as to why we couldn't be together. All that was left was me and her and a love that would no longer be contained.

There would never be anyone else—not for either of us. Maybe it was because of that that the next step felt so simple.

"It's more than wanting you though, more than even loving you." I tilted up her chin so that her eyes met mine. "I want forever with you, sweetheart—although even that doesn't sound like enough. And I think you do too."

The look she gave me was both wistful and exasperated. "About time you figured it out, Maris."

She stared at my mouth, looking almost insultingly astonished as I grinned at her.

"I've learned that fate doesn't always grant second chances." I leaned forward, catching her lips in a quick kiss—a reminder of the one so long denied. "And that tomorrow is never certain. Right now, I don't want to wait another second, not with you." It was my turn for my tone to falter, old fears bubbling up despite the certainty in her eyes. "That is, if you'll have me."

"Of course I will," Quinn breathed.

A thread of my light squeezed between our interlaced fingers, binding us together. This light didn't aim to burn or break—it was warmth and love and something that felt like home. Her hands glowed in response, a mix of blue and red, as her magics melded with mine.

The world around us seemed to pause, grinding to a halt. Even my swirling light came to a standstill, like those twinkling orbs were holding their breaths. There was a strange resonance to my voice as I murmured the ancient words that would bind us eternally.

"You are my beloved."

The acceptance slipped from her lips like those four words came from her soul itself. "And I am yours."

Our lips met and the world burst back to life in endless color. This kiss was magic and wonder, joy and eternity, and a love so deep I could feel it in my soul. I gasped as I realized there was more to it—that the growing echo of the love in her heart was merging forever with mine.

It was a refuge and a reckoning. The slow build of a friendship blossoming into more, and desire so absolute that it might never be sated.

It was the way a single glance spoke volumes and the shared silences that felt as full as a conversation. It was the rawness of being known and the possessiveness of belonging to another.

And it was all building into a storm both dizzying in its strength and entirely consuming—one I would gladly weather with her by my side.

Most of all, it was a homecoming. The simple knowledge that no matter how the world shifted around us, and no matter what happened next, I would forever and always be hers.

My eyes opened to an explosion of light; both the blue and red of Quinn's magics entwining with my own power. Her healing and blood magics weren't warring with each other—no, they complemented the other so completely I wondered if they weren't one and the same. My lightning streaked harmlessly around us, its branches an echo of the veins leading to our hearts.

I laughed, the unencumbered sound taking me by surprise. Quinn stared at me, her mouth parting.

After so long of not letting myself feel, it felt like I was drowning in her love. And I hoped with all my heart that tide would never stop sweeping me away.

I was hers. I always had been.

"I would live through all of it again," I whispered against her lips. "If it meant we ended up here."

Her joy echoed along our bond, like sunlight warming my face. I slipped the strap of her nightdress off her shoulder, tracing the line where silk met skin. Her desire merged with mine, the primal need to consummate this much more than simply some magical imperative.

"I wasted far too long denying this to waste another night without you." It seemed like insanity now that I had ever tried to push her away. This was how we were meant to be, the two of us eternally bonded to each other. And if anyone tried to get in the way of that…if Silvius tried to hurt her, I would sear the flesh from his bones.

Quinn's eyes widened at the same time I felt my power flash, like a bolt of lightning behind my corneas.

"What's wrong?"

Of course, she had felt the change in my emotions.

"If anything happens to you," I gritted out. "The closer we are to a cure, the more danger you're in. The thought of him trying to hurt you…"

"Your turn to breathe," Quinn demanded. "Silvius will pay for what he did."

"I don't want to hear you even say his name," I growled. "I don't want him anywhere *near* you."

Quinn just raised an eyebrow. I exaggeratedly drew in a breath, holding in for a quick four count, before releasing it. Whatever protectiveness I already felt for her had somehow multiplied, the need to eradicate the threat to her life almost consuming enough to distract me from my need for her.

She rolled her eyes. "Once more, Maris. With feeling this time."

I obediently drew in an exaggeratedly loud inhale, and a soft smile curved her lips.

"You could always list off five things you can hear…"

I pressed a kiss behind her ear, my voice low as I commanded, "Remind me the other four?"

"Four things you can see, three things you can touch, two things you can smell…" Quinn's breath stuttered as I dragged my lips down the side of her neck. "…and one thing you can taste."

I smiled against her skin, then whispered directly into her ear. "I like that method. I'm dying to taste you."

Her back arched as I nipped at her earlobe. Her voice was breathless as she asked, "Oh?"

"But first…tell me what you can feel." My fingers dug into her thighs, lifting the hem of her nightdress. She gasped as my fingers grazed the thin lace separating me from my goal. "You're already soaked for me, sweetheart."

"I feel…" Her eyes were heavy-lidded as they met mine, her mouth slightly parted, begging to be kissed. I had dreamed of that look; thought about it with my hand wrapped around my cock too many times to count.

I slipped my finger inside her. Her core clenched around me even as her thighs fell open. "You feel?"

"Whole." She let out a whimper as I brought that finger up to circle her clit, rubbing her wetness around her. "Like I was alone before, and now…it feels like my soul is smiling. I feel *you*."

I could feel her need for me like a burning ache, her desire licking down my spine. She was wound so tight already. But I wanted to be inside her before I felt that tension snap.

With one twist of my wrist, I tore that bit of lace away.

Quinn laughed. "If you don't stop doing that, I won't have any clothes left."

"Good," I rasped. "I've had a long, long time to imagine every filthy thing I want to do to you, Sagray. Clothing isn't necessary for any of them."

The heat in her eyes matched the pulse of need across our bond. Slowly, Quinn tugged her nightdress over her head, revealing herself to me entirely.

I stopped breathing.

She was more perfect than I ever imagined, and I drank in every inch of her like a man drowning. The long line of her legs, the curve of her hips, her dark, peaked nipples, and what lay between her thighs. Her throat bobbed as I continued my blatant perusal.

I was so hard that it was physically painful, the thin sleep shorts I wore hiding nothing.

"Is that what you wanted?" The sultry edge to her voice nearly brought me to my knees.

Yes. But what I *wanted wasn't the goal here.*

"It's a good start," I said hoarsely.

She smirked as she looked down at the evidence of my arousal. With a sharp tug, she yanked my shorts down, leaving us both completely nude.

"Tell me what you want," I insisted. "Because I need to be inside you, in any way you'll have me."

"I want…" Hesitancy twisted down our bond as Quinn pressed her hand against my chest.

Her scent, her closeness, it was all intoxicating. And yet, I understood what she wanted in an instant. I leaned back, letting my head rest on my pillow.

"You want control?" I murmured. "Then take it."

It was something I had never willingly given anyone. The few trysts I had allowed in this realm before my capture had been transactional—a moment of release and a means to an end, with the boundaries agreed upon ahead of time. They hadn't been who I pictured as I made them come.

But for her…for her, I'd give anything.

As though sensing my acceptance, she moved forward until she straddled me. It would barely take a tilt of my hips to bury myself inside of her, but I waited for her next move.

I didn't have to wait long. Her hips lowered, grinding against my hard length. I swore under my breath as she took just the tip of me inside her.

"You've always been the one in control, sweetheart."

With a mangled moan, she sunk down, her wet warmth engulfing my cock. That sound mixed with the rightness, that endless love flooding me like an eternal tide, almost made me lose myself right there. The world narrowed to that blissful heat and pressure as she lifted herself up, then lowered again—taking exactly what she needed from me.

My hands gripped her ass, angling her against me. I was rewarded with the sight of her eyes rolling back in her head, her lips parting in a gasp.

"Eyes on me," I ordered, yanking her down as I thrust upward.

Her eyes flew open, red overtaking the amber as her hand flattened against my chest.

"I feel your heartbeat." Quinn sounded faintly amazed. "And feel how much you love me. I feel…"

Her hand dug into my chest almost painfully and her inner walls tightened rhythmically around me. My hands braced her hips, urging her to go faster. It didn't take long for that tension to reach a crescendo; her pace grew faster as her body started to shake.

A deep groan vibrated through me. "That's my girl. Don't stop."

"Yes, sir," she breathed, and I nearly lost it right there. She leaned forward, bracing her hands on either side of my head as she panted against my mouth. "Come with me."

I kissed her, hard. Then I pushed up into her, watching her breasts bounce tantalizingly with each hard thrust. That telltale pressure built at the base of my spine as I felt her start to shake. Her pleasure merging with mine brought me right to the edge.

"Quinn—"

Her climax took her a heartbeat before mine—the feeling of her clenching around me paired with the explosion of her release utterly unraveling me. I plunged deep inside her, filling her as wave after wave of her orgasm rolled through her. I barely noticed the lightshow of our magic as my light rained down around us, streaks of blue and red intermingled throughout like our own personal fireworks.

Quinn collapsed against me, her face tucking into the space between my neck and shoulder as we caught our breath. My fingers traced down her back, reverently memorizing the bumps and dips of her spine.

"I love you," she breathed, the echoing emotion so unbearably vivid I kissed her again.

Gently, I slipped from inside her. She rolled from the bed, bare feet padding across the floor as I watched the sway of her hips, utterly entranced. She disappeared into the bathroom, and even that short time away felt too much to bear. When she returned, I pulled her into bed, then curled around her, watching the slow flutter of her lashes as her exhaustion caught up with her.

"I love you too," I whispered, feeling like those three words would never be enough.

Though maybe now, she could feel its depth. The emotion I had spent so long burying behind bars had only grown stronger over the years, waiting for its chance to escape and feel the sun.

With every shared inhale, I could feel her love like my own heartbeat. That unbreakable bond pulsed between us as we fell asleep in each other's arms.

CHAPTER 39
TOBIAS

I woke before sunrise with Quinn's hair tickling my face. Even with last night's interruption, I couldn't remember the last time I slept this well. Or when I last opened my eyes without expecting to feel the cold, claustrophobic pressure of my mask against my face.

Instead, I was warm. Almost too warm with my *anima* wrapped around me.

I should have told her the truth sooner—the one that seemed obvious the second I let myself acknowledge the depth of my feelings. Quinn clearly had guessed based on her lack of surprise last night.

There was an unexpected relief in realizing I could be loved after so many years abandoned in that cell as that cold, cruel mask dripped ice into my soul...and that I could love her as much as she deserved. For so long, I had believed I was so damaged that there was only room for vengeance and loneliness in my heart.

And yet all along, it had beat for her.

I should've known that she'd prove me wrong.

It was peaceful listening to her steady breaths and the synchronized beats of our hearts. She needed the rest, not only after what we had done last night, but from the continual drain on her magic as she poured it into the cure. Quinn had worked until the last possible minute yesterday, preparing each of the life essences to ensure everything was ready for Eva and all the others Silvius had infected.

She had poured everything she had into it, as I knew she would with what was at stake. Then again, she always did.

I also knew Quinn wouldn't be happy with me if I let her sleep in. After all, today was the day we had been striving for if all went to plan—my literal blood going into it, along with our figurative sweat and tears. Today we would save my sister. Although Silvius was still out there, we would undo the damage his virus caused before defeating him together.

Counting each second, I blew out a slow breath...though for once I didn't feel the need to. I felt safe with her in a way I hadn't felt in a long time.

Quinn stirred slightly, perhaps roused by the feeling of my excitement. I couldn't help but press a soft kiss against her lips.

"Hi," Quinn mumbled, her smile brushing against mine.

"Hi," I whispered stupidly back.

Against her, I hadn't stood a chance. I never had.

I lifted my chin, brushing the barest of kisses against her forehead. Trailing them across her cheeks, her eyelids, the point of her ear...

She yawned, blinking open her eyes as she snuggled closer. "How long do we have until the lab opens?"

I should have known that would be her first thought. Her single-minded determination brought a smile to my lips as I gently chided, "It's still dark, Sagray."

She gave an exaggerated sigh. "I thought we were finally on a first name basis."

I smirked. "Old habits die hard. But you have *some* time if you want to get a little more rest." I ran my fingers down her spine, tracing lazy circles onto her back. "I'll wake you when it's time."

Stubbornly she shook her head. "I'm up. I won't be able to get back to sleep, not when there's so much to do today." Her brows scrunched together. "Did the others ever make it home last night?"

I frowned, straining to hear any sign they returned. "I'm sure they would've told us is something went wrong."

Unless they were in too much danger, or worse. I was only too aware of the methods Silvius had for keeping one silent.

Quinn reached for where a pad of paper sat on the bedside. "I'll send a note to check in, just in case."

My reply lodged in my throat. I could feel the metal of the mask, icy against my skin as I tried to push that recollection back down. It felt more difficult than usual to picture the cells that once held me, even as that steady drip of moisture echoed in my ears...

The warmth of her hand brought me back as it rested on my cheek. "Where did you go?"

I tried to sound casual as I asked, "When?"

Her gaze sharpened, as if debating whether to call me out. "When you lost the light in your eyes, Tobias. When I couldn't feel you anymore."

For a heavy beat, I couldn't find my voice.

"Back to my cell," I whispered.

I wouldn't—*couldn't*—lie to her anymore. I didn't want to anyway.

I had raised my walls instinctively, unthinkingly blocking our bond. Her concern now bled through the cracks in my shield, wearing away at the barrier between us like water against sand.

"You don't have to anymore," Quinn said though without any judgement. "Talk to me. Before you bury your feelings again, try to remember that I'm here and I'll help you through it."

I swallowed the lump in my throat. "I'm sure they're fine. But the thought of Silvius silencing them somehow...I spent four years with that psychopath. Four *years* listening to him talk about how I wasn't worthy to be in his King's presence, never mind the fact that I would've given almost anything not to be. Aviel may have been my torturer, but Silvius was the mastermind of it all. He was the inventor of the band around my neck and the mask that hid my face, and the one behind the silence I grew so accustomed to that I'm still working to find my voice again. Aviel may have orchestrated it...but Silvius was the one who broke me."

"You're not broken," Quinn protested. "And you never broke, or I wouldn't be here with you now. That silence saved me too."

"Just promise me you'll be careful," I rasped. "If anything happens to you..."

Quinn nodded, like she understood. And maybe she did, considering what I must be sending across our bond.

"This is going to take some getting used to," I muttered. "I didn't even realize that I blocked you out." Taking her hand, I brushed a kiss against the back of it, relishing in the soft flutter of her response across our bond. "I'm sorry. I'll do better."

I knew she could sense my determination and regret, along with the truth of my apology.

Quinn pursed her lips. "That's one thing you've never been good at, you know."

"And what's that?"

"Asking for help."

I continued kissing my way up her arm, determined to wipe the remaining concern from her face. She squirmed a little as I reached a sensitive spot on the inside of her elbow, and I noted it for later.

"And you know me so well?"

Quinn rolled her eyes. "I know everything about you."

"Oh yeah?" I raised one eyebrow. "What's my favorite color?"

She smiled like it was obvious. "Yellow."

Her laugh made my heart skip a beat.

"Yellow, huh?"

Those amber eyes sparkled. "Nothing garish. Warm and golden, like the magic that flows down your sword. Like—"

My gaze fell to where her necklace sparkled against her chest. "Like sunflowers."

Her breath caught. My eyes slid up slowly to see the blush coloring her cheeks.

Of course, my favorite color was yellow. It reminded me of her.

Yellow like the sunflower amulet she hadn't taken off for as long as I could remember, its pale diamonds shining above her heart.

Yellow like the sunlight playing across her cheeks as we sparred in the courtyard.

Yellow like the dress she had worn when she danced with me in a perfect, stolen moment.

Yellow like the field of flowers in Soleara I once watched her walk through from the shadows of my room—a voyeur as she spread her arms wide and fell back into them. I had stared at her through my window, wishing I could find the courage to go to her and fall into the flowers too.

I picked up her necklace, the backs of my fingers brushing against the curve of her breast. Its diamonds glimmered, golden and alive, as I watched Quinn's slow swallow move down her throat.

"You're right," I said. "It's yellow."

The smile she gave me could have rivaled the sun. The morning light painted her hair with an angelic glow, that smile growing as I gently tugged her amulet so the chain brought her closer.

I twirled the sunflower in my fingers, feeling each dull point against my thumb. "Now, are you going to make me guess yours or is it still yellow too?"

She told me that once, a lifetime ago. When we were teens on an early morning car ride and Eva had fallen back asleep in the backseat.

Yellow, like the sunrise, she said as the early morning light set her amber gaze aglow.

I remembered being thankful she had her eyes on the road since it gave me the excuse to watch her unobtrusively. Though given the way she had accidentally missed a green light, there was a chance she noticed.

"Hmm," she murmured suggestively. "I know a way you can get the truth out of me."

I leaned in, unable to resist the allure of her arousal, the entirely intoxicating feeling of her need for me. When we were home in Soleara, I would spend a lifetime worshiping her and spend each day in awe that she was mine. For the first time in a long time, I not only had a future—I was looking forward to it.

"You are my sunrise, Quinn Sagray, and I never want to wake up without you again." My voice was steady and sure, even as I sent a silent plea to the universe that I always would. "I hope you're prepared to be sick of me because I'm never letting you go again."

"About time, Maris," Quinn said with a laugh.

I kissed her again.

CHAPTER 40
QUINN

Despite the lack of sleep, I had never felt more awake.

I dressed in a hurry, making sure I strapped my dagger to my waistbelt. In addition to the obvious need for it, there was something grounding about the familiar silver blade on my hip. Whether or not I needed it, today would indeed be a battle—one I was determined to win.

"As soon as the lab opens, we'll confirm dosing and head back to Morehaven," I said again, repeating my mental list like doing so would calm my racing heart. "Dolion said he'll handle the rest of the infected, but I want to administer it to Eva myself."

Tobias knelt between my thighs, hands sliding down my legs as he fastened my boots.

"Stop that, you'll distract me."

"And if that's my goal?" The look in his eyes was downright devilish, though I could feel his worry twisting across our bond. If he *was* trying to distract me from my own anxiety, it was working. Tobias had put on pants—black, of course—but his shirt still draped open, the undone buttons showing off the stark lines of his abdominals. It was an effort not to push him down and trace that path with my tongue. He had already strapped his sword to his back, ready for the return trip.

Tobias must have sensed my desire because his gaze heated.

"Let's save your sister first," I chastened, though it was more to admonish myself. "Then you can distract me all night if you want."

"Just one night?" He smiled, the sight of it leaving me breathless. "I was hoping for forever."

I couldn't resist Tobias when he was smiling—a lazy, teasing smile, but a real smile nonetheless. But it faded as he no doubt felt my uneasy mix of dread and anticipation.

"Do you think she'll be surprised?" I bit my lip. "When Eva wakes up, do you think she'll pretend she always had an inkling?"

He wrapped his arms around me. "I think she'll be happy for us. I know I am."

Tobias's joy fluttered down our bond, light and airy. Paired with the comforting, all-encompassing feeling of his love, it felt like my heart might burst.

I couldn't wait to tell my best friend the news.

✧

Tobias brought me a plate full of breakfast, though I barely noticed what I was eating as I stared at the door to our suite, willing it to open. I wanted to send another missive to Pari but didn't want to risk alerting anyone to her presence. If she hadn't answered yet, there must be a reason she couldn't reply.

Maybe the magic of last night had bled into today, and Silvius was already in custody. Maybe Yael, Rivan, and Pari would return any second with him in chains and a cure in hand. But I couldn't shake the feeling there was a far more sinister reason for their lack of response.

The lab would open soon. But if our friends were in trouble…

"We should split up," I said even as I knew what Tobias's answer would be.

"No," he snapped, his voice like iron.

My immediate annoyance was mitigated by the way I could feel his terror at the thought. Not concern, not fear, but a flash of something entirely overwhelming before he tamped it down, like the idea of letting me out of his sight physically hurt him. A surge of protectiveness took its place, reaching down our bond like it might wrap around me.

"I can get the cure to Eva, especially with Dolion's help," I said calmly. "If something happened to our friends then someone needs to go after them. And we can't trust anyone else. Telling the wrong people might lead to more trouble."

His shoulders were so tense I could see every muscle of his back as his shirt strained against it. "Leaving you isn't an option."

"Neither is abandoning our friends," I retorted. "Let's not waste time arguing about it when you know I'm right."

I lifted my tea, taking a sip as Tobias opened his mouth to argue. The door slammed open.

Rivan rushed in, Pari in his arms. They were covered in blood—too much blood. Pari's arms hung limply from where Rivan clutched her to his chest. Blood covered the bottom half of her face, even more of it splattered onto Rivan's neck and chest.

The sound of my mug shattering brought me out of my shock.

"Help her," Rivan pleaded. He looked more scared than I had ever seen him, his chest heaving with exertion.

My magic flared to life, reaching for the blood and the lifeline of her veins. I didn't care if Rivan noticed the red tinge of my eyes or knew what it meant. Not when my magic told me that Pari's heart was still beating, which meant she could still be saved.

"Put her on the bed," I ordered.

Rivan crossed the room in two long strides, bringing her not to her room, but his.

"Grab a towel and a bowl of water to clean her off," I ordered Tobias as I hurried passed him. His eyes were wide and scared, but he nodded as I rushed to Pari's side.

Rivan gently set her on the bed, his careful movements a sharp contrast to the tension vibrating through him. His hand still cradled the back of her head, tangling in her hair, its silver dark and matted with her blood. Only when I reached for Pari did he back up to stand by the head of the bed.

My magic seeped into her body like a fish in a stream, fighting through the current to find the right path. I already knew what I would find—after all, I had spent my every waking moment since Eva's wedding studying the virus that was attacking her.

Pari's blood told the same story. The nosebleed dried on her lips, the loss of consciousness...the fog had already begun to surround her brain. I could feel it working to block my magic even as I attempted to push it back. Soon, the virus would replicate until the mist solidified and she was out of my reach.

"How long since she was injected?"

Rivan stared mutely at Pari. His hands shook as he gathered a clump of her silver hair now red with her blood and separated it from the rest. His thumb rubbed against it like he could remove the stain.

"Rivan."

"An hour ago, if that," he rasped, not taking his eyes from her. "I healed what I could as I brought her back, but she still hasn't woken up. The fog was already there."

My stomach plummeted. "That's too fast. Eva was injected nearly a half day before her nosebleed. Which means..."

"He's created a more potent strain," Tobias said from behind me.

I stared at my *anima* as he handed Rivan a damp towel and a steaming bowl of water.

"What?" Tobias looked vaguely put out at my surprise. "I pay attention."

"The cure should still work," I said as I checked Pari for any additional injuries. A long gash down her arm looked newly knitted back together, along with a few scrapes—no doubt Rivan's handiwork. "Even if there's higher transmissibility, it shouldn't affect its effectiveness."

Rivan barely seemed to hear me as he wiped the blood from Pari's face and neck. His hands shook as he reached back for fresh water.

I placed my hand on top of Rivan's, gently taking the blood-soaked towel from him. "Rivan, what happened?"

His voice trembled as he whispered, "It was meant for me."

"What was?"

"The syringe." He let out a low, wounded sound. "She saw the syringe when I didn't. And she put herself between us, between me and the coward who tried to sneak up to plunge it into my back. She—" His voice cracked. "She's like this because she saved me."

"It's not your fault," I said adamantly. "And it's going to be okay. The cure is ready. We just need to get to the lab and..." I froze as I realized the implication of what he said. "Wait, if the vial was meant for you, it shouldn't have worked on her. Unless..."

Tobias's eyes met mine, narrowed in understanding. "Unless there's a new version of the virus that doesn't need a blood link." Tobias filled a glass of water from the bedside, passing it to Rivan who downed it in one gulp. "Back up. How did this happen in the first place?"

"Pari convinced her contact to help us gather Silvius's supporters tonight," Rivan said, his gaze never leaving her face. "On the way back, I insisted we visit one of the remaining buildings along the tunnel route. A few of our rangers were there to make sure there isn't another entry point for Silvius to use." His voice was thick with recrimination. "Instead, we were greeted by a faction of guards. I should've realized something was off the second we didn't see our people. As soon as we walked inside, they turned on us. We fled into the next room only to find our own rangers unconscious and covered in blood."

I swallowed against my dry mouth. "Were they—"

"Infected," Rivan confirmed grimly. "Then one of the guards touched the wall behind him and we suddenly couldn't use our magic. It was some sort of ward I haven't seen before, set up in the building itself. More were waiting on the floor below, blocking the exits." He shook his head. "We're lucky we made it out alive."

I handed him a fresh towel. "Is Yael safe?"

"She's with our rangers, helping bring the wounded back to the Enclave." He blew out a breath. "I ran ahead."

Ran. He ran with Pari in his arms for gods knew how long.

"I'll have to run a few tests, but the cure should still work on her and the others," I said, mentally crossing my fingers. "She'll be okay."

My magic receded. The greenish gray glow of Rivan's healing magic took its place, its light noticeably dim.

He must have poured his power into her for it to be this weak, especially if he hadn't been able to access it during the fighting.

"Keep her comfortable until we get back," I said gently. "We won't be long."

Rivan nodded, still focused on wiping the blood from Pari's hair. I followed Tobias out of the room, taking his hand in the same moment that he reached for mine.

The lab was open by now. Dolion was likely already wondering where we were.

I hesitated when I heard Rivan's voice. He had knelt beside the bed, silhouetted by the doorframe. A blood-covered towel was clenched in his fist. His forehead pressed to the back of Pari's limp hand, his long braids shielding his face as he bowed over it.

"I'm sorry," Rivan said hoarsely. "I'm sorry, okay? I'm begging you...don't let the words I said in anger be the last thing you ever hear me say." His voice broke. "I don't want you compliant. I want you to argue with me every day for the rest of our lives. I want your passion, I want your fight, I want... everything with you." A sob choked from his throat. "Please, Pari..."

His shoulders shook as I turned away, despite it being far too late to give them privacy. I exchanged a look with Tobias, who held the door to the hallway open for me.

Rivan's whispered plea snuck past it before the door shut behind us.

"...come back to me."

CHAPTER 41
QUINN

We sprinted down the halls side by side. Our urgency pulsed between us, an anxious thrum that grew louder the closer we got to the lab. The halls were mostly empty with our late start, though a few heads turned as we rushed past. I fleetingly wondered how quickly it would get back to Queen Sariyah that the visitors from Soleara were armed and running through her research wing.

Dolion had assured me he was keeping her updated on our progress, so hopefully we weren't about to cause a diplomatic incident. If so, the formal apology would have to wait until my friends were safe and healthy.

I skidded to a halt in front of the laboratory's iron door, pressing my hand against the access pad. A skitter of apprehension crossed our bond before Tobias reached past me, yanking the iron door open.

"I'm sorry we're late—"

Tobias threw me behind him, raising his dagger in the same movement. The once-sterile environment had been reduced to ruin. Shards of glass glittered everywhere: the remnants of precision instruments broken beyond recognition. The cold storage that held the cure we had worked so hard for now hung wide open, its contents gone. Taken, considering the carrying cases Dolion had stacked next to them to prepare for today were missing as well.

Blood streaked across the floor like a body had been dragged across the lab. Dolion's familiar pack was strewn around in its wake, his notebooks torn or damaged by seeping reagents.

They had him. And they had the cure.

My shock and fury echoed right back to me. Everything we had worked for had been stolen from us on the cusp of success. The cure we had fought for—bled for, suffered for—was undoubtably on its way to Silvius. And Dolion, my friend who made it possible, was likely fighting for his life.

Glass crunched underfoot as Tobias stepped forward, his gaze sweeping across the empty lab for threats. "This *just* happened." He knelt by the blood on the ground then looked back at me. "This is fresh. Besides, nothing can survive the overnight sterilization, and we're barely late. Which means—"

"They haven't gone far." I shoved my panic aside, focusing on what little we knew. "How did they even get in?" I glanced behind me. "The door was locked. Unless they made Dolion open it for them when he arrived?"

"The real question is how they got out," Tobias said thoughtfully. "Either they dragged a bleeding Dolion through the research ward during the busiest time of the day..." Tobias ran a hand along the wall as he slowly walked along the edge of the room, avoiding a dark stain. "Or there's another way out of here."

There wasn't any blood in the hallway. I glanced around the lab, desperately searching for anything we had missed in our long hours here. "Surely Dolion would've noticed a glamour in here."

Tobias paced around the perimeter of the room. I could feel his steady determination, his confidence that there was something hidden in plain sight.

I scanned the debris, looking for the vital information from our research in the pages littering the ground. From what I could see, anything I could use to recreate the cure had been stolen, the pages left behind filled with our failed efforts.

"We need to tell someone," I murmured into the quiet.

I knew better than to call for help, especially after double agents had infected Pari. There was too great a chance any nearby guards could be compromised. Alerting someone we didn't trust was worse than telling no one at all.

Dolion's desk had been torn apart, more papers littering the floor around it. I carefully walked over, avoiding the trail of blood as I leaned over to grab a pen off the floor along with a torn notebook. "I'll let Rivan and Yael know what happened, and Queen Sariyah too. If you're wrong, they could still be somewhere in the Enclave."

As I straightened, I did a double take. The storage room. The one that I had never seen unlocked let alone open…

Its door was ajar.

Tobias noticed in the next second, likely from the shock sparking down our bond like a livewire. I found myself holding my breath as he ran over, then threw the door wide open.

It was empty. Completely empty. None of the dangerous substances I had expected after Dolion's explanation about why it was locked. Not even storage.

Nothing but empty shelves.

Suspicion spread across our bond, the sensation curdling in my gut. Tobias reached his hand forward, and I stared in shock as it vanished.

Tobias swore, yanking his hand back. "Another glamour. Add it to the notes." He gestured at the pen and paper still in my hands, his voice tight. "We can't wait for them to get here."

He paced as I did so, sending each missive off in a flare of blue magic.

"Let's go then," I said grimly. "If there's any chance of finding Dolion alive, and retrieving the cure, we don't have time to waste."

From the tremble of worry across our bond, I knew Tobias had reached the same conclusion. "If something happens to you…"

"We don't have time to argue," I said firmly. "*Pari* doesn't have time for us to argue. And if you think I'm staying behind, you don't know me at all."

"You're right, I just…" Tobias stopped pacing. "Bringing you to him is my worst nightmare come to life, and I'm having a hard time coming to terms with it." His eyes met mine, the outright fear in them making my heart clench. But at least he was facing it, and talking to me, rather than pushing it away. "But that's my problem, not yours. Just promise me…Promise me that if it comes down to a choice between saving me and saving yourself, you'll put yourself first for once."

"I'm not making that choice, Maris." I reached out, and he took my hand automatically. "I'm choosing us, every time. We're getting through this together." I squeezed his hand reassuringly. "Besides, you'll have to try harder than that to get rid of me."

His jaw flexed, but he nodded. Drawing in a deep breath, we raised our blades in unison as we walked through the wall together.

. . .

✧

The winding stairway was so narrow we were forced to take it one at a time. Tobias insisted on going first, ignoring my grumblings.

"This isn't about whether you can take care of yourself." I could practically hear his eyeroll. "You need to conserve your magic for once we get the cure back."

The limestone walls matched the stairs, the steps blurring together as we hurried downward. Fresh blood smeared across the middle of each one in a macabre marker we were on the right path.

Was Dolion injured? Or had they infected him with the virus, and its first symptom had left this trail.

"We need Silvius alive," I reminded him threateningly. "We have to question him on this new version of the virus. And we need to see if he has his own antidote on hand in case he already destroyed ours."

Though something told me he hadn't—not when he could use our research to help inform his own. He hadn't gotten this far by being rash, and he certainly wasn't stupid.

"We also need to figure out what part Dolion plays in this," Tobias said hesitantly. My surprise must have traveled across our bond because he added, "This tunnel went directly to his private laboratory, and you think he's innocent?"

There had to be an explanation, and one that didn't mean my friend was in league with Silvius. If there was one, though, I couldn't think of it.

"He's been helping us," I protested weakly. "They attacked him…"

Tobias ran a hand through his hair, agitation written in every line of his body. "Just because they turned on him, doesn't mean he's innocent."

"He…"

There *had* been something off since we arrived in Mayim. A disconnect from our time in person that felt different than the easy tone of our letters. I assumed that Dolion was simply more comfortable writing his thoughts down, as could be the case with scientists prone to spending their days shut in their laboratories instead of socializing. But what if there was more to it?

There was that note naming Seawater on his desk. Maybe he hadn't written it down because he heard about our surveillance there, but because he had also been given a place to meet, just like the others who sought to support Silvius.

What if his sudden standoffishness since our arrival reflected his shift in allegiance or an attempt to play both sides?

What if in trusting him, I led us to this moment?

"He's my friend," I said quietly. "Even if you're right, we still need to try to save him."

Tobias nodded. "As long as you go in there with a seed of doubt." His features tightened. "Don't let your guard down. We don't even know if that blood is his."

I bristled though I was forced to acknowledge his point. Even if I didn't want it to be true, that doubt was there—and it was enough to make me wary.

As we walked further down the stairs, Tobias's light swirled around me almost playfully, in sharp contrast to their master's stern expression. A few twirled around my ankles, one winding down the curl that had fallen in my face, its light touch warming my cheeks.

The question left my lips before I could stop it. "Why doesn't your light burn?"

Tobias stumbled, nearly missing the next step. His shoulders drew together, his entire body stiffening like he was bracing for a blow. "Why would it?"

His emotions felt muted like he had tamped down on them instinctually —not blocking our bond, but his own reaction.

"Because when Aviel stole your magic, it did." I wished I had stayed quiet. This wasn't the right time for this conversation. "And I thought…"

"Aviel had no interest in the nuances of my power," Tobias said disdainfully. "He stole it to trick the realm and to hurt those who stood between him and the crown he wanted to steal."

The stairwell widened slightly, enough that I could stand beside him. We had to be getting close.

"So this—" I lifted my hand, and those familiar balls of light swirled down my arm to circle my fingers. One rested on my ring finger like the jewel of a wedding ring. "—won't burn unless you want it to."

"It's no different than your blood magic." Tobias reached back to hold my hand, his light scattering as he did so. "You can use it to help or to hurt. It's in the intention."

"Here I was so certain you'd hate my magic after what blood magic was used to do to you," I admitted, the way my voice strained betraying my attempt at lightheartedness.

Tobias shook his head. "I could never hate anything about you."

A lump formed in my throat, a smile coming to my face despite the situation. I nearly tripped over my own feet as we reached the end of the stairs, my knees buckling at the unexpected stopping point. Tobias pulled me against him, wrapping an arm around me to keep me upright before moving me behind him.

"No one's here," I hissed, pushing past him. I kept my dagger raised anyway.

The blood led to the middle of the room, where it abruptly disappeared. I carefully avoided stepping in it as I reached out with my blood magic, trying to sense a heartbeat.

Nothing.

"Maybe they stopped the bleeding so it didn't lead us straight to a glamour?" I didn't need our bond to sense Tobias's frustration. "There has to be one. Or..."

I knelt near the end of the bloody trail, my eyes fixed on the space around it. It looked off somehow, like the stone was misaligned.

"Here."

Tobias was at my side in a second. "What is it? Did you find..."

He trailed off with a curse as my hand sank into the stone, disappearing into the glamour in the floor. Pulling it out, I took his hand and wrapped it around my waist.

"Hold on." My other hand tightened around my dagger. "I'm going to stick my head through far enough to see what's beneath us. Lift me up when I squeeze your arm."

Tobias looked ready to argue. I didn't wait for permission as I leaned forward into the floor, flinching as my face went through the seemingly solid marble. It felt like diving into a dense fog, the stone pulsating around me as I held my breath instinctually.

A wayward curl poked through the ceiling just before my face did. I recognized where we were in an instant.

I squeezed Tobias's arm. He pulled me back with such force he fell backwards, catching me on top of him.

"The mirror," I gasped as I tried to untangle myself. "We're above the mirror in the tunnel, the one that led to Silvius's lab. It's beneath us."

Tobias stared at me, slack jawed. "That's why we couldn't figure out how Silvius was entering the Enclave."

"The top of the mirror is close enough that it wouldn't be hard to climb down, or up." From the bottom, I hadn't realized that the frame's looping exterior formed an easy ladder to climb. "There's no one there. They must have gone through."

Tobias's brow furrowed. "The gate, it's open?"

"For now," I said. "We need to hurry in case Silvius closes it again."

Tobias's lips pursed. "I take it the guards stationed down here are either working against us or dead?"

"I didn't see anyone."

He was likely right.

Tobias held up a missive, waving it at me. "This showed up while you were head down. Yael's on her way with reinforcements."

I recognized her cramped penmanship as I took the note from his hand. Reaching into my pocket, I retrieved a pen, then scribbled:

The closet in the lab leads to the mirror in the tunnels. We're going through. No magic in the lab.

I let out a heavy sigh, then added one more line.

Don't trust Dolion.

"Once we walk through that mirror, there's no magic," I reminded Tobias too. "Is there anything you want me to add before we lose contact?"

"No." A muscle flexed in Tobias's jaw. I knew the worry tumbling down our bond wasn't for himself. "I don't suppose I can convince you to wait to go through it until those reinforcements join us?"

I shook my head. The note disappeared in a flare of magic—not my healer's blue, but a red I knew reflected in my eyes.

Dolion was in imminent danger, no matter what part he played in this betrayal. Pari too, considering I had no idea how fast the new strain of this virus worked, and Eva was comatose and counting on me.

My blood magic reddened my fingertips. No matter what, I wouldn't let Silvius get away again.

"Would you let me go without you?"

Tobias's face darkened. "Fair enough." His hands found the invisible edge of where the glamour covered the hole in the stone. "My turn first this time."

His fingers gripped the edge as he lowered himself down until they were all that was left of him. When Tobias let go of the wall, he disappeared entirely.

I swung my legs over the edge. A scream caught in my throat as Tobias's hand gripped my ankles, guiding my feet onto something solid. His hands slid up my thighs as I crouched down, my head popping through the glamour last this time.

We perched precariously on the top of the mirror. I immediately grabbed its frame, the highest of its eight twisted points cutting into my hand. Though the tunnels weren't tall, we were still two or three body lengths from the ground—a much longer distance than I had realized from the bottom.

The puddle of blood in front of the mirror looked a long way down.

"Don't look down," Tobias murmured. His hand fastened around one of the brass loops that decorated the edges of the glass, his foot finding another. "And don't rush."

Trembling, I copied him on the opposite side, focusing on the next rung. My heartbeat thundered in my ears as I looked down, the sheer drop below making my head spin with vertigo.

My foot slipped, and I gasped.

"Quinn."

After so long whispering, his panicked shout echoed far too loudly down the hall.

"Fine," I said quickly. "I'm fine."

Or at least I would be once my feet were on solid ground.

Tobias's lips quirked across from me. "I never realized you were afraid of heights."

Of course, he could feel my fear, even if he couldn't see the cold sweat now dripping down my back.

"I would argue it's not the height, but the fear of what would happen if I fell from it," I countered wryly. My foot slid against the curl of the next rung and my breath caught in my throat, my chest tightening.

"Don't all fears have a source?" Tobias looked thoughtful, despite the situation. "I'm afraid of open spaces because I spent so long trapped in that cage that being outside…it feels like I'll float away. But the fear isn't of the space itself, it's the fear of losing control, of unpredictability." Despite his calm façade, his emotions crossed our bond in a whirlwind I couldn't fully untangle. "I'm not afraid of the dungeon below Morehaven, but what waited for me in it: the promise of pain, both mine and others. Of losing my voice along with my autonomy."

It had taken more bravery than I realized for him to go on this adventure with me—and to merely exist in the long months since he found his freedom.

My feet hit the ground, and I launched myself at him in the space behind the mirror. Tobias let out an oomph of surprise even as his arms wrapped around me.

"You've faced plenty of your fears here, and found a way through," I reminded him. "But there's no rush to this kind of healing. When we get home, we'll take it one day at a time."

Taking his face in my hands, I kissed him, trying not to think that it might be our last chance to do so. There was an urgency in the way he kissed me back, his mouth demanding like he was thinking the same.

Reluctantly, I pulled away. Light streaked across his irises, flitting from eyelash to eyelash as if mutinying before being stifled.

Tobias pressed a kiss against my forehead. "As long as you're with me, I think I can manage that."

I walked around the mirror, careful not to get too close this time. Its surface slowly undulated like it was reading my intention. Tobias's face tightened, no doubt doing the same.

"We can't wait for reinforcements," I said grimly. Dread twisted in my gut, though I tried not to let it cross our bond. "The mirror could close at any second. Even if it's still open by the time Yael gets here, there are too many people at risk. We need that cure."

Rivan's desperate face flashed in my mind along with the pure terror in his voice as he begged me to help Pari. Even if there was more between them as I suspected, Pari had no *anima* bond to protect her from the effects of the virus like Eva did, nor did any of the patients waiting for the cure in the hospital ward. And there was no telling how quickly this new version of it would progress.

A shout rang out down the tunnel. The metallic ring of a sword being unsheathed filled the room a second later as we drew our blades in unison,

Tobias's sword gleaming brightly. The tension was palpable across our bond. It was too soon for reinforcements, as much as I hoped Yael's voice was about to announce her arrival.

The sound of a single pair of footsteps stumbled forward. Tobias shot me a look—a warning not to say anything before we knew what we were up against. Light blossomed in the palm of his free hand, a spinning orb growing larger as his power built behind it. One false move and I knew our opponent would be eviscerated before he could take another step.

A figure stumbled through the mouth of the tunnel, his sword clanging against the stone. He wore the uniform of the Mayimite guards, though it was soddened and stained with blood like he had come straight from a battle. With the way he leaned forward, his hood blocked his face from sight.

There was no telling whose side he was on.

Tobias's voice was deadly as he demanded, "Not another step."

The stranger came to a halt, swaying as he did so. As he straightened, his hood fell back. Blood ran down his chin, his eyes cloudy.

My gasp echoed through the hall. "He's infected. Recently, considering he's still conscious."

The light disappeared from Tobias's hand in an instant. "He must've been guarding the mirror."

The stranger let out a strangled yell, then charged forward, swinging his sword wildly.

I raised my hands, stepping in front of Tobias. "Don't hurt him, he thinks he's fighting."

"Yes, he's fighting *us*," Tobias said exasperatedly, but he lowered his sword.

The guard stumbled, nearly falling as he came within striking distance. He lunged toward Tobias, missing him entirely. Tobias seized the opportunity. Ducking under the next wild swing, he expertly plucked the sword from the guard's hands. The guard whipped around, but I darted behind him, placing my hands on his sweat-slick temples.

The guard crumpled into my arms. His weight nearly toppled me before Tobias helped me lay him down.

"He'll be out for a bit," I murmured as my magic surged to check the virus's progress.

The fog was so thick it felt impenetrable. There was nothing I could do for him. Not until I had that cure back.

Tobias reached out a hand, helping me to my feet. My eyes fixed on the mirror. I took a step forward, then another, my hand curling around my dagger as I eyed the ripples on its edges for any sign they might freeze over.

A message appeared by Tobias's hand. He snatched it from midair, his eyes scanning the paper. "They doubled back to enter through the tunnels since it was closer. It shouldn't be much longer, if we want to wait for backup."

I hated waiting, hated the feeling of inaction when there were people that needed my help—but it was the smart thing to do as long as the mirror stayed open. My eyes fell to where a pool of blood lay in front of the mirror.

Or at least, I thought there had been. The floor was now clean.

Tobias's voice sharpened. "What is it?"

My eyes narrowed as I walked closer, trying to make sense of it. There was a strange familiarity I couldn't quite identify; a nagging feeling in the back of my mind like a whisper in the dark.

"Wasn't there a bloodstain there—"

I realized my mistake a moment too late.

My foot went through the solid ground, my momentum propelling me forward. A scream tore from my throat as I fell through the glamour.

I twisted midair, reaching for Tobias.

He lunged across the distance, wrapping himself around me.

Then we plunged into the darkness.

CHAPTER 42

TOBIAS

I wasn't sure how long we fell through the darkness, only that I was able to wrap Quinn securely in my arms during our plunge. My only thought when I heard her scream was to reach her in time. To make sure that, wherever we ended up, we went together.

We slammed down, hard. Pain shot up my leg as it crunched beneath me. Quinn landed on top of me, knocking the breath from my lungs. The hilt of my dagger jabbed into my hip. My sword still lay somewhere above us after I dropped it in my wild leap for her.

Silvius expected us to follow. Of that much, I was certain.

Once again, he was one step ahead.

"*Quinn*," I gasped, trying to catch my breath.

Her hands found my face in the dark. "I'm okay."

My light exploded around us, searching for a way out. It illuminated four stone walls, the matching floor beneath us, and the ceiling we had fallen through. It was barely larger than…

My cell.

Terror cut through me like a knife. My light faltered, flickering like a candle in a breeze as my hold on it went haywire.

The only thing that was missing was the screams. As if that thought had summoned them, their ghosts played in my ears, blocking out my ragged breathing.

"Breathe," Quinn demanded, her fingers digging into my jaw. "Tobias, please."

The walls were pressing in, my vision darkening.

There wasn't any air. There wasn't any *air* in here...

I couldn't survive this again.

My chest spasmed, that band tightening around my throat.

And worst of all, I brought her here with me.

"*Tobias*." Her voice broke. "I need you."

Blue light reflected in her eyes as it poured from her hands, trying to fix what had long since been broken.

I needed to block it out. To push it down. To get it together before they could tear her away from me. I had to—

"I love you."

Quinn's thumb stroked my cheek, her touch grounding me in reality—in that place that felt like home. The icy grip of my panic waned, its hold on me slipping away. The warmth of her hands on my face reminded me of the sun I once loved.

Her love flowed through our bond, certainty and hope overtaking my fear. Not hiding it away where it would only get worse, not blocking it to face another day—but tempering it with something stronger.

My light burst from me, brightening into something dazzling.

I sucked in a breath, then another. On my exhale, I managed a heartfelt, "Thank you."

"I told you," Quinn gently chided before pressing a chaste kiss to my lips. "No more hiding."

She got to her feet, a wince crossing her face as she rubbed her lower back. A pained cry escaped me as I tried to put weight on my leg to join her. Quinn's face tightened with concern. Her hands were back on me in a heartbeat, her magic running down my leg. I bit down hard at the feeling of bone sliding on bone, holding in a scream.

"It's broken." Quinn swore under her breath. "In two places."

"Don't drain yourself trying to heal it completely."

There was no telling what we were about to get into, no matter how quiet our current tomb.

Quinn stubbornly shook her head. "If we end up magicless again, I can't risk you being hurt without a way to fix you."

I knew better than to argue, especially when she was right. Blue light wrapped around my leg in interconnecting strands before disappearing under my skin. The pain lessened, immediately more manageable than before.

"Be careful on it." Quinn's teeth sank into her bottom lip. "I did enough to keep you upright, but it needs time to mend."

I took a deep, fortifying breath, pushing through the remainder of the pain. She reached into her pocket, retrieving a piece of paper, then wrote a missive that disappeared in a flash of deep red. "A bit embarrassing admitting we literally fell for Silvius's tricks."

"Then let's find a way out of here before Yael has to fish us out," I said as Quinn helped me to my feet.

I limped over to the nearest wall, careful to avoid putting too much weight on my leg. My hand pressed against the stone like it would yield a secret way out, even as I tried to ignore the sinking sensation I knew Quinn could feel.

There were no handholds, no ladder. No sign of a shimmer that could indicate a glamour. Nothing but sheer, slick stone.

"That glamour we fell through wasn't here last time, or it wasn't open," Quinn mused. "He must have someone like Rivan whose magic has an affinity with stone to build this beneath."

"He planned for us to come back."

I almost finished my circuit of the walls when I realized what she was staring at: the glamour. The edges shimmered slightly in the light, close enough that…

"Get on my shoulders," I ordered.

"You don't mean…" Quinn looked between me and the ceiling. "Your leg won't hold my weight. Besides, even if I can make it back through, there's no way I can pull you up."

Nor were there any ropes in the tunnels she could use to assist her.

"Yael should be close."

"Oh, don't you dare, Maris. I'm not leaving you in here alone." She held up a hand as I started to argue. "I'm not sure what self-sacrificing gene runs through your lineage, or if it's just a knack for reckless courage, but you and your sister both need to quit it."

The worry she had mitigated crept back like it was seeping from the walls. One of us needed to get out of here. And we both knew it wasn't going to be me.

"It's simple, Sagray," I said pointedly. "You're the doctor. *You're* the one who has a chance at figuring out a cure if we can't get it back from Silvius."

"And you're the godsdamn King of Soleara. You're—"

"Replaceable."

"You're not," Quinn snapped, heartbreak in every word. "Not to me."

I could sense the panic she was barely holding back like a wave of static. It tightened around my ribcage, constricting my next breath.

"Five things," I reminded her, as I tried to push a sense of calm her way in the same way she did for me. "Tell me what you can hear, what you can see…maybe you'll find something we're missing. But unless you see a rope in here, this is the best plan we have."

As if on cue, a note appeared as if blown in by a gust of wind. Yael's words took a second to decipher, having obviously been written in a hurry.

Ambush. Hold tight.

"Tobias…"

The alarm in Quinn's voice made me spin toward her, my dagger raised. My panic rose to match her own.

White particles hovered above us like mist swiftly moving downward. My light soared to meet it, forming a wall as I tried to sear them from the air.

The gas only seemed to multiply in response, though perhaps it was being pumped in faster. Quinn turned to me, her eyes wide as the air grew thick with fog.

Helplessness clogged my throat.

There was nothing I wouldn't do to save her. And nothing I could do.

This time, there was nowhere to run as the gas descended. I fell to my knees as it choked its way down my throat, thickening in my lungs. Before my light was extinguished, I pulled Quinn into my arms.

Her body went limp just as our bond slackened. Then everything went black.

CHAPTER 43
TOBIAS

The chains around my wrists bit into my skin. It wouldn't be long before my wounds reopened. They never seemed to fully heal, especially when Aviel left me unconscious and hanging from them.

My legs had fallen asleep from the awkward way they were folded beneath me, my neck and shoulders screaming at the way my chains held me upright. But there was something different. Something was missing, even if something gnawed in my brain that there was more to it.

"Tobias, wake up."

Quinn. If she was in my dream, I didn't want to wake. Her voice washed over me, soothing despite the edge in it. I was thankful it wasn't real—that she wasn't seeing me like this. Maybe Aviel had finally gone too far, and I had finally lost my mind. Maybe her voice was the last thing I would hear before I left this earth.

"Tobias, *please*."

She sounded terrified. If she needed me…

You'll fail as you've done so often, and then you'll lose her forever.

I couldn't breathe around the tightness in my chest. My eyelids refused to cooperate, like they had been weighed down, even as my soul strained to go to her.

She needed me.

"Tobias…"

Quinn. My *anima.*

Not a dream. A minute ago, we had fallen through the floor. She should still be in my arms—

My eyes flew open.

The laboratory was familiar. Silver countertops. No windows, or any way to tell where in the realm we were.

And a cage.

Except this time, I was looking at it through the bars. And Quinn was stuck in here with me.

"You're awake." Her voice shook, her eyes glimmering with tears. "I thought…I can't heal you here. I couldn't even tell if you were breathing…"

Chains held her in place. I lunged for her on instinct. My body snapped back, my shoulders screaming in pain. I hissed as my shackles cut into my wrists. Quinn flinched, her hands tightening into fists where they were fastened above her.

I reached for my magic on instinct—and slammed into a wall. The sudden loss tore through me like an old wound ripped raw.

"Tobias?"

"I'm okay." I wasn't, but my voice was miraculously steady as I asked, "Are you hurt?"

Fear threatened to drag me under all over again, cold and familiar. But I forced a steady breath. I refused to fall apart—not when she needed me.

With a panic I was thankful she couldn't feel, I examined her head to toe, trying to catalogue her injuries. Thankfully, I found none. But the sight of her chained?

I was going to skin Silvius alive.

Quinn shook her head. "I'd be better without these shackles, but I'm fine otherwise."

My brain felt fuzzy, likely from the aftereffects of the gas. There was something I felt like I was forgetting…something important. Worst of all, I couldn't feel her. Whatever it was about this room that blocked our magic also blocked our bond.

"I'm going to kill him slowly," I snarled.

I thought I saw a hint of red tinge those amber eyes as Quinn met my gaze, before violence narrowed them into slits.

"Good."

She nodded at the dark, flat mirror. Not even a reflection shone back at us. "The others might be looking for us, but they won't be able to get through. So we're going to need to find another way out, unless we manage to reopen the gate."

"Simple enough," I said wryly and was rewarded with the slightest of smiles. "Do you have any give in your chains?"

Quinn shook her head. "I can't reach the bars from here, and I'm guessing you can't either."

Gingerly, I lifted my hands, inspecting the iron encircling my wrists. I turned around, wrapped my hands around the chains, and tried to tear that iron bolt from the wall.

It wasn't long before I was forced to admit defeat. I knew these manacles all too well. If four years of trying hadn't made them yield to me, I doubted I was about to find a way now.

I pressed my forehead into the stone, forcing air into my lungs in a careful four count.

Quinn's chains rattled behind me. "Tobias, are you okay? What do you need?"

Everything I had done in that cell, and everything I had done since, had been to keep her safe from exactly this. And despite all of it, she was stuck here with me.

"I need you to survive this."

A short laugh. "Right back at you."

I pulled against my chains, knowing I couldn't reach her, but trying all the same. "I need *you*, Quinn. It's selfish—"

"It's not."

Her chains stretched taut behind her as she leaned toward me too.

"We could have been together for months," I said, angry at myself for that wasted time. "If I hadn't fought this...we could've had more time. And now..."

I didn't need to feel her emotions to see the determination in every line of her body.

"Don't you dare give up on me, Maris," she demanded. "We'll get that time. You and me? We'll have forever."

No matter what, I wouldn't let her die down here. Whatever it took.

"I'll never give up on you, sweetheart." I managed to smile, even as my vision swam. "It's a date."

I leaned against the wall, feeling queasy. A concussion from our fall, maybe, considering Quinn didn't seem to have any lasting effects from the gas. Using the wall to brace myself, I slid down against it until I sat on the floor, my arms suspended uncomfortably above me.

Telling Quinn would only make her worry, especially when she had no magic to fix it. But those amber eyes seemed to stare right through me, as they always did.

"Tobias?"

My mouth snapped shut as a door appeared in the solid wall across from us. A shiver I couldn't help skittered down my spine as three fae walked into the lab—though my eyes immediately fixed on the one in the center.

Silvius.

CHAPTER 44
QUINN

Tobias went completely still as he stared at Silvius. His eyes blazed with hatred, his face tight with fury that looked a breath away from breaking loose. Silvius bowed slightly in response, sneering. Two guards flanked him, both clad in nondescript black leathers. Their expressions were distant, their eyes almost unfocused as they stared mindlessly at their leader.

It was strange finally seeing the person responsible for so much harm. Silvius was shorter in stature, though he held himself like a king. His long gray hair was tied back into a no-nonsense ponytail. A permanent frown etched his forehead and a pronounced droop pulled at his lips.

He had the look of someone who had lost too much weight too quickly—like he wasn't quite at home in his own skin. His spotless white robe billowed behind him as he walked into the room, similar to the ones the healers wore in the Enclave.

A familiar silver dagger was attached to his belt. *My* dagger. My gift from Tobias.

"Apologies for the delay in welcoming you," Silvius said with faux enthusiasm. "I'm afraid I had to change after getting some blood on me."

Dolion.

My hands formed into fists. "Where is he? What did you do to Dolion?"

"Finally, you're asking the right questions," Silvius said snidely. Tobias's chains creaked as Silvius's gray eyes focused on me. "Does that mean you've figured it out?"

The surprise must have shown on my face because Silvius tsked as he came closer. "I'll take that as a no. There are two answers to that question, and both are, in a way, correct."

Tobias let out an exaggerated sigh. "You always liked hearing yourself talk."

"A shame you're now able to talk back," Silvius sneered. "Now *her* I understand not recognizing me. The second I saw you at her side, I was worried you would find me out." He glanced between us. "How lucky I am that you were too busy staring at each other to look too closely at your companion."

Tobias's face slackened in disbelief. Something like horror crossed his face, gone before I could be certain.

"What is it?" I demanded, hating the fact I couldn't feel him. "What's he talking about?"

Silvius laughed, high and cruel. The hair on the back of my neck stood up.

"He hasn't been breaking in," Tobias said stonily. "He walked through the front door."

Silvius tipped his head toward him in acknowledgement. One eyebrow raised as he looked at me. "Don't you recognize me? Perhaps a different skin would help."

His features blurred, his stomach deflating as he stretched taller and taller. His hair and skin darkened; his shoulders grew broader. Horror tightened in my gut like a fist as the insufferably smug look on his face changed into the features I had seen almost every day since our arrival in Mayim. The color of Dolion's sharp gray eyes stayed the same, though dark eyelashes now replaced Silvius's sunken gaze.

Silvius was a shifter.

I didn't even realize I backed up until I felt the stone wall against my back. Tobias trembled with rage, the rattle of his chains echoing through me.

"You were there the whole time," I said shakily. "Why did you even let us get as far as we did?"

I was going to be sick.

"I would've thought that was obvious," Silvius sniffed. "I wanted a cure on hand, should I need it. And I thought it best to keep an eye on you before you could administer it to the only person in this realm whose magic might be able to stop my creation outright."

That was why Eva had been infected first. Not as some sick form of revenge, or at least not solely for that reason. Silvius had made sure the magic of the land couldn't be used to cure anyone.

He had been planning this from the beginning, had been standing next to me since the first day we arrived. Worse than that, if he had been the one writing me letters, he had orchestrated everything even earlier than I imagined.

"Was it always you?"

I had to keep him talking—something I doubted would be difficult. He was far too self-impressed not to brag about his accomplishments, especially now that we were under his control. His hubris and his certainty that he was smarter than us might make him careless enough to reveal too much.

Silvius was used to answering my questions after so long working together. It wasn't much...but I would use it to my advantage.

"Dolion was my way into the Enclave after my fall from grace." Silvius's mouth twisted. "It took some time to tempt him out of his laboratory, but I needed someone with his level of access. It was easy enough to have those loyal to me get me close. Once I had the right face, it was a simple matter of getting him alone." His eyes darted from Tobias back to me. "The mist is an aerosol version of the serum I created to knock fae out as well as temporarily incapacitate their magic. My own invention." He looked at me like I should be impressed by that fact. "Much more civilized than a hilt to the head. You should be thanking me."

He was *delusional.*

It was an effort to keep my voice civil as I asked, "If he wasn't part of this, how did his lab connect to the mirror? Unless you have someone who's able to connect the tunnels?"

"Very good." He said it like I had succeeded in correctly imbuing another cure rather than unraveling the secrets of his plotting. "The tunnels below the castle already existed, of course. From there, it was a matter of having the earth elemental in my employ inconspicuously work their way up."

Tobias shifted, but I didn't dare look at him, not when Silvius was finally giving me answers. I kept my tone neutral, careful not to betray anything other than clinical interest. "So you took Dolion's place in order to take over his lab?"

Silvius stroked his chin. "I needed somewhere to work after I lost my laboratory in Morehaven. When I saw your letters sitting on his desk, I knew I had a singular opportunity to lure you here." He looked at Tobias, a cruel smile splitting his face. "The fact that you brought my favorite test subject was an unexpected bonus."

My blood boiled. If only I had my magic, I would make him crawl. I would make him *beg* for the chance to survive me.

Tobias's jaw flexed, but he said nothing. Sweat beaded at his brow, the only sign of his nerves. I wasn't sure whether he was holding his tongue because he knew what I was up to, or because his voice refused to work.

"And Dolion..." My voice wavered, but I forced myself to remain purely inquisitive. "Is he still alive?"

"For now." Silvius gave me a thin smile. "He's been my guest ever since and will be as long as he still remains...useful. Just as I hope you will be, my dear."

I didn't let myself react to the pet name, though I saw Tobias's fists clench. Hopefully that meant poor, innocent Dolion was nearby somewhere. But if that wasn't Dolion's blood on the stairs, who had Silvius dragged down them? There was no way the blood was his, or he wouldn't still be standing.

Silvius leaned against the iron bars between us, wheezing as Dolion's face faded away. His hair lost its color, graying from root to tip. Then his features sagged, his face paling as lines traced his forehead one by one. His eyes, the same ones I had grown used to, stayed the same shade: a flat, lifeless gray.

His hands tightened on the bars like he was wringing someone's neck. I was suddenly aware of how vulnerable I was, chained and magicless, if Silvius came into our cell. I chanced a look at Tobias.

If looks could kill, Silvius would already be flayed alive.

"I take it you shifted to hide yourself from capture," I said quickly, drawing Silvius's attention back to me. "Considering no one's been able to track you down. Lucky that you hid that particular ability."

Silvius's face twisted in a scowl. "Luck had nothing to do with it. My magic has a divine purpose—one that led my King to find me in the first place. His Majesty was a siphon, not a shifter. I earned my place as his most trusted servant."

"He took your magic to look like his younger self," I whispered as it dawned on me. Tobias shook his head in disgust. His hair hid his eyes from me as he leaned forward, the muscles in his back pulled taut.

Silvius smiled, cold and cruel. "He borrowed that power from me. And it was my honor to do so."

There had been a mention of shifters in some of the research I had done on blood magic. Something nagged at me in some far corner of my brain as I resisted the urge to press my hand against my temple. Something that I was too distracted to fully remember.

I opened my mouth, but Silvius raised his hand. "Enough questions. We have more work to do together, my dear."

Together? Surely, he didn't think I would assist in his research.

"She won't be going anywhere with you," Tobias growled.

My voice trembled with barely contained fury as I ground out, "I have no intention of helping you."

"I think you'll change your mind." Silvius reached into an inner pocket, removing an iron key. A shudder traveled through Tobias as he placed it into the lock. "After all, helping me isn't just the only way to save everyone you love, it's your *only* way out."

The cell unlocked with a loud click. Tobias flinched so violently his chains clattered.

A grim wave of helplessness surged through me, pressing down on my chest. I couldn't even touch him, let alone comfort him—not when I couldn't even help myself.

Silvius glanced behind him, nodding once. One of the guards strode across the laboratory towards the dark, frozen mirror. I exchanged a confused look with Tobias as he reached it.

Then he drew his sword, raising its hilt high above his head.

I realized his intent a moment before he brought the pommel crashing down. It hit the dead center of the glass, its frame vibrating with the force of the blow.

No.

My gasp was eclipsed by a sharp crack. Tiny fractures spiderwebbed outward, the sound scattering through the silence like a rock breaking through the surface of a frozen pond.

The guard brought his sword down again. My heart caught in my throat as those cracks multiplied, his grunt of exertion drowning out their brittle dissonance as they spread.

Everything seemed to stand still as he raised it one last time.

With one final blow, the mirror shattered.

CHAPTER 45
TOBIAS

My face stared back at me in a thousand different pieces. The shattered mirror quivered tauntingly, its broken shards only reflecting my own despair.

There wouldn't be any help coming. Nor was there a simple way out.

My head swam, my mouth going dry as I tried to swallow. A cold sweat broke out across my forehead and each beat of my heart pounded loudly in my ears. Once again, I wouldn't be able to save my sister, or anyone else counting on us.

My nightmares had come to life, and they were so much worse than I ever imagined.

Silvius straightened his robes as a guard walked into the cell. I strained against my bonds.

"Don't you fucking touch her," I warned him.

"You should know by now that you can't stop me." Silvius sounded almost bored as he brushed a speck of dirt from his sleeve. But the only thing I cared about was that Silvius had turned his attention on me.

"Let her go," I pleaded. I wasn't above debasing myself if it meant saving her. "I'll do anything you want—"

"I don't think so." Silvius's voice dripped in condescension. "After all, I need her. But I have no doubt you will do as I ask this time. As will she." The guard removed a smaller key ring, lifting a single key as he reached Quinn. Silvius turned his focus on her. "It's simple, really. You're going to help me, or he'll die."

Something dangerous flashed in Quinn's eyes. "Help you with what, exactly?"

"The next step, of course." Silvius frowned, looking almost disappointed. "A virus's purpose is to spread. While I managed to circumvent the need for a subject's blood in my latest version of my creation, it still requires an injection. Which is where you come in."

Quinn's eyes widened in alarm. "If this becomes viral, you have no control over how it'll spread. Or how it'll mutate."

"Which is why we're where no one can reach us," he said condescendingly. "When it's over, the city will be mine, as will anyone who attempts to breach it. I'll be free to conduct my research with willing participants. And Agadot will suffer for not choosing the True King when they had the chance."

The chains echoed my shudder. But there was honest curiosity in my voice as I asked, "Do you think the rest of the realm will simply let you keep an entire kingdom?"

Silvius's smile chilled me to the bone. "I think they'll be too scared of being infected to try to stop me."

The guard gestured at Quinn to raise her shackled hands. Her eyes darted to mine, surprise flashing across her face.

"I wouldn't try anything once you're unchained," Silvius cautioned.

Quinn looked up at him, then back to the guard releasing her manacles. "And why's that?"

"Because I have the cure you need." He said it like it was obvious. "Or did you not want to save your Solearan friend before her mind goes?"

The look on Quinn's face seared deeper than any wound.

How long did we have before it was too late to cure her?

Quinn's chains fell to the floor with a loud clang that seemed to reverberate through my brain. My jaw clenched as her hands moved to her wrists, rubbing the area where the iron had been.

She looked unsure. "You'll give the cure to Pari?"

"She was never my target. I told them to infect the warrior who brought down the mountain." Silvius sighed, shaking his head. "No matter. The Solearan won't last long before some of the effects become permanent, if she survives at all. The latest strain is particularly unstable without the infected's blood to balance it."

My stomach bottomed out. That quickly—she would succumb that quickly. The room seemed to tilt and sway, the cage moving sickeningly around me.

Quinn's eyes narrowed. "You'll get her the cure immediately if I help you?" I could see her mind working, the pinch between her brows. "Because she needs it now, not later."

She was smarter than him, and he knew it if he was this desperate for her help. A grim smile tilted my lips.

He was foolish to underestimate her.

Silvius tilted his head in assent. "I'll send someone first thing tomorrow if you do as I ask. But today, I get your mind."

Quinn swallowed hard. I knew she wouldn't help Silvius, not really. I also knew she was far too crafty not to play along. If anyone could find us a way out of here with that cure in hand, it was her.

Silvius gestured at the table, where one of the guards dumped a stack of leather-bound books, as well as a few familiar ones. "My own research, for your perusal, as well as ours in case you need it for reference." His eyes narrowed. "Now, come."

I lurched forward instinctively as the guard next to her drew his sword. To my relief, he didn't point it at her. Instead, he took two steps closer, pressing its tip against my throat.

My smile widened into a grin, even as my neck stung where the blade nicked the scar banded there. Silvius needed Quinn's help, which meant he wouldn't risk hurting her, at least for now.

"Don't hurt him," Quinn pleaded. "I'll help you."

She raised both hands in submission but took a step towards me. Silvius tutted as she got too close.

"If she tries to do anything to free him, make sure he bleeds," he ordered my guard.

Quinn froze as the blade scraped against my skin.

Her eyes met mine as she slowly backed out of the cell. Silvius slunk toward the door, hiding behind the safety of his guard.

Quinn eyed him up and down in a way that would make most cower. "I won't trade anything I come up with until I have proof that Pari's cured."

"You're hardly in a position to make demands, my dear." Silvius pressed his hand against a panel at the side of the door. It looked identical to the ones in the Enclave. “But I’ll consider it. I’ll even bring you some help.”

“Help?” Quinn looked troubled. “Please don’t force anyone else to—”

Silvius ignored her, walking out the door. It vanished behind him, the glamour hiding it almost seamlessly, integrating it into the wall. I squinted, noting the faint sheen of magic I had missed before—the only flaw in the façade.

Considering the only panels I had seen like that were in the Enclave’s laboratories, I doubted we had left the city. If that panel had been keyed to Silvius alone, then we would need him to escape without the mirror as an option. That didn’t mean there wasn’t another way out.

“I need some water, and something to eat if you want me able to focus,” Quinn said testily to the guard by the door. She glanced back at the one by me. “And so does Tobias.”

The guards stayed silent.

Her hand trembled as it curled into a fist, the only sign of her nerves. “Do you hear me?”

The door reappeared. Silvius walked back through it a moment later.

“If you want me to be able to do what you’re asking, we need food and water,” Quinn demanded imperiously. “Your guards don’t seem to understand that.”

“They only take orders from me,” Silvius said simply. “I’m afraid my earlier test subjects couldn’t retain much more than the ability to fight and function. Though I suppose that’s all I need from them.”

I stared at the guards in renewed horror.

Quinn’s look mirrored my own. “Who were they?”

Silvius shrugged. “Does it matter?” He turned to the closer guard, his hand still on that panel. “Fetch some refreshments for our guests. Do be quick about it.”

The guard slipped through the doorway just before two more walked through, half-carrying, half-dragging someone between them. They dropped him to the floor in front of Silvius’s feet. I winced as his palms hit the stone.

The real Dolion had lost so much weight he was barely recognizable. My stomach lurched as I saw the blood dried on his wrists and the visible bruising on his arms and face. Blood stained his hands, seeping into the bottom of his robes like he had been kneeling in it.

Yet my focus lingered on the band that was fastened around his neck.

I couldn't stop my shudder at the sight of it, but more important was what it meant. We may not have our magics in this room, but outside that door? The only reason Dolion would be wearing that band was if there was somewhere here where we could access it—or at least some way to undo the block on our power.

My eyes met Quinn's, who gave me a subtle nod.

She took a hesitant step forward. "Dolion?"

He searched her face, looking bewildered.

"I'm Quinn Sagray," she said quickly. "I…we wrote letters…"

"Quinn." Dolion's hoarse voice sounded so much softer than the one Silvius had taken on to mimic him. "I'm so sorry."

"You have nothing to apologize for," I gritted out, glaring at Silvius.

Dolion's gaze flicked to me, his face hardening as he took in my chains.

Silvius cleared his throat. I didn't miss the way Dolion shrank back from the noise. Aviel may have been a sociopath and a sadist, but in many ways, Silvius was far worse. He was a genius, and his fixation on his research above all else meant he was just as dangerous yet far more unpredictable. His utter disregard for life and lack of conscience made him the worst sort of psychopath.

He didn't care who survived as long as he learned what he wanted from them.

A guard returned with a tray of food and a jug of water, placing it on the table in the middle of the room. Dolion's throat bobbed convulsively, the hunger on his face far too familiar.

"You two have one day." Silvius looked at Dolion first, who quickly nodded, then Quinn, who held his stare. "One day to trade the answer to my problem for the cures you need."

Dolion's mouth opened in protest. "Without magic, without samples to test—"

"I said I wanted your hypotheses, not your grunt work," Silvius said flatly. "I know better than to give you access to your magics. I suggest you work fast before I decide you need more motivation."

Quinn's eyes sparked with defiance. I knew that look—she was about to test how far she could push him.

She lifted her chin. "And if we refuse?"

The guard at my side straightened as if on some unspoken cue. Silvius nodded, a cruel smile twisting his lips a second before the guard's boot rammed into my freshly healed leg.

There was an audible crack. My vision went black, the sudden agony so overwhelming it nearly blocked out Quinn's scream.

Then the darkness swallowed me whole.

CHAPTER 46
TOBIAS

I came to with a blade to my throat, the pain radiating from my leg waking me as easily as it had pulled me under. Tears streamed down Quinn's face as she watched me from the opposite side of the bars.

"—a lesson that chains or not, you are still under my control." Silvius finished, the sound of his voice making me wish I had stayed unconscious. "Any more questions?"

Quinn didn't answer, looking stricken.

I hung limply from my chains, trying and failing to push away the pain. It wasn't the first time my bones had been broken. I wanted to tell Quinn it wasn't her fault as I watched the guilt mix with the tears on her face, but it was all I could do to breathe.

He hadn't hurt her, though. A grim smile came to my lips. She was far from safe, but at least she wasn't in this cell.

Quinn's hand shook as she filled up a glass of water. Steeling her jaw, she looked at Silvius, then the guard beside me. "Please, can I…I'm not going to try to free him. Just make sure he's okay."

Silvius smiled benevolently. "Of course, my dear. But do be careful."

My eyes narrowed at the obvious threat. Silvius nodded at the guard. He backed away one step, the movement jerky, then lowered his sword.

Lucky for him. If he hadn't acquiesced, I knew she would have found a way to get to me, whether or not it meant going through him.

Silvius turned on his heel. The guards followed except for the one next to me, the door vanishing behind them once it closed. The wall shimmered in that uncanny way now that I knew what to look for as I stared at it, trying not to pass out again.

Quinn hurried back into the cell, barely glancing over at the guard as she reached me.

She could easily overpower him. But there was no way out if she did, and I knew Silvius would take it out on me—something I was sure she realized as well. We would have to put up with his presence until Pari was cured.

She fell to her knees in front of me, hands forming into fists as she took in my injury.

"Hey Sagray," I drawled as best I could, my voice gravelly. I relished in the way her amber eyes widened. "Miss me already?"

She glared at me. "This isn't the time to flirt."

"I wasted too much time not flirting with you to worry about the timing, sweetheart."

I leaned in, my chains going taut as my lips brushed hers. Her hand cupped my cheek as she returned it, the taste of her the best sort of distraction.

It was over far too soon. A ghost of a smile flickered across her face, gone before I could appreciate it. Then she swallowed hard. "Tobias, your leg..."

I glanced down, then immediately wished I hadn't. My knee jutted to the side in an angle that left me even more nauseated.

"He would've done that no matter what," I said softly. "He was just waiting for an excuse."

Her lower lip trembled. She firmly pressed her lips together.

"I need to splint it until I can heal you." She glanced at the guard, but his sword remained at his side. "This will hurt. I'll get you comfortable after, I promise. You're going to lose circulation to your hands if you keep hanging like that."

I already had. "Ready when you are."

Her thumb pressed into my boot. "Can you wiggle your toes?"

It took a second before I could. Quinn let out a relieved exhale. "Good. That should mean the fracture's isolated to the bone and there isn't major nerve damage."

Dolion stumbled forward, two metal rods in hand and a roll of what looked like tape. "I took these from the ring stands not in use. And found some parafilm to help bind the splint."

Quinn gave him a nod in thanks. Then she reached down, gathering her shirt in her hands before ripping it to expose her midriff.

"Padding," she explained. Her mouth twitched as she caught me blatantly ogling her exposed skin. At least the pain hadn't blocked my ability to see her.

I winked. "I'd have to be dead not to admire you."

Seeing her smile, as tremulous as it was, was the best sort of balm.

The guard shifted his weight as Dolion entered the cell, but didn't stop him. Not that he was much of a threat—he looked like a strong breeze could knock him over. He laboriously knelt next to Quinn, then dipped his head to signal he was ready.

I choked back a cry as her hands touched my leg. It was about to get much worse. I bit my tongue, trying not to make Quinn feel any guiltier as the pain and pressure swiftly became unbearable.

She pressed down. The second my leg shifted, my vision went dark, but the mercy of unconsciousness lasted barely a second. I found myself momentarily thankful our bond was blocked as I held in the scream building in my throat—though I doubted I was fooling either of them.

Quinn had gone pale, her hands trembling as the two of them worked to wrap my leg in tandem. My breathing came in ragged pants, my ears ringing by the time they finished.

I brought my forehead against my sleeve, wiping away my sweat before it dripped into my eyes. Quinn didn't look much better. She trembled as she got to her feet, returning with a stool from the other side of the bars.

"Now we need to get you situated," she said with a cheer she could barely muster.

The guard gazed at her blankly, though his sword arm twitched in a way that made me want to throw myself in front of her. She ignored him.

Quinn's arms wrapped around my middle, lifting while Dolion kept my broken leg steady. I straightened my good leg, trying to help. Pain exploded in the other the second I shifted, my breath escaping me in a hiss.

I sagged onto the stool behind me, leaning back against the wall so abruptly my shoulders slammed against the stone.

It was harder than it should've been to shove the pain away, even after years of practice. When I finally managed to catch my breath, Quinn reluctantly pulled away.

Dolion watched us, sadness shadowing his expression. "I'll get you something to eat..."

"Tobias," I supplied. "Nice to *actually* meet you."

His eyes flared in surprise. "The northern king?"

I nodded, then winced at even that small movement. The pounding in my head almost matched the pulsing pain in my leg.

"Your Majesty, I'm Dolion," he said, then grimaced. "Though I suppose you already knew that."

"Let's drop the honorifics, shall we?" I gave him what I hoped was a welcoming smile. "That goes for when we get out of here too."

With a weak smile in return, Dolion backed out of the cell, his gait uneven. Quinn bent to pick up the glass of water. She was shaking so hard it sloshed over the rim.

"Easy," I said, my voice gentle. "Breathe or I'll make you start listing five things out loud."

She obediently drew in a breath as she lifted the water to my lips. I drank the entirety in two large gulps, a few drops dribbling down my chin.

As she wiped them away, I asked, "Are you alright?"

"You don't need to worry about me, Maris," Quinn said, her tone both amused and agitated. "What about you?"

"I'll be okay," I said, wishing that was at all true. "Nothing you can't heal as soon as we get out of here."

Dolion returned with three dry rolls and apples that had seen better days, passing me one of each. He cradled his roll before taking a careful bite, as if afraid to waste a single crumb.

I waited until he swallowed before asking, "Who else is here?"

He blinked in confusion. "What?"

"*Cures*, plural," I clarified. "That's what Silvius said. Who are you trying to save?"

"He didn't tell you?" Dolion's hand started to shake. "My queen. He has her."

"Queen Sariyah?" I nearly dropped my roll. Mayim had to be in chaos. "How?"

"I don't know, only that she's in bad shape." Dolion looked bleakly at where the door had disappeared into the stone wall. "They brought her here today. I refused to help Silvius until now…but with her life at stake, I can no longer. This realm needs her."

My respect for him rose. He had been through hell and hadn't broken. Not until they found the right leverage.

Quinn's mouth dropped open in horror. "The blood on the stairs…"

"Silvius must've told her we had the cure," I said grimly. "Lured her to his lab. Then infected her before bringing her through the secret passage."

"From the look of the lab, she put up quite a fight first," Quinn said admiringly.

My fists clenched, squashing my roll. The queen had been nothing but helpful in the short time I knew her, and Silvius had taken advantage of that. With the secrecy involved, I doubted she had even brought her guards.

"He said he wants her compliant for what comes next," Dolion said thickly. "But with her blood loss, she'll be lucky if she survives the fever. Without my magic…I can't heal her even if he would let me."

While Silvius might want to use her as a puppet, Aviel's supporters would rejoice in her death after their failed uprising against her during the war.

Either way, there was no way Silvius would allow Dolion to cure her.

I winced as I repositioned myself. "His goal was never just revenge."

"Oh, Silvius wants revenge." Dolion fished an apple from his pocket, taking a loud bite. "On you, on the High Queen, and on everyone who took part in destroying his so called 'True King'. He plans to follow in the False King's footsteps and force the realm to bend to his will. He *wants* this virus infectious in order to take down this entire city, so only he and his followers have the cure. *'Only those who pledge allegiance will be allowed to live'*." His imitation of Silvius's aristocratic tone was uncanny. "And those who stand in his way will find themselves trapped in their minds and essentially lobotomized." He shuddered, gesturing at the eerily still guard at my side. "We don't need to worry about what we say in front of this one. He's a shell. A living corpse. He'll fight back if we attack or try to escape, since those are his orders. But if there's anything else to him, it's been erased."

Quinn looked skeptical. "And you know this all because…"

"Silvius likes to talk," I muttered just as Dolion said the same. His eyes narrowed at me, his gaze locking on my neck—and the scar banded around it. He gave me a nod of understanding.

"Seeking sanctuary here was no accident," Dolion continued. "Without the Enclave's resources, there are few who would be able to create a cure that could stop Silvius's plan. And without the High Queen and her use of the magic of the land to cure the realm, there's no telling how many he could infect if we go along with this."

The room was silent for a long beat.

"Can it be done?"

I didn't want to know the answer even as I asked the question. Quinn and Dolion exchanged a loaded look.

"There's little that can't with magic, intention, and the right research," Dolion said heavily.

"And time," Quinn added, her voice bleak. "Though even if we had all the time in the world, we can't go along with this. I can't speak for Queen Sariyah, but Pari is my friend. She would never forgive us if we traded her life for innocent people. Especially since there's no telling how far this could spread."

Of course we couldn't. But that didn't mean I was about to give up yet.

"Can we trick him, somehow?" I kept my voice low, though the guard showed no sign he understood me. "I don't know how long we were unconscious, but Pari needs that cure yesterday."

I knew Marin and Rivan would do everything they could to keep her stable. But without an *anima* bond and someone in her mind fighting alongside her to keep her memories, her very *self* intact...

"Or we use the time to find a way out of here," Quinn murmured. "Do you know where Silvius could be storing the cure?"

Dolion shook his head. "It's not far but that doorway is keyed to Silvius's blood alone. We're trapped here until he returns. Even the guards can't go anywhere without him."

"I could try to ambush him when he reenters," Quinn said hesitantly.

Dolion could barely stand up unassisted, and I was chained to a wall. She would be on her own.

I shook my head. "With that gas in play...we can't risk it without getting the cure first."

"Without my magic, I won't even be able to tell if he gives us the real one." The despair in Quinn's voice made me want to gather her in my arms and promise everything would be okay, though I couldn't do either. "Or if he does, whether he's tampered with it somehow."

"Tamper with ours right back then." They both stared at me. "You two are the geniuses. There must be a way to give him a plan with a fatal flaw but still be believable enough for him to hand over the cure. Then we demand he send Quinn to administer it to Pari. Her magic will be able to confirm if it is what he says it is."

"I'm not leaving you," Quinn protested. "Dolion can—"

"He knows you're my *anima*," I said exasperatedly. "That you'll come back for me. It's the perfect leverage, especially if he wants to ensure you don't replicate the cure while you're there."

Quinn's gaze was sharp and searching. "Then *you* should go."

"I'm not getting anywhere fast," I said, nodding at my leg. I didn't bother to add that there was no way Silvius would let me leave. "You and Dolion are the only options."

"He won't agree." Dolion sighed, leaning against the bars. "He'll want to go himself, wearing my face." His voice shook on the last three words, disgust tinging his horror. "His plan is to return with my queen at his side once he can control her. To use her to infect the entire city until everyone is under his control, or dead."

It was a solid plan, especially since Silvius wouldn't need to keep up the façade for long. Once the Enclave fell, its greatest minds erased? There would be little anyone in the realm could do to stop Silvius.

"Let's worry about that once we have a way to trick him," I said. "He's counting on the fact that he can use the ones we love against us, but I promise you, what he hasn't accounted for is that he's up against someone smarter than he is." I nodded at Quinn. "This can work, as long as we stay ahead of him for a change."

Quinn's lips formed a tight line, but she nodded. "We can try."

Dolion hesitated, his eyes dropping again to my neck.

I tapped my finger once against the banded scar, ignoring the way my chains rattled. "The dagger Silvius stole from Quinn—the silver one on his belt. If we can get it back, I can remove that for you. Though his blood should also do the trick."

The diamond on its pommel was Bash's mother's creation—and had the ability to draw magic into it.

Quinn blinked at me in surprise. "When you gave me that gift, I didn't realize..."

"That I was giving you the key to my freedom, should I ever need it again?"

Quinn swallowed hard, then nodded.

I shrugged. "Maybe I wanted to make sure you had the key to yours."

Quinn didn't say anything. She only took my face in her hands and kissed me.

I never wanted it to end, but this time I was the first to pull away. "Get to work, Sagray. I'll be here if you need someone to check your notes."

Her smile was fleeting before she left the cell, Dolion by her side. The guard looked down at me as I crossed my arms. His empty eyes sent a chill down my spine.

Quinn's and Dolion's low voices blended together as they started working through the notebooks, the faint scent of leather drifting my way as they looked for an answer and a loophole.

I was grateful they were facing the opposite direction as I closed my eyes. The pounding in my skull was only getting worse, the sense there was something wrong multiplying by the minute.

If what I suspected was true, she couldn't know. Not when she needed to focus on saving everyone else.

Besides, there was nothing she could do.

CHAPTER 47
TOBIAS

The fog wrapped around my feet, curling up my legs as I ran. It tugged at me like it was trying to drag me down. Her footsteps echoed around me, her laugh ringing in my ears even as it scattered in every direction.

"Quinn," I gasped, looking around wildly. "Wait for me."

She only laughed again. I couldn't see her, couldn't find her in the mist. The ground shifted unnaturally beneath me as if it was breathing.

I let out a desperate scream, yet it sounded as weak as a whisper. "Quinn..."

The fog rose higher, wrapping around my wrists and neck. The more I struggled, the tighter its grip became, like sinking deeper in quicksand. It wasn't just the pressure on my body. It was the crushing, claustrophobic realization that every movement sealed me in tighter, as if the fog was a living thing bent on destroying me.

I sucked in a breath right before it covered my face. It blinded me until all I saw was a cloudy, endless white. I sunk beneath the surface, those tendrils dragging me under—smothering me into a submission so complete I couldn't even scream.

The laughter stopped.

I had to get to her, even if it killed me. The fog held me back as I kept resisting, the mist solidifying into iron bonds.

This time, as the mask stole the heat from my skin, I knew there was no help coming. This time, there was no way out.

I tried to shout her name—

. . .

✧

My chains caught me as I lurched forward, pain ricocheting from my broken leg as my knees hit the stone. It was an effort to catch my breath as the world flickered around me.

Blood dripped from the wounds on my wrists, painting my forearms in lines of red. Another iron scar to add to my collection if I survived this.

Quinn's face snapped toward me. "*Tobias*."

She jumped to her feet; the pen she was holding clattering to the floor.

"I-It was a dream," I said weakly. "I'm fine."

I wondered if she could sense it for the lie it was, even without our bond. The guard shifted in place but didn't move as she ran to me, helping me back onto the stool. A cry of pain slipped from my throat.

"You're not." Something about her tone made me sit up straighter. "Your blood...Tobias, it's flowing too fast..." Quinn sucked in a sharp breath. "I can feel your heartbeat."

Even across the cell, I could see the change in her eyes—the deep blood red of her irises.

Dolion turned to her, his mouth open in astonishment. "Your magic shouldn't be able to work here."

Maybe not her healing magic. But perhaps something else.

She looked at me intently. "Can you reach your light?"

I barely attempted it before I shook my head. I had tried and failed already.

"Can you access your healing magic?" I asked cautiously. "Or just your..."

I glanced at Dolion only to see realization dawning on his face.

He leaned forward, gripping the edge of the table so hard his knuckles turned white. "You have blood magic?"

He didn't sound judgmental. He sounded elated.

Surprise flashed across Quinn's face. "I assumed that you wouldn't think that's a good thing."

I couldn't think around the pain in my head. Why was he looking at her like she was the answer to all of this?

Quinn blinked. "But how did you know?"

Dolion was staring at her so intently it was an effort not to tell him to step back. "Bodily magics all come from the same internal source. And it's hard to hate a power that's about to save our lives."

I loved that look on her face—the furrow to her brow, the faraway look in her eyes, the slight pucker to her lips. I could practically see the wheels turning in her brain.

Quinn sucked in a breath. "I'm an idiot." I opened my mouth to protest when her next words stopped me cold. "Shifting is a form of blood magic. Whatever Silvius did to make this room resistant to Elemental and Celestial magics, he made sure his power was the exception."

Dolion nodded, looking expectant.

"I-I should've realized." Quinn looked down at her hands, her fingers splaying. "If he can shift in here..."

Then she could use her magic. At least, half of it.

"The mist," I murmured. "The aerosol serum had a magic blocking component. The effects of that must have taken longer to wear off."

Quinn closed her eyes. Her fingertips glowed a faint red.

"I didn't realize until you started bleeding, especially without my healing magic," Quinn whispered. "They've always felt like two sides of the same coin, like one balanced out the other. After hiding my blood magic for so long, it's become second nature not to use it. And with my healing blocked, I didn't recognize..."

"You can get us out of here," Dolion whispered excitedly.

The guard beside me lurched forward like the words woke him from his stupor. Before I could move, Quinn raised her hand.

He went completely still. Her fingers splayed apart, trembling with tension.

Dolion gasped as the guard's entire body contorted, each limb extended like an unwilling marionette as her magic forced him against the wall. His sword fell to the floor with a clatter. Then his body followed, crumpling into a heap.

"New plan," I croaked. "We make Silvius pay."

Quinn looked at me, then did a double take, her triumphant smile sliding away. The fear on her face made my heart spasm. Dolion's eyes widened as he followed her gaze. The loaded look they exchanged felt like a swift, silent conversation.

"Tobias...are you feeling alright?" The gentle words were a sharp contrast to how quickly she hurried over.

"I'm—" It was harder than I thought, lying to her. "Fine, Sagray. Why?"

Her voice was strained as she whispered, "Maybe you should lie down." She knelt next to me, then looked back at Dolion. "Can you check the guard for the keys to his locks?"

Even without our bond, Quinn's panic was plain.

"Quinn..."

Her thumb gently brushed against the skin above my upper lip, the touch so fragile it hurt. When she pulled away, my focus narrowed on the blood darkening her fingertips.

The look in her eyes...that terror was entirely for me.

My tongue darted up to lick my lip. The taste of iron confirmed what I already knew.

"I thought..." I gestured up at my face. "I thought I had more time."

"You knew?" The hurt in her words felt like it was cutting into me. She shoved against my chest, her hands curling atop my heart. "You *knew*?"

"I suspected," I admitted, leaning into her touch. "When the nosebleed didn't start sooner, I hoped I was wrong. I didn't want to alarm you when it was only a suspicion."

There was nothing she could do. Even with her blood magic, she had no way to heal me. And putting her into a coma to keep me stable definitely wasn't an option.

Dolion stopped patting the guard down, shaking his head. "Silvius must have them."

The telltale drip from my nose was coming faster now, dark spots crowding my vision as I swiped my mouth with my sleeve. Dolion removed the guard's cloak, silently passing it to me. The blue immediately turned black with my blood.

His voice was kind but measured, a doctor speaking to his patient as he asked, "How long, exactly, have you suspected?"

I leaned forward as a dizzy spell overtook me. It was almost a relief not to hide the signs anymore even as I fought against their pull.

"Not long after I woke up," I confessed. "I thought whatever he used to knock us out was the culprit, but then it only got worse. It would've been easy to infect me while I was unconscious, especially since he already created a virus keyed to my blood."

We literally handed my blood to him that first day in the lab. The stricken look on Quinn's face told me she had just now realized it.

I coughed, then spat out blood. "I'm only surprised Silvius didn't mention it as leverage against you."

Quinn laid the back of her hand against my forehead. "Low-grade fever. Though the fact you haven't passed out yet is promising."

I nodded blearily, then immediately regretted it at the ensuing vertigo. "Happy to hear you're impressed by my stamina."

Quinn's mouth twitched with a hint of a smile before her worry stole it away.

"Once we get the cure, you'll be fine," she said reassuringly, her tone carefully calm. But I could've sworn her hands were shaking.

My hand covered hers, my thumb rubbing against the blood smeared on her palm. "Promise me you'll do what you need to do, no matter what."

"No matter what happens to whom? To you?" Her voice wavered, a thread of desperation weaving through her words. "Nothing's going to happen to you, Tobias. I'm going to make sure of it."

I opened my mouth, then closed it again, trying to find the words to comfort her only to find the lies caught in my throat.

This had always been Silvius's plan. He had targeted this virus for me from the beginning. And, unlike the rest of them, he personally wanted to see me dead.

Quinn's eyes were fiery as that red intensified. "I can't heal what's wrong. But I think I can slow your heart rate and repair the blood vessel damage enough to keep you conscious. It'll have to be enough for now."

One hand moved to my cheek, the other pressing against my heart. I didn't say anything as Quinn closed her eyes in concentration. My nosebleed slowed to a trickle.

I dropped the bloody cloak, leaning my head back against the stone. I didn't even have the energy to wipe the remaining blood from my lips.

A glass was lifted to my mouth, and I took a grateful swallow.

"I won't let you die," Quinn said in a voice so low she might have been talking to herself. "And that's a promise."

CHAPTER 48
QUINN

My magic reached for the unconscious guard, dragging him to his feet like a puppet master moving a marionette. I was grateful for the blond length of his hair covering his face enough that Silvius wouldn't be able to tell he wasn't in charge of his limbs any longer.

It was no wonder blood magic had earned such a sinister reputation when this was the least of what it was capable of. The web of his veins made it only too easy to bend him to my will, though a voice in the back of my mind whispered this was exactly the sort of use that had made blood magic forbidden. And yet, the only part of this that felt wrong was making the guard point his sword at Tobias. This power, this control…it was liberating in a world where I had so often had neither.

Tobias had long since stopped trying to act like he was okay. He leaned forward with his face in his hands, his breathing shallow, though he still clung to consciousness. I was aware of his every breath along with the pulsing rhythm of his blood as Dolion and I worked.

There was nothing more I could do for him until I had the cure in hand or my healing magic to help him. I ground my teeth together. Even when Eva had gotten sick, I hadn't felt this helpless.

Whatever version of the virus this was, the symptoms were moving more slowly than Eva or Pari, considering he was still awake. There was nothing to do but watch and feel the quickened beat of his heart as his body fought the virus invading his bloodstream—and try to ignore the trickle of uneasiness in my veins that whispered there was something I was missing.

Dolion held a fresh notebook in front of him with the plan he and I had spent the night working on: entirely unethical ideas on how to spread a virus both of us knew was too dangerous to allow. For a bloodborne virus to be altered to spread, several biological and structural changes would need to be engineered to enable it to survive long enough to infect others. My understanding on how to do that came from coursework on how to identify potential pandemic threats, not how to create them.

Given the magic of this city, there had been one way that made the most sense, even as the thought of it actually happening turned my stomach.

It would have to be waterborne.

A bloodborne virus was far too fragile to survive in the city's water supply, yet it was up to us to devise a plan convincing enough to make Silvius believe viable particles could be spread that way. We worked the rest of the night—or what I assumed was night based on how tired I was. Even Dolion looked concerned at how believable our proposition was by the time we finished.

When the door finally appeared again in the stone, I was ready.

The guard I controlled jerked to attention as two more vacant guards entered, a prone form carried between them. Matted black hair covered her face as her head lolled against her chest. I didn't need to hear the gasp on my left to confirm her identity.

Queen Sariyah.

Her long braid unraveled where it dragged against the floor. What had once been an ocean blue dress was now mostly the rust-colored brown of dried blood.

The papers in Dolion's hands shook. "My queen…"

She didn't move.

Silvius shuffled in behind them, another two guards at his back. The door slammed shut, then disappeared into the wall.

Tobias slowly raised his head to glare at Silvius. I couldn't tell whether he was conserving his strength or that was all the vitriol he could muster.

"I see you've finally noticed my handiwork," Silvius said, looking insufferably smug as he took in the blood covering Tobias's shirt. "I do hope you went ahead with your plans to create the next phase of the virus. If not, you won't be able to save him."

It was an effort not to stop his heart. To make him bleed and see if he still felt like celebrating.

First, we needed the cure.

Silvius gestured imperiously at Dolion, who handed our research to the nearest guard. The smile that crossed his lips—the first real one I had ever seen from him—filled me with the visceral urge to punch him in the face.

"You offered to cure Pari," I gritted out through clenched teeth. "Why infect Tobias?"

Silvius's mouth curled in pure hatred. "Maybe I want him to suffer."

The bottom half of Tobias's face was stained with his blood despite my efforts to wipe it away. He looked like he was on the verge of passing out, though he managed to hold Silvius's gaze.

"And I wanted to be certain you'd bring the plans I requested to life," Silvius said, looking back at me. "After all, I did promise motivation."

I couldn't help my shudder. He would have used Tobias to force me to continue working for him. Without my blood magic to save us, would I have bowed to Silvius if it meant saving my *anima*?

It was lucky I didn't have to make that choice. Not when it would have cost me my soul.

"We have your plans," I said snippily. "Where's the cure?"

Silvius took a black box from an inner pocket. Inside was a vial and two syringes.

The vial was labeled in my handwriting...but I had to be sure. I wouldn't put it past Silvius to switch out the contents or somehow negate the cure we created together.

"How are we supposed to trust that's what you say it is without our magic?"

"That's why I brought her." Silvius nudged Queen Sariyah's leg with the tip of his boot. "It seems that most of my loyalists were targeted in a plot to bring them to justice. One loose thread rounded them up. Most were captured by a faction led by your friends. Some killed." He clicked his tongue. "A pity."

His utter lack of concern for those that had given him sanctuary was chilling. For him, they had only ever been a means to an end.

Silvius cleared his throat. "My plan to use the queen for my goals won't work anymore, especially as it seems that his face"—he gestured at Dolion—"will no longer do for a disguise."

Yael.

A smile lifted my lips despite the seriousness of the situation. At least our last messages had served their purpose.

"You're smiling," Silvius scoffed. "You won't be for long. Your actions have forced me to take a different direction—a far more aggressive one. One in which every single person in Mayim will be infected far sooner. And one in which I don't require the queen to live."

Dolion tensed beside me, his hands curling into fists. For a fleeting moment, I thought he might lunge at Silvius. Instead, he lifted his chin. "If you kill her, I won't help you."

"Kill her?" Silvius's laugh lacked any hint of warmth. "I'm going to *cure* her." He extracted a syringe, carefully filling it. "We still need to test it, after all. She'll remain here as my prisoner, of course, if she survives. I wasn't expecting her to fight me as much as she did when I brought her with me."

He knelt beside the queen, then slapped her cheek. Dolion flinched, but she barely stirred.

Dolion stepped forward only for Silvius's guards to raise their swords. "Please, let me..."

Before he could finish, Silvius jabbed the syringe into Queen Sariyah's upper arm. Dolion and I exchanged a startled look.

"Here's how this will work," Silvius said as he emptied the syringe. "I will take the Northern King and the Southern Queen with me before I remove the block on the magic in this laboratory. Then you two will create this waterborne option within three days, or you'll get to watch them both die a slow and painful death."

"I'll need our research," I said quickly, my stomach turning at how closely I had worked with him all this time. "And everything you took from the lab."

"Of course," Silvius simpered, his voice grating on my last nerve. He looked imperiously at one of the guards, who retrieved a satchel from his back. The guard lumbered forward, then dropped the bag on the closest counter. Tobias's careful notes spilled out onto it, mixing with my own. "I destroyed nothing of importance. You'll need to create a cure for the new version, after all, just to be safe."

I looked away so I wouldn't betray my excitement at having my hopes confirmed, nodding stiffly. "And Pari?"

Silvius closed the box with the vial and remaining syringe. "There's more than enough left for her. However, to make sure no one tries to replicate it, I must insist on going myself."

"No." Tobias's voice held no trace of weakness though he remained slumped against the wall. "They won't trust whoever you hide yourself as. They know Dolion's compromised. It has to be Quinn."

I knew Tobias wanted to be sure the box was safely in my hands before we moved to the next stage of our plan. But the cruelty in Silvius's flat gray eyes told me we were out of time.

My blood magic should feel drained from the effort it took to hold the guard still. And yet, I felt unstoppable.

This was true power—alive, electric. I could hear every one of the hearts beating in this room. I could feel them like I held them in my hands, warm, fragile, and entirely at my command. And I could sense the blood surging through their veins, urging me to reach out and finally give in.

Silvius's face twisted as he faced Tobias. "Do I need to remind you who's in control here?"

He looked at the guard I still held upright like a puppet. A flicker of confusion crossed his face.

"No," I said coldly. "Because *I* am."

My vision turned red as I let the magic roaring to be released consume me. I ensnared the remaining guards between one breath and the next, my magic reaching through them to control every vein, every single blood cell.

Then I reached for *him.*

Silvius's eyes went wide as his body betrayed him. I could feel each panicked beat of his heart, the way his muscles tried and failed to counteract my control. His fingers trembled as I forced them apart, extending the arm holding the cure toward me against his will.

"You..." Silvius forced out. "You have..."

"Blood magic."

Silvius let out a choked sound. Every one of his guards reached for their weapons, then dropped them to the floor in a clatter of metal. I sauntered closer as Silvius struggled—a fly caught in a spider's web.

It would only be too easy to block an artery and make him hurt for what he had done to Tobias, to my friends, and to so many others. I could stop his heart right here and feel each vessel die a tiny death until he was cold and still.

I barely noticed as Dolion rushed forward, taking Queen Sariyah into his arms. Not as I watched Silvius tremble.

"Quinn?"

Tobias's voice sounded far away, drowned out by the accelerating thrum of Silvius's heart beat in my ears.

This monster had tortured my *anima* for years. He created the mask that haunted his nightmares and had infected him with the virus now ravaging his body.

Killing him would be the least of what he deserved.

"Sweetheart…" Tobias's voice broke, pure fear tinging the endearment. "While I'm all for revenge, you're the one who told me we need him alive. And I-I need you to come back to me." The waver in his voice tugged at me from far away. Then his tone sharpened into a command. "Five things, Sagray. Listen to my voice and then find four more things, okay?"

I stood motionless, suspended between the intoxicating pull of power and the tether of his love. And then I started to count.

I could hear the whoosh of blood rushing through the veins of everyone in this room.

I could hear Silvius's choked breaths as I restricted his blood flow, his face turning red.

I could hear Dolion's murmured pleas for Queen Sariyah to wake, oblivious to the battle being fought within me.

I could hear the faint clang of metal on metal as Tobias leaned forward, his chains shifting.

And I could see...

Him.

My vision cleared as I focused on Tobias's face, taking in the worry in those gold-flecked eyes. An encouraging smile lifted his lips, just enough for that dimple to form.

With a gasp like I was resurfacing for air, I shoved my bloodlust away. Silvius's fingers twitched. I snatched the box with the cure from his outstretched hand, its handle digging into my sweaty palm.

"Now bring the guards to the cell," Tobias instructed, the concern in his voice plain. "Then you can let go of it."

With a shaky breath, I focused on putting one foot in front of the other, one body at a time. Sweat beaded on my forehead as I made their blood bend to my will. The jerky movements sent a chill down my spine.

Maybe they had once aligned themselves with Silvius. Now I doubted they even knew who they were.

"Keys," I gasped as the last guard entered the cell.

Dolion gently set Queen Sariyah down. "I saw them."

My heavy breathing blocked out the rest of his sentence as he limped toward Silvius, rummaging through his pockets. This magic was instinct, intrinsic in a way that felt even more natural than my ability to heal. But I hadn't trained for this, and my hold was fading fast.

"Hurry," Tobias said tightly, his eyes fixed on me.

Dolion rushed into the cell, the keychain rattling as he removed Tobias's shackles one by one. He wrapped an arm beneath Tobias's shoulders, fully supporting his weight as he helped him to his feet.

The world swayed around me. That red encroached on my vision, my eyelashes fluttering. The cell door slammed closed with a loud clang.

Two hands closed around my shoulders just as I heard a key turn in a lock.

"Let go of it," Tobias pleaded.

He caught me as my knees buckled, and we both went down hard.

"*Quinn.*"

He sounded so scared. I lifted my hand to his cheek, touching the corner of his lips, the stubble along his jaw. Drawing the scent of him, like smoke and safety, in with each breath. I leaned in eagerly, tasting his lips—letting him ground me.

One thing I could taste.

I let out a slow breath as I let that power recede completely. My vision cleared in time to watch the guards fall to the floor unconscious, like puppets whose strings had been cut. Silvius slumped against the bars behind him. Dolion immediately held one of the guard's swords level at his throat.

There was no resignation on his face, no trace of fear. Only a quiet, unsettling anticipation as he studied Tobias.

"Now we just need to get back to the Enclave." I glanced at the mirror as I got to my feet, then helped Tobias to his. The silver backing reflected a faint imitation of my likeness, ghostly without the glass strewn across the floor like a constellation of broken stars.

Dolion's borrowed sword wavered. He looked like he barely had the strength to hold it. "To leave the room, you need Silvius's palm print. I never saw a way out of this compound other than the mirror, but there must be a way."

I looked at Tobias's broken leg, then Queen Sariyah. "We'll need our magic back before we can go anywhere."

My heart twisted at the thought of everyone who needed this cure. We didn't have time to blindly search for an exit, not when so many people depended on us.

But Tobias was staring at the keypad. "When Pari was infected, Rivan said that one of the guards touched a wall before his magic was blocked."

"Silvius would need the ability to turn it on and off for this laboratory to be of any use," I mused.

Tobias looked at Silvius—who barely blinked as Tobias limped toward him—and then at Dolion. "And the bands he created are locked with blood…and can be unlocked with the same."

The two of us thinking through a problem in a lab together was strangely comforting.

"The access pads in the Enclave work similarly to control the wards that keep excess magic leaking out," Dolion added.

It stood to reason the merging of the two was the key to returning our magics.

"So maybe all we need is his blood on the access pad," I theorized. "After all, Rivan watched one of his supporters trigger it without Silvius there."

Dolion stepped back, lowering his sword as Tobias finished crossing the distance to Silvius. In a flash, Silvius reached into his robes like he had been waiting for this. Before I could so much as scream, Tobias's hand shot out, clamping around his wrist. Silvius grunted, twisting against him, but even in his current state, Tobias was stronger.

There was a gleam of silver as he wrenched a dagger from Silvius's hand. Then he slammed its hilt into Silvius's nose.

A crack split the air, followed by a wet-sounding curse. Blood streamed down Silvius's face, too reminiscent of the virus's initial symptom for me to feel even a flicker of sympathy for him.

The diamond on its pommel winked at me. I had almost forgotten that Silvius had stolen my dagger from me. Tobias, obviously, hadn't.

He pressed it to Silvius's throat. Silvius hissed as the edge grazed his skin, a thin line of blood appearing in its wake to match the red splattered down his no longer spotless robes.

"How do we get out of here?" Tobias's voice was chillingly calm. "Don't think I won't kill you if you don't tell me."

"You wouldn't," Silvius whispered, though he sounded less than certain. "You...you can't..."

That cool mask slid down Tobias's face, the impassive look in his eyes chilling me to my bones.

"Tobias...this isn't justice," I reminded him softly. "This is revenge."

Tobias nodded without a hint of concern. "Your point?"

I swallowed hard. "But you just said..."

"We both know you're better than me, sweetheart," Tobias murmured, staring intently at the blood dripping down his blade. He was breathing hard—too hard. It was a miracle he was still conscious let alone upright. "Besides, he owes me his blood after stealing mine for so long. Though there's one thing I want more—the end of his miserable life."

The blade pressed in. Tobias's cool façade cracked with a hint of a smile that chilled me to the bone.

"You were right," Silvius gasped, his voice frantic. "My blood...the access pad...just bring me to the access pad and my handprint will open the door. I'll show you the way out. And this..." He shakily gestured at his bloodied face. "It will remove the block."

"I knew I could count on you to still be a coward," Tobias spat. He pulled the dagger back, raising it high in the air.

I gasped as he brought it down.

The blade sliced across Silvius's hand. His shriek echoed through the room as blood dripped from the wound.

Tobias didn't look away from the blood as he said, "Would you like the honor?"

He wrenched Silvius's hand forward, forcing his bloody fingers against the collar on Dolion's throat.

Dolion nearly dropped his sword as his free hand flew to his bare neck. His voice hardened as he passed Tobias the band. "Oh, this is all yours."

Silvius shrank back, but with the bars behind him, there was nowhere to go. Tobias nicked his thumb, his blood welling as he pressed it against the band's open clasp.

He smiled as he closed it around Silvius's throat.

CHAPTER 49
TOBIAS

My walls were crumbling as the virus ravaging my system disintegrated them bit by bit. One last time, I made myself picture the dungeon I built in my mind—not to cage my emotions within, but to keep that fog from slipping through the bars.

While the others had worked, I had painstakingly rebuilt the cells I knew by memory. But this time, the bars were made of light, not iron. They burned a pale, perfect yellow, bright against the onslaught of the cloudy white haze.

I shoved Silvius forward toward the doorway. Dolion looked remarkably steady as his blade leveled at Silvius's back, its tip slicing through his ruined robes.

"If he doesn't cooperate, feel free to stab him," I drawled scornfully. "After all, we only need his hand."

Black dots multiplied in the corners of my vision as I tried to limp back to Quinn, nearly falling before she rushed over to help me. Bile lurched up my throat, but I forced it down along with everything else. Her hand shook as she draped my arm around her shoulders.

When she was safe, I would let myself feel this. For now, it was all I could do to remain standing—silently praying this would succeed, even as something inside me whispered it was too easy.

Quinn shot Silvius a look sharp enough to cut. The flicker of red in her eyes told me she was ready to take control the second he tried anything.

The door reappeared as they neared. Another poke of the sword, and Silvius raised his hand to the access pad. His blood seeped into the stone.

For one agonizing moment, I thought Silvius tricked us yet again…

A familiar current zipped through my veins. The crackle of light momentarily blinded me, surprising me in its intensity. I hadn't expected to still be able to access my magic, not when Eva had lost hers almost immediately after the virus's first symptoms. And yet, mine traveled between each fingertip in celebration, its power immediately bolstering me.

"Now into your cell," I said coldly to Silvius. "I'll keep you alive as long as you're useful."

Two lines he had so often said to me. Silvius's eyes narrowed, his face calculating, but he stayed silent as he staggered to his cage.

Dolion unlocked it, then shoved Silvius inside. He slammed the door behind him with a clang that made my heart plummet before locking him inside. I let out a breath I hadn't realized I was holding. The bluish glow of Dolion's power immediately flared at his fingertips as he rushed back to his fallen queen.

Quinn knelt beside me, her fingers pressing against my rebroken leg as I leaned heavily against a cold, steel counter.

"Save your strength," I muttered raggedly. "You'll need it to find the way out of here."

Quinn lips pursed. "I am. You're too heavy to carry and you can barely walk as is."

And yet, for some reason I couldn't fathom, I was still standing. Still… functioning, despite the virus attacking my brain. I closed my eyes as her magic faded into my thigh, its blue glow bright behind my eyelids. The relief barely registered.

"*Kill him*," Silvius demanded.

I opened my eyes a split second too late. A horrible crack echoed through the room. One of the guards had wrapped his arms around another, his neck already snapped. There was nothing I could do as his lifeless body slumped against the stone.

A moment later, everyone in the cell but Silvius went completely still. I didn't have to see the rise and fall of their chests to know Quinn had incapacitated them.

Quinn's blood red eyes glared at Silvius. "It's over, don't you get that? Why did you…how could you…"

Silvius let out a bitter laugh. "You may get out of this room, but now you won't get out of here alive."

The sinking feeling in my stomach solidified.

"If you want to survive this, you'll explain that," I growled. "The two healers you captured may feel some moral obligation not to let you bleed out in the same cell you used to torture us, but it's no less than you deserve."

"It *is* over," Silvius agreed. "*That*"—he gestured at the mirror—"was your only way out. We are deep beneath the Enclave, far beneath the earth. There's no way out now. The tunnels leading here are completely blocked thanks to my stone wielder, and *he*"—a dismissive glance at the body—"was the only one with the magic to reopen them." His gray eyes bore into me. "If I die here, then so will everyone who killed the True King, including your bitch of a sister."

I stared back at him as the world around me blurred. Silvius only smirked.

"He's lying," Dolion gasped. "There's no way he would entomb us down here…"

My voice sounded foreign to my ears as I whispered, "He's not."

For four years, my survival had depended on knowing every tick of the fae in front of me, every tell, every mannerism and mood that might signal what torture I had in store. He might be a psychopath and a murderer…but he wasn't a liar.

Quinn turned to the desk behind her, hastily scrawling a message. "We just need another Elemental who can reopen the tunnel, and Rivan—"

Silvius laughed as the slip of paper disappeared only to reappear in his outstretched palm. A line formed between Quinn's brows, before she whispered, "A spyfinder."

Aviel had used the same magical barrier to stop messages from escaping when his forces decimated the Mayimite army during the war. The price for that magic was in lives willingly given. Though something told me the lives he had taken to maintain it had likely lost their minds first.

Silvius only watched me, the smug look on his face begging for me to plant my fist into it. "I should also mention that I put a failsafe in place that triggered the moment you used my blood to unblock your magics. Should I not return to disarm it within the hour, you'll all be reacquainted with a familiar airborne serum, except this time there will be no one to shut it off." Blood streaked his teeth as he smiled at me. "Unless you all want to die down here, I'm afraid your only option is to let me free."

Letting Silvius go wasn't an option. I was once again caged beneath a castle, with no way to claw my way from it—and Quinn was trapped here with me. The muted feeling of her fear tore into my racing heart, each beat demanding that I figure out how to save her before I lost the ability to do so.

There had to be a way. Someone who could...

My brain felt unbearably sluggish as I looked at the shattered mirror, the broken pieces sparkling like sunlight on sand. I blinked, as though that might clear the fog away, limping closer.

Light glowed at my fingertips—some intrinsic part of me knowing the answer before my brain fully put it together.

My eyes dropped to the jagged shards of the mirror left in its frame, trying to remember the exact process—one I had only read about. The silver backing of the mirror was still in place, my dull reflection staring back at me. Two balls of light consumed the space where my eyes should have been.

I knew what I needed to do.

"Tobias?"

Quinn's voice seemed far away as I burrowed deep into my power. But I didn't have time to explain, not when I could feel myself weakening with every breath. The tether to my magic felt impermanent—like if I were to let go of it again, it would fade from my grip forever.

I drew a deep breath in, letting it steady me even as the world blurred at the edges. When I let it out, light arched from my hands, turning into the burning bands I had once learned to fear. They painstakingly wrapped around every piece of glass, reflections scattering in every direction as I lifted them from the floor. Zaps of lightning darted between them as I reached for each tiny shard, the smallest already binding back together from the heat.

Closing my eyes, I let the charge build up within me. Tunneling down and down and down into my magic, I welcomed that same heat that seared my skin so many times—the scent that lingered in my nose after every nightmare.

Aviel had never understood the intricacies of light and heat, let alone the true depth of my power. This wasn't fire, despite the inferno growing inside me, nor could light alone create this warmth. The brilliance that burned within me was born of loss, its untamed chaos too bright to be contained. This was the magic that had blazed inside me for months, building in power until I thought it might consume me.

The air thickened, a sharp metallic taste coating my throat. My hands extended forward, my fingers splaying wide as I felt for that invisible channel through the air.

A low, electric hum curled around me, not quite sound, not quite silence. The hair on my arms rose, my skin prickling as the tension built in a feverish crescendo.

I couldn't contain it anymore, but I no longer had to.

My eyes flew open.

Pure power flew from my hands like a long-silenced scream, a blinding, jagged bolt of lightning streaking across the room with a sharp crack. The sudden heat slammed into me like I had inhaled pure flame. It branched apart like the limbs of a tree, striking every single piece of glass I had forced together.

The sharp, clean scent of ozone filled my nose as the glass glowed like it contained the sun itself. I took one step forward, then another until I stood before it. Not daring to look down, I sliced a deep cut across both palms.

If this didn't fucking work...

I thought I was done being burned, that I had suffered that pain for the last time. Maybe that was why I finally gave in to the roar of agony and long repressed rage as I pressed my hands against the white-hot glass. As magic and my blood—the blood of Soleara's king—melded into the molten, glowing mass.

The mirror shuddered as its light-covered surface undulated beneath my fingers so violently I feared it would break. My teeth ground together as I forced the glass to bind against the silver, bonding it at a molecular level. The edge of my endurance began to fray, my magic pouring into it until I thought it was me who might shatter.

"Tobias."

Quinn. I couldn't feel her anymore. Couldn't sense her like I should. She stood far too close to me, too close to the lightning that seemed to stretch from my very soul.

My blistered hands clenched into fists. The last of my light seared my palms as I cut it off at the source.

The room went dark. Only the ghostly shape of those branches remained, suspended where my magic tore across the space an endless heartbeat ago. I forced myself to breathe through the pain.

It was nothing compared to the ruins of the fallen walls in my head.

A familiar blue light cut through the dark as the blind spots in my vision receded. My vision was tinted a milky white as Quinn wrapped her hands around mine, the chill of hers shocking against the heat of my skin.

"Holy gods," Dolion whispered from behind me. "How did you know that would work?"

Only then did I realize that the mirror wasn't just whole.

It was *rippling*.

"I didn't," I croaked, my throat raw. My eyes found Quinn's. "When lightning hits sand in the desert it creates glass. Someone I love mentioned it once."

Her lower lip trembled. My arms wrapped around her, far too weak for how tightly I wanted to hold her. Yet the bond between us still felt muted—silent despite the emotion all over her face.

Quinn seemed to realize something was wrong in the same heartbeat. "Tobias?"

Dolion swore as the mirror began to ripple more urgently, lifting up his sword. But the figure who came through the mirror was familiar, one of the same Solearan soldiers who once welcomed me to this realm. Quinn's gasp of surprise turned into a shout.

"Akeno."

Quinn was safe. Pari and Eva would be too, now that we had their cures. They had to be.

I stared into those amber eyes, committing them to memory as my vision went cloudy. There was nothing left to stop the endless white as it bore down on me, intent on erasing the broken pieces that finally felt whole.

My gaze dropped to the sunflower glinting around Quinn's neck—the familiar yellow shining like a beacon through the fog.

That last wall crumbled, and so did I.

CHAPTER 50
QUINN

Tobias sank to his knees, his dead weight dragging me down along with him. It was my turn to wrap my arms around him, his sweat damp hair too hot against my skin as his head fell against my chest. Dread coiled in my gut, my scream trapped behind clenched teeth.

I couldn't feel him.

He shouldn't have been able to fix the gateway home—shouldn't have had any access to his magic at all, not when the virus stripped everyone else of their power almost immediately. Whatever magic he had left was gone now though and it had finally allowed the fog to take hold.

Both parts of my magic streamed into him, trying to keep him stable. Akeno ran forward, eyes wide with fear, as more Solearan soldiers I recognized rushed through the mirror, swords in hand.

"Yael called us for backup," he gasped. "What can I do?"

I pointed at the open case that held the vial needed to fix this. "We need to replicate that cure, and quickly. Eva and Pari need it as soon as possible, as well as all the infected being treated in the Enclave. And Tobias—"

A cruel laugh cut me off. Blood gleamed on Silvius's teeth as he smiled at me.

"The cure won't help him," he sneered.

Terror clogged my throat, even as I forced my words past it. "What exactly is that supposed to mean?"

"Exactly what I said. The cure won't work on him." Silvius leaned forward, one hand tightening around the bars that caged him. "I made sure of that."

The look in his eyes was worse than malice. It was pride. Pure, callous delight mixed with heartless indifference to the suffering he had caused.

I stopped breathing. "What did you do to him?"

"It's a strain created to thwart the cure we made together, my dear." Silvius's voice was weak but triumphant. "You may have beaten me, but I'll take solace in the fact that my favorite test subject won't survive this. At least not as he was."

No.

Dolion picked up the case, his hands shaking. "You can't trust anything he says."

"Try it," Silvius urged. "You'll see soon that it won't save him."

I stared at Silvius, trying to determine if what he said was true or if this was one last trick. Finally, I turned back to the others. "Between that vial and our research, we should have everything we need to make more."

"I'll handle it," Dolion said from behind me. I turned to find him clutching the satchel that held our research. Two Solearan soldiers helped Queen Sariyah to her feet, who already looked markedly better. "I'll create more for everyone who needs it, even if I have to put the entire research ward to work on it, and test dosage levels between the strains." He glanced over to the cage where a few of the guards wandered aimlessly. One stared blankly at the wall in front of him. "Maybe we can even make it work for them."

The cure had worked for her. The cure *worked.*

Now I needed it to work for him.

"We need to get everyone out of here," I stammered. "I almost forgot the mist...Silvius's failsafe for intruders..."

Queen Sariyah brushed the guards helping her off before imperiously smoothing her skirts. "I'll keep the mist at bay. And make sure there aren't any poor souls left trapped in here before we depart." She turned to Dolion. "Use whatever resources you need to get that cure distributed and administered quickly."

"We need to get Tobias somewhere we can monitor him." Only the feeling of his chest rising against my hand with each breath kept my voice calm. Tobias didn't have time to waste when every second could mean the difference

Thorin stepped out from behind Akeno. "Take him back to Soleara. Take him home. We'll help you."

Home.

But it wouldn't be home anymore, not if I didn't save him.

"And Silvius?"

He glared at us from behind the bars. His hands clawed at his collar, yanking at it as if it were strangling him—frantically fighting against his own cruel invention.

Queen Sariyah cleared her throat. "Leave him to me. After what he put my people through, he'll spend the rest of his days in a dark cell after we force the names of his collaborators from him."

A fitting end. Silvius's eyes had grown round with terror, and I allowed myself one last, smug look in his direction. He deserved to suffer for what he done.

If his fate was a cold, dark cell, I hoped he lived a long, long time.

✧

Tobias still hadn't woken up.

Dolion had long since delivered the cure through the mirror in Soleara before racing back to Mayim. All I could do was wait…and destroy the syringe I used to inject Tobias with the miracle we had created together, not wanting him to see it when he woke up.

I hadn't yet left Tobias's bedside to change from my bloody clothes when Marin had sent a message with an update: Queen Sariyah's army of healers had been dispatched to administer it to everyone infected, including Eva. She and Bash would soon be woken from their stasis. Rivan had sent a missive to confirm that the healers had treated Pari as well, though she also hadn't woken up.

Queen Sariyah seemed to have no lasting effects from the virus, though that was hardly a baseline as she was one of the last to be infected and the first to be given the cure. But it gave me hope. She had sent me a personal note confirming the infected patients at the Enclave had also received the cure—and made me promise I would keep her updated about Tobias's recovery.

I could only pray the cure had reached them all in time to make a difference.

Try as I might, I couldn't stop thinking about Silvius's promise that I couldn't save Tobias. Maybe it was an empty threat—the final attempt at hurting us now that he was out of options to do so. But if Silvius had told the truth, I hoped the cure's imbued magic would be enough to eradicate the fog, even if Silvius had successfully mutated the virus to be resistant to our cure.

It *had* affected him differently. Either Tobias was oddly resistant to the virus's effects or the blood magic I used to suppress the virus's initial symptoms had delayed them. It didn't explain why he was able to use his magic to fix the mirror when it should have been completely blocked.

Nor did it explain why he hadn't succumbed to the fog until his light was completely drained.

Marin showed up as the day faded into darkness, bringing food I barely touched.

"Eva's showing enough improvement that we took them out of stasis, though neither she nor Bash have woken up yet," Marin said as she gently washed some dried blood I missed from behind Tobias's ear. "What you created is a miracle."

Science had a habit of producing those.

I absentmindedly stroked my thumb up and down Tobias's hand. "Any word from Rivan and Dolion?"

Marin shook her head, her brow wrinkling. "Not yet. But it sounds like Pari—"

My heart jumped into my throat as Tobias's eyelashes fluttered.

His lips moved, but no sound came out. Marin brought a glass of water to his lips, as I gently lifted his head.

"Tobias," I said in a rush, his name a lifeline.

His voice was barely a whisper. "Quinn?"

Of course he still knew me. He'd known me since his first breath, after all.

It also meant I had no idea how much he remembered.

He swallowed, the motion exaggerated as if even that small act took effort. "Where am I?"

"You're safe," I breathed. "We're okay. You saved me."

I sucked in a shaky breath, brushing away the wetness from my cheeks with my sleeve.

"We're okay," he repeated, his voice painfully unsure.

My healing magic poured through him, only to crash against the fog like surf against stone. I tried again to no avail, searching for anything I might have missed.

"Tobias..."

His breathing turned ragged. "I...I can't see you."

The fog in his eyes now entirely blotted out the gold. He was getting worse, not better.

Silvius hadn't been lying.

I let out a choked cry as realization turned to heartbreak.

"There's something I'm forgetting," Tobias mumbled. "Something I'm... something I can't forget..."

My blood magic reached for him this time, only for my effort to have the same effect. I could still feel his heartbeat—but his mind, his memories, the things that made him *him*—were caged within the fog. I wanted to scream, to sob...to plead with the universe to save him and allow us our happy ending.

"Don't forget me," I begged. "I can fix this if you just hold on. I-I love you."

It was a risk saying it when I didn't know what he remembered. But I couldn't bring myself to regret it.

His eyes slowly blinked, trying to focus on me and failing. "I love you, Quinn. I always have. N-nothing will ever change that."

I wiped my face on the back of my sleeve, even as more tears took their place. Each heartbeat was slower, more irregular—his heart working far too hard for his weakened state, struggling to save a body that was shutting down. The heartbreak on his face mirrored my own, and I knew.

Whatever this was, Silvius had miscalculated...or perhaps this had been his plan all along. The virus wasn't simply taking his memories.

It was killing him.

I turned to Marin so abruptly she startled.

"He's dying," I whispered. "Whatever Silvius did, it's not just his mind at risk."

"But the cure..." Her magic ran over him, the green glow fading into his body. Her face dropped as she confirmed what I already knew. "How can I help?"

A reckless plan formed in my mind as if I had always known what I had to do.

"I need you to put me under like you did for Eva and Bash." Marin opened her mouth to argue, but I cut her off. "I have to try."

It was the clarity of desperation. Of one last chance.

"I'm going to dreamwalk to him."

CHAPTER 51
QUINN

I would bring him back no matter what the cost.

Was Tobias trapped in those mental cells, caged once again in the prison of his own making? He said we had torn those walls down together, but if he was a captive in his own mind, I had a horrible feeling he used his time last night to rebuild if only to bar the pain I couldn't save him from. My heart shattered as I pictured him, alone and scared, trying to keep the fog out with iron bars and dank stone.

"This isn't like Eva." Marin's worry sharpened each word. "He's dying, Quinn. And if he dies with you in there with him, you'll…"

I didn't care. I didn't so much as consider the impossible odds or the slim chance of rescuing him with his mind intact because it didn't matter. Not when there was still a chance of saving him.

This wouldn't be the first time he'd come back from the dead.

And if he didn't…

"He'll take my soul with him either way," I countered, my voice firm. "Stop wasting time and help me, or I'll find someone else who will."

Her eyes flickered with concern, even as I saw the resignation on her face.

The moment she whispered a terse, "Fine," I slid into bed beside Tobias. He was a living furnace despite the number of windows I opened to let in the crisp air. The damp cloth on his forehead instantly heated every time I applied a cool compress.

I dipped my head in a nod, bracing myself. "How does this work?"

"Reach out to him as I put you under," Marin said curtly. "Try to feel your way to him across your bond. Picture him, and don't let yourself get distracted."

I wrapped my body against his side, laying my head on his chest as I placed my hand against his heart. Its sluggish rhythm was a sharp contrast to the frantic drumbeat of my own. My blood magic answered automatically, urging it to continue—every part of me begging him to stay with me.

Marin touched two fingers against each of our temples, her magic flickering in the corner of my vision as it streamed into me.

I pictured Tobias's face: the cleft to his chin, the dimple I adored, the rare but precious way his eyes crinkled when he laughed.

I remembered the way he had watched me as we worked, like he couldn't help himself, his gaze attentive and patient and full of a quiet admiration that made my chest ache.

I thought of the look in his eyes the first time I told him I loved him, and the smile I had received in return, all the more precious for its rarity.

I would give anything to see it again.

"Good luck," Marin whispered. "I hope you find a way—"

Between one word and the next, I was gone.

✧

I ran through Soleara, its streets eerily empty. My footsteps echoed strangely as the cobblestones swirled unnaturally beneath my feet. A thick fog blocked the rooftops from sight, the two magnificent peaks of the mountain hidden from view. The bronze castle ahead was nearly covered with clouds, its normally vibrant luster dull and fading.

No, not clouds.

Fog.

"TOBIAS."

My scream was swallowed by the dense mist, only a muffled, ghostly echo bouncing back at me. A cold sweat trickled down my spine as I turned in a full circle, frantically searching for him and finding no trace. My breathing came quick and shallow as I broke into a run.

The healing magic at my fingertips seemed to mimic the glowing orbs of Tobias's as it reflected against the fog. It pressed in with every step, my power barely holding it back from touching me. I was so focused on avoiding it that I didn't notice the feeling of wrongness engulfing me as I sprinted toward the familiar bronze castle.

The second I reached it, I knew he wasn't inside.

My hand curled into a fist against the castle doors, my gasps starting to sound like sobs. It was impossible to breathe—not when he was lost, or worse.

"Tobias, please," I begged aloud. "Where are you?"

A breeze whipped around me in a whirlwind of dust, spinning me around. My yellow skirt twirled around me, the wind fluttering along the long slit up my thigh—the same dress I wore to Eva and Bash's catastrophic rehearsal dinner. A flurry of dust caught my gaze as it raced across the drawbridge, sparkling like glimmers of glass.

Something inside my chest tugged me forward as surely as Tobias's heart beat against my palm. I chased that pull, my heels clattering along the bridge. I knew without a doubt who was waiting on the other side.

As soon as I made it across the drawbridge, my heels sank into the grass. I sucked in a breath at the sight before me.

Tobias lay on his back in a meadow beneath a cloudless sky. Flowers bloomed all around him in a sea of yellow, so bright they couldn't be real. Yarrow, daffodils, hibiscus…and so many sunflowers, a swath of smaller ones blooming around his head like a crown. Rows upon rows of them towered around the meadow, their golden faces raised in defiance as they kept the fog at bay. But the ones closest to me spread apart, creating a tunnel for me to walk through.

He looked so at peace, far more than I had ever seen him in real life. His arms were crossed behind him, cradling his head as he looked up at the sky. He was barefoot, his pants and unbuttoned shirt a soft, ethereal white.

A smile curved his lips, that dimple firmly in place.

"I forgot how much I loved the sun," Tobias said quietly. "That warmth and light didn't need to mean pain. That the openness of the sky could feel like freedom."

Slipping off my shoes, I carefully stepped through the flowers. Their leaves tickled my toes, petals brushing pollen against the inside of my ankles as I passed. It felt so real that for a heartbeat I imagined it was—that we were here and safe together.

Tobias lazily reached out a hand for me. The second I took it, he tugged me down next to him.

A surprised laugh left me as he caught me in his arms. He pulled me close, my legs tangling with his. My hand tucked beneath his shirt to rest against his heart. There was no sign of the fever flushing his cheeks, the chills wracking his body. No hint of his chapped lips and sweat soaked skin.

Those silver scars remained, the band around his neck even more stark against the healthy flush of his skin. I was glad—the scars were part of his story.

"I thought I'd find you beneath Morehaven," I admitted.

Tobias shook his head, his eyes finally opening. The gold of them caught the sunlight as he gazed into my own. "I couldn't go back into that cell even if I wanted to after we destroyed it. I tried to rebuild it, but it wouldn't hold anymore. So I thought I'd come home, one last time." He pressed a kiss against my forehead. "I should've realized how well I know every detail about you, to recreate you so perfectly."

I stiffened, pushing onto my forearms. "I'm not some daydream, Maris. I'm *here*. This dream isn't home—" My voice caught. "Home is where I'm going to bring you back with me."

Horror overtook his calm, wind whipping through the flowers as Tobias jerked upright, his arm crushing me against his chest.

"You can't be here," he whispered, his voice tight with fear.

"Then come back with me," I demanded. My hands moved to his face, my thumb stroking his cheek. "I'll follow you anywhere, Maris."

"I-I can't," Tobias stammered. "Do you think I didn't try, Sagray? I started at the top of the mountain, and the fog flooded through every room of our home. It followed me, chasing me down every step to my castle, and then it took my city too." His next words were hesitant, like they were being ripped from him. "I tried to get back to you, but I can't keep running. It was all I could do to find my way here."

I shook my head, refusing to accept it. "I can cure you...I just need time. I need you to keep fighting. I need...you."

Tears welled in my eyes, my lower lip trembling.

"Silvius said there was no cure for me," Tobias reminded me unnecessarily. "That the version of the virus he made for me was specifically created to work around what we made together." His throat bobbed, his eyes searching my face like he was memorizing each detail. "We both know I'm dying. But I made my peace with death once before, if it meant saving you. You need to get out of here before I take you with me."

The acceptance in his tone made me want to murder him.

"Not without you." I wasn't sure if it was a threat or a plea as my breath splintered into desperate, shallow gasps.

"Breathe, Sagray," Tobias ordered, distress bleeding into his tone. "That's it. Breathe for me."

I focused on the timbre of his voice, instinctually responding to his instructions. Tobias's hand stroked my cheek.

"That's my girl."

I was his. And he was *mine*.

"Only one of us is getting out of here," he continued gently. His voice was so assured, so convincing, that for a heartbeat he almost convinced me. "Which means you need to go, before the choice is taken from you. If anyone can survive the breaking of our bond, it's you. You've always been stronger than me."

If we survived this, I was going to throttle him for his utter lack of regard for his own self-preservation—and for how blindly he dismissed how losing him would affect me.

Because it would shatter me.

"I don't accept that," I seethed, resolve sharpening my tone. "You need to give me a chance to try. If I can keep you stable like Bash did for Eva, then Dolion can find a fix for whatever Silvius changed. There has to be an answer in one of those notebooks, or in his lab, something we can find before you..." My voice cracked, unable to finish the thought. "Don't you want to live? To have a life with me?"

"Of course I want that," Tobias said forcefully. "But not if the price is you."

I couldn't bear the quiet surrender in his voice; the wistful way he was watching me.

A frown crossed his face, beads of sweat appearing between the lines on his forehead. "The cure. Did it work for my sister?"

I nodded. "She's not awake yet, so we don't know the extent of the damage. But Marin said she's doing better. Our cure worked."

A fleeting smile. The knot in my throat threatened to choke me at the resignation in his gold-flecked eyes.

"If I don't live and Eva does, I'd say it's a fair trade," Tobias choked out. "The years since the first time I died feel like borrowed time anyway."

His eyes darted to the drawbridge. The fog had crept closer, a steady countdown to what he thought was inevitable. Fear dissolved into fury, and I was drowning in it.

"You don't need to sacrifice yourself to save Eva," I hissed, my hand stubbornly tightening on his. "You don't need to sacrifice yourself to save anyone."

Tears slipped down my cheeks as I watched his face go ashen with pain. The fog started to slip through the sunflowers, reaching gnarled hands into the formerly sunny sky—now an ominous gray. Flowers swayed around us as the wind picked up, their petals falling like colorful snow.

"I don't think I have a choice, sweetheart."

That healthy glow faded until he stared up at me through shadowed eyes, his face pale and covered in sweat. His heartbeat slowed beneath my hand, like it too was giving up the fight. My own heart was being eviscerated with every irregular beat.

"Loving you was worth every single moment," Tobias said, his voice ragged. "As much as I wish we had more time, I'm thankful for every minute we were given."

I glared at him mutinously. "Don't you dare say goodbye to me, Maris."

The wind whipped around us, the fog graying the corners of my vision. We were in the eye of the storm. A funnel of swirling gray spiraled inward, narrowing by the second.

He only held me closer. "There's so much more I wanted to do with you. I wanted to explore this realm with you by my side, now that the sky feels safe again. I haven't seen enough yet…don't think I could ever see enough of you, not even if we were given all the time in the world." His breathing came more labored now, like each one took effort. "I've known you since my first breath, Quinn. And I'll love you long after my last."

His hand slipped from my side as he fell back into the flowers. One overlarge sunflower formed a pillow behind his head.

"I always thought the afterlife would be soft," Tobias mumbled. "After all those nights sleeping on stone, I hoped it would be like this."

"Tobias." His name was a prayer and a demand, both begging him to stay with me. "Please don't leave me."

"Sorry Sagray," Tobias murmured blearily. "It-it hurts. I can't hold it off much longer."

It hurt. And I couldn't heal him.

Tears blurred my vision. I reached for him, needing to do something—*anything*.

My magic sprang to my fingertips, reaching for him as surely as I did.

My mind reeled; my thoughts racing faster and faster. I couldn't heal him from the outside because the fog blocked my path. But now, I was inside the storm, inside the last circle of safety before that fog fully descended.

And so was our magic. Maybe I couldn't destroy the fog, but I could reach him.

"*Quinn*." The plea in his voice nearly broke me. "Whatever you're thinking, stop. You need to get out of here before..."

He didn't have to say it. Soleara had disappeared entirely into the fog. Sunflowers waved violently in the wind, a circle of them tightening around our clearing as the fog moved ever closer.

Our last line of defense before the inevitable.

I raised my chin, squaring my shoulders as I kept my eyes locked on him.

"I'm staying right here," I said, the words a promise.

His voice was strained and utterly desperate, but a fight finally flared in his eyes. "Don't you fucking dare."

I ignored him. "Can you feel your magic?"

Without waiting for an answer, I placed both hands on his chest, my hair whipping into my face. The blue of my healing magic swirled with the red of my blood magic, their glow leaking through my lashes. Wielding them together was simple, easy even, like they had always been meant to function this way.

Together, they battled against the virus that had taken hold of his blood.

"What are you...?" Tobias's voice trailed off as he sucked in a deep, shuddering breath. Color returned to his cheeks, his eyes clearing enough to meet mine. Even the sunflowers seemed to bloom brighter.

It wasn't enough to cure him, only keep the virus at bay—but it was enough to keep hope alive.

"This isn't over yet," I breathed, willing him to believe it too. "I need you to fight this with me, Tobias, because I'm not leaving you. I have no desire to exist in a world without you again. So if you won't fight for yourself, then fight for me."

I saw the moment he realized he wasn't going to convince me to go; the way the glassiness in his eyes gave way to pure determination. The sunflowers had multiplied, their swaying stalks reaching up to the white sky.

"You're the best problem solver I know," Tobias murmured. "So solve me."

"You're not a problem."

That dimple winked at me. "Debatable."

I let out a choked laugh, blinking away tears.

"Right now, Sagray," he ordered.

Closing my eyes, I made myself focus. I could sense the cure we had so carefully created together, the components and magic somehow not enough to stop this virus from invading his blood, even if I could hold the fog back from his brain.

I needed to think. There had to be another way.

The virus hadn't affected him like the others. I thought it was because of the changes that Silvius made to it, but now I wasn't so sure. Tobias had stayed conscious after the nosebleed, not because of me but because he had his own defense against it. His magic may have been blocked, but it was still present in his body…and in his blood.

It wasn't until he depleted his power that he finally succumbed.

His light, the heat he told me he had learned to fear…that had to be the missing piece. The lightning that lived in his veins that liked to jump between his long, dark eyelashes. The light that swirled around me like tiny stars, playful yet destructive.

That was the key to this.

Heat can kill viruses, I had told him not long ago. *That's exactly why the body's natural response is to raise its temperature. But the effectiveness depends on the virus, the duration, and how hot you can get without killing the host along with it.*

What he had done to recreate the mirror gateway hadn't been enough alone, because it hadn't been focused on the right place. But this time, the components of the cure were in his system. I could wrap my healing magic around him like a shield while using my blood magic to target his lightning exactly where it was needed.

Unlike the last time I thought I lost him forever, this time I had the means to save him.

This time, I wouldn't let him die.

"I have an idea," I whispered. Granted, it was a desperate, reckless idea verging on pure insanity…but I was out of options.

"I'm in, Sagray," Tobias drawled. "Should I be worried or just mildly terrified?"

The wind whipped my hair around me, flowers flying into the air as my eyes met his. "Burn it. Burn all of it. I need more than a lightning strike this time—I need a storm."

This could work. It had to.

Tobias looked up at me, startled. "Burn…"

"The fog." I gritted out, pouring my power into him. "You were able to use your magic despite the fact that the virus should've blocked it. Even Eva wasn't able to use the magic of the land against it, and yet you were able to stay conscious. Your light…I think Silvius left a sort of magical loophole for his master's stolen light when he originally made this virus. Or maybe it's just the biology of heat and viruses, considering that lightning lives in your veins." I swallowed, praying I was right. "My magic may not be able to stop it…but I think yours can. Or at least they can together."

Lightning danced between his eyelashes. Every muscle in my body went tight as I felt that power flow through his veins—each and every blood cell burning as electric, white light gathered inside him.

For some reason, I expected his magic to hurt, to burn. Instead, it swirled around mine, the light a warm embrace—the gentle touch of a lover. A few bobbing balls of light fought against the wind as they joined the sunflowers standing guard.

"*Now*, Tobias," I urged. "If you want me to live, if you want us both to survive this, then I need you to burn it all away."

The moment stretched taut. The wind intensified, a hurricane of yellow petals whirling around us.

Tobias's eyes glowed an unearthly white. My own squeezed shut as his magic exploded.

A crack resounded in my ears as lightning split the sky, tearing into the fog in a million tiny strikes. His light flooded all around me in a vicious torrent—consuming me, though it didn't burn.

The world turned red as my blood magic reached out, locking onto his. Carefully, I guided his power into his body to where the virus hid within each host cell. His magic burned it from his blood as I immediately healed the damage.

Working in tandem, it didn't take long to destroy every last trace. After all, we had always worked best together.

Sunlight warmed my face; the last of the fog burned away. The sweet scent of sunflowers filled my nose as an army of them swayed around us. His arms held me close, even our breathing in sync.

I searched Tobias's face for any sign of discomfort—any trace of the pain he endured while fixing the shattered glass of the mirror—but that dimple flickered on his cheek.

The last of my magic faded, its glow beneath my fingertips weakening into nothing. I could only hope it would be enough as the world around me dissipated into the warm, bright light.

My arms tightened around him, refusing to let go—no matter what came next.

CHAPTER 52
TOBIAS

I was struck by the inescapable feeling that I was forgetting something. Something vital. Something more important than anything.

An acrid scent filled the air despite the breeze, smoke going up my nose. How fitting that I should die in a fire after how this journey began. I was on my back with my eyes closed. Every muscle ached as I tried to move, seizing like they no longer remembered how to work together.

A warm weight lay on top of me. The hair tickling my face gave away its owner, even if I hadn't memorized the exact feeling of my *anima* against me.

Quinn wasn't moving.

Panic gripped my chest in a vise. I coughed, trying to open my eyes—

"Were you trying to burn down the whole damned castle?"

Marin's voice pierced the inside of my skull. I opened my mouth, but nothing came out.

Forcing my eyes open, I blinked through the haze. We were in my room —the one I rarely slept in, inside the bronze castle of Soleara—though I barely recognized it. The curtains had been reduced to ash, the desk split in half and smoldering. My armoire was now on its side, charred clothes spilling out. The breeze was apparently courtesy of a smashed window, the shattered glass littered across the floor.

At least the bed remained in one piece.

"I managed to put the fires out," Yael said from the doorway, twirling a small twister of her air magic with one finger. "Removed all the air that was fueling it. Though I won't deny it was a challenge."

Marin grimaced beside her, adding, "You're lucky your people found cover in the mountain above."

Quinn groaned, shifting slightly. Her skin felt hot where it rubbed against mine. With a start, I realized we were naked, our clothes entirely burnt away.

I reached for the sheets only to have them crumble apart in my hand.

"We're alive," Quinn croaked. She smiled at me, utterly exhausted yet grinning from our victory. The light, playful giddiness along our bond was a welcome relief.

I stared at her, slack jawed. This determined, unyielding creature had followed me into the throes of death and pulled me back with sheer strength of will.

And I'd been so close to losing her. To taking her with me.

Her fingers traced my palm as if reading the future that she refused to surrender.

"You could've died," I rasped. "Coming after me was a risk—"

Her amber eyes burned. "And I'd do it again."

Stubborn to a fault. I was fully aware that her tenacity had saved my life.

"Of course you would, Sagray."

"You absolute idiot, if I hadn't—"

Before she could finish her sentence, I kissed her. One hand gripped her cheek, tilting her face up to mine. The other wrapped tightly around her bare waist, dragging her closer.

Yael cleared her throat and we broke apart. A burst of air spread a towel over us a second later—apparently, we had left the bathroom intact.

Marin chuckled under her breath. "Perhaps a quick once-over and a bath before we celebrate. Eva's asking for you both."

"She's awake?" Quinn squeaked, trying to sit up, then fell back against me with a groan. "And remembers us?"

Her elbow dug into my gut. I only grunted in response, the last of my remaining energy entirely extinguished by that kiss.

Marin tutted under her breath. Her magic glowed at her fingertips as she placed a hand on both of our foreheads. "I would lecture you about the dangers of burning out your magic, but considering what you pulled off… well, I'll save it until you don't look like you're on the losing end of a battle against charcoal."

"Pari," I forced out. "D-did she…"

I couldn't even say the words.

Marin shook her head, smiling. "Rivan dreamwalked to her. He kept her alive long enough to administer the cure. Luckily, the second strain of the virus wasn't as deadly as the first despite its faster onset." She smirked. "Last I heard, they threw Dolion out and locked the door."

"He…" Quinn's eyes met mine, her excitement flurrying across our bond. "I *knew* it."

Good for Pari. I was happy for them both that, after fighting it for so long, they had found their way together.

"The other victims are being treated now," Marin added. "Most should make a full recovery after some magical rehabilitation of their neural pathways. Queen Sariyah dedicated a wing of the Enclave to their therapy and is running it herself."

We had done it. Against all odds, we had not only survived…we had won.

I looked at Quinn, without whom none of this would have been possible. She was selflessly brave and impossibly brilliant in a way that left me awestruck.

And she was mine.

My cock twitched, the only part of my body with any energy, apparently. Quinn grinned at me as she moved her thigh to keep it from tenting the towel.

"As much as I'm enjoying the nude audience, I could use a bath…or three, to get the smell of smoke out," Quinn sighed, sniffing at her hair.

Yael laughed. "I think the bathroom's mostly unscathed. Let me get the bathtub running, and we can go from there."

Marin's lips quirked as she eyed the singed clothing that remained. "And I'll go hunt down something for you to wear."

I sank back into the charred pillows, smiling despite myself.

"I don't forgive you," I murmured into Quinn's hair, relishing the feeling of her weight on top of me—of holding her, even if doing so used all the strength I had left. Her exhilaration spilled across our bond as well as the stunned disbelief we had somehow both survived, just as I was sure she could sense my quiet contentment.

We would have a lifetime of this. An eternity.

Quinn propped her chin on her hands, smirking. "I don't remember offering you an apology."

CHAPTER 53
QUINN

It was humbling being as weak as a kitten, especially with my reserves so drained I couldn't even heal myself. Tobias and I slowly bathed each other, and I couldn't help but giggle at our sluggish progress. Marin and Yael got us both dressed—with only a little ribbing—before they brought us to a room with a bed less likely to collapse. Between one heartbeat and the next, Tobias and I passed out in each other's arms.

Sunlight warmed my face as I awoke, painting the inside of my eyelids a deep red. When I reached out across our bond to find my *anima*, my heart stopped.

Tobias wasn't there.

My eyes flew open. A pair of familiar gold and hazel eyes met mine—but not the ones I was expecting.

Eva perched on the edge of the bed, her finger holding her place in her book. She also wore pajamas, with a cozy robe wrapped around her. Her irises swirled, those gold flecks catching the light. She looked pale and gaunt—the virus had obviously taken its toll.

But she was *awake.*

A smile stretched across her face. "About time you woke up."

She spoke more slowly than usual, as if each word took extra effort. It was a common aftereffect of the virus, one that should get better with time and healing—especially now that I was here to help.

"About time *I* woke up?" A laugh burst out of me. I scrambled across the bed, throwing my arms around her. "You're awake. You're okay. You're—"

The sob that tore from me took me entirely off guard. My shoulders shook, and Eva's grip on me tightened. Everything that happened since the last time I saw her crashed down at once, the weight of every terrible *what if* threatening to swallow me whole.

I had come so close to losing her. So close to losing them both.

"I'm okay," Eva repeated, rubbing my back in slow circles. "Because of you."

"I wasn't sure if—" I let out an embarrassingly loud sniffle. "You were asleep so long..."

Eva plucked a tissue from a box on the bedside without letting me go, then offered it to me.

"I'm a little slow," she admitted softly. "Marin said my speech is already improving. But even with whatever magic Marin used to keep my muscles from atrophying, it's been an adjustment getting up and about." She released a huff of exasperation. "Bash may have carried me here. Even my magic feels raw, like I'm relearning those pathways...so I haven't been able to heal myself much either. I don't remember much between the rehearsal dinner and now, only that Bash was with me."

I let out a wet-sounding laugh. "I'm surprised he isn't attached to you currently."

"Speaking of which..." I pulled back to find Eva frowning, a lingering sheen of tears still glimmering in her eyes. "It seems I'm not the only one with an overprotective *anima* to deal with. I only got my brother to leave your side by telling him that I'd stay here until he got back, and even that took some cajoling. He's off getting us all breakfast."

She didn't look half as surprised as I expected.

A blush warmed my cheeks. "I'm sorry...I would've told you if I could've. I-I didn't realize my own feelings until all this forced us together." I was babbling and apparently couldn't stop. "And by then...well, I wanted to tell you, but I couldn't, obviously, but I hope you aren't..."

Eva's laugh cut me off. "Are you kidding? We've always been sisters, but now it'll really be official." Her grin was infectious. "I'm just thrilled I won't have to watch my brother pine over you for eternity."

My eyes widened. "You *knew*?"

"Suspected." She shrugged, looking far too pleased with herself. "He's been making doe eyes at you since high school. You were the one I wasn't so sure about, and I didn't want to pressure you. But I hoped you might feel similarly, especially when I saw you two dance."

Some part of me had known long before that, despite how long it had taken us to get there. If fate and circumstance hadn't kept us apart, I wondered if our *anima* bond would have managed to break through the amulet's hold in the human realm.

But I couldn't bring myself to regret the path that had taken us here—not when it had brought us together in the end.

The door swung open. Tobias walked in beside Bash, who was holding a tray laden with so much food I almost laughed. Bash's eyes found Eva's, a soft smile curving his lips, before his gaze zeroed in on me.

He hurried past Tobias, placing the tray on the coffee table before falling to his knees beside my bed. My greeting caught in my throat as his head bowed. One arm crossed his chest, his fist resting above his heart as his mismatched eyes lifted to mine.

"I owe you so much more than a thank you, Quinn Sagray. Until the day I die, if there's anything you ever need that I can give you, consider it yours." He got to his feet, taking my hand between his. "You saved my heart and my soul, and I won't ever forget it."

I gaped at him, unable to find anything to say in response to that speech.

"I...I appreciate it," I stammered. "But you don't owe me anything. I'm just glad we're all together again."

Bash simply smiled. "Open offer, whether it's tomorrow or in a hundred years."

Shadows swirled in his eyes, wrapping up his arms. I didn't miss the tendril of shadow that looped around Eva's fingers like a curled extension of her wedding ring.

Smoothing down my nightdress, I nodded. A groan escaped me as I sat up, then I slid off the bed onto my feet.

Tobias straightened from where he was making two plates of food. "Get back in bed, Sagray."

"If you can walk to the kitchen, then I can at least make it across the room," I argued, taking the plate from him and turning away. I winced as an ache flared through me at its weight. "Just because we destroyed your room doesn't mean I want crumbs in my bed."

"*Our* bed," Tobias corrected. He begrudgingly followed, pulling the chair out for me. "But if you insist."

He draped himself into the armchair next to me. Reaching underneath my chair, he tugged—moving my chair, and me, right next to his. I couldn't help but smile up at him.

Eva plucked a pastry from the tray before she flopped onto the couch opposite us, Bash close behind.

She looked thoughtfully at her brother. "You seem…better."

"Well, I can indisputably blame Quinn for that," Tobias said dryly. He spooned some fruit onto my plate before stealing a piece of melon with his fingers.

Eva cocked her brow. "For what exactly?"

"I'm not entirely sure what this emotion I've been having is, but it might be happiness," he admitted, his voice soft. "I don't want to scare it off."

Eva let out a startled peal of laughter. I couldn't help but join in as an affectionate tendril of emotion crossed our bond, warm and bright and so full of love I choked up. Tobias passed me a cup of tea, his brow furrowing at the tears in my eyes.

He reached up, brushing them away.

His fingertips ran back and forth across my knuckles as we ate and talked. It wasn't long before Eva's eyes grew heavy. When she moved to the bed "to close her eyes for just a second," I settled back in bed next to her. Her soft snores drifted through the room as I fought a losing battle against my own closing eyelids.

Bash picked up the now empty tray, murmuring, "I'll be right back. Take care of her, will you?"

"Always will," Tobias said with a solemn nod.

He settled on my other side with a book in hand, one he must have retrieved from his ruined room before I woke. I recognized it—the one about mirrors and their creation that had somehow survived the lightning strikes. The cover was faintly singed; the pages were smoky but still readable. Tobias thumbed through to reach the spot he bookmarked near the end as my eyes fluttered shut.

That book had saved our lives. I supposed the least he could do was finish it.

CHAPTER 54
TOBIAS

My face lifted as soon as I passed through the doorway, drinking in the sunrise.

We were set to travel to Morehaven later for Eva and Bash's long-delayed bonding ceremony celebrations. Quinn insisted on waking up before dawn so we had time to train together. She had been a menace about me sticking to the physical therapy plan she had made for us as we recuperated. My arms were aching after an hour of exercises and swordplay, but from the stubborn look in Quinn's eye, I knew we were far from done.

She had been working with Eva daily as well on building back her speech and strength, spending so much time in Morehaven I had barely seen her. I had also been busy taking a more active role with the daily duties of running Soleara—a job I had undeservedly been welcomed back to with open arms by Pari, Akeno, and Thorin. While making sure our kingdom flourished was part of their responsibilities as representatives of Soleara's senate, I had a newfound appreciation for everything they did while I stayed behind the scenes.

Akeno and Thorin had accepted my apologies as easily as Pari had, but I was careful not to throw my weight around. Though I hadn't been able to resist teasing Pari about her blush every time a missive arrived in a flare of greenish-gray magic—which was often. Turnabout was fair play for all the ribbing she gave me about my obsession with Quinn's most minor habits.

Akeno and Thorin mercilessly made fun of us both for how long it had taken Pari and I to realize that fighting the pull to our *animas* was a losing struggle.

I supposed we were all just idiots in love.

Pari's speech occasionally stuttered, a lasting effect of the virus she hadn't been able to completely shake. I was careful not to point it out, knowing how much any hint of pity annoyed me. But when my own words stumbled for the first time in a while, her look of commiseration was met with a smile.

Quinn's next blow nearly knocked me over. "Where's your head at today, Maris?"

"Just imagining all the better ways we could be getting sweaty this morning," I drawled, raising my practice sword.

"You need to build back your strength."

"What I *need* is to—" I lunged forward, ducking under her sword arm, only for her dagger to press into my jugular.

My hand found the nape of her neck, yanking her lips to mine.

She melted into me, though her blade stayed right where it was. My practice sword fell to the ground as I held her closer, plundering her mouth with my tongue until we were both flushed and panting—and not only from our workout.

"Let's go home," I murmured. I loved the way that word meant something mutual, something that was ours. "If you want me to continue my workout, I have another idea in mind..."

✧

I carried Quinn out of the shower, jealous of the drops of water that got to touch her too. She gave a little gasp as I sucked them from her skin, taking my time on her neck, her breasts. The towel I had wrapped around us both dropped onto the floor. I didn't care that I was leaving a trail of darkened footprints, only that I wasn't inside her.

Her eyes widened as she noticed the silk rope I had tied to the headboard.

"You seemed stressed," I casually explained. "I thought I could help with that. I seem to remember promising to tie you to the headboard not too long ago, if you're still interested."

Her bright laugh made me smile. "Remind me to be stressed more often."

My lips twitched. "Let's try for the opposite."

I laid her beneath me on the bed, my hands roving her body as I worked my way up her arms. Kissing each wrist, I wrapped the rope lightly around them before securing it in the middle. It wasn't our first time doing bondage, though this rope was new. Her arousal heated our bond, urging me onward as I tightened her bonds.

Once I was done, I kissed her again before working my way down her throat, spending extra time on the spots I knew made her moan. I played with her until she was writhing, begging me both with her body and aloud. She tugged on the ropes instinctively as her hips moved, seeking friction.

I brought her nipple between my teeth, lightly biting down. Quinn gasped, her breathing heavier as I moved to the other, sucking it into my mouth. Then I kissed her roughly, her lips feverish as they moved against mine.

She let out a soft whine into my mouth as my fingers traced down her midline. Finally, my hand slipped down between her thighs, tauntingly avoiding the spot where I knew she needed me most.

"Oh sweetheart, I've barely gotten started," I crooned. "And you know how I like to take my time."

I pressed my lips against the pulse in her neck, and her heart thundered beneath my touch.

"Please," she moaned. Her hips bucked as my fingers circled too lightly, seeking more pressure. Her eyes were half-lidded as she looked up at me. "I need you."

She was playing dirty. Those three words never failed to make me fold.

"My fingers?" I slipped two inside her, making sure she was ready for me. "Or..."

"Tobias..."

Her desperation across our bond grew in tandem with her lust. It was almost enough for me to take pity on her.

Almost.

I kissed my way down her midline, taking my time as I took in every inch of her splayed before me.

"My mouth?"

I knelt between her legs. She let out a loud whimper as my tongue flattened against her clit.

"Don't stop," she begged.

I didn't think I could even if the world was on fire. I pumped my hard length once, my grip nearly painful as my tongue swirled against her. She was getting close—so achingly close, her body already starting to tremble.

"Or my cock?"

I knocked her knees open with my own, spreading her wider, fitting myself against her entrance. I paused.

"Sir, please," she keened, eyes glassy with desire.

"I love it when you beg," I growled in approval. Then I plunged in to the hilt.

Quinn's legs clamped around my hips as I drove all the way out, and I moaned aloud of the blissful sensation as I slowly thrust back in again. It only took two deep thrusts, and my fingers picking up where my mouth left off, to drive her over the edge I had left her on.

I bit down on my lip, holding myself back from coming along with her as she clenched around me like a vise.

She was so perfect; so beautiful as she came. The flush on her chest, the arch of her back showing off her heavy breasts, her full lips parted as those breathy moans escaped her. I slid out of her, glistening with her wetness, before gliding back in. I was trembling with restraint by the time her tremors died down.

The sound she made as I shoved myself until I was fully seated was somewhere between a gasp and moan—and it was all I could hear. I needed more. Needed to bury myself so far inside her we could never be parted again.

My hands dug into her ass, tilting her hips to find that perfect angle to begin our next round. Then I paused.

"What time do we have to get to Morehaven?"

Quinn blinked at me, then smiled like a cat given cream. "Not until dinner."

"Good," I drawled. "Because I plan to make you come so many times that you can't walk straight down the aisle tomorrow."

✧

When we were finished, I had carried Quinn right back into the shower to rinse off. At least the marks clawing down my back from when I finally untied her and the love bites on my neck would still mark me after the water washed the rest away. Quinn had, however, insisted on healing everything visible over my jacket collar

"Help me with this, would you?" Quinn turned around, offering me the hook and clasp of her amulet. I took it from her carefully as she lifted her hair from her neck. Her dress was backless, and, at my request, the same shade of yellow I often saw in my dreams. I wanted to run my tongue along the indentations of her spine…

"Don't you dare start that again, Maris, or we'll never make it out of this room," Quinn said as I pressed a kiss to her back, then another. "We can't be late for this rehearsal dinner. With how the last one ended, they deserve a perfect redo."

I fastened the amulet, kissing the back of her neck before Quinn let her hair fall.

"As long as you promise me a dance," I conceded.

She laughed. "You can have them all."

Tonight was for us, Eva had explained. A celebration before tomorrow's big event with the group that had ensured it would finally happen.

Tomorrow, I would walk my twin sister down the aisle in front of the entire realm. But this time, the thought of the open space and the marble floors of Morehaven didn't scare me. Not anymore.

I hadn't needed to hide away my fears. Not for a long while now.

Not when I finally felt safe.

Not when I finally believed in forever.

EVA

EPILOGUE

Cascading arrangements of roses, wisteria, and lavender spilled from towering golden vases by the doorway. Garlands of greenery and bright colored blooms hung from the ceiling of the great hall, transforming it into a fairytale forest as the crowd sat in wait. It barely looked like the same room as candelabras cast the hallway in a warm, romantic glow, and faerie lights scattered amongst the greenery like fallen stars.

White, I had been relieved to learn, was a mortal tradition. My dress was gold. Enormous gold lace roses covered every inch of the full skirt, each hand sewn and utterly unique. The dropped-waist bodice was sleeveless, a sweetheart neckline showing off the silver star amulet around my neck. My chestnut curls cascaded down my back, gold strands intermingled throughout.

The actual ceremony would be quick—after all, Bash and I had said the same two sentence blessing we would repeat today the night we had accepted that bond.

You are my beloved.

And I am yours.

My brother looked more like himself than ever as he stepped up beside me, ready to walk me down the aisle at last. The glow of his magic lit his eyes as he watched Quinn from where she chatted animatedly with Pari and

Rivan across the room. Phantom's tail wagged happily as Marin fed him treats, Yael scratching behind his ears.

The music swelled. This would all begin soon.

I couldn't help but smile at the way he looked at her. "I take it you're next?"

My words still felt a bit stilted, like my mind took a beat too long to find the one I wanted. But today, I barely noticed.

Tobias frowned uncertainly. "For what?"

"A bonding ceremony."

His eyes darted back to Quinn, a strange expression crossing his face. "I...well, it's your day."

"Toby," I said imploringly. "If it's my day, then I should get what I want, no?"

Shushing me, he looked again at Quinn to make sure she was occupied as he led me behind a nearby veil of flowers. The blooms acted like drapery, so dense they hid us nearly completely from view.

My brother looked uncharacteristically nervous as he reached into his pocket. "Can you keep a secret?"

Tobias took out a ring. I sucked in a sharp breath at how lovely it was—how perfect it was for her. The pale-yellow diamond looked like an exact match for Quinn's sunflower amulet, the classic emerald shape set on an intricate golden band.

"I had a jeweler here reset one of Mom's rings once I found the right diamond," Tobias whispered. "I picked it up this morning. Quinn and I already said the only vows that matter...But I was thinking of taking her to a field outside Soleara once we're home. Just us, a few friends, and my completely unimportant twin sister, now that they're in bloom."

"Now that what's in bloom...?" I started, then realized I already knew the answer.

"Sunflowers," we said in unison. Tobias let out a beleaguered sigh at the twinness though I saw his smile. Then footsteps sounded around the corner. He hastily shoved the ring back into his inner pocket.

Bash poked his head around the drapery. "Is everything okay, hellion?"

I could feel his awe as he saw me—the first time seeing me in my dress—across our bond. The love and wonder and blatant lust streaming across it nearly bowled me over.

"You look…" It was rare to see him so speechless. "You look too lovely to be real."

It was nice to see him looking at me without the hint of worry crinkling his eyes that had been present ever since I recovered. He woke up from nightmares more often than me these days, reliving the moments when I had almost slipped away.

I winked at him. "What happened to waiting for me at the end of the aisle?"

Bash shrugged. "The realm gets everything else. I thought I'd take one moment just for the two of us."

Tobias placed a hand on Bash's shoulder, giving it a familiar squeeze. "I'll give you two a moment then." He glanced back at me with an easy smile—one that had become wonderfully familiar. "Let me know when you're ready, sis."

He walked away, beelining straight to Quinn and wrapping his arms around her from behind. Her face glowed as she smiled up at him. I quickly looked away as he placed a kiss on her bare shoulder. While I was happy for them both, I never wanted to know the details my best friend normally shared with me. Considering the hickey placement I noticed when Quinn adjusted her dress, I knew far too much already.

Bash took my hands, pulling me closer. His lips met mine in a chaste kiss that I quickly deepened into more.

"Tell me something true," Bash whispered against my lips.

There were tears clouding my vision as I looked at Bash. His smile dropped as he immediately held me closer.

"I can't believe this is real," I said, my voice wavering. "That we're here together, after everything. That you're mine forever."

"I told you I'd collect." There were tears in Bash's eyes too, that swirling storm of green and blue glistening like the sea. "Whatever comes next, we'll face it together."

There was so much left to do, especially when it came to bringing change to a realm whose concept of power and who deserved it were firmly entrenched in hierarchy and tradition. But real, consequential change had never come without persistence. It was up to me to challenge the systems that benefited from keeping things the same—to build a better world with my friends and family by my side.

"I'm hoping the only thing next, for today at least, is finally getting to kiss you at the end of the aisle."

Bash smiled as he led me forward to where our family waited. "I think we can manage that." A tendril of shadow looped around our fingers, binding them together until they were entwined as tightly as our souls. "I have to admit, as much as this feels like a spectacle, I'm looking forward to showing the realm how lucky I am that you walked into my life."

"More like fate and ill-intentions sent you to kidnap me."

Bash smirked. "Semantics."

My smile widened. "Did you ever think this would happen the day you found me on the other side of the mirror?"

Bash shook his head, the expression of his face almost rueful. "Not in my wildest dreams could I have imagined how entirely I was about to fall for you."

My darkness swirled around us, hiding us from view for one more minute before the ceremony began. The voices around us muted as Bash's shadows joined them—their streaks of gray like a storm forming against the deepest night.

Then I kissed him, knowing he could feel the way my heart beat for him, just as his did for me.

"Until the stars fade from the sky," Bash breathed. His thumb brushed against my cheek, his gaze drinking me in like he could be content to stay in this moment for eternity.

My joy unfurled like a rosebud finally opening wide—the feeling rebounding right back to me.

"And forever after that."

Thank you for reading! Did you enjoy? Please add your review because nothing helps an author more and encourages readers to take a chance on a book than a review.

And don't miss more in the from Dana Evyn coming soon and keep up-to-date on all the news at danaevyn.com

Then, read THE BOUNTY OF BLOOD AND NAILS , by City Owl Author, N K Brown. Turn the page for a sneak peek!

Also be sure to sign up for the City Owl Press newsletter to receive notice of all book releases!

SNEAK PEEK OF THE BOUNTY OF BLOOD AND NAILS

BY N K BROWN

It was almost time.

The final night, the crescendo, the climax. The other charlatans would be turning up the fires, pouring out the charm, increasing the danger, the difficulty, the disbelief. I had to remain stoic. Isolated, yet approachable. Alluring, yet aloof. They didn't *need* to know what I could see, yet I appealed to them, like a whispering siren. A craving. An urge. An itch.

There was only one I needed to satisfy tonight.

I shivered as night rose around me. The air thinned, laced with a refreshing chill as the last of the sun's color bleached from the sky. One by one, fairy lights popped to life. Green, amber, purple, silver, all small fiery splotches of color suspended from spindly wires looping between the stalls. A gentle breeze rumpled the cloth in front of me, evoking the small tinkling of bells that hung weighted at the edges of my table.

The gentle twang of a harp filtered through the calm night. A few isolated notes of a violin chased after it, attempting to warm the pre-magical atmosphere. The wooden sign suspended above my stall creaked in the breeze.

A low whistle snagged my attention. I placed the tarot deck upon the velvet cloth and brushed the deep hood from my face, allowing a glimpse of the stall across the aisle to the left. The candy man grinned, dimples puckering his cheeks. I didn't know his name, nor age—somewhere in his mid-twenties surely, but the high-waisted tan trousers and star-studded suspenders made him appear twice that age. Or perhaps transported in time from a century ago.

I wasn't doing anything to subvert the stereotype either. Black cloak with scarlet trimmed hood. Sleeves that dripped down past my hands allowing only a flash of red nail polish and multiple silver rings to emerge as

I tapped confidently upon the chosen card, eager to bestow my knowledge of the future upon the lucky client.

Candyman ran his hand around the gold-rimmed edge of the floss machine. Cotton candy swirled around his finger, interlacing like a fat pink chrysalis. He slowly brought his finger to his lips, maintaining eye contact, sucking the chrysalis into his mouth. I knew what he would taste like later. Sugar and caramel and a hint of rum—kept in a not-so-secret bottle under his stall. I swear that when I looked away, he would dab himself with the candy floss like sticky cologne, knowing that it would make me kiss him harder, that it would entice my tongue to caress his skin, my teeth to nip in all the right places.

Though tonight, there would be no fun for either of us.

I let the hood fall back across my face. The music picked up, a thrum of excitement charging the air from a crowd of people I couldn't yet see. If I was successful, there would be no time to lose myself amongst the bags of sugar, the mounds of sweets, the warm, roving hands of Candyman. If she came and it worked, I would have to dissolve into the dawn, putting as much distance between myself and the Collectors as possible.

Sweat prickled my palms, threatening to slide down my skin and pool upon the velvet tablecloth. I forced my breathing to deepen, my lungs to expand past the point of recoil.

From under the peak of my hood, I caught sight of the first eager footsteps rushing the aisle. The grass lay trampled, blades permanently bowed from the weight of passersby this past week. Yet, for the last six days, she had not come.

She must tonight.

My heart ticked like a bomb, speeding toward the deadline. Sixty days it had taken me to find this one. She was reclusive, a shadow. I didn't know what she'd done, but I wasn't surprised they'd ordered me to track her down. Her bounty was impressive. If I could be as stealthy as her, we'd both disappear into the ether, no tracts, no guilt, transformed into legacy.

Candyman handed a large paper bag stuffed with toffees to a small girl. He bent over the stall, deftly flicking the top cube into the air and snapped his teeth shut around it. He winked as the girl giggled, her mother affectionately patting her braided hair.

So that is what he would taste of later. Cinders and treacle. I swallowed, holding his gaze which had floated not-so-innocently to mine until he turned to the next customer, a broad grin lapping at his cheeks.

The music hung thick now in the air, twined with shouts and laughter. From my right, the swoosh of a lit torch rippled a wave of heat toward me. Marianne didn't only eat fire, she commanded it, molding it into shapes like smoke rings from a cigar. Some of the magic here was real, parlor tricks, really. Just enough to make people part with their money, but not enough to be arrested.

Sweat trickled down my spine. At least now I could blame it on the heat in the air.

Once the first rush of visitors subsided—those who instinctively knew where they wanted to go or were dragged by small children—the timid arrived next. These were innocents, virgins to the fayre. They'd come for a specific reason. Perhaps to catch the eye of one of the performers, eagerly hoping to be chosen as a volunteer to levitate ten feet into the air before being caught by the toned biceps of the magician. His shirt sleeves rolled up, winding ink crisscrossing his flesh.

On more than one occasion I'd seen his tattoos morph into the mirror image of the person he wanted to tempt backstage. How could one resist when your face was clearly visible etched permanently upon his body? It was fate of course, and so one did not resist.

My first client was here. It wasn't who I needed to see, but I doubted I'd be lucky enough to escape so early. She was a young woman of nineteen or twenty. Her cheeks were flushed, and she gripped the arm of a young man, tugging him toward me. She would never have ventured this far by herself, and yet, the eagerness in her eyes told me I was who she'd come to see.

Shame I was a fraud.

I gestured silently to the bench in front. She sat carefully, scooping her long skirt beneath her, the bells tinkling seductively as she rustled the tablecloth. The man stood behind, one hand on her shoulder. The sinews popped from his hand; his fingers almost clawed, but he stopped short of releasing that pressure onto the bare skin of her neck.

I riffled the tarot cards in my hand. The deck was pristine, the pattern on the back that of a simple silver skull upon black, the kind you could purchase anywhere. The satin cloth and silver ribbon binding them also looked new, like I'd exchanged them for a handful of pennies a week ago when the fayre opened.

A trained eye would see the con, could smell the treachery a mile away. I could scrunch the deck, bend the edges and yet wasn't this whole place one large trick? A parallel realm an ordinary being could wander into for only seven nights per year and be transported into a land of magic and fun and frivolity. One where they could step out of their ordinary, meagre lives and succumb to their dreams. Or so the proprietors would have you believe.

"Are you sure, my dear?" The man's face stretched tight. His mouth was obscured beneath a manicured moustache. "We have talked about your disposition toward the supernatural at length. Have you forgotten?"

I flattened my palm and raised my hand toward him. My nails wanted to extend, the gift coursing through my bloodstream like poison.

"Oh yes, honey," she answered. "It's only a bit of fun. I won't take any of it to heart, I promise." Her mouth curved downwards as she spoke, her dark eyes beseeching.

They all wanted the same reading from me this week, *will I marry the crown prince?* No one was so bold as to outright say it, but it was written in the singe of heat on their cheeks, in the coil of hair they twined nervously around a finger. But not this one. She needed something else.

The man tutted and fumbled in his waistcoat for coins. He withdrew two coppers and dropped them into my open palm, returning the pounds and gideons that were ostentatiously brandished amongst them back to the pocket.

I nodded, tipping the coins into my cloak and returned my hand to the tarot. I tapped the skull on the uppermost card as my thigh knocked against the table leg, silently cracking a vial of incense. The perfume seeped out, infusing the air with a faint shimmer. The young woman's eyes widened, her chin lifting as she inhaled deeply.

"That's my nana's smell," she whispered. "Roses."

The man above her said nothing, everything he wanted to utter explained in the twitch of his mouth and the tightening of his hand upon her shoulder. If she wasn't so enraptured by the aura, she would be able to feel the bruises pooling beneath his fingertips, blemishing the smooth skin beneath.

I turned the first card over. The Grim Reaper. It was my favorite to start with. Everyone knew someone who had died or was dying. That was life.

"You have lost someone whose wisdom meant a lot to you." The crack in my voice was not intentional. I needed to get a grip on my emotions.

Another pulse ricocheted through my veins as the magic struggled to escape.

She inhaled sharply. Her hand pressed to her breast, but not over her heart. Her fingers rested on a gold brooch shaped like a butterfly pinned to her green dress.

I turned the next card face up revealing two entwined skeletons with empty sockets gazing at one another, bony arms encircling barren ribcages. The Lovers.

Her face faltered. She stared at the card, her knuckles blanching as she gripped the brooch.

"You see," the man interrupted, pulling her back from the table, "it's us. Now, let's go."

I turned over the next card, pushing it in front of the others and toward her. A man dangled upside down from a spiral pillar, his legs entangled with a serpent, a crown of thorns encircling his head.

"What's that one?" He lowered his head, squinting at the table.

"The Hanged Man."

He choked, jerking backward. He grabbed the woman's shoulder again to half-drag her from her seat. "Come on, we're leaving."

When he released her and turned to straighten his waistcoat, I slipped the final card across the table. The woman took it, glancing quickly at the picture and the inscription before slipping it back face down.

"You know what she would have said," I whispered. "Because that's what you believe as well. Trust your instincts."

She swallowed, her eyes wide, cheeks drained of color. She bestowed a small smile upon the man as she delicately took his arm, as if suddenly repulsed by the thought of touching even his clothing. As they walked away, she turned back to me and nodded. My chest tightened as my breath paused on the inhale. Good. No one should be trapped by another.

I reined in my emotions, crushing them beneath years of well-trained lies. The air thinned again as the cool breeze drained the incense.

Perhaps there would be time to linger when the fayre closed, and the patrons had departed. We could all finally be ourselves. I did love toffee, probably more than the small caramel droplets Candyman kept in a bowl for melting. Maybe tonight I would line the small candies down his chest, arranging them like stars, before using my tongue to trace swirls and patterns and galaxies as they melted from his body heat...

There she was.

Everything stopped. The dragon of fire Marianne shot into the air paused, a great tongue of jade flame cauterized from its mouth. The jaunty spring from the bow of the violin froze on the strings. The clouds of pink candy floss strangled the white stick.

Then the breath whooshed from my lungs, adrenaline igniting my body as the world revolved once again.

She was here.

I'd studied every inch of the small portrait I had been given when assigned this task. Ingrained the details onto the corrugations of my mind while traveling through wood and dale, skirting cities and plowing through barren countryside.

As I closed in and navigated the labyrinthine streets of this town, I imagined every conceivable change of hair color, added wrinkles or frown lines, each blend of fabric she could opt to wear. I had questioned the baker, the tailor, the midwife, all in a roundabout, casual tone, painting an amicable smile on my face while secretly probing their answers for the minutiae.

Dully, she was as expected. Mid-forties, brown hair streaked with gray, thick glasses perched upon a straight nose. Her clothes were average—well-pressed, but clean. She hid her wealth in the diamond necklace that peeked out of her frilled collar and the pointed shoes inlaid with golden thread and satin bindings which serpentined up her ankles.

What had she done? And, more importantly to whom? Maybe it was better not knowing. Then I was just doing a social service—for a hefty fee. The chase had been fun, the funneling of the hunt heart-pounding. But the kill? I may not be directly slitting her throat, but I was handing over the knife. My stomach flipped, the sweat beading upon my palms.

I flicked the top card at her. It fluttered on the breeze, dying at her feet.

She stooped to pick it up, turning toward me with a cock of her head as she considered what I could deign to offer her. I raised my face, allowing the color from the fairy lights to fall upon me as the hood lifted, unmasking the shadows. I gestured toward the empty bench.

Don't run. Don't flee. I don't want to have to chase you.

She moved closer, a smirk stretching her lips. "That was a silly little trick." Her voice stretched, the sarcasm snagging the attention of passersby. "Is this my likeness?" She twirled the Death card in her fingers.

"A warning," I said.

She didn't believe in the power of the deck, for her fortunes were not told in fables and fairytales. She would sit just to prove a point. To prove how ridiculous this was.

The crowd grew steadily around her, magnetized by her scorn.

My heart hammered and my mouth dried. The hood flapped back over my face as she settled herself, elbows planted upon the velvet cloth, the bells cackling wildly with the movement.

Don't leave.

Don't hate me.

"I don't need a fortune read," she said. "What else do you have?"

I pulled the tarot toward me and positioned them perfectly square at the edge of the table. I held out my palm hoping she wouldn't notice the sheen of congealing sweat.

She extracted a dainty coin purse from the depths of her outfit and handed over one copper. "You can have more if these fine folk are impressed." She waved her hand, inviting the hovering people closer.

A small throng had gathered. It wasn't surprising. She was well known, respected, and feared. It had been difficult getting anyone to talk about her, to reveal even the smallest morsel of information. Once they sniffed where the conversation was going, they rapidly scurried away. Being tantalizingly close for such a long time had been half the fun. They were as curious as I was about the woman underneath.

I reached under the table and pulled up a velvet-draped divider. It was a foot high and the same width with an ebony cloth attached. She watched me intently as I reached across and gently lowered her left arm. I moved it to the side, palm down, fingers splayed. I slid the board along the table and into the crook of her arm, arranging the cloth over her left shoulder so she seemed to melt seamlessly into the fabric.

Next, I flopped out a doll's arm. Stuffed, pink and plump, perfectly proportioned to her own body size. I slid the severed end under the cloth, positioning the hand and unpainted nails exactly like her real one.

Candyman's eyes lingered on mine through the packed bodies as they jostled for a better vantage point, but the flirtation had gone. His brow furrowed, a fleeting look of worry marring his features until my view of him was engulfed by the crowd again.

If this went wrong, I would need access to all his hidden rum. Gorging on sugar and drinking myself into a stupor would be a good swan song for my life thus far.

I tugged the two strands of silver ribbon out from under the tarot. I ran each length along the fake arm and her real one simultaneously. Her brow furrowed, a small crinkle of disgust burrowing into the skin above her nose.

"Do you feel this?" I asked.

She huffed, her eyes darting to those closest before answering, "Of course I do."

I stopped stroking her real arm but continued to slide the ribbon up the doll's arm. "And now?"

She scoffed again. "Yes."

A small murmur arose from those watching. The woman stilled, her blue eyes narrowing on me.

I nodded. "Very well."

Returning the ribbons to the corner of the table, I scooped up a handful of fire jacks from an alcove underneath. Marianne had kindly lent me a few dozen at the beginning of the fayre, in return for a doctored reading of ill omens when her ex-wife visited.

I cracked one of the jacks between my fingers, tossing it quickly into the air as a small ball of white-hot fire cracked into life. It hovered for a split second before sizzling into ash and drifting toward the table. I shifted in my seat, pressing my thigh into the table leg where another aroma waited. This would release the charred scent of burning flesh, raising the air temperature by a few degrees with it.

I took another jack between my fingers and squeezed, dropping it quickly onto the doll's arm. As it landed, I cracked the vial with my leg, the noise lost amongst the woman's shriek.

She gaped at the fake arm and the charred circle marring its pink wrist. The crowd tittered. Whispers of, "Did you really feel that?" and "She's part of the act." I waited until they quieted and took another jack to her real arm. She couldn't see over the screen, hadn't even noticed my arm move to the side as she stared transfixed at the black stain on the doll's arm.

I cracked another and rested it on her real hand. It ignited, a brief ripple of heat firing into the crowd. They drew back, some gasping, a few honks of nervous laughter, but the woman did not move.

She frowned at me, then swiveled to assess the crowd. I reached out to tug on the fake arm. "Sit still please." As if I'd pulled her physically, she turned back and settled. The crowd gasped again.

I pushed the remaining jacks aside, willing the tremble in my fingers to cease and pointed toward an elderly lady to the right of the woman. She wore an elaborate jewel-spattered hat, braided with ribbons and flowers.

"A pin, please." She extracted one, a fine specimen, two inches long with a diamond head.

I started on the woman's real hand. Gently, the pin sunk into the flesh between her fingers, skewering her to the velvet table as if she were a butterfly. She made no sound, nor even flinched. The crowd was silent, sensing the finale, their eyes wide, muscles tensed as they hung on every little movement.

I pulled the pin out slowly, a smear of blood coating the barb. Moving toward the fake arm, I gently prodded the flesh of the forearm. The woman jumped. I did it again, and she flinched. Hovering the pin just above the fake skin, my eyes locked with hers beneath the hood.

My right hand crept toward her real arm, nails silently extending. Power coursed through my body, pooling with a tingle in my fingertips as I dragged my nails down her arm, the jagged ends biting into her flesh.

She didn't move an inch.

I fought to stop an exhale of relief as the magic rushed out, my body yearning to lay limp as if exsanguinated.

A young boy popped up beside the woman and crammed himself next to her on the bench. "What's going on, Ma?" He shoved a pink and green swirled lollipop into his mouth and stared at the fake arm with my pin hovering over it, before peering past the barrier.

My stomach twisted. She had a child?

It was too late, but the real question was, would it have stopped me?

I smoothed the blood away using the velvet tablecloth and tugged down her long sleeve. Unfolding the cloth from her shoulder, I returned the barrier beneath the table and lowered my head. The audience broke into applause.

In a daze, the woman cautiously wound her arm in as if the nerves had all come loose. Coppers rained onto the table, bouncing off one another until the excited voices turned away to see what other wonders the fayre held.

Midnight had barely struck, but I was done.

When I pushed the remaining fire jacks toward the boy, he pocketed them gleefully. I waited until his mother had fully roused herself and shepherded the boy away before tugging down the wooden sign above my stall. Candyman was obscured again in the rush of customers who had left my performance, blocking my last view of him. I scooped up the coppers, left the tarot and other equipment, and headed toward the far end of the field.

Once the grass began to tickle my knees and the colorful glow from the fayre had dimmed to an ashy firelight, I doubled over and retched.

When there was nothing left in my stomach, I straightened, wiping my mouth on my sleeve. The woods bordering the field were thick and almost impenetrable, but I had scoped out my retreat already. Picking my feet high along a narrow game trail, I made for the other side, a distance of only a few miles if I stayed true.

I didn't know how much time I had before the Collectors came. They wouldn't snatch the woman at the fayre, it would be too public. On her way home, perhaps? Maybe they had a shred of decency left and would wait until she'd tucked her child into bed, sparing him the eternal nightmares. It would be better to wake and find her vanished than the alternative.

This, I knew firsthand.

The wood pressed in around me, brambles snagging on my cloak and razor-thin spiderwebs caressing my face. Where were the night creatures? The hooting owl, the mouse rustling through the fallen leaves? Even the bats were not silhouetted against the dark clouds.

I ignored the acid roiling in my stomach, the ever-deafening roar in my ears to turn back and spend the night in the warm embrace of Candyman. Safely tucked up amongst people and far away from the darkness that lurked everywhere else.

A twig snapped like bone from just ahead.

Is that why the animals had fled? The Collectors were already waiting?

Crunch.

I tried to submerge the screaming of my subconscious mind, the instinct for self-preservation and pushed through toward a small clearing.

A figure emerged from the shadows on the other side.

Don't stop now. Keep reading with your copy of THE BOUNTY OF BLOOD AND NAILS , by City Owl Author, N K Brown.

And sign up for Dana Evyn's newsletter to get all the news, giveaways, excerpts, and more!

Don't miss more from Dana Evyn coming soon and get all the news on her website at danaevyn.com

Then, discover THE BOUNTY OF BLOOD AND NAILS , by City Owl Author, N K Brown.

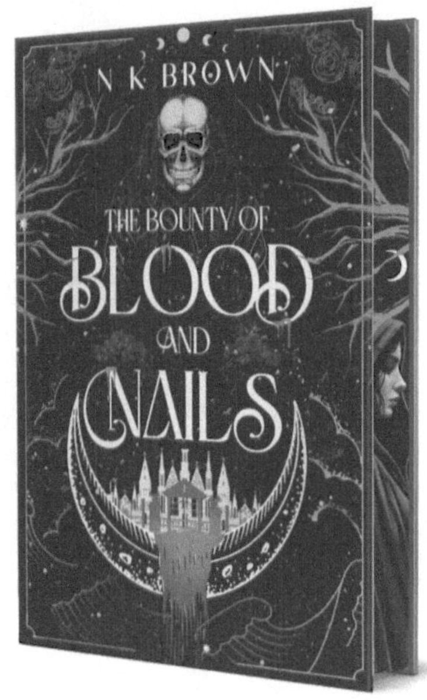

Tam is a heartless, ruthless bounty hunter—or so her handler would have you believe.

With her ability to use forbidden blood magic, Tam tracks and captures her prey. The same blood magic that curses her to a life of servitude under a cruel handler—one wrong move and not only her life, but her family's will be at stake. But when she's sent to a remote, superstitious northern town where even a glimmer of magic will send you to the gallows, she's forced to confront the darker consequences of her work.

After the murder of her bounty, innocent townspeople are blamed—and Tam's conscience begins to stir. But there's no turning back. Her handler raises the stakes, and her next mission is even more dangerous: infiltrate the royal castle and capture the enigmatic Prince Bellinor. Disguised as a maid, Tam is drawn into a world of deadly secrets, where her words are whispered into the prince's ears through an ancient magic she's never faced before.

To get close to the prince, she befriends his loyal bodyguard, Clement, but the deeper she digs, the more she realizes that Clement's destiny is tied to the prince. With time running out and the castle tightening, Tam is forced to watch the trial of the people blamed for her own prior actions. But will she complete the mission—or risk it all as she falls in love with the person whose life she must destroy?

In this fast-paced, thrilling tale of magic, betrayal, and forbidden love, Tam will have to decide if being the bad guy is worth losing everything.

Please sign up for the City Owl Press newsletter for chances to win special subscriber-only contests and giveaways as well as receiving information on upcoming releases and special excerpts.

All reviews are **welcome** and **appreciated**. Please consider leaving one on your favorite social media and book buying sites.

For books in the world of romance and speculative fiction that embody Innovation, Creativity, and Affordability, check out City Owl Press at www.cityowlpress.com.

ACKNOWLEDGMENTS

This book is especially close to my heart as my dad has been fighting Huntington's disease for decades—a diagnosis that changed my family's fate, and so many others who have loved ones with forms of dementia. While I wish I could write a happily ever after for him, there was something cathartic about creating a memory sickness that could be healed and writing characters with the power to do so. I only hope that one day we'll find a cure for the sicknesses that have rewritten so many lives, and that no one else will have to watch someone they love fade piece by piece ever again.

Writing this series has been an emotional whirlwind on so many levels. It's both wonderful and completely bittersweet to see this story come to a close. This trilogy changed me to the core and made me an author, and I'm so thankful to everyone who took part in this adventure.

First, I need to thank my readers. Some of you have been with me from the beginning, some of you only recently went through the mirror and have become some of my series' most vocal supporters, and some of you have even become friends along the way. Thank you, thank you, thank you for sharing, for reviewing, and most of all, for reading. A huge thank you to my street team for being the best group of hellions a writer could ask for!

A heartful thank you to my IRL three-star book club, Teresa, Mel, Sam, Leah and Colleen, for making me fall in love with romantasy in the first place. Thank you Sam, Mel, and Colleen for being the best alpha readers a girl could ask for, and for making this a better book. And thank you to my friends Hope, Minako, Mandy, and Stacey for being so endlessly supportive, no matter how many book signing I invite you to.

To the amazing author friends I made along the way—I'm so endlessly grateful this journey brought me to you. To Jaclyn and Berkeley, and our coven of bi chaos. To Sheila, for always understanding and whose voice notes kept me going more than once. To Sophia, for the coffee dates and for being such a light. To Fleur and Gretchen, my fellow patrons of the arts, for enabling the addiction. To Alison, for all the advice and pizza dates. To Ariella, for being there from the beginning and for all the best fanfic recs. And, of course, to The Emotional Damage Collective—Harper, Kate, Hillary, Morgan, and Gretchen, for the commiseration and cupcakes.

To Sav, the best PA I could have ever asked for, and an even more amazing friend. I'm so glad you've been there since the beginning.

To my agent, Jackie, and the team at Focused Artists: thank you so much for believing in me, and for your support in my next chapter.

Thank you to my wonderful editor Danielle, without whom this trilogy would have been a duology. To Jenny for your thoughtful copyedits, to Tina for all the work behind the scenes, and to my fellow owls.

To my mom, for always going above and beyond, and who insisted on reading the smutty scenes. To my little sister, Katie, who skipped them, and my little brother, Charlie, who listened when I told him he's not allowed to read my books at all. To Nick, for being my fellow grumpy to our sunshine spouses. To my amazing in-laws, Bryant and Esther, who have been such cheerleaders—and my brother-in-law Warren for the "conversation starter" books he keeps in his office.

To my husband Shane for being the real romantic in our relationship, my forever favorite ginger, and the literal loudest supporter of my books. I couldn't have done this without your love and support. And to Chloe and Sloan, I love you, but please never bring my books to school for show & tell ever again.

To my luck dragon/golden retriever Dallas for being the best foot warmer, and my demon cat, Mia, for always reading over my shoulder.

And once again, to my readers—thank you for going through the mirror with me one last time.

About the Author

DANA EVYN is a romantasy author who has been lost in her daydreams for as long as she can remember, and finally started writing them down. When she's not writing, she's usually reading a good book—especially one with an indomitable female lead, a unique magical world, and a dark twist you don't see coming. She lives in Kirkland, WA with her two tiny humans, ever-supportive husband, giant golden retriever, and tiny demon cat.

To learn more about Dana's books, please visit danaevyn.com.

instagram.com/danaevyn
tiktok.com/@danaevyn
x.com/danaevyn
danaevyn.substack.com

ABOUT THE PUBLISHER

City Owl Press is a cutting edge indie publishing company, bringing the world of romance and speculative fiction to discerning readers.

Escape Your World. Get Lost in Ours!

www.cityowlpress.com

facebook.com/YourCityOwlPress
x.com/cityowlpress
instagram.com/cityowlbooks
pinterest.com/cityowlpress

www.ingramcontent.com/pod-product-compliance
Lightning Source LLC
LaVergne TN
LVHW041057080826
845145LV00007B/1600

* 9 7 8 1 6 4 8 9 8 6 7 6 5 *